Dear Mr. Mauro,

Actually Isaac predicted the end of world in the year 20[...] I saw my job as a modern minute man to prevent that by moving it up a tad, to 2018. Through work as brilliant as yours, I am sure you will understand my presentation. Your and my job is to present information so that we are prepared and it never happens. The US military is listening, but I'm not sure but few others. Keep up the good work,

Daniel
Lion '05

The George Washington Vision

By

Daniel Lion

authorHOUSE™

1663 LIBERTY DRIVE, SUITE 200
BLOOMINGTON, INDIANA 47403
(800) 839-8640
WWW.AUTHORHOUSE.COM

First published by AuthorHouse 03/19/05

ISBN: 1-4208-1079-0 (sc)

Printed in the United States of America
Bloomington, Indiana

This book is printed on acid-free paper.

ABOUT THE BOOK

In his sequel to *The George Washington Prophecy – Before 9/11 and Beyond,* Daniel Lion heads into the future as David Lion and his two grown sons return to battle the forces of evil that assemble once more at the gates of the United States. In the gripping overlay of the third and final attack on the United States, the books of the Bible are presented with startling realism that constantly raises the question: Could it be true? Could this be the destiny for the United States that George Washington foresaw?

As the descendent of a Revolutionary War soldier who passed down the vision in order to help the president during the United States' third century avoid the attack on America, Lion feels compelled to tell this gripping, amazing story to protect future generations! For more details go to the website: www.georgewashingtonvision.com.

THE WHITE HOUSE
WASHINGTON
March 2, 2004

Mr. Daniel Lion
Post Office Box 581
Wildwood, Maine 04222

Dear Mr. Lion:

On behalf of President Bush, thank you for your letter and the copy of your book. The President appreciates hearing your views and concerns.

President Bush remains confident in the faith and resolve of our Nation, and he is confronting our country's challenges with focus, clarity, and courage. As the President has said, these are times of great consequence, and he is working for a prosperity that is broadly shared, strengthening domestic programs vital to our country, and answering every danger that threatens the American people.

To accomplish these goals, President Bush welcomes suggestions from all Americans. Thank you again for sharing your ideas.

Desiree Thompson

Special Assistant to the President
and Director of Presidential Correspondence

**This book is dedicated to
my God,
my family, my brother
and my country.**

ACKNOWLEDGMENT

I would like to thank Monsignor Charles Murphy, whose parish at Holy Martyrs in Falmouth, Maine gave me the inspiration to identify the precognition of 9/11 and to try to stop the evil from happening in the only way a good citizen can, by writing to our leaders.

I pray that the United States of America will return to the simple, wholehearted belief in God upon which George Washington and his peers founded this country. Their faith in God has been passed down through the ages not only in my family but also in the families of the servicemen and women who protect us and our free beliefs.

I hope that someday our Muslim and communist brothers of the world will see that we are trying to help them find freedom, hope, and prosperity under faith in God. Then they will recognize the radical elements that have led them astray and leave these radical elements behind.

TABLE OF CONTENTS

ABOUT THE BOOK..v

ACKNOWLEDGMENT.. xi

THE PAST xvii
    Prelude xvii

THE GEORGE WASHINGTON VISION.............................1
    George Washington and His Vision..............................2
    The Revolutionary War Years 8
    The Civil War Years 12
    The Twentieth Century 14

DAVID LION'S LIFE AND BOOK 19
    The Enlightenment 19
    David's Book: Prologue 20
    David's Book: Dedication 21
    David's Book: Foreword.. 22
    David's Book: Out of the Sadness 23
    David's Book: In Search of Peace.............................. 27
    David's Book: Finding the Right Place to Ski............. 32
    David's Book: Purgatory 34
    David's Book: Fearing Nuclear War 38
    David's Book 1981 40
    David's Book: "Averting the Holocaust".................... 44
    David's Book: Changing My Skiing Goal – Skiing for
    Peace 48
    David's Book: A Fateful Event................................... 52
    David's Book: Time Out 55
    David's Book: Becoming a Good Father..................... 58
    David's Book: Six Years of Loneliness...................... 62
    David's Book: Ending the Journey 64
    David's Book: Sugarloaf: The Inspiration.................. 66

THE BEGINNING OF SORROWS 70
    "Fire Falling From the Sky"...................................... 71
    The Vision of the Mountain 74
    The Epiphany.. 77

The Vision of the Scroll 81
The Confession: A Cleansing Before Becoming "Born
Again" 88
The Presentation 90
OUT OF THE DEPTHS 92
The Sorceries of Ward P666 93
Faith in God vs. the Sorceries 98
Samuel Adams: Thunder and Lightning 102
Salem 105
Warning the Leaders 107
The Fraud of the Sorcerers 110
The Hippocratic Oath 115
A Page from David's Paper Twenty Years Later 117
September 11th 120
Hospitalization Aftermath 123
THE PRESENT 129
Post 9 / 11: Inspiring Our Leaders With the George
Washington Vision 130
David Studies Islam: The Mahdi vs. Ad-Dajjal 139
THE FUTURE 145
The Code 146
Science of Mind 150
The Senator 152
The Next Generation: The Hawk and the Eagle 153
The Final Vision 156
The Eagle Competes 159
The U.S. Space Force 162
Area 51 166
Oh Holy Night 170
Hacker Attacker: The Kujinator 173
The Red Peril 176
Hawk and Databyte Cowgirl 178
True Love 180
The Wahhabis 183
More Study of Islam and the News: Saudi Arabia 187
Muslims Victories before the Dajjal's Appearance 191
The Kaaba and the Capture of Osama bin Laden 193

Son of Atta 198
The Mortal Head Wound 202
The Whole World Was Amazed 204
King of the South 212
The Oilfields 214
The Russian Equation 217
Kings of the East 221
The Third Red Revelation 225
The Red Sky 227
And the Dragon Knocked the Stars from the Sky 230
The Red Light of Europe 233
Red Sun Rising 235
Top Secret Bombs 237
General Mark West 240
Centcom Headquarters 242
The Eagle Soars 245
China Doll 248
An Angel Opens Her Eyes 250
The Unholy Spear 257
Shattered Dream 259
Broken China Doll 261
The Revelation 264
Ride 'em, Cowgirl 269
An Airborne Hawk 271
Bathe Seoul with Fire 275
Centcom Rules 276
The Koptenators 278
The Lake of Fire 282
Christ Appears in China 284
Lion's Den 289

AFTERWORD 291

APPENDIX A The START Treaty 293

APPENDIX B David Lion's Letters to National Leaders 295

APPENDIX C David Lion's Drawings of His Defense Ideas Such as the Peace-Ball 323

THE PAST

Prelude

The year was 1666. Isaac Newton was sitting up late one night in the study at Westminster and had his Bible open to Daniel, Chapter 7. He was tired, but he kept working on figuring out the exact date of the end of the world. He knew the Bible prophet Daniel would have the answer.

He read that in the first year of Belshazzar king of Babylon, Daniel had a dream. When he woke up, he wrote down the dream, recording the main facts. Then Daniel spoke, saying, "I saw in my vision by night, and behold, the four winds of heaven were stirring up the Great Sea. And four great beasts came up from the sea, each different from the other. The first was like a lion, and had eagle's wings. I watched till its wings were plucked off; and it was lifted up from the earth and made to stand on two feet like a man, and a man's heart was given to it. And suddenly I beheld another beast, a second, like a bear. It was raised up on one side, and had three ribs in its mouth between its teeth. And they said thus to it: 'Arise, devour much flesh!' After this I looked, and there was another, like a leopard, which had on its back four wings of a bird. The beast also had four heads, and dominion was given to it. After this I saw in the night visions, and behold a forth beast, dreadful and terrible, exceedingly strong. It had huge iron teeth; it was devouring, breaking in pieces, and trampling in the residue with its feet. It was different from all beasts that were before it, and it had ten horns. I was considering the horns, and there was another horn, a little one, coming up among them, before whom three of the first horns were plucked out by the roots. And there, in this horn, were eyes like the eyes of a man, and a mouth speaking pompous words."

Daniel was perplexed by this vision, so he asked about its interpretation. This is what he learned:

"I, Daniel, was grieved in my spirit within my body, and the visions of my head troubled me. I came near to one of those who stood by and asked him the truth of all this. So he told me and made known to me the interpretation of these things: 'Those great beasts, which are four, are four kings which arise out of the earth. But the saints of the Most High shall receive the kingdom, and possess the kingdom forever, even forever and ever.' Then I wished to know the truth about the fourth beast, which was different from all the others, exceedingly dreadful, with its teeth of iron and its nails of bronze, which devoured, broke in pieces, and trampled the residue with its feet; and the ten horns that were on its head, and the other horn which came up, before which three fell, namely that horn which had eyes and a mouth which spoke pompous words whose appearance was greater that his fellows. I was watching and the same horn was making war against the saints, and prevailing against them, until the Ancient of Days came and a judgment was made in favor of the saints of the Most High, and the time came for the saints to possess the kingdom.

"Thus he said: 'The fourth beast shall be a fourth kingdom on earth, which shall be different from all other kingdoms, and shall devour the whole earth, trample it and break it in pieces. The ten horns are ten kings who shall arise from this kingdom. And another shall rise after them; He shall be different from the first ones, and shall subdue three kings. He shall speak pompous words against the Most High, and shall intend to change times and law. Then the saints shall be given into his hand for a time and times and half a time.

"'But the court shall be seated, and they shall take away his dominion, to consume and destroy it forever. Then the kingdom and dominion, and the greatness of the kingdoms under the whole heaven, shall be given to the people, the saints of the Most High. His kingdom is an everlasting kingdom, and all dominions shall serve and obey Him. And in the latter time of their kingdom, when the transgressors have reached their fullness, a king shall arise, having fierce features, who understands sinister schemes. His power shall be mighty but not by his own power; he shall destroy fearfully, and shall prosper and thrive; he shall destroy the mighty, and also the holy people.

"'Through his cunning he shall cause deceit to prosper under his rule; and he shall exalt himself in his heart. He shall destroy many in their prosperity. He shall even rise against the Prince of princes; but he shall be broken without human means.

"'And the vision of the evenings and mornings which was told is true; therefore seal up the vision, for it refers to many days in the future.'

"And I, Daniel, fainted and was sick for days; afterward I arose and went about the king's business. I was astonished by the vision, but no one understood it."

Isaac Newton pondered Daniel's prophecy. He believed that the Bible is literally true in every respect. A substantial portion of his enormous energy went to the study of the Bible and Biblical texts and history. He read the Bible daily throughout his life and wrote notes regarding his study which were over a million words in length..

Newton was a formidable Biblical scholar, was fluent in the ancient languages, and had extensive knowledge of ancient history. He wrote two treatises on Bible prophecies, "Published Observations Upon the Prophecies of Daniel" and "The Apocalypse of St. John."

Daniel's prophecy recorded above is called the Revelation, with respect to the Scripture of Truth, which Daniel was commanded to shut up and seal till the time of the end. Daniel sealed it until the time of the end, and until that time comes and the Lamb opens the seals, it will remain sealed. This means that the prophecies of Daniel and John will not be fully understood until the time of the end. However, it also means that some men should prophesy out of it. When they interpret the prophecy, they will be in an afflicted and mournful state for a long time. Their interpretations will be dark, so as to convert but few. But in the very end, the prophecy should be so far interpreted that it will convince many.

Newton commented on this verse: "Then said Daniel, many shall run to and fro, and knowledge shall be increased." He said, "Tis therefore a part of this Prophecy, that it should not be understood before the last age of the world; and therefore it makes for the credit of the Prophecy, that it is not yet understood. But if the last age, the age of opening these things, be now approaching, as by the great success of late Interpreters it seems to be, we have more encouragement that ever to look in to these things. If the general preaching of the Gospel be approaching, it is for us a dour posterity that these words mainly belong: In the time of the end the wise shall understand, but none of the wicked shall understand. 'Blessed is he that readeth, and they hear the words Prophecy, and keep those things that are written therein.'" (Daniel XII 4, 10, Apoc. I 3).

Newton had been working on a three dimensional pyramid of Greek letters which dealt with the three prophecies concerning the end of the world and Christ's return to Earth. He created a mathematical matrix of algorithms in order to develop a calculation of the year of Christ's return so he could warn men of God and His future actions and thus awaken men to their purpose. He held his mathematical matrix up to the candlelight, and this is what he saw:

ΟΧΙΛΙΑΡΧΟΣΔΕΕΦΟΒΗΘΗΕΠΙΓΝΟΥΣΟΤΙΡΩΜΑΙΟΣΕΣΤΙ
ΝΚΑΙΟΤΙΗΝΑΥΤΟΝΑΔΕΔΕΚΩΣΤΗΔΕΕΠΑΥΡΙΟΝΒΟΥΛΟΜΕΝ
ΟΣΓΝΩΝΑΙΤΟΑΣΦΑΛΕΣΤΟΤΙΚΑΤΗΓΟΡΕΙΤΑΙΠΑΡΑΤΩΝ
ΟΥΔΑΙΩΝΕΛΥΣΕΝΑΥΤΟΝΑΠΟΤΩΝΔΕΣΜΩΝΚΑΙΕΚΕΛΕΥΣΕ
ΝΕΛΘΕΙΝΤΟΥΣΑΡΧΙΕΡΕΙΣΚΑΙΟΛΟΝΤΟΣΥΝΕΔΡΙΟΝΑΥΤ
ΩΝΚΑΙΚΑΤΑΓΑΓΩΝΤΟΝΠΑΥΛΟΝΕΣΤΗΣΕΝΕΙΣΑΥΤΟΥΣΑΤ
ΕΝΙΣΑΣΔΕΟΠΑΥΛΟΣΤΩΣΥΝΕΔΡΙΩΕΙΠΕΝΑΝΑΡΕΣΑΔΕΛΦ
ΟΙΕΓΩΠΑΣΗΣΥΝΕΙΔΗΣΕΙΑΓΑΘΗΠΕΠΟΛΙΤΕΥΜΑΙΤΩΘΕΩ
ΑΧΡΙΤΑΥΤΗΣΤΗΣΗΜΕΡΑΣΟΔΕΑΡΧΙΕΡΕΥΣΑΝΑΝΙΑΣΕΠΕ
ΤΑΞΕΝΤΟΙΣΠΑΡΕΣΤΩΣΙΝΑΥΤΩΤΥΠΤΕΙΝΑΥΤΟΥΤΟΣΤΟΜ
ΑΤΟΤΕΟΠΑΥΛΟΣΠΡΟΣΑΥΤΟΝΕΙΠΕΝΤΥΠΤΕΙΝΣΕΜΕΛΛΕΙ
ΟΘΡΟΣΤΟΙΧΕΚΕΚΟΝΙΑΜΕΝΕΚΑΙΣΥΚΑΘΗΚΡΙΝΩΝΜΕΚΑΤ
ΑΤΟΝΝΟΜΟΝΚΑΙΠΑΡΑΝΟΜΩΝΚΕΛΕΥΕΙΣΜΕΤΥΠΤΕΣΘΑΙ
ΟΙΔΕΠΑΡΕΣΤΩΤΕΣΠΟΝΤΟΝΑΡΧΙΕΡΕΑΤΟΥΘΕΟΥΛΟΙΔΟ
ΡΕΙΣΕΦΗΤΕΟΠΑΥΛΟΣΟΥΚΗΔΕΙΝΑΔΕΛΦΟΙΟΤΙΕΣΤΙΝΑΡ
ΧΙΕΡΕΥΣΓΕΓΡΑΠΤΑΙΓΑΡΑΡΧΟΝΤΑΤΟΥΛΑΟΥΣΟΥΟΥΚΕΡ
ΕΙΣΚΑΚΩΣΓΝΟΥΣΑΡΟΠΑΥΛΟΣΟΤΙΤΟΕΝΜΕΡΟΣΕΣΤΙΝΣΑ
ΔΔΟΥΚΑΙΩΝΤΟΔΕΕΤΕΡΟΝΦΑΡΙΣΑΙΩΝΕΚΡΑΖΕΝΕΝΤΩΣΥ
ΝΕΔΡΙΩΑΝΑΡΕΣΑΔΕΛΦΟΙΕΓΩΦΑΡΙΣΑΙΟΣΕΙΜΙΥΙΟΣΦΑ
ΡΙΣΑΙΟΥΠΕΡΙΕΛΠΙΔΟΣΚΑΙΑΝΑΣΤΑΣΕΩΣΝΕΚΡΩΝΕΓΩΚ
ΡΙΝΟΜΑΙΤΟΥΤΟΔΕΑΥΤΟΥΛΑΛΗΣΑΝΤΟΣΕΓΕΝΕΤΟΣΤΑΣΙ
ΣΤΩΝΦΑΡΙΣΑΙΩΝΚΑΙΤΩΝΣΑΔΔΟΥΚΑΙΩΝΚΑΙΕΣΧΙΣΘΗΤ
ΟΠΛΗΘΟΣΣΑΔΔΟΥΚΑΙΟΙΜΕΝΓΑΡΛΕΓΟΥΣΙΝΜΗΕΙΝΑΙΑΝ
ΑΣΤΑΣΙΝΜΗΔΕΑΓΓΕΛΟΝΜΗΤΕΠΝΕΥΜΑΦΑΡΙΣΑΙΟΙΔΕΟΜ
ΟΛΟΓΟΥΣΙΝΤΑΑΜΦΟΤΕΡΑΕΓΕΝΕΤΟΔΕΚΡΑΥΓΗΜΕΓΑΛΗΚ
ΑΙΑΝΑΣΤΑΝΤΕΣΟΙΓΡΑΜΜΑΤΕΙΣΤΟΥΜΕΡΟΥΣΤΩΝΦΑΡΙΣ
ΑΙΩΝΑΙΕΜΑΧΟΝΤΟΛΕΓΟΝΤΕΣΟΥΔΕΝΚΑΚΟΝΕΥΡΙΣΚΟΜΕ
ΝΕΝΤΩΑΝΘΡΩΠΩΤΟΥΤΩΕΙΔΕΠΝΕΥΜΑΕΛΑΛΗΣΕΝΑΥΤΩΗ
ΓΓΕΛΟΣΜΗΘΕΟΜΑΧΩΜΕΝΠΟΛΛΗΣΔΕΓΕΝΟΜΕΝΗΣΣΤΑΣΕΩ
ΣΕΥΛΑΒΗΘΕΙΣΟΧΙΛΙΑΡΧΟΣΜΗΔΙΑΣΠΑΣΘΗΟΠΑΥΛΟΣΥΠ
ΑΥΤΩΝΕΚΕΛΕΥΣΕΝΤΟΣΤΡΑΤΕΥΜΑΚΑΤΑΒΑΝΑΡΠΑΣΑΙΑΥ
ΤΟΝΕΚΜΕΣΟΥΑΥΤΩΝΑΓΕΙΝΤΕΕΙΣΤΗΝΠΑΡΕΜΒΟΛΗΝΤΗΔ
ΕΕΠΙΟΥΣΗΝΥΚΤΙΕΠΙΣΤΑΣΑΥΤΩΟΚΥΡΙΟΣΕΙΠΕΝΘΑΡΣΕ
ΙΠΑΥΛΟΣΩΣΓΑΡΔΙΕΜΑΡΤΥΡΩΤΑΠΕΡΙΕΜΟΥΕΙΣΙΕΡΟΥΣΑ
ΛΗΜΟΥΤΟΣΣΕΔΕΙΚΑΙΕΙΣΡΩΜΗΝΜΑΡΤΥΡΗΣΑΙΓΕΝΟΜΕΝ
ΗΣΔΕΗΜΕΡΑΣΠΟΙΗΣΑΝΤΕΣΤΙΝΟΣΤΩΝΙΟΥΔΑΙΩΝΣΥΣΤΡ
ΟΦΗΝΑΝΕΘΕΜΑΤΙΣΑΝΕΑΥΤΟΥΣΛΕΓΟΝΤΕΣΜΗΤΕΦΑΓΕΙΝΜ
ΗΤΕΠΙΕΙΝΕΩΣΟΥΑΠΟΚΤΕΙΝΩΣΙΝΤΟΝΠΑΥΛΟΝΑΝΑΔΕ
ΗΣΑΝΟΥΣΤΕΣΣΑΡΑΚΟΝΤΑΟΙΤΑΥΤΗΝΤΗΝΣΥΝΩΜΟΣΙΑΝΠ
ΕΠΟΙΗΚΟΤΕΣΟΙΤΙΝΕΣΠΡΟΣΕΛΘΟΝΤΕΣΤΟΙΣΑΡΧΙΕΡΕΥ
ΣΕΙΝΚΑΙΤΟΙΣΠΡΕΣΒΥΤΕΡΟΙΣΕΙΠΟΝΑΝΑΘΕΜΑΤΙΑΝΕΘΕ
ΜΑΤΙΣΑΜΕΝΕΑΥΤΟΥΣΜΗΔΕΝΟΣΓΕΥΣΑΣΘΑΙΕΩΣΟΥΑΠΟΚ
ΤΕΙΝΩΜΕΝΟΝΠΑΥΛΟΝΝΥΝΟΥΝΥΜΕΙΣΕΜΦΑΝΙΣΑΤΕΤΩΧ
ΙΛΙΑΡΧΩΣΥΝΤΩΣΥΝΕΔΡΙΩΟΠΩΣΑΥΡΙΟΝΑΥΤΟΝΚΑΤΑΓΑ
ΓΗΠΡΟΣΥΜΑΣΩΣΜΕΛΛΟΝΤΑΣΔΙΑΓΙΝΩΣΚΕΙΝΑΚΡΙΒΕΣΤ
ΕΡΟΝΤΑΠΕΡΙΑΥΤΟΥΗΜΕΙΣΑΔΕΠΡΟΤΟΥΕΓΓΙΣΑΙΑΥΤΟΝΕ
ΤΟΙΜΟΙΕΣΜΕΝΤΟΥΑΝΕΛΕΙΝΑΥΤΟΝΑΚΟΥΣΑΣΔΕΟΥΙΟΣΤ
ΗΣΑΔΕΛΦΗΣΠΑΥΛΟΥΤΟΕΝΕΔΡΟΝΠΑΡΑΓΕΝΟΜΕΝΟΣΚΑΙΕ
ΙΣΕΛΘΩΝΕΙΣΤΗΝΠΑΡΕΜΒΟΛΗΝΑΠΗΓΓΕΙΛΕΝΤΩΠΑΥΛΩ

Isaac Newton sat alone in the dark, working on the numerology equation from the Bible in Daniel, Chapter VII. This Biblical code* would provide him with the approximate date and year of Jesus Christ's return to earth. Never had a mind such as Newton's existed. A pale man who never married, he came up with the theories of gravity and escape velocity needed to attain orbit around the planet. It became clear from his equations that the planet's gravitational fields were holding everything in balance. What would upset that balance on the earth? Huge earthquakes and fires perhaps? Gigantic explosions of an impact which no one had ever seen before? He didn't know for certain, but as he worked through the Biblical history, he checked every aspect of the Bible prophecies and revelation. He could not find even one inconsistency.

As Newton sat in the dark, it was as though the whole room became illuminated and he was in the middle of a giant holographic pyramid, looking at Hebrew letters. Arranged and assigned concurrently were Greek numerals, together forming a matrix. This illumination was provided by the divine and deep spiritual introspection which he had done throughout his life. He wrote the number of the year of his final calculation down on a piece of parchment. The next day, he expired. Isaac Newton had gone to the heavens. He had spent his earthly life pursuing ideas for the betterment of mankind and especially for the benefit of those who would live far in the future.

Although his discovery was unknown to the world, before his death Isaac Newton gave it to Peter Lion, who immigrated to America in the 1600's and brought it with him. Peter Lion passed it to his grandson, Daniel Lion I, who became a colonel in the continental army in 1775 and served in the 14th Virginia regiment under General George Washington.

*Note: It is a historical fact that Isaac Newton actually did develop a numerology equation or code based on the Biblical prophecies in the book of Daniel.

THE GEORGE WASHINGTON VISION

George Washington and His Vision

"While the stars remain, and the heavens send down dew upon the earth, so long shall the Union last." (George Washington's Vision)

In Valley Forge during the winter of 1777, American forces were fighting against the British, the most powerful nation in the world. The Americans were freezing, starving, bleeding, dying, and about to give up hope. George Washington knelt in the snow to pray. Colonel Daniel Lion happened upon General Washington, alone and on his knees in the snow. Washington was praying to God while tears ran down his cheeks. The General was so consumed with emotion that he did not realize that Colonel Lion was present. What both men saw next was recorded by Washington; his document now resides in the Library of Congress.

This is George Washington's vision: "This afternoon, something seemed to disturb me. Looking up, I beheld standing opposite me a singularly beautiful female. So astonished was I, for I had given strict orders not to be disturbed, that it was some moments before I found language to inquire the cause of her presence. A second, a third, and even a fourth time did I repeat my question, but received no answer from my mysterious visitor except a slight raising of her eyes.

"By this time I felt strange sensations spreading through me. I would have risen but the riveted gaze of the being before me rendered volition impossible. I assayed once more to address her, but my tongue had become useless, as though it had become paralyzed.

2

"A new influence, mysterious, potent, irresistible, took possession of me. All I could do was to gaze steadily, vacantly at my unknown visitor. Gradually the surrounding atmosphere seemed to rarefy, the mysterious visitor herself becoming more airy and yet more distinct to my sight than before. I now began to feel as one dying, or rather to experience the sensations which I have sometimes imagined accompany dissolution. I did not think, I did not reason, I did not move; all were alike impossible. I was only conscious of gazing fixedly, vacantly at my companion.

"Presently I heard a voice saying, 'Son of the Republic, look and learn,' while at the same time my visitor extended her arm eastwardly. I now beheld a heavy white vapor at some distance rising fold upon fold. This gradually dissipated, and I looked upon a strange scene. Before me lay spread out in one vast plain all the countries of the world; Europe, Asia, Africa and America. I saw rolling and tossing between Europe and America the billows of the Atlantic and between Asia and America lay the Pacific.

"'Son of the Republic,' said the same mysterious voice as before, 'look and learn.' At that moment I beheld a dark, shadowy being, like an angel, standing, or rather floating in mid-air, between Europe and America. Dipping water out of the ocean in the hollow of each hand, he sprinkled some upon America with his right hand, while with his left hand he cast some on Europe. Immediately, a cloud rose from these countries and joined in mid-ocean. For a while it remained stationary, and then moved slowly westward, until it enveloped America in its murky folds. Sharp flashes of lightning gleamed through it at intervals, and I heard the smothered groans and cries of the American people.

"A second time the angel dipped water from the ocean, and sprinkled it out as before. The dark cloud was then drawn back to the ocean, in whose heaving billows it sank from view. A third time I hear the mysterious voice saying, 'Son of the Republic, look and learn.' I cast my eyes upon America and beheld village and towns and cities springing up, one after another, until the whole land from the Atlantic to the Pacific was dotted with them.

"Again, I heard the mysterious voice say, 'Son of the Republic, the end of the century cometh, look and learn.' At this, the dark

3

shadowy angel turned his face southward, and from Africa I saw an ill-omened spectre approach our land. It flitted slowly over every town and city of the latter. The inhabitants presently set themselves in battle array against each other. As I continued looking I saw a bright angel, on whose brow rested a crown of light, on which was traced the word 'Union.' He bore the American flag which he placed between the divided nation, and he said, 'Remember – ye are brethren.' Instantly, the inhabitants, casting from them their weapons, became friends once more and united around the National Standard.

"And again I heard the mysterious voice saying, 'Son of the Republic, look and learn.' At this the dark, shadowy angel placed a trumpet to his mouth, and blew three distinct blasts; and taking water from the ocean, he sprinkled it upon Europe, Asia and Africa. Then my eyes beheld a fearful scene: from each of these countries arose thick, black clouds that were soon joined into one. Throughout this mass there gleamed a dark red light by which I saw hordes of armed men, who, moving with the cloud, marched by land and sailed by sea to America. Our country was enveloped in this volume of cloud, and I saw these vast armies devastate the whole country and burn the villages, towns, and cities that I beheld springing up. As my ears listened to the thundering of the cannon, clashing of swords, and the shouts and cries of millions in mortal combat, I heard again the mysterious voice saying, 'Son of the Republic, look and learn.' When the voice had ceased, the dark shadowy angel placed his trumpet once more to his mouth, and blew a long and fearful blast.

"Instantly, a light as of a thousand suns shone down from above me and pierced and broke into fragments the dark cloud which enveloped America. At the same moment the angel upon whose head still shone the word 'Union,' and who bore our national flag in one hand and a sword in the other, descended from the heavens attended by legions of white spirits. These immediately joined the inhabitants of America, who I perceived were well nigh overcome, but who immediately taking courage again, closed up their broken ranks and renewed the battle.

"Again, amid the fearful noise of the conflict, I heard the mysterious voice saying, 'Son of the Republic, look and learn.' As the voice ceased, the shadowy angel for the last time dipped water from the ocean and sprinkled it upon America. Instantly the dark cloud rolled back, together with the armies it had brought, leaving the inhabitants of the land victorious!

"Then once more I beheld the villages, towns and cities springing up where I had seen them before, while the bright angel, planting the azure standard he had brought in the midst of them, cried with a loud voice, 'While the stars remain, and the heavens send down dew upon the earth, so long shall the Union last.' And taking from his brow the crown on which was blazoned the word 'Union,' he placed it upon the standard, while the people, kneeling down, said, 'Amen.'

"The scene instantly began to fade and dissolve, and I at last saw nothing but the rising, curling vapor I at first beheld. This also disappearing, I found myself once more gazing upon the mysterious visitor, who, in the same voice I had heard before, said, 'Son of the Republic, what you have seen is thus interpreted: three great perils will come upon the Republic. The most fearful is the third, but in this greatest conflict the whole world united shall not prevail against her. Let every child of the Republic learn to live for his God, his land and the Union.' With these words the vision vanished, and I started from my seat and felt that I had seen a vision wherein had been shown to me the birth, progress and destiny of the United States." (Library of Congress document of George Washington's vision)

Colonel Daniel Lion I was present at the scene of Washington's vision and saw the vision himself as he stood behind a bush. Lion was a young officer from Virginia who had fought alongside General Washington. He was so trusted by the General that he was his personal attaché officer. Through the mist, he witnessed the same events and vision of the future.

The Lord God did indeed bestow inspiration upon George Washington, who went on to lead the American nation on to victory in the Revolutionary War. The first woe was passed. Washington knew that God had protected him during the war because several times during battle he was grazed with bullets which pierced his outer garments but did not inflict a wound. He was rewarded with the presidency twice, and declined a third term because his love for his country prevented him from leading it as a monarch.

A pact with God had been established with the United States of America. Almost all the founding fathers and signers of the Constitution were deeply religious men who believed that God would lead the country out of any difficult situation provided that the country remained unified in belief in Him. Consider these words from George Washington, the Father of our Nation, in his farewell speech on September 19, 1796: "It is impossible to govern the world without God and the Bible. Of all the dispositions and habits that lead to political prosperity, our religion and morality are the indispensable supporters. Let us with caution indulge the supposition that morality can be maintained without religion. Reason and experience forbid us to expect that our national morality can prevail in exclusion of religious principle."

General George Washington's private words also reflected his deep faith. His Monday Morning Prayer began: "O Eternal and Everlasting God, I presume to present myself this morning before thy Divine majesty, beseeching thee to accept of my humble and hearty thanks, that it hath pleased thy great goodness to keep and preserve me the night past from all the dangers poor mortals are subject to, and hath given me sweet and pleasant sleep, whereby I find my body refreshed and comforted for performing the duties of this day, in which I beseech thee to defend me from all perils of body and soul."

To the soldiers who fought under his command, including Colonel Daniel Lion I, General George Washington said, "I hope and trust that every officer and man will endeavor to live and act as becomes a Christian soldier defending the dearest rights and liberties of his country. To the distinguished character of Patriot it should be our highest glory to add the more distinguished character of Christian."

And how did General George Washington portray his personal role in the Revolutionary War? "I was but the humble agent of a favoring heaven, whose benign influence was so often manifested in our behalf, and to whom the praise of victory alone is due."

Like its leader, the United States of American had established a pact with God. Almost all the founding fathers and signers of the Constitution were men of great faith. Further evidence of the Christian character of the country is found on every dollar bill in the phrase, "In God We Trust." The birth of the United States had happened as described in Washington's vision: "I cast my eyes upon America and beheld villages and towns and cities springing up, one after another, until the whole land from the Atlantic to the Pacific was dotted with them."

The Revolutionary War Years

Conditions were terrible during the winter of 1777 at Valley Forge. The British had just captured Philadelphia, and the Continental Army was struggling to keep itself alive. Lacking food and clothing, the men were dying of exposure and starvation. Certain political leaders – many of them jealous of Washington – began to whisper that the general's cause was hopeless.

But the men who served under Washington felt differently. Washington was a leader like no other, and he inspired their loyalty.

In today's "anything goes" culture, intense striving after moral excellence is rare. But it was the reason Washington's men were willing to sacrifice for him, even when their cause appeared hopeless. Later, Washington's striving after moral excellence was the reason he was chosen as our first president.

Many soldiers were taken as prisoners of war by the British. General George Washington heard reports of abuse on the prison ships, and in 1777 he wrote to the ranking British officer, General Lord William Howe. He wrote, "You may call us rebels, and say that we deserve no better treatment, but remember, that supposing us rebels, we still have feelings ..."

The terrible conditions faced by prisoners of war during this time are described in the following report from the National Archives. It is a testimony of just how committed Washington's men were. This account was given by Daniel Lion II, son of the man who fought with Washington:

Daniel Lion II related, "that he frequently and repeatedly heard his father, the said Colonel Daniel Lion I, relate his service in the Revolutionary war, and that he first enlisted (as well as his son now recollected) in Albemarle county, Virginia in the year of 1775 or 1776. That enlistment was under Captain Thomas Holt of one of the Virginia regiments. (The son no longer remembers the number of the regiment his father originally joined nor the name of the commander of the regiment). The son frequently heard his father relate stories of some of the battles which he distinctly yet recollects, to wit, the battle of Brandywine, the battle at Monmouth, the battle at Germantown, and the battle at Long Island (which he said was the hardest and toughest of any). After the 14th Virginia Regiment was split up from General Washington, Daniel Lion I was in the siege of Charleston in South Carolina, where he was taken prisoner by the British and put aboard a dungeon ship about nine months. During that time he never saw land. He was confined in irons while prisoner, and his legs and ankles were made extremely sore by the irons. His son had seen the marks and sores caused by the irons on his father's legs while a prisoner. One William Westbrook was taken a prisoner by the British at the same time as Daniel Lion I and was confined in the dungeon in irons upon the same vessel. The son frequently heard Westbrook and his father, Colonel Daniel Lion I, relate together the same story about the being taken prisoners at Charleston and about their escape. They described how they made their escape from the British somewhere at or near Quebec in Canada. They were able to escape while the vessel lay near the shore one night because they had the irons taken off their legs on account of the extreme soreness and danger of their wounds becoming mortal. They returned home together to Albemarle County, Virginia about the year 1782. The son repeatedly heard the said Colonel Daniel Lion I and Westbrook speak of their services and sufferings in the war and say that they had been massmates together while in the service. At the time of this writing, Westbrook has been dead a number of years; he died in Virginia. The son heard Colonel Daniel Lion I say often that he had seen two horses shot dead from under General Washington during battle."

Colonel David Lion I was one of the first prisoners of war of the United States, living in dreadful conditions of starvation, disease, and death. Nights were especially bad. Lion would fall asleep thinking of the vision he had seen with General Washington. He saw the coming of a new, free country in angelic and heavenly dreams. To get through the night, he shared the prayer that General Washington had given him with William Westbrook, who was chained to the same mast. "Oh, eternal and everlasting God, direct my thoughts, words and work. Wash away my sins in the immaculate blood of the Lamb and purge my heart by thy Holy Spirit. Daily, frame me more and more in the likeness of thy son, Jesus Christ, that living in thy fear, and dying in thy favor, I may in thy appointed time obtain the resurrection of the justified unto eternal life. Bless, O Lord, the whole race of mankind and let the world be filled with the knowledge of thee and thy son, Jesus Christ."

Days aboard the prison ship, the Esk, were not much better than nights. The men were confined in three-foot cages much of the time. Colonel Daniel Lion I shared moldy bread and foul water with William Westbrooke. Thousands died of disease and malnutrition; the conditions were inhumane. Epidemics that could have been stopped by good nutrition emptied the prison ships by death. "Turn out your dead," the jailers would yell each day on the rounds of the prison ships.

The prisoners looked sickly and ghastly. Some cursed the day they were born and the God above. Others would pray the "Our Father" until they became delirious. At times like these, Colonel Daniel Lion I had visions of his descendents walking in a new America, free of British oppression.

The British offered the American prisoners a way to escape their suffering. They told them that if they would join the British forces, it would mean freedom from the prison ship. Great numbers of prisoners did just that. For the officers, who perhaps knew secrets about American military tactics, the offer came daily. The temptation to desert to the British grew as the months progressed. But Colonel Lion persisted in the prayer, "lead us not into temptation." As the shackles that were on his wrists and ankles bit through his skin to the bone, his single solace was recalling the sight of George Washington when they had together witnessed the vision at Valley Forge. He called it the George Washington Vision.

Colonel Daniel Lion did not give up information to the British, nor did he tell them of his vision with George Washington at Valley Forge. He told no one except family members, and they have become a long line of servants to God and the United States. I, Daniel Lion VII, am one of his descendents. I first heard the original story of the George Washington Vision from my Great Aunt Hazel. She said, "You are descended from a man who fought by General Washington's side!" I am the seventh generation of that man: I am the news bearer to the present citizens of the United States.

The Civil War Years

Almost a century passed before the second peril of George Washington's vision, the Civil War, began. During this time, three generations of the Lion family also passed.

The country was on the verge of "brother against brother," the second peril that my ancestor had witnessed in the George Washington Vision. The Union Army was trying to defend the city of Washington from being besieged by the Confederate Army. General Daniel Lion IV was in the tent of General George Brinton McClellan, commander of the Union Army, and they were talking strategy. Already, they had been through a bloody campaign in which tens of thousands of Americans had died. General Lion related the George Washington Vision to General McClellan, and then they retired for the night.

As General McClellan was sleeping, an amazing thing happened. At 2 a.m. that early morning in March of 1862, with the Confederate Army surrounding Washington, the locked door to his quarters was thrown open. A voice said, "General McClellan, why do you sleep at your post? Rouse you, or ere it can be prevented, the foe will be in Washington." The voice continued, "General McClellan, you have been betrayed! Had not God willed otherwise, ere the sun of tomorrow had set, the Confederate flag would have waved above the Capitol and your own grave. But note what you see. Your time is short." The spirit of George Washington then raised his hand over McClellan's head and thunder boomed as the mortal man awoke. On his map table he saw a map marked with the exact positions of the Confederate Army. At dawn, General McClellan re-positioned the Union Army around Washington, and they saved the city. General McClellan summarized his account of his vision with these words: "Our beloved, glorious Washington shall again rest quietly, sweetly in his tomb, until perhaps the end of the Prophetic Century approaches. When that time brings the Republic to a third and final struggle, he may once more lay aside the crements of Mount Vernon and become a Messenger of Succor and Peace from the Great Ruler, who has all Nations of the Earth in His keeping." (This is a true, historical account which was documented in the Portland, Maine newspaper).

Abraham Lincoln was aware of the George Washington Vision when The Union was tested in the Civil War. The second woe of the vision was upon them. "The end of the century cometh, look and learn....The inhabitants presently set themselves in battle array against each other....casting from them their weapons became friends once more, and united around the National Standard." Lincoln achieved the fulfillment of Union. He was a martyr for the vision.

The Twentieth Century

Almost another hundred years passed, and the time was halfway through the twentieth century. Three more generations of the Lion family also passed. There was much debate among scholars about the third and final woe of the George Washington Vision which was yet to be faced by the United States of America.

The Lion family was still a stronghold of patriotism. Deep within the heart of a patriot is a love of his God, family, and country. Many patriots are born that way, while some are formed through adversity. In the Lion family, patriotism was deliberately taught and learned. Colonel Daniel Lion I, the officer who fought alongside Washington and shared his vision, passed patriotism down through seven generations of his family until that responsibility fell to David Lion, Jr. By the time David Lion Jr. was ten years old in the year 1969, it was evident that he was a patriot.

David Lion, Jr. was born into a military family. His father, General David Lion, was a fierce patriot, and instilled that love of country into his son. At the age of ten, David was awarded a certificate for "outstanding quality and content of an essay on patriotism."

In his award-winning essay David wrote:

"I think Memorial Day should be a patriotic holiday to keep America and Americans aware of all of its courageous men who went before them into the field of battle. They risked their own lives for the lives of others.

"I believe it is only right to honor those who died for their country. As long as I live, I will respect a soldier who is not thinking about his life, but the lives of his countrymen.

"I know that many Americans feel the same way I do about keeping Memorial Day to honor the men, young and old, who gave their lives for America. Therefore, as long as there is an America, we should keep Memorial Day to honor the men and women who stood up for their country, the United States of America."

David's father, General David Lion, was considered a military genius by many. He helped design the landing gear on the lunar exploration module (LEM), which was the first space vehicle to land on moon. He wrote a paper called "Mule on the Moon" which described the significance of America winning the "space race" to the moon before the USSR. (The Mule was the Army mascot and represented the Army securing the higher ground of space for free people and the United States). As General Lion said, "Many people do not know that we won the race to the moon by only a week as the USSR rocket burnt on the launch pad." General Lion personally selected many of the astronauts who went to the moon, and his presence went to the moon with them. On one mission, they used duct tape to put up a lunar map he made for the mission in the lunar rover. This created a fender so that moon dust would not obscure their vision. That rover, which is now on display at the Smithsonian Institution, still has the duct tape and General Lion's map in it.

David looked up to his father. "Wow," David thought, "What a great man. People joke and call him the smartest man in the world, but I think he really might be the smartest man around. Well, if I were to follow in his footsteps, I would choose to go to MIT and be an Army engineer at age 14 like my dad did."

On the fateful day in July, 1969 when Americans landed on the moon, David was filled with such pride. He felt as though all of mankind, whatever their differences, stood together on planet Earth on that day. They were united in the miracle of the moon landing achievement. It was a testimony to American ingenuity, technical expertise, and purposeful pursuit of a single objective.

David was especially proud because he knew that his father had designed the landing gear for the LEM. That was his father's LEM on the moon! As he was watching the lunar landing on TV, he almost burst with pride when he heard the astronauts say, "Houston, the Eagle has landed." Armstrong stepped down the ladder onto the moon and said, "That's one small step for man and one giant leap for mankind."

David watched as his father tried to take pictures of the LEM sitting on the moon. Astronauts Neil Armstrong and Buzz Aldrin were bouncing off the legs of the spacecraft which he had helped design.

Later, David went outside to look up to the sky. Looking at the moon, he felt that nothing was impossible. He thought, "What's next for this great country? I'm so proud to be an American!" David wished that all people on earth could be free to control their own destiny.

General Lion continued the habits his family had honored for generations ever since the American Revolution. Every Sunday General Lion took his son to church to pray. Their church was built on land that had once belonged to George Washington. David liked to sit in the front row of the chapel before church and think about George Washington. He still believed in the forefathers' pact with God. He looked up at the thirty foot tall stained glass image of General Washington kneeling in the snow and imploring the Lord for help. David believed that he could pray like George Washington did. If he prayed hard enough and stayed honest and virtuous, his prayers could reach the same importance level of our founding father, and they would be answered.

In the spring of 1970 his faith was put to the test. Boy, did he ever pray fervently and need his prayers answered then!

Apollo 13 was launched and had problems with the air supply rapidly leaking. Because his father had been so close to the space program, David felt as though these astronauts were like extended family. They were trapped in the command module with the Lunar Module attached. To stay alive they climbed into the LEM, and by firing the engine on the LEM, they were able to get close to earth.

But they were not close enough, and they were going to run out of air. David knew they might die.

David went to church and knelt before the George Washington window and prayed "Our Fathers." He prayed so hard that he entered another level of consciousness, similar to the experience of a Tibetan monk. David prayed specifically for the crew of Apollo 13 to get back alive. It was all he could do, but he believed in the power of prayer. He believed they would make it! The rest is history. As David watched the carrier rescue, he thanked God for saving the astronauts' lives.

Agnostics would say that it was technical expertise, training, and hard work that brought Apollo 13 back. David would tell you that God put all those forces together and achieved the miracle though the reunification of all the parts which he had made: the incredible human brain and the ability to strive for the single unadulterated purpose of saving lives. Quite simply, the astronauts were saved by having prepared to the best of their worldly abilities in combination with the prayers of many people.

As "Army brats" often are, David was forced to move that year when General Lion was reassigned to the War College. His new home was in Carlisle, Pennsylvania.

As David got older, he became more aware of the threat of nuclear war. When he was in 5th grade, a teacher told the students that if Washington, D.C. were hit by a nuclear bomb that the ripple effect would kill them even though they were over 100 miles away in Pennsylvania. David was shocked.

Then, his friend Chip Munson and he got really into the "Planet of the Apes" movie series. In part two of this series, there is a group of post-nuclear apocalyptic mutants who are worshipping the last underground bomb under the subways. They chant Catholic chants to it, "We believe in one bomb..." Later the apes invade the subway, and Charlton Heston, although wounded, falls on the bomb. This sets off a chain reaction which blows up the whole planet.

Everything seemed to make David became more fearful of nuclear war. On the news, he saw that both the United States and USSR had thousands of nuclear missiles pointed at each other.

Nuclear annihilation seemed to be a frightening possibility at the end of a real sequence of events.

As David contemplated the possibility of nuclear annihilation, he knew he was destined to write a book – a book about his family, a book about his life – which would become an inspiration to a generation.

DAVID LION'S LIFE AND BOOK

The Enlightenment

"The moment I read these words, I beheld another universe and became another man. All at once I felt my mind dazzled by a thousand lights; a crowd of splendid ideas presented themselves to me with such force and in such confusion that I was thrown into a state of indescribable bewilderment."

- Jean Jacques Rousseau, Philosopher of the Enlightenment

David's Book:
Prologue

This is an uplifting book about how one family played a part in making peace on the earth and about the catharsis of bringing peace to their own hearts and family. In an era of nuclear weapons, one thing is being constantly destroyed – the nucleus of the family. Every family should sit at the dinner table and discuss the many things that are important to them individually, within the family, locally, nationally, and internationally. Some of these things must be taught in historical perspective.

This book is an exciting journey of my attempt to find peace. It is a story of adventure, speed, excitement, family, and religion. The intent of the book is that I may share my values with the reader. I hope these values and this book will keep as many families together as possible throughout the world.

David's Book:
Dedication

I would like to thank my family and friends who stuck with me through thick and thin to help me find happiness.

David's Book:
Foreword

Sometimes we put our loved ones, friends, and family through much doubt and pain through our actions and our words. Maybe this happens because we have a goal for happiness that they can't understand. We can not explain our goal to them through speech, thoughts, or written words because it might hurt them. I think many times we sacrifice our needs for the needs of others so much that sometimes we need to just do something for ourselves. It can be a little thing, like taking a walk by the ocean, or skiing, or anything which makes us feel peaceful inside.

The key to this is inner peace. Many times our inner peace is so interrupted by our everyday lives of serving others. We take care of them in every aspect of our daily life and neglect ourselves to the point that we slowly start to lose our own inner peace. Day by day, bit by bit, our inner peace slips away.

The following story is one that needs to be told as a testament to this truth: Don't lose faith. Faith is the only way we will all find inner peace.

David's Book:
Out of the Sadness

Our journey begins when I was twelve, living in the most beautiful city of San Francisco, California. The ocean meets the bay, forming whitecaps under the giant towers and cables of the red Golden Gate Bridge. The bridge seems to reach the sky. Rocky cliffs rise up on either side of the bridge, with mountainous terrain to the north and a sandstone cliff to the south. This cliff is called Old Fort Point, and it still stands at the entrance it used to guard from any attacks at the Sea Gate. To the north are green tree-covered hills and little coves that each flow over the horizon until they vanish out of sight. Small white sailboats dot the deep aqua blue water, and fog horns drone like sick cows in the distance.

Angel Island lies in the middle of the bay. It is a majestic piece of land covered with trails and fragrant with the smell of pine trees. Alcatraz Island is next, right of center, with its old prison house rising above it. The "Birdman" lived there. He had many birds, but alas, no man could fly off "the Rock." Like the Birdman, I have looked through barred windows, past the blue sky as it meets the ocean outside the gate, beyond the bridge as the water disappears into the west, stretching on infinitely.

When my family moved to this paradise, I was only 12 years old, but in reality, I was a man with a child. Let me explain. The year before we moved to San Francisco, my father headed off to Vietnam. He boarded the plane with men dressed for battle, full rucksacks on their backs and carrying M-16 rifles. It occurred to me that the next day these soldiers would land and be at war. My father was going to be shot at and possibly killed. He might not be coming back. He shook my hand and said, "You are the man of the family now." My brother John was only one. I had a baby to take care of! I took that to heart, changing his diapers and being his constant playmate.

At the end of the year, my father returned from war, thanks to many prayers. The one sniper shot that had his name on it had just missed his head. He was rewarded with a reassignment to the Presidio of San Francisco.

My brother was like a son to me, and he was my best friend. My feeling of being John's "father" carried over through our move to San Francisco. Even though my father was with us now, I took care of John in the afternoons. He was a four year old hanging out with fourteen year olds. My mother became concerned that friends my age might be too rough and John might get hurt. So one afternoon, she said "you play football with him for a little bit and then I'll come and pick him up."

After an hour or so of playing, I saw the family station wagon pull up. I said, "There's Mom. Go, John!" And he ran and got in the car. I continued to play with my friends until the end of the game in which I caught a winning touchdown pass. I was exhausted as I proceeded to walk up the 50 stairs to the road. I saw my sisters, Mary and Suzanne, running across the football field screaming, "John's been hit by a car!" It was surreal. I can replay that scene over and over in my head like a movie. We ran home, and my Dad was on the phone. When he got off the phone, I asked him, "How is he?" I had never seen my father cry, and he was crying uncontrollably. He said, "Pretty bad, David."

The next weeks were filled with going to the hospital to see my dear brother's

bruised face and depressed skull. I would talk to him, and he would kick his legs like he was running. I knew he would never be the same. I went to church and I prayed for God to take him. His brain died. His heart soon followed. My parents arranged to have a service at the church. Since I was the leading altar boy, I stoically marched up to the altar and back again after the Mass. My Dad remarked out of sadness that someone told him, "Good to see Dave leading the troops up."

Arrangements were made to fly John's body back to Arlington Memorial Cemetery. No arrangements were made for me to go, although my older brother Daniel was allowed to go. My Aunt Agnes and I took care of the family until my parents and Daniel came back.

My mother blamed herself for years because she had run across the street after telling John he was supposed to stay in the car. However, he got out and then tried to cross the street behind her, only to be hit by oncoming traffic.

Now I must pass on the lesson of this tragedy. Teach your children to listen to you as parents. Teach them to look both ways when they cross the street. Hold their hands. Cross with them. Never, ever, run across the road ahead of them, for blood is thicker than water, and if water flows in a river, blood sticks together like glue. A child's instinct to run after his mother is like sharing of blood in the womb.

This lesson was not observed by my family a few years ago while on vacation. We were at Nags Head / Kitty Hawk, North Carolina. It is a beautiful stretch of sand that meets the ocean. The Wright brothers chose this as the place for man's first flight.

My wife's family has been going there for years. So has our family. Naomi, my wife, her sister Molly, and her family came down. My best friends in the world, Cheryl and Dan Sleepwel and their family decided to come and rent a place across the street from us. We were all walking home from dinner one night. Naomi was pregnant. I was holding my son John's hand. (He was named after my deceased brother). Molly was behind me. Suddenly, and without explanation, Naomi darted across the busy road with cars flying by at 45-50 miles an hour to go say "Hi" to the Sleepwels. My son saw her and ripped free from my grasp and attempted to follow her across the road. Molly grabbed him and prevented him from being hit by an on coming car.

Family saved him. My job and experience as the leader of the family is to protect them, and sometimes I need help. That experience was an exact re-creation of the way in which my brother John had tried to cross following his mom. The similarities were uncanny, except this time Molly saved him. Learn from your mistakes and help protect your family.

After the death of my brother, my father bought Neil Diamond records to bring him solace. As his father's son, I also found music to be a great source of comfort. Before John's death, I was always whistling in my house, so much that my father called me "the whistler." My whistling stopped on the day John died. He was my best friend. My sister Karen bought me Elton John records in order to bring me peace. They did. My favorite songs became "Sunshine on my Shoulder" by John Denver, "Candle in the Wind" by Elton John, and "Shower the People with Love" by James Taylor.

An important part of the enlightenment is to choose some music to help you hum, sing, chant, and just elevate your spirits. Trust me. It will. It can be any tune that makes you happy. If you are in distress, put this book down and do that right now.

David's Book:
In Search of Peace

Inside, all of us are searching for an inner peace with which we can live our lives in the grace of God. We should be so strong and peaceful that we spread peace to others – our friends, or families, and our children. When we slip and fall and are not peaceful, it is up to our families to help us find out what is the matter and help us return to that peace.

When I was 14, I was trying to find peace. John was dead, and his loss was with me every minute of every day. Dad took us all up to Heavenly Valley, California to get some R&R. I met and skied with Sonny Bono up there. I wanted to share with Sonny my deep sadness that he and Cher were splitting up, but I didn't feel it was really any of my business. I could see the pain etched on their daughter Chastidy's face I think it took Sonny's death and funeral for me to see that same despair on Cher's face as I watched his funeral on TV.

I bought ski magazines while at Heavenly Valley, and I read about Spider Sabich and Claudine Longee and Andy William's marriage. Spider was one of the top skiers in the U.S., but he was lustful and had to have someone else's wife. In the end, he was shot dead. A true-life lesson of "Thou shalt not covet thy neighbor's wife" (Deut. 5:21) if ever there was one! Interestingly enough, many skiers wear Spider sweaters on the mountain in spite of his disgrace.

Well, skiing at Heavenly Valley was just that – heavenly. My instructor, Denny, was a short, gnome-like little guy, but he walked around the area like a king with big ski boots. He taught me how to ski fast. I didn't think that I was ready when he picked me to go up the big chair lift, but boy was I ready! The chair lift rose above the clouds, and we got off. I followed Denny closely through white mists and green pine trees again and again. We skied in the sound of silence, as light crystalline flakes of snow began to fall, each so well defined that you could see the crystal shape.

I went home that night and knew that skiing was the most wonderful way for me to ease the pain of my brother John's death. I read on in my ski magazines. I read about Hank Hashawa, a bow-legged champion who had won many races. I read about Jean Claude Killy, the Frenchman who won three medals at the Olympics on dynamic VR-17's. I read also about a young downhill champion named Franz Klammer.

This was an exciting world of heroes. I wanted in on it! My next time skiing was up at Dodge Ridge in the beautiful Sierra Nevada redwoods. It is a wide open area with runs made for wide open skiing. Ted and Jim Hammaker were there. They had been skiing many times, but I was bound and determined that I would be faster then they were. Jim was on the left, Ted on the right, and I set a course straight down the middle of them without turning a ski! I almost lost my balance. My right leg can still feel that moment of apprehension and balance. I was on the complete and utter edge of total explosive wipeout! But my balance held, and at the bottom we all let out a collective, "Wow!" It was exhilaration beyond belief.

The California sun burnt my face that day. Oh yeah, Betsy was there too, and she was in love with me. That night Betsy and I ice skated around and around a rink. I love to skate fast. I believe the balance learned from the disciplines of skiing and skating go hand in hand, with skating using single edges, while skiing is riding on a frozen surface on a pair of metal edges, balanced and turned on edge. I went to bed that night and thought, "I could become a really great skier!" as I drifted off to sleep.

That spring, the U.S. Army moved our family to Moline, Illinois. My father needed to be closer to his mother in Decatur, Illinois and to be able to find peace over the death of my brother John. But the move did absolutely the opposite for me. I was in ninth grade when

John died, and within six months I lived in Moline, Illinois. Alone. Away from my new-found happiness in skiing. No friends. It was a far cry from all the friends I had skiing.

My sister Karen saw that I was lonely and not at peace and she reached out and tried to do something for me. I urge all family members to be as observant and kind as she was. If someone is hurting from loneliness or despair, reach out to them in any way you can. Do not feel uncomfortable about it. It does help.

In high school, in Mrs Bernardi's class, we read a short story called "By the Waters of Babylon" by Stephen Vincent Benet. This story is about a primitive tribe in the future that lives by a bridge pillar that says "Ashington" on it. Well, it was just a clue, but it turned out that the pillar was a cracked piece of the George Washington Bridge and the tribe was surviving in a post-atomic blast of New York City. In the end, a boy ends up searching the burnt-out remains of New York and returning to his tribe as a man and a priest. As I mulled over the story, I wondered, "Is the 'Babylon' referred to in the Biblical Book of Revelations New York City? And why has the George Washington Bridge been blown up? Does the United States of the future break the Pact with God? Can I prevent this from occurring?" Heavy thoughts for a 16-year-old man-boy.

I did find peace by being in the ski club and taking ski trips to northern Illinois, Iowa, and Wisconsin. However, again family stepped in. My mother's brother, Uncle Jack, invited me to his ski house in Jackson, New Hampshire to gain some peace through skiing. He couldn't believe that I was skiing so well by this time.

Wildcat Mountain, where we skied, wears its name with pride. It is across the valley from Mount Washington, New Hampshire where winds in excess of 225 miles an hour have been recorded. There are mountain cats' names for the runs like "Pole Cat," "Bobcat," and "Lynx." On sunny days it might be below zero. On cold days, you could freeze part of your face off.

One particularly chilly, windy, snow-blowing morn, my cousins Mikey and Duffy Winnan and I climbed onto the chair lifts. The thermometer was 76 degrees below zero. The wind blew the chairs 25 degrees, and it swept all the snow off the trails. As we came down the mountain, it was like skiing on a giant black ice cube.

We had sharpened our edges with flat files and we cut into the icy surface, left, then right, and then did it over again. When we arrived at the ski patrol shack, we bought big mugs of hot chocolate and held our faces over them. Still, to this day, when it gets really cold, a patch of my cheek stays white like a snowflake of frostbite. My mother said, "You ruined your face!" A word of advice to you would be to try to completely avoid skiing in weather that is this extremely cold. I was fortunate to come away from it with only a white patch on my cheek.

It's hard to define that single moment when one becomes (as my Uncle Jack puts it) "bitten by the skiing bug." But for me it happened on that cold, cold Wildcat Mountain in the beautiful Mount Washington Valley, in the George Washington Forest, as we were flying down a narrow trail. I scraped the edge of a rock face and sparks came streaming from the metal edges of my skis. This is where Henry David Thoreau received his inspiration. I also received my inspiration here as my life became poetry through writing and skiing into the George Washington vision.

The inner peace which skiing gave to me began to alleviate the pain of the loss of my brother. This is something that people should try if they have lost a loved one.

My family at home was still sick about the loss of John. There were no elaborate counseling nets set up to help people in those years. My Dad would just sit in his easy chair and listen to his records. I did the same. I listened to everything from the Beatles to the Grateful Dead. My father became so distraught during this time period that my mother was thinking of leaving him. I convinced her to stay, telling her that he was a great man, and that we all needed her. She stayed. Whenever there is a question of family unity or division, I believe "united we stand, divided we fall." As I thought about the subject of unity, I remembered the words from the George Washington vision, "As I continued looking, I saw a bright angel, on whose brow rested a crown of light, on which was traced the word 'Union.'"

Winter came in 1976 and with it came the Olympics from Innsbruck, Austria. As I watched the Olympics on TV, I saw majestic jagged mountains cut upwards into the sky and gray mountains wind all the way down into Innsbruck. If you imagine, you can hear the music from "The Sound of Music." The Austrians have always prided themselves on their downhill racing team and in 1976 they produced a beauty of a team. Franz Klammer literally flew down the course on the very edge of control, sometimes on just one ski, sometimes on a small part of the edge of a ski. In his yellow suit and red helmet, he crossed the finish line in the #1 position. It was certainly one of the most dramatic victories in downhill skiing up to that date. As I watched the TV, they replayed his run to the tune of Dan Fogelberg's "There's a Place in Their World for the Gambler." I told my Mom that I could do this. She looked at me mortified. She had already lost one son and didn't want to lose another.

David's Book:
Finding the Right Place to Ski

Everyone must find their home. This is also true for skiers. They must find the area where they like to ski best. Some would call it the skier's "home area." David was looking for a home.

The San Juan Mountains surround Durango, Colorado. They are part of the western slope of the Rocky Mountains. In the San Juans, you can see Engineer Mountain rising over 14,000 feet above sea level. Just before you get to it, there is an area called Purgatory. There is a view across from it of the Needles Mountain Range, jagged smaller mountains which are all about the same size, so they almost look like one mountain, frosted with powdered sugar valley lines between gray ribs.

My first year of skiing at Purgatory was incredible. The snow kept falling. The snowflakes fell down and were as big as your hand. The thick powdery snow was five feet deep, and it became hard to turn in, so it worked every single muscle in your body. We would do Native American Snow dances and chants to try to make it snow more. We chanted, "En-a-a-en-a-a ah-en," and moved in circles with our hands reaching up to the sky and then down again with palms outstretched. And it snowed and snowed. That season it snowed almost 200 feet!

It was a snowy week before Thanksgiving, 1978 in Durango, Colorado. The snow fell in torrents, huge flakes as big as crystalline silver dollars, scurrying downward to the earth. "Champagne powder, Buddy!" Mike Butler said to me. And he was right. The snow began to pile up, and with the elevation and temperature preserving the crystallization, the deep piles sparkled at even the slightest ray of light. It was like being in the "Winter Wonderland" that Bing Crosby used to sing about on Christmas albums.

As we drove up into the mountains in all this snow, we had one objective: to make it to the ski mountain called Purgatory. I was so excited! But we could barely see. It was like driving through a cloud. It was a "white-out" like my cousins and I had driven through on the dangerous Kankamangus Highway to Loon Mountain in New Hampshire.

My new mountain of Purgatory brought back happy memories. I met all the ski instructors, racers, and patrol at the lower mountain lodge. I was inspired and excited to be skiing at this mountain of champagne powder! The trip home was long and careful, but when I got home, I knew I had found something that would bring me peace throughout my college years.

David's Book:
Purgatory

When you think of Purgatory, you think of a place half way between heaven and hell, in which a lot of people are in limbo, praying to try to get to heaven. At the ski area, however, I used to say, "It's heaven when you're flying and hell when you're falling."

I started skiing at Purgatory with a reasonable goal – to be a better and a faster skier yet have good control. The first chairlift ride I took up to the top of Purgatory was with Butler, Becky, and Betsy.

As the chair lift dropped us off, I saw a beautiful Colorado day of sun reflecting off the white crystalline snow. Mike grabbed the boda bag containing wine, closed his eye, and asked, "Hey girls, have you ever seen an eyeball drink?" He answered his own question by showing them an eyeball drink – he squirted some wine on his eye! Then he turned and skated off with his skis. Straight downhill. No turns. I followed. I had to.

If I were to learn how to ski really fast, I knew I had to ski with the best of them. I needed to find them. Mike was the son of a Navy doctor who retired and made it big in Las Vegas. He had broken his back cliff diving and had nursed himself back to health. He had skied at racing school in Squaw Valley, USA where the 1960 Olympics took place. More importantly, he had skied in a circle of friends that included the world speed record holder Steve McKinney, The late Steve McKinney's record at the time was over 125 mph. Interestingly enough, Steve was not killed on skis, but was struck by a truck when he pulled over to the side of the road to sleep. Steve's sister, Tamama McKinney, was a former U.S. ski team member.

Mike's favorite story about Steve McKinney was that he was on some talk show on the radio and a lady called in and asked, "Steve, was Robert Redford's portrayal of the life of a downhill racer in the movie "Downhill Racer" an accurate portrayal of the life of a downhill racer?" There was a pause. Finally, Steve McKinney responded, "You can imagine." Then there was a longer pause. Then the radio announcer said, "OK, next question for Steve."

We all laughed and that became our mantra. I followed Mike through independent leg and ski motion, uphill ski unweighting to total downhill ski weighting at any moment. He told me, "Skiing is like anything else. You have to practice, practice, practice."

I took his advice to heart. It was not so much enjoyment as it was training for me to learn how to ski with edge turned faster and faster. My outfit was a red wind breaker on which I sewed the Wild Cat, New Hampshire patch and black corduroy pants which were tight like ski pants. I didn't have enough money for ski pants.

The trail map at Purgatory literally reads like a division of heaven and hell. On the front side there is the River Styx, Upper Hades, Lower Hades, 666, Catharsis, Pandemonium, and … well, you get the picture. On the back side is Peace. On many runs I remember being up on the chair lift all alone with only the sound of snowflakes hitting my hood. It was as close to heaven as you could get. I would say "Our Fathers" and pray for peace on the chairlift above the run called Peace.

As I began skiing faster and faster down the mountain I became somewhat of an icon. From the chair lift, I would be so happy I would yell out, "Whoa" at the top of my lungs so that it would echo off the trees and mountains. Many other skiers followed my example and yelled out too.

The ski patrol was always chasing me around. One time when I was flying down the mountain with Billy Newcombe, they stopped us, grabbed our passes from around our necks, and said, "You're skiing way too fast. Make more turns or we'll take these away!" Ha! We laughed after they left. How would we be us, then?

One morning, it was crystal clear snow. The grooming machines had flattened everything nicely and the snow was crisp. I was flying down the River Styx on my VR17 American Flyers when I got out of control and just sat down. I slid for 100 feet on my butt sending a 30 foot plume of a frozen cloud into the air. Hank Thurston, who now runs a ski shop at the base of Aspen Mountain, came over to me and said, "Speed demon, give me your pass." The name stuck. I was the "speed demon of Purgatory" skiing for peace of mind and international peace from nuclear war.

I was in business school then because I knew that I would need a job when I graduated and that there would most likely be a recession due to Jimmy Carter's policies. Business school was quite demanding. It was sort of like having to do tax returns, profit-loss statements, marketing reports, and computer analysis all day long for no pay. I really got into political science, and U.S. foreign policy was very interesting to me. I wanted to be a skiing ambassador to try to stop nuclear war.

But my source of solace was skiing. I didn't have a car, so I would hitchhike with my skis until someone picked me up. Once I was up on the slopes, the peace I felt was indescribable. However, I will try to describe my experience: Crystal blue sky. Air so clean and cold it singes your lungs going in with freshness. Mountaintops meeting the sky as if God Himself used artists' tools and trowels to make them, working them into just the right ripples and rolls that he wished. Sometimes warm sun, basking bright, or rolls of pillowy, feathery clouds moving across the sky.

Whatever the conditions, I was to ski to the best of my ability and as fast as I could to honor my God and His creation in combination with my God-given ability. I was at peace. The body is mostly water and snow is crystalline frozen water. When a ski comes between the body and the snow, a giant bubble of water forms. In effect, you are hydroplaning. Without metal edges as a way to check gravity and cause friction, a skier would flow down the mountain like water along the fastest, most direct path possible.

Some skiers call this the fall line. When I ski, I ski the way water flows down the mountain. This is the accelerant which gives me peace, for I know I am glorifying my God in the way he intended me to, for all those watching from the chair lift to see. One night as I slept, I had a dream that I skied with God. I couldn't really see Him, but we knew it was a race. He let me use 444 cm skis. (This is about twice as long as the longest Olympic skis – about as long as a station wagon). I flexed them. Then I mounted them and I tucked in an egg and did my fastest run of my life. At the bottom of the hill I heard, "Beat ya." Every run was the same as the last. Never try to beat God. He knows all and has done all. That's why he made all the rules, the Ten Commandments, to keep us out of trouble. If you break the rules, you will get into trouble, and God help you.

David's Book:
Fearing Nuclear War

President Jimmy Carter might have been concerned about nuclear war, but he had allowed the conventional military forces to deteriorate to the point that Soviet forces outnumbered us two or three to one. In most areas, such as tanks and planes, the Soviets were superior. There was actually no way that the U.S. could build enough military strength fast enough to repel an attack in Europe.

Our military came up with a plan of "mini-nukes" or tactical theater nuclear weapons. The Pershing II was one such missile. It was mobile on big tractor trailer trucks, going on the Autobahn or on all terrain, and at a moment's notice it could be ejected straight up into firing mode.

My Father, General David Lion, took charge of this phase of the rocket's development to make it more accurate. That he did, with satellite repositioning. It was said that the Pershing II could explode within ten yards of its intended target.

In 1981, protests were being held all throughout Germany. Sting, the rock star, wrote a song that said, "Mr. Reagan says he will protect you.... I do not subscribe to this point of view." The song ends with bells tolling and the question, "Who will save my little boy from Oppenheimer's little toy?"

Clearly, there were global tensions. I became a student of American history and foreign policy and took many courses in the study of wars. I took a Master's honor program on war and peace in which the department heads of psychology, anthropology, sociology, history, economics, business, and political science came in to teach the origins of war from the viewpoint of each department. For example, the anthropologist explained territorial rights, food, and women as a cause of war. He showed how tribal warfare dated back to cavemen. The head of the economics department explained war in economic terms. Through the business and economic cycles, he showed that war had evolved into a vital and necessary part of the world's economy. He gave the example of war reparations on Germany following World War I, and he said that they led to World War II. It was a most interesting seminar.

I began fearing that the implementation of my father's missile, the Pershing II, might start nuclear war. I subscribed to the *Bulletin of Atomic Scientists* which had moved the tick of the "Doomsday Clock" one tick closer to the midnight of nuclear war. Einstein had said, "If we do not destroy nuclear weapons, then they will destroy us." It looked like his prediction was getting closer to coming true.

My goal was to prevent nuclear weapons from destroying us. I entered an essay contest given by the *Bulletin of Atomic Scientists* which was called "Ending the Threat of Nuclear War in Europe." My paper was entitled "Averting the Holocaust." In it I proposed that we destroy missiles such as the Pershing II. Secondly, I proposed to make the current weapons obsolete by a system of satellites and particle beam weapons. The ideas presented in my paper became the elements of the peace process in which the Pershing II missiles were offered up by the Americans. The Soviet's gave up the SS2O's, and both types of weapons were destroyed. They are now side by side in the Air and Space Museum in the Smithsonian Institution right by the Wright brothers' plane.

My last idea ended up being in President Reagan's Star War speech two years later. It was not easy trying to take the role of peacemaker, but I felt as though it were a vital role so that we would have a planet where we could raise the next generation. Dad and I would argue at the dinner table and in the house about my ideas.

David's Book
1981

"When I have finally decided that a result is worth getting, I go
ahead on it and make trial after trial until it comes."
(Thomas Edison)

In 1981, my father's rocket program had turned to the
development and implementation of the world's most accurate and
devastating tactical nuclear missile, the Pershing II. I went to the
same church where I'd prayed more than a decade earlier for the
Apollo 13 astronauts. This time I prayed that the world would not
end in a nuclear holocaust.

I was studying U.S. and world foreign policy, and what concerned
me the most was that these mobile missiles would be put into the
hills of Germany, moved around on the back of a large tractor trailer
truck, and could be erected for launch anywhere, anytime, within 30
seconds.

"My God!" I thought. "Fifteen minutes …..at any time…. That
is how far away we are from nuclear war!" To make matters worse,
the USSR had the same thing on the other side of Germany. Not only
that, but they had superior numbers of tanks and could overwhelm
American forces decisively, so it made fielding this weapon a
necessity. Mutual Assured Destruction (MAD) battle plans were
drawn up in which the USSR and Warsaw Pact countries invaded
West Germany with overwhelming numbers of tanks. Once our
forces were overrun, the U.S. would shoot off these weapons. It was

a nuclear deterrent, but they would be crazy to do it. MAD – Mutual Assured Destruction – truly was mad. The most incredible part was that some of our leaders were twisting this and making it look like nuclear war was survivable! A whole group of "survivalists" cropped up in America. They stocked up on provisions and moved away from the cities to avoid being killed in a nuclear holocaust. Who was really crazy?

Thinking about this scenario made me look into the abyss. I saw the truth of what Nietzsche once cautioned, "The abyss will look back at you." I studied all the effects from a nuclear detonation: instant vaporization, complete implosion of building, electromagnetic pulses, instant blindness, and a slow, painful death from lingering radioactivity. I began studying the Bible and found references in the book of Revelation. I read that the most treacherous work of the Antichrist will be misleading the whole world before the return of Christ with world-wide catastrophic results. These verses greatly impressed me: "It worked for the beast whose fatal wound had been healed. And it used all its authority to force the earth and its people to worship that beast. It worked mighty miracles, and while people watched, it even made fire come down from the sky. This second beast fooled people on earth by working miracles for the first one. Then it talked them into making an idol in the form of the beast that did not die after being wounded by a sword." (Rev. 13:12-14) Such evil would not happen, if I could prevent it. The fire falling from the sky had to be from nuclear weapons!

That year I was twenty one years old. I was writing my thesis, "Averting the Holocaust," to try to show the world how to avoid nuclear war. I lived with my parents during the hot summer of 1981. Meanwhile, my father was working on the Pershing II missile, which was the most accurate and deadly nuclear missile ever made. We lived at Fort Belvoir, Virginia, about 5 miles from Woodlawn Plantation, which was one of George Washington's favorite properties.

President Ronald Reagan noticed the work my father, General Lion, was doing and felt it was a way to break the "evil empire" of the Soviet Union, so the President sent former Vice President George Bush and General Colin Powell to be briefed on it. Then my father gave a presentation to NATO on the implementation of the Pershing II in Germany and it won final approval.

At the same time that my father was being hailed as a military hero, I was becoming more and more concerned with the world's rapid approach toward nuclear warfare. During those hot summer days at home, my father's and my differences in political and military ideology resulted in conflict after conflict. I would often go have a few beers after work so that I would have an easier time broaching the subject with my stern father, who was hell-bent on peace through scaring the be-Jesus out of everybody – including me. I told him, "No way can you put those missiles into Europe, Dad! It'll result in total nuclear war!"

I ran every day in dry land training for the upcoming ski season. "Better, farther, faster," I would tell himself as I sometimes ran up to 26 miles at a time. One July evening, I ended up running down the grass beside the long, tree-lined road that lead through the military base to Route 1. Once at Route 1, I ran north, past the baseball field and horse stables, until I saw Woodlawn Plantation. I crossed the busy road and boldly climbed over the fence surrounding the property. I ran up the steep hill of the front lawn, which was covered in high, three foot tall summer grass. I had run about 300 yards when I came to the mansion. Around the right side was a small sitting area that had a doorway to both the front and back of the house. I sat down to absorb the "vibes" of the place. I imagined that George Washington's spirit might have been there since he had frequented the place in life. I prayed out loud, "Help me, George Washington, and give me strength and guidance to figure things out for my God and my country!"

I sat there for awhile, halfway expecting a vision of a ghost or something, but none came. It was quiet, though. Dead silence. Eerie silence. I felt as though someone was watching me. Then, in the mist, the vision of George Washington came to me. He said, "Your forefathers shed blood with me! Do not be deterred from what people may say about you, David, but I am to give you information and inspiration to write a paper which will save the United States of America from the third and greatest peril which she shall face. People will scorn you for this vision and you will be imprisoned until the Constitution sets you free. You will become aware of it only upon its revelation and fulfillment. Study your Bible and make sure the leaders of the United States comply with the Pact with God. Woe to the Union and the world if a president arises who violates this sacred Pact which I have established. Godspeed." With that, the vision disappeared.

I felt a chill run up my spine as I left through the gardens and ran down the front lawn. On the way home, I knew that the spirit of George Washington would help me. It always helped inspire the great men of our country rise to the occasion to save and protect the United States from destruction. I felt the George Washington vision within me.

That same night in July of 1981, I wrote my thesis, "Averting the Holocaust." This was my inspiration:

"And again I heard the mysterious voice saying, 'Son of the Republic, look and learn.' At this the dark, shadowy angel placed a trumpet to his mouth, and blew three distinct blasts; and taking water from the ocean, he sprinkled it upon Europe, Asia and Africa. Then my eyes beheld a fearful scene: from each of these countries arose thick, black clouds that were soon joined into one. Throughout this mass there gleamed a dark red light by which I saw hordes of armed men who, moving with the cloud, marched by land and sailed by sea to America." (George Washington's vision)

I submitted my thesis to *The Bulletin of Atomic Scientists* in a contest on ending the threat of nuclear war in Europe.

David's Book:
"Averting the Holocaust"

The Rabinowitch Essay Competition
The Bulletin of Atomic Scientists
David Lion
July 1, 1981

War has been an integral part of man's existence since the beginning of group survival. In all of recorded history, mankind has seen few years of global peace. There have always been wars, and there will continue to be wars. In this century, two major conflicts have disrupted the lives of many millions of people in the most widespread and destructive wars in history. In Europe during World War II, German technology offered a new dimension to warfare, and the V-1 or "buzz bomb" was launched from Holland to pinpoint targets in England. The V-2 followed as the first modern rocket, which was fortunately only in its infancy by V-E Day in 1945. World War II ended with the beginning of a new type of war when Hiroshima and Nagasaki were incinerated by the explosions of the first atomic bombs, the most destructive weapon ever developed by mankind People inside the cities were instantly vaporized. Not too far away, others were scorched in shock waves of radioactivity, and further away witnesses were blinded. Mutants still live in Hiroshima and Nagasaki as testament to nuclear war. The prospects and possibilities for eliminating the threat of nuclear war in Europe must be considered in order to avert the holocaust which would result from the exchange of modern nuclear weapons.

Dr. Robert Oppenheimer was in charge of operations in the development of the atom bomb. He and the most respected scientists in the United States developed the bomb in the name of peace to bring an end to the war. Ultimately, hundreds of thousands of American and Japanese lives were saved by the immediate surrender of Japan. In Europe, the Soviet Union considered the bomb to be another example of "capitalist imperial warmongering."

In the midst of bilateral agreements over Europe between East and West, the USSR developed its own atomic weaponry. With Germany and Europe split, the race had begun to secure national interests militarily. This translated into terms of range and payload of the superpowers' nuclear arsenals. As a result, the hydrogen bomb was developed in order to insure the supremacy of the United States. (Dr. Oppenheimer and other scientists protested the development of the hydrogen bomb). The USSR followed suit, and intercontinental ballistic missiles (ICBMs) were introduced to insure the delivery of these bigger payloads via advanced rocketry. Submarine launched ballistic missiles (SLBMs) entered the race as the fear of nuclear war grew among the peoples of the world.

During the Cuban missile crisis, the threat of nuclear war became a reality in the political decision making of world leaders while the world balanced on the brink of fiery destruction. Mutual assured destruction became the mad political policy, with the theory that neither side would initiate conflict because both would be destroyed. The Soviet Union eventually backed down in the crisis. They feared greater damage to their countryside in light of the nuclear superiority of the United States. This spurned the Soviets into development of a vast conventional capability. It was based primarily on large numbers of tanks and armored infantry divisions, and it was prepared for "blitzkrieg" offensive strikes.

Nowhere is the imbalance of strategic conventional forces more ominous than in Central Europe where the armies of the two superpowers are aligned at a common border. The Soviet forces outnumber NATO forces at a ratio of nearly three to one. Tactical nuclear weapons are in place to counterbalance this threat.

The tactical nuclear weapons are to be used against conventional weaponry in the event that Soviet tanks attack in overwhelming numbers. The Pershing II and the ground launched cruise missile (GLCM) are intended to be used in battlefield strikes to destroy the Soviet conventional weapons, but their presence creates the possibility of retaliatory strikes of ballistic missiles from the Soviet Union. Such a sequence of events could bring an end to the nuclear age once and for all.

In the nuclear age, three types of conflicts can occur: class X, Y, or Z wars. Class X is the conflict with conventional weapons between small states, with one or the other (or both) being supplied by the superpowers. For example, all Middle East Wars have been fought in this manner. Class Y is a conflict in which one of the superpowers must become directly involved, where it will fight primarily against weaponry provided to the opposing state by the other superpower. Vietnam and Afghanistan are examples of this type of conflict. Class Z is the direct confrontation between rival superpowers and their respective allies. A war in Europe would entail this situation. Class Z wars are the most dangerous possibility for the introduction of tactical nuclear weapons, progressing ultimately to the launching of bigger and further ranged missiles armed with multi-independently targeted re-entry vehicles (MIRVs) intended for industrial and populated areas. This will create a situation of worldwide nuclear holocaust if these weapons are allowed to reach the earth with their payloads of megatons of mass annihilation. Nuclear proliferation in Europe dramatically increases the chances of thermonuclear global exchanges which would poison life, the atmosphere, and the earth.

The ideal way to end the threat of nuclear war in Europe would be mutual and unconditional disarmament. However, the situation is similar to two men in a room pointing guns at each other – neither will lay down his weapon for fear of being shot by the other. Strategic arms limitations talks (SALT) have failed for the reason of mutual mistrust. Current spending plans for the United States alone indicate an unprecedented nuclear arms buildup in Europe.

Another possibility is removal of all land-based nuclear weapons. Both sides could still be allowed to maintain a sense of power by turning these weapons into SLBMs because submarines are hard to locate, much less destroy. Since both sides would still have nuclear weapons, they would be deterred from initiating conflict. However, this solution is still closer to a mad policy than a dedication to a peaceful world.

Scientists are obligated to promote peace and eliminate the threat of nuclear war in Europe. To achieve this, nuclear weapons must be made obsolete by the creation of new technology to surpass the threat of nuclear holocaust. It is the tradition of paradox that we forge ahead in a volatile world, evidenced in the Nobel Peace Prize. The prize was named in honor of the man who invented dynamite. He developed it for peaceful purposes, but it was also used as a weapon which killed many men in war. The atom bomb was used in a similar manner. Perhaps if the Japanese had been allowed to view final testing of the bomb once we were certain of its power, surrender could have been reached without the loss of lives.

The new weapon on the horizon which will eliminate nuclear war is the particle beam. Once installed in defense satellites and the space shuttle, it will eliminate the threat of nuclear war by destroying the missiles before they destroy us. Science must develop this weapon completely in order to deter nuclear exchanges. But this weapon must be used in the promotion of peace. Demonstrations of a peaceful nature will have to be made in order to prove the uselessness of nuclear weapons against the concentration of light rays of high intensity assisted by computer tracking, guidance, and delivery systems operating from the new frontier of space.

The threat of nuclear war in Europe will be eliminated only when nuclear missiles are removed. This will occur only if they are perceived as obsolete, a product of man's war-torn past. The scientist must strive to develop and demonstrate this technology in peace in order to promote, preserve, and protect peace.

David's Book:
Changing My Skiing Goal – Skiing for Peace

"God blesses those people who make peace. They will be called
his children!" (Matt. 5:9)

After submitting my thesis to *The Bulletin of Atomic Scientists,*
I realized that my diplomatic efforts might take too long to be
useful if they were all that I did for the cause of peace. Therefore, I
decided to train full time, while going to school, for the 1984 Winter
Olympics at Sarajevo, Yugoslavia. I wanted to win so I could
stand on the medal stand. I knew that if I won I could get speaking
engagements and begin to talk to people of the region about peace.
I felt as though Eastern Europe would be the place where war would
break out because World War I had started when Archduke Franz
Ferdinand was shot. Also, when Hitler invaded the Sudetenland,
Czechoslovakia, Hungary, and Poland, World War II began. I felt
that perhaps I could through speaking engagements, if not through
my paper, play a role in averting World War IIII.

The future looked bleak at that time. It was the age when nuclear
weapons were depended on for the survival of man and the planet.
The two chief nuclear powers in the world were the USSR (Soviet
Union) and the United States. Sarajevo was right in the middle of
East vs. West. War would happen there. I thought this might be the
place that would spark "all out" nuclear war, and I hoped it could be
the place to end the threat of nuclear war once and for all.

Since that time in the early 1980's, war is exactly what has happened in the region of Eastern Europe. Young American lives have been wasted to keep the peace there. The ski jumping hill landing area, the site of many ceremonies, has since been destroyed by mortar fire. One half of the Olympic mountain is in Serb hands, the other half in the opposition Croat control.

I wanted to get to Sarajevo to speak for peace, so I trained for the Olympics every day. I would run up and down the mountain to school. I got to class so sweaty that I felt I had to take my shirt off. My softball team leader, Rick MaHorn, and my basketball team captain named me "Captain Dave." Later, Jeffery Spears found a "Captain" hat which he gave to me. I kept it in my Wildcat windbreaker and wore on the chairlift.

Some pros came up one day and asked me to join their tour, but I refused in order to keep myself pure. Boy, I really needed the money I could have made on their tour to buy food and equipment. However, I remembered the story of Jim Thorpe, and how they had taken away his Olympic medals because they did a background search and found out he had played football on a Sunday afternoon for a few dollars. My friend Dan called me "Jim Thorpe" after he saw me demolish a team on a football field one Saturday afternoon. I had always considered Thorpe an idol since I ran my first kickoff back for a touchdown at Indian Field in Carlisle, Pennsylvania, the same field where he ran. I would not make the same mistake Thorpe had made.

I was skiing better than ever. I had become the "speed demon of Purgatory." I tried to emulate and integrate things that I had read about famous skiers. For example, Billy Kidd always swung his skis up and down on the chair lift to keep them warmed up, so I swung my skis too.

People began to emulate my style, both on the mountain and on the chair lift. I remember one snowy afternoon, I saw someone swinging their skis a few chairs ahead of me. I recognized him from one of my classes. His name was Stan Florida. He was carrying a boda bag and had apparently been skiing and drinking all day long with friends. He flew down the Upper Hades-Lower Hades track, disappearing and tumbling in a mass of snow. I skied much more carefully down, and I noticed red streaks in the snow. As I skied closer I saw him lying in the snow, injured. His ski pole went though his abdomen and out his back side. He had been completely skewered. Time was of the essence. We cut off both ends of the pole on either side, loaded him on a sled and brought him down to the patrol hut. When they started an IV in him, he said to me, "David, I'm so cold." I warmed his hands and began saying the Lord's prayer silently to myself. He said, "I'm so tired." I said, "Just stay awake, Stan." We were afraid he would bleed to death or go into a coma from the loss of blood.

I caught a ride halfway home to Hesperas with a ski patroller who said, "I haven't seen anything like that since Nam." I walked 13 miles that night saying Our Fathers for Stan. God would make him live! I stopped by the hospital and he was still in surgery. He was in surgery eight hours in all. The pole had punctured his large intestine sixteen times and exited without puncturing any other organs. Today he is alive and well and lives in Southern California.

Stan's accident certainly taught me never to ski after consuming alcohol, especially at the speeds I traveled, because it could literally mean death. Interestingly enough, I had pulled Stan off the mountain at the bottom of the trail named Lower Hades.

My skiing was coming along great. While I spent many days in school, I spent Tuesdays, Thursdays, and weekends flying down the mountain. My speed was becoming a concern for some. My mother worried and so did my dad. Betsy, who had known me many years, told me that she believed that the only reason I had not been killed was because my little brother John was my guardian angel. To this day I still think she might be right.

As my skiing got better and better, I believed I would have a shot at the Olympics. I won or placed in some of the regional races that I could compete in, but I could not travel to ski with the U.S. team. Traveling would take money that I didn't have I figured it would take $10,000 to make a run at it, and I had spent all my money on the college tuition bills. I went home and asked my father for the $10,000 I figured I would need to ski with the U.S. Olympic team. He said he didn't have the money to give me.

I graduated in the spring of 1982 with a business degree. My Dad and I cashed in my bonds that I had saved since I was a child and they totaled only $1,000. I was heartbroken. My dream of skiing was starting to die.

The $1000 from the bonds was barely enough to get a car, but I needed one. I bought a car and put a dynamic skis sticker on the fender. That summer I also purchased a pair of Rossignol VAS (Vibration Absorbing System) skies that Tamara McKinney used in the Olympics. I thought those skis might get me to the Olympics.

I worked that summer and fall but barely saved up enough to pay for anything but rent and food. In the early1980's, our country was in the worst economic recession since the Great Depression. The head of racing at Purgatory got me a job with Durango Threadworks, and I started training again. However, I trained with despair in my heart because the Olympics were so coming up so quickly that I felt like clock was ticking. I barely had enough money to buy a ski pass, let alone make a run for the World Cup. I was Director of Intramural Ski Racing and I co-managed a little area at Chapman Hill. Then came my crash.

David's Book:
A Fateful Event

I had always been a good athlete. When I found snow skiing, I knew I had found my sport. It gave me tremendous peace from the pressures of this world which seemed to be heading towards a nuclear holocaust. I left Virginia in August of 1981 to continue to ski faster and faster in Purgatory, Colorado. I had always skied fast, and now I was entering in competitions.

I remember the days at Purgatory like they were yesterday. On one of them, I remember stretching my hamstrings, and boy, were they tight. As I was swinging my legs back and forth to loosen up, I met Walt Garrison, former running back for the NFL football Dallas Cowboys. He had a chew in, "just a little pinch," from the company that was helping sponsor the race. He said, "Good luck, David." "Thanks, Chief," I replied.

It was time for me to get into the starting gate. I got in the starting house and they started the count-down. "Racer ready... five ... four ... three ... two ... one" BANG! I kicked high and pushed forward with my poles and skated strong with my left toward the first gate, a right hand turn. I approached the turn at high speed and cut a sharp ski edge into the snow. SHHHHHHHHH. I cut a straight fall line and came so close to the gate that I grazed it with my shoulder. FLOP! The gate sprang to the ground since it was spring loaded.

"Looks like he's done this before," shouted the announcer as I started cranking through the top of the course. I was picking up speed now, and was going around 45 to 50 mph, and I was low in my tuck. I could hear the wind whistle through my helmet. I saw a rut coming around the next gate, so I entered it very low now near the gate. It was a perfect turn as I felt my long 215 cm skis snap back under the angulations of my knees and hips to get ready for the next turn. No margin for error. Perfect timing, a body in sync with the snow. Flow like water. "Liquid smoke" streamed from the snow spray from the back of my skis as I blew through the finish line, snapping the shutter of the timer with a forward outstretched hand, arching a big turn to stop, all within one half of a second. That was it! The margin of victory! I had won a chance to train with the U.S. Olympic Team.

I hoped I could win a medal and present ideas to begin a reduction of nuclear weapons in the subsequent interviews. Perhaps the leaders would notice the wisdom of this! I would present ideas from my paper, "Averting the Holocaust," which was actually a culmination of my work in the war and peace seminar. I hoped this would lead to the reduction, removal, and the elimination of nuclear weapons on the planet.

The next race was a qualifying downhill run at Purgatory on the NCAA sanctioned run called Upper-Lower Hades. Upper Hades was a speed burner blue slope that lets the racer get up to speeds of over 70 mph. Of course, how fast you can ski depends upon how low you can get in your tuck and how well you can hold it. I had practiced this over and over, getting lower and lower into an egg position.

My hands would be out in front of my face in a steering position, with my elbows barely overlapping the outside of my knees. Maintaining this position for longer than a minute or two sends the thigh and calf muscles screaming in pain due to the lactic acid building up in them. The only way to build up the endurance needed to do this was training and mountain running down the trails as fast as one could. In the summer and fall I had put on old ski gloves with holes and run down this same trail, in the same path which water would go. I ran fast!

Now it was winter and I was in great shape. I needed to be! After the compression on the bottom of Upper Hades was a lip that began the steep cliff, and then there was a tight right hand turn at a gate at the top of the back of Lower Hades. This lip could act as a catapult if the skis hit it and flew off the top. To compensate, the downhill racer had to "get up and get down." It was an act of pre-jumping the lip, in an act of essentially flying over the lip without hitting it, so as not to be sent airborne as in a ski jump.

I was in the starting gate. The countdown wound down. Kick start out of the start gate. Giant skate with giant 222 ski wings. Down into my tuck. 45 ... 50 ... 55 ... 65 mph past the first six gates. Wow! "I have never skied Down Upper Hades this fast before!" ran through my mind. Perhaps that split second thought threw me back. A racing friend said once, "You think about it too much. Just don't think about it!" In other words, just let your body see it, feel it and react. I saw the transition lip. Ready for the pre-jump. A split second too late! I was airborne, arms flailing back and forth to find a center of gravity and a downhill landing edge in order to make the sharp right turn. It had to be the uphill edge of the left ski. There was no way I could get it down. The right ski hit the snow first and I lost control. I spun off the course and flew over some hay bales on the edge of the trees. I was traveling straight for a tree. Sudden death! I extended my left arm high in the air, and my right arm low towards the snow. I flew by the tree like a bird, coming so close to the tree that I saw the details of the bark. Then I felt enormous pain in my shoulder, and then in my legs. Then all was black.

David's Book:
Time Out

A brilliant light shone so brightly that I felt blinded. I was lighter than the clouds. The pain had disappeared now. I could feel myself rising over the snowy mountaintops up to heaven. Through the bright lights, I could see Jesus Christ, beckoning me. He said, "Stay with me, David."

Then all went black. I opened my eyes slowly, and through a blurry fog I could see my dad. As my vision became focused, I could see my father was smiling at me. I saw the surroundings of a hospital room and the pain returned slowly to my shoulder, ribs, leg, and head. My shoulder had been acutely dislocated. My ribs, thumb, and collarbone were broken. My right leg had a compound fracture of the femur which had lacerated the skin from the inside out. Although I had missed the larger tree on the perimeter, I had flown another twenty feet and my helmet had struck a small sapling, shattering the helmet like an eggshell. My head had been lacerated and I had suffered a severe concussion which had caused brain swelling. I had been in a coma for ten days and a priest had administered the last rights.

My father said, "Here's the doctor who saved you!" He introduced a well-built man in his middle thirties with a crew cut. I didn't remember this man at all. What I did remember was a long-haired man in the bright light working on my head. I stared at the doctor in disbelief and said, "Thank you." To this day I still don't believe that he was the one who saved me.

I was alive! But was my dream of a skiing in the Olympics still alive?

Rehabilitation was slow and arduous. Each injury had to be worked on separately. The shoulder was best treated by swimming. The legs were strengthened by weights. I also found out I had shattered a disc in my lower back. Therapy did not help it so I had to undergo spinal fusion surgery. It was another setback that I could not overcome. With a heavy heart, I gave up the Olympic dream.

By 1983, relations between the U.S. and USSR had worsened. President Ronald Reagan called the USSR an "evil empire." In the United States, weapons of mass destruction such as the TRIDENT submarine-launched nuclear missile, the MX missile, and the B-2 bomber were being developed or deployed with all possible speed. The centerpiece of this aggressive 1980's defense policy was the intermediate range Pershing II missile, destined for deployment to West Germany to counter the Soviet SS-20. Proposals to make nuclear war "survivable" were embodied in attempts to proceed with anti-ballistic missile "Star Wars" funding and civil defense programs.

I watched the movie "The Day After." It raised American anxieties over the possibility of nuclear holocaust. In the movie, a Midwestern town is hit with a bomb. The voice on the radio trying to reassure the American people sounded strangely like President Reagan's voice.

The presidential administration tried to stop the airing of this mini-series. The graphic depictions of people dying from the horrible effects of radiation from nuclear war influenced American culture against continued nuclear proliferation. Many arms programs were halted, had their funding cut, or were scrapped altogether as a concerned nation increasingly questioned the wisdom of the notion that nuclear war was "survivable."

What had my paper said? This very thing. Nuclear war was not something we should risk and try to survive.

Over the next four years, massive anti-nuclear demonstrations around the world helped restore rational thinking to nuclear policy making. In 1987, President Reagan and Mikhail Gorbachev signed the Reykjavik accords in which the two heads-of-state withdrew the

Pershing II and SS-20 from Europe. It was called the START Treaty. (To read the message from President Reagan to the Senate about this treaty, turn to Appendix A at the end of this book).

My paper was being fulfilled as it lay in a trunk in my basement. I had forgotten all about it.

David's Book:
Becoming a Good Father

When I met Leza, I fell in love. Her dad had founded Mountain Airways. He was my kinda guy. I hoped that maybe he would sponsor my skiing. He flew Leza and me up to Aspen to ski for the day. Aspen is where all the little rich boys who throw cocaine parties ski. When they used to come to Purgatory, I would smoke them down the hill, right from the starting gate.

Leza called me from Denver in January, 1983 to tell me she was pregnant. My skiing dream was only a heartbeat from death.

My duty was clear: I had to go to Denver, face the recession, and use my degree to obtain a job. I saved up enough money, set out in my Datsun S10, and headed up the mountains to Denver. A police officer pulled me over to tell me he had noticed my engine burning oil. He recommended that I head back and get a mechanic to look at it. I kept going. My car seized up on Monument Pass. Snow started falling.

I was picked up by a truck that took me to downtown Denver. I was confused, hungry, and didn't know Denver. I found Leza's apartment. Her mother was there. She started yelling at me. I went out and slept in the stairwell.

I loved Leza, but I had no money. I called my friend Andy Carpenter and he and his mom Carna took me in. I slept for months on their couch. I applied for jobs, typing my resume on the same typewriter I had used to compose my "Averting the Nuclear Holocaust" paper. My car was still stuck on Monument pass, so my friend Mark Weener agreed to go and get it towed off the mountain so that I could rebuild its seized engine.

Leza would not allow me to see her. I was so in love with her. All I wanted to do was try to get a job to support the baby. Job interviews were hard to come by. It was the greatest recession ever. I figured out the difference between a recession and a depression. A recession is when everybody else doesn't have a job. A depression is when you don't have a job.

The winter snows came hard, heavy, frequently, and wet. When I went job hunting I would wear my business suit and snow boots and carry my shoes in my overcoat pockets. The slush walking up to University Boulevard in Denver was enough to make my pants wet.

500 people applied for a job with Razor, USA. I came out in the top 50 applicants. I went back for my second interview and was able to sit before John Johnson, a guy from Boston in a double breasted blue suit. He didn't give me the job. I was saddened, but I was not through yet.

Summer came and went, my car was still not rebuilt. I had never done major car repairs before, but I bought the *Chilton's Manual* for my car and saved up enough to buy the rings and bearings the Datsun needed. To be truthful, the cam shaft was in need of turning, and Carpenter told me this, but I didn't accept his advice.

I finally got a job as a telemarketer for First Solar Sales. I worked nights in phone rooms trying to get appointments for First Solar Sales representatives to try to sell $10,000 - $20,000 solar heating system to moms and pops across Denver. At that time people were very interested in heating their homes with solar heat as an alternative source of renewable energy.

I worked after dinner, so every day I had to rush home from my job interviews for a "real" family job, ride my bike for over six miles to get to the phone rooms, wolf down some fast food, and begin dialing every minute for appointments. I made my pitches using a "canned" script. I received minimum wage, but it was enough to pay Carna for my share of her electricity and water bills, as well as my food, clothing, and bus fare downtown for the next morning's job interviews.

Then came a big break! Mutual Insurance Company wanted me back. They took me to a Japanese steakhouse restaurant to celebrate. However, on Monday morning, the man who was to be my boss, Tom "Christmas" Carroll, called me in to tell me final approval had to be made by the home office in Dallas. I felt so important! They flew me to Dallas, and that plane food was the most well-rounded meal I had had in months. It was August 10, 1983, and when we landed in Texas it was 108 degrees in the shade. There was a cab waiting for me. I went through a series of meetings with old men. They looked like salesman who had "B.S.ed" or "butt-kissed" their way up to the top.

One fellow, who had a Boston accent and a gold Rolex watch, asked me, "Dave, do you know what your biggest problem is going to be?" I told him, "No, Sir, I don't, but I don't think I'll have any problems!" He said, "Yes you will, and your biggest problem will be fear of rejection. Do you think you will still be able to pick up the phone after continual rejection?" I said, "Yes, Sir. I won't have a problem with that." He said, "Good," and stood up and shook my hand.

I was really tired by this time, and I thought I had been hired. But they benignly sent me to talk to an old gnome-looking relic of a guy. I thought, "O.K., they still haven't hired me, so here's the close."

The strangest thing was that this man reminded me of Leza's old Grandfather, Edward Binan, who had said, "I really like that David." That was before Leza's mother and grandmother made him hate me for getting Leza pregnant. She was now 8 ½ months pregnant, so the heat was on.

I showed the old Mutual Insurance gnome all my achievements: my scholarships, debate championships, achievements as a ski racer, coach, and director, and my softball captain awards and championships. I wasn't sure he heard me all the way through. Finally he asked me, "So Dave, since you are so talented, why do you really want this job?" I told him I had gotten my girlfriend pregnant and I wanted to do the right thing and get a job to support and raise the baby. He told me that his son had gone through that. He said sometimes it works out, and sometimes it doesn't.

On the way home, I was still not sure I had received the job. But in my naiveté, I couldn't believe the cans of worms that I had opened up concerning work, family health insurance, and mental care for me and my family.

When I went back to work the next morning, everyone was acting weird. I had an upset stomach. I felt nervous. Tom "Christmas" Caroll called me into his office and asked me if there was anything I wanted to tell him. I said, "No." He said, "Well I heard you told someone in the home office that your girlfriend was pregnant. Why didn't you tell me?" He felt as though I we had an employer-employee relationship and that he should know everything. He said sometimes people are jerks, but then they could change, and that he didn't know about me. He said he had called my dad, and he was a pretty good guy, and he might be my best bet. He told me he had to let me go.

I had struggled for over six months in a cruel, cold job market and I had failed. I was crushed. I called home to mom and dad. Leza had already called. She was now 8 1/2 months pregnant. I had given it my best shot. I boarded a plane for Washington, DC, the birthplace of the George Washington Vision. Within two weeks I had a job as an insurance salesman with the Insurance Company of America.

Ava, my daughter, was born the day after I got my job. It was September of 1983. The Olympics would be in February, the next winter, but I didn't care. I sent Leza half of my first paycheck that I earned at the Insurance Company of America. My Olympic dream was dead, but I was not a dead beat dad. I wanted to be the best dad in the world!

David's Book:
Six Years of Loneliness

Being an insurance salesman is a lonely job. Every night I made phone calls to set up appointments with people who would allow me to give a sales presentation in their home. The following week, at their kitchen table, I would try to convince them to purchase more insurance. We sold all kinds of insurance, but we primarily sold life insurance.

The man who hired me, Mr. Small, was a squirrelly little ball of a man with a fat little stomach that stuck out of his cheap shirts like a feather pillow. He had chubby, stubby little fingers that were stained with nicotine. He chain-smoked Marlboro Light 100's. He was so addicted to cigarettes that he would chain-smoke by lighting one on the end of the other before it was finished. Hell, he smoked so much that my secretary Sandra Sodrean's beautiful blue eyes were bloodshot from being in the same building with him.

The most peculiar thing about Mr. Small was that I don't think he could tell the truth. I know he couldn't look you straight in the eye. He would look at you with a lazy eyeball. His gaze switched back and forth. First he looked at the wall, then at you, then at the desk, then at the floor, and then back again. It drove me crazy. My father told me never to trust a guy who couldn't look me straight in the eye. In fact, that's how my dad would determine if I were telling a lie or not. He'd say, "Look me straight in the eye and tell me that."

One day I told Mr. Small that I was tired of him lying to me and my clients. I told him to look me straight in the eye and repeat what he had just told me. He screamed, "I am looking you in the eye!" But to me it still looked like he was looking at a fly on the wall. He was a crook. He was cheating people out of their dividends. I had abandoned my goal of world peace to work for a crook.

David's Book:
Ending the Journey

It was 5 months after Ava was born, and I had made the decision to be in the insurance business instead of pursuing my goal of competing at the Olympics at Sarajevo.

Bill Johnson won for the Americans in downhill skiing at Sarajevo that year. (To bring you up to date, on Johnson, he recently tried to make a comeback, but he hit a snow fence and went into a coma. He recovered and is currently in Idaho trying to rehabilitate after breaking his broken hip while out skiing again. I guess old ski racers never die).

I was very discouraged. I had been spending all of my time doing something demeaning – selling life insurance. While Bill Johnson was winning in Sarajevo, I was sitting in a dingy office in Triangle, Virginia, working until 11 p.m. and trying to make sales over the phone. Mr. Small made a mockery of my dream by starting a sales contest which was titled "This is your Olympic Game." The contest was based on the number of sales each employee made. My playing piece was "Vucko the Wolf," the mascot of the games. Every time I made a sale, Vucko would move across the board toward the finish line. I won that game. I don't think he meant anything ill by the contest, he was just trying to get the maximum number of sales out of me.

The only solace I had was being in Washington, DC. The George Washington Vision was born there! In the spring, Washington is one of the best places on earth. The majestic monuments, especially the Jefferson Memorial, are surrounded by thousands of cherry blossom trees. Their beauty is reflected to the sky by the tidal basin and reflecting pool. Inside the Jefferson Memorial, the words of this noble and strong Virginian ring for all time against all forms of tyranny. Jefferson's words are the cornerstone of the building blocks of our country's democracy.

I quit working for Mr. Small and formed my own insurance agency. How beautiful capitalism is! It's great to be able to go off on your own, to free yourself from corporate corruption, and found your own company!

Nevertheless, I spent nearly twenty years in the place of being nearly being dead to myself.

David's Book:
Sugarloaf: The Inspiration

I had taken care of my family well, and it was time for me to do something for myself. I decided I wanted to ski again. I went to sleep one night and got up the next morning and hit the road. "Up with the sun, gone with the wind." I was still undecided about where my new ski area was going to be. My choices were Sunday River or Sugarloaf.

I ate breakfast at a breakfast cafe that morning. I ordered blueberry pancakes because blueberries are the food that is highest in antioxidants and I wanted to get into shape for skiing. As I ate, I tried to decide where to ski. Ten years previously, I had skied at Sunday River and had won the Nastar gold medal for beating their "pacesetter" or top guy on the mountain. It was a weak victory, but still, he was almost half my age. However, I had heard that it was too crowded at Sunday River. You see, the way I ski, crowds can be dangerous. This is because I try to pre-pattern where everybody below is going to be when I get to them, I do this so I can make little adjustments in my fall line that enable me to not be even close to other people when I pass them. That way it is less dangerous for them – and for me. Any wrong move and I could be sent into the trees. Again.

I asked the waitress who served up the pancakes about where to ski. She said, "The Loaf." She gave me directions on how to get to Sugarloaf. She wrote them down on a napkin, and I still have it.

I drove up Route 27. As I got closer, I saw the Cassabassett Valley Academy. I stopped there, told them about myself, and asked if would they have a position for an aged ski racer. Their director was on vacation. "Nuts!" I said. However, they gave me her card and it's still in my wallet. I told them about my two children and their predisposition to ski and snowboard. They said this would be a perfect place for them to ski.

I got back onto the road and kept driving. I made the left turn into Sugarloaf and drove up, up, the winding road. There was a chapel right in the parking lot. I wanted to go in and say a prayer, right then and there. I checked the front door, but it was locked.

It was lunchtime, so I took my peanut butter and jelly sandwich, apple, and Gatorade, and asked a couple sitting on the bench to the right of the chair lift base if I could join them. I sat, looking at Sugarloaf while I ate. I saw that the large mountain to the left rises gradually, not sharply like the Rockies. It is rather smooth and looks bluish green due its tree cover. Then it just drops off at an almost exact 45 degree angle, lowering itself into the clouds. The clouds were like those rolling ribbons of stratus which you sometimes see when you are in an airplane. Then, out of nowhere to the right, rising up is a triangular peak. But then beyond that, as far as the eye can see, is the blue-green of trees all the way to ocean. I thought, "If someone sees this and doesn't believe in God, something is wrong." I wanted to ask the couple if they believed in God, but I was too embarrassed for that. The woman took a picture of it and I said to her, "That was the best picture you took... ever!" She nodded in agreement.

So this was the view. But what about the mountain I would be skiing on? I rented a room at the Sugarloaf Inn, a loft bed up on the top. When I opened the curtain I couldn't believe the mountain I saw. It was so lush and green, and the trails were gentle and nicely cut. It was not at all like the blasted rock of many ski areas in the East. It had a rainbow adorning the left top part of it. My kids and I refer to that as a "Mainebow." I spent time looking at each trail and imagining the path I would be coming down when I would ski it.

Then I decided, "Enough of this!" I had to talk to a realtor, so I called Jeff Kennedy. I told him I needed a place where I could get away to find peace and quiet and to write my book. I wanted to get the best deal for the coming winter before prices went up. I also wanted a perfect place for my family to find the peace that I find from beauty, nature, and skiing. I sensed gold medals in skiing coming from this mountain for my sons. (At that time I had not even heard of Bode Miller, a local boy who had gone big in skiing. In the winter Olympics the following year he won a medal).

Jeff and I went and looked at houses. I was moved to tears at one little old A-frame house with butterflies on it because it made Sugarloaf seem like the answer to my sojourn to find a new mountain.

The next morning I awoke and decided that if Sugarloaf were to be the mountain where I would bring my family, I had to mountain run all the way up to the top of it and sprint down it. I had to traverse it as the water flows, looking at the deep gouges here and there where dirt had given way to rounded stone, where water had chosen its natural path.

The run I chose was the competition one, of course, so I began walking up the hill in the tall grass. My feet and pants got wet from the mountain dew. Wildflowers of yellow, white, and purple abounded. I came upon some wild strawberries that had been nibbled on by little bunnies, and I finished them off.

I crossed over drainage ditches of water which were man-made. You could tell they weren't natural because they flowed across the mountain and were somewhat stagnant. I was getting hot even though it was only 7 a.m. and the temperature was only 60 degrees. The constant walking and running made me sweat. I took off my shirt and left it there. My hat and sunglasses must have fallen off, but I didn't miss them until later on. I came upon the culvert which channeled water's natural path down the mountain. I wove my way up the mountain, past white and yellow flowers. I found some wild raspberries and ate them.

Before I turned to run down the mountain, I found a rather fresh, greenish stick that looked like sugarcane. It was perfect for my run down. (I had recently had knee surgery for a torn meniscus and needed to protect my knee). I ran down the mountain, watching carefully for rocks or boulders, jumping over the drainage ditches.

It felt great. I slowed down and stopped when I came to the place where I had shed my red L.L. Bean jacket on the ascent. My chest was heaving. As I picked up my shirt, I was very surprised at how wet with sweat it was from the ascent. I put on my Boston Red Sox hat and matching red sunglasses and pumped down the mountain for the finish. I was within sight of the lodge! I finished fast and had an exhilaration pumping through my body which I hadn't felt in twenty years. It was kind of like John Denver's "Rocky Mountain high."

Near the bench where I had eaten my lunch, down below in the parking lot, I looked at the chapel which looks up to the sky and mountains. There are plaques on the outside of the building dedicated to the religious skiers who had built this church. They were men and women who share my vision of glorifying God and nature to find peace in our discipline of skiing.

I chose this "Chapel in the Sky" as the place I wanted to have my tenth year anniversary Mass. The hotel is perfect for it. I have never seen a ski mountain with such utter beauty and glorification of God. I have asked Father Matthias to preside over this Mass, and he has accepted. I pray also that the Father will understand more and help me get a publisher for this story, so that the proceeds can be used to help people

I feel as though the good works which God has done at the church are miraculous in my own life. I believe that His works are so holy and good that his church is overflowing with people who have come to his flock to share in this feeling of good work. I'm just so hopeful and euphoric.

The End of David's Book

THE BEGINNING OF SORROWS

"Fire Falling From the Sky"

"From the waist up, it was glowing like metal in a hot furnace, and from the waist down it looked like the flames of a fire. The figure was surrounded by a bright light, as colorful as a rainbow that appears after a storm. I realized I was seeing the brightness of the LORD's glory! So I bowed with my face to the ground, and just then I heard a voice speaking to me." (Ezekiel 1:1-28)

The twenty years of David's life covered in his book were full of dramatic changes and challenges, but the biggest challenges were yet to come.

During the middle years of his life he met and married his wife Naomi. They had two beautiful daughters, Ava and Angel, and two handsome sons, James "Hawk" and John "Eagle." He founded his own insurance company in Northern Virginia.

Problems arose, however, when his premonition of an attack on America caused him to move his family from the area of George Washington's house in Virginia to Maine. He wanted to get his family out of the path of danger. Once in Maine, he began taking his family to a new church, as his father had taught him.

On July 15th, 2001, David, now age 41, took his family and his mother-in-law, Ruth, to church. They attended the fortieth anniversary celebration of Father Matthias' ordination as a priest. David and his wife had already met with Father Matthias several times. This ceremony was very crowded because the man was very popular. David personally credited Father Matthias with helping to bring him closer to God.

David sat next to his mother-in-law, Ruth. At the "Peace be with you" part of the ceremony, he said to her, "God is helping us." He went to the back of the church where the kneelers and candles were and lit a candle. He prayed to God. He had a vision in which he saw Ruth with a large fire burning close to her. Ruth lived in New York, just outside the city. He began to think this was a premonition of a greater evil. Later he would know that it was.

After praying at the back of the church, David went to his car. His kids, his wife, and his mother-in-law were there waiting for him. He didn't say a word during the entire drive home because he was very concerned about the vision he had had. Did it mean Ruth was going to burn in hell? He decided to spend a few days away from his house so he could think. He dropped his family off at home, packed his shaving kit and enough clothing for a few days, and drove to the Fortune Inn.

David spent that night at the Fortune Inn. He had brought a card of Father Matthias' with him for religious inspiration. He went to the grocery store and bought a bottle of Jack Daniels. He made himself a drink with some ice and water. He flicked on the TV.

On TV he saw an interesting documentary about John Wayne, "The Duke." When he was a ten, David had loved to go to John Wayne movies with a quarter in his pocket on Saturday mornings. He poured himself another Jack and water. He turned back to the TV show and saw that John Wayne had lost everything in his life because he was such a prolific drinker. "That's so damn sad," David thought. "Drinking ruined his life! That's enough for me." As he turned off the TV, he poured his drink down the sink drain and went to bed.

The next morning when he awoke, he was not hung over, because Jack never did that. The water also helped because it was nice and pure and had been through charcoal filtering. But if he had drunk cheap stuff, he would have been hung over. He sat down and mapped out where his life was going to take him. He had spent the last twenty years building a business to support his family without taking time for himself. He had moved his family to Maine to get them out of the "Blast Zone." He needed to do something for himself.

He sat down with a pen and tried to write down which way his life was going to take him. Like the Duke, except without whiskey. What had been delayed in his self-actualization? His skiing! He needed to re-find a mountain. On the Fortune Inn "Guide to Restaurants" he wrote down, "Find a ski mountain."

David checked out, jumped into his car, and headed up Route 1. He stopped at a breakfast cafe and ordered blueberry pancakes and a cup of coffee. The waitress looked like a "snowboard chick," so he said to her, "I'm an old ski racer. Where should I go to ski – to Sunday River or to Sugarloaf?"

"If you ask me, Sugarloaf," the girl replied.

"Why?" David asked.

"It's just more of a mountain," the girl retorted.

"I'm there!" said David as he gave her a napkin to write down directions to Sugarloaf.

The Vision of the Mountain

At last David arrived at the mountain resort. It was raining when he checked in. He climbed three flights of stairs to his room, which had a loft with a giant plate glass picture window.

Outside of the picture window was the most beautiful mountain David had ever seen, green with summer foliage. He lay down on the soft double bed and continued looking out the window at the mountain. It was gently sloping at first, then rapidly rising to an elevation over 4200 feet. It had ski lifts rising right in front of his view, ascending all the way to the summit. Plush green trails broke between the ash colored tree trunks, gently adorning the mountain like green Christmas garland. He was home! After all the pain he had experienced in Purgatory, God was giving him this mountain to ski on!

The rain stopped, the clouds formed a ribbon on the mid-section of the mountain, and the bright sunshine shone on top. A brilliantly colored rainbow arched directly over Sugarloaf Mountain. It shone with the darkest shades of red, blue, and purple David had ever seen in a rainbow. He slowly began to close his eyes and drifted off to sleep.

He dreamed that he was above the mountain. He had his skis on and was looking down between them as he was being lifted up into heaven. The sun beamed through the clouds and a vision of General George Washington said, "You are not finished on Earth."

When he awoke, he was so stunned at the beauty of the experience that he decided to run up to the top of the mountain. Running up from the main super quad lift pole line, David crisscrossed on a slightly worn path through waist-deep grass, going up the same way water would come down. As a skier, he recognized the fall line, or the steepest line of ascent and descent possible. It was hot halfway up, so he took off his shirt. His bare chest was heaving. He spotted some wild mountain strawberries which he picked and ate for breakfast. He kept going and reached the steepest part, where water had washed out some rocks. In winter this run was known as "Competition Hill". David sensed Olympic medals coming from this place. He turned and observed the splendor of all the surrounding mountains.

David had not run down a major mountain as fast as he could in over twenty years, so as he criss-crossed down the high summer grass, he watched closely for boulders and smaller stones which could mean death for a now middle-aged man. He kept the brakes on, using the contour of the mountain to slow him down. Toward the bottom, he saw the chair-lift. He knew the terrain was flattening out so he allowed himself to pick up speed to finish hard. Some tourists saw him and gave him that "You're crazy" look that people give to mountain men. He used to relish that! He was back! David sat down to observe the mountains all the way to the coast. He thought, "How could anybody look at this and not believe in God?"

He looked across at the top of the Appalachian Trail where there is a ridge called the "Sleeping Indian." It looks like an Indian chief lying down from left to right with his toes in a pointy pyramid. His legs rise to a little hump of his hands on his chest. Then you see his chin, his face, and his forehead. On his face is a washout of rocks heading downward from his eyes which looks like a line of tears.

David called home to tell Naomi about his finding a new mountain which would bring him peace. He told her he might come home in the morning. She wanted him to come home, but she stayed aloof.

The next morning, when David awoke, his first thought was that he wanted to stay on and explore the new ski mountain. Then he began thinking about his kids and about teaching them how to ski race on this mountain, so he left for home. When he got there and he saw Ruth, the troubling vision of the "fire falling from the sky" near her came back to him. David needed to be alone so he could try to figure this out. He went down in the basement and found some of his things that had been lost in the move. Among them, he found his paper, "Averting the Holocaust," and he re-read it.

The Epiphany

How things had changed in twenty years! David suddenly felt old and tired. He was deeply troubled. His mind raced as he though of spiritual things like the visions of the Virgin Mary which pious children in Eastern Europe recently had.

Late that afternoon while he was reminiscing, Ruth approached him. He ended up spending the entire evening telling her about the mission of peace he had been on twenty years previously and how he hoped to help end the cold war. He concluded his story by telling her, "You know, Ruth, the issue of missiles and war are coming back again and the United States is in grave danger." She replied, "I know." Although she pretended to agree with everything he said, she was convinced he needed help. She would not accept this type of behavior in her eldest daughter's house. She continued to badger him, "What's the matter David? Don't you love Naomi anymore?"

That question was too much. His face developed a blank stare as his spirit retreated from Ruth. He was like a crab going into his shell. He was looking into the abyss again, and the fiery sight frightened him.

As he and Ruth ended their conversation, she stood at the top of the stairs and took his hands and squeezed them. His hands were cold while hers were amazingly warm. There was some kind of spiritual energy, a strange warmth, passing from her hands to his. She asked him, "Can you feel it?" At first he wouldn't admit it, so she pressed on, holding both of his hands in hers. He wanted to break the grip, but she would not release him until he admitted it that he felt something. It was weird. It was like the passing of the Holy Spirit. He babbled something about the Virgin Mary being sighted by kids in Europe. He was so tired that he just wanted to go to bed. He wanted her to just leave him alone.

David went to bed but was so over-tired and sad that he couldn't go to sleep. All the things in his paper had come true: the removal of the Pershing II and SS20 Missiles from Europe, the proclamation of Reagan's Star Wars plan. But it had not been completed. He stared praying "Our Fathers" about the nuclear threat to the world. "Oh, no," he said. He saw a vision of a near miss of a missile intercept. Unbeknownst to him, a few days before his vision a test had been performed in California. The test was aborted and declared a failure.

A part of George Washington's vision sprang into his mind: "And again I heard the mysterious voice saying, 'Son of the Republic, look and learn.' At this the dark, shadowy angel placed a trumpet to his mouth, and blew three distinct blasts; and taking water from the ocean, he sprinkled it upon Europe, Asia and Africa. Then my eyes beheld a fearful scene: from each of these countries arose thick, black clouds that were soon joined into one. Throughout this mass there gleamed a dark red light by which I saw hordes of armed men, who, moving with the cloud, marched by land and sailed by sea to America."

"Oh, my God!" he thought. "We are going to allow missiles in and we will be attacked. World wide war will begin!"

His vision made him remember what he had learned about Dr. Carl Jung. Late in 1913, Dr. Jung had a vision that changed his life. He saw images in his mind of a giant flood engulfing most of Europe. Jung wrote that he "saw thousands of people drowning and civilization crumbling" and water turning into blood.

When World War I started in August 1914, Jung believed his vision had been a precognition. That was the start of his belief in what he called the collective unconscious, the psychic connection between an individual and all of humanity.

Once again, thoughts of national destruction arose in David's mind. He thought, "America is leaving herself vulnerable to missile attack. This is like a launch countdown!" The vision was the combination of all that he had studied, past and present, coming together in a horrible premonition of attack

That night, the vision continued. As he was deep in prayer, David's frightful vision kept coming. More "Our Fathers." Faster, faster. He had a vision of a building imploding and collapsing totally. Then he suddenly felt released from it all, as a vision of bright light and bright spots like snowflakes overwhelmed his mind. A lady in white was holding hands with children, leading them from the destruction up to the bright light of heaven. "Oh, no," he thought. More "Our Fathers." In the strange green light of the room, his mind was racing. His mind was like a demonstration of the inside of a computer that he had seen. There were streams of numbers coming so fast that he was not able to decipher them. Some did not look like numbers at all, but rather like Greek or Hebrew symbols, all arranged in a code. He had it! It was some sort of launch code! The United States, having failed to complete a missile defense system as he had outlined years earlier, was about to come under a missile attack. Was it the fulfillment of the third and most terrible section of George Washington's vision? He lay in his bed. What to do next? He was almost asleep when a train came by the house awakening him to the thought, "Time is running out!"

"Oh, my God!" David thought. "The enemies of the United States are coming to attack us!" Next, he saw a time of worldwide conflict between Christians and Muslims. "What should I do? Whom should I tell?" David, suddenly very weak, slipped back into bed. Try as he might, he could not get to sleep. Was it possible that the paper he had written so many years ago contained some sort of prophetic message? Had he carried this message with him since birth? He'd better protect it, then, and get it to the proper people. Maybe his dad, maybe Father Matthias, maybe the president. He didn't know to whom. He went down in the basement, got his paper, and put it safely under his bed.

He had seen "the code." The code that Daniel had written, the code that Isaac Newton transformed into the date of Christ's return. Newton had given this information to David's forefather, Peter Lion, and it had come down through the family to him. Now it was up to him to interpret it and deliver it to the president.

There was no longer any question in David's mind. His vision was the beginning of the third woe which General Washington had seen and recorded thus: "Throughout this mist there gleamed a dark red light by which I saw hordes of armed men, who, moving with the cloud, marched by land and sailed by sea to America. Our country was enveloped in this volume of cloud, and I saw these vast armies devastate the whole country and burn the villages, towns and cities that I beheld springing up. As my ears listened to the thundering of the cannon, clashing of swords, and the shouts and cries of millions in mortal combat, I heard again the mysterious voice saying, 'Son of the Republic, look and learn.' When the voice had ceased, the dark shadowy angel placed his trumpet once more to his mouth, and blew a long and fearful blast." (from George Washington's vision)

The Vision of the Scroll

"The LORD said, 'Ezekiel, son of man, I want you to stand up and
listen.' After he said this, his Spirit took control of me and lifted
me to my feet. Then the LORD said: 'Ezekiel, I am sending you to
the people of Israel. They are just like their ancestors who rebelled
against me and refused to stop. They are stubborn and hardheaded.
But I, the LORD God, have chosen you to tell them what I say.
Those rebels may not even listen, but at least they will know that a
prophet has come to them. Don't be afraid of them or of anything
they say. You may think you're in the middle of a thorn patch or a
bunch of scorpions. But be brave and preach my message to them,
whether they choose to listen or not. Ezekiel, don't rebel against
me, as they have done. Instead, listen to everything I tell you. And
now, Ezekiel, open your mouth and eat what I am going to give
you.'"
(Ezek. 1:2-8)

Twenty years ago, David had read Ezekiel while writing his
paper, "Averting the Holocaust." Now David imagined that his little
paper might be the little scroll mentioned in Ezekiel because it was
so bitter. He was beginning to have such an intense pain in his side
that he thought he was going to die! Perhaps he never should have
written those things in the first place!

Every passing train awoke David with the reoccurring thought of
a missile attack on the U.S. He felt that somehow his paper, written
twenty years earlier, was key evidence in proving his premonition

correct. He had hid the paper under his mattress to protect it. He still couldn't sleep. He was so tired. He finally drifted off to sleep, and began dreaming. His dream was one of a crucifixion.... his! As he awoke from the dream, he felt a sharp pain in his side, so sharp he though he was going to die. He thought of the part of George Washington's vision where he wrote, "I now began to feel as one dying, or rather to experience the sensations which I have sometime imagined accompany dissolution." At the end of David's dream there was of a Roman soldier standing over him, pulling a long spear out of the point of pain in his side. He heard a voice say, "You killed my son the first time and I'm not going to let you do it again!"

As he emerged from sleep, he was still exhausted and feeling the deep pain in his side. He could not get up, but he was so miserable that he writhed in pain in a fetal position. His wife came in and saw him writhing, and she thought it was a diabetic seizure. He said to her, "Call the ambulance." She held off and ran downstairs to talk to her mother. She had called his parents who would be arriving soon, and she wanted to wait for them so they could help her decide what to do.

David had no choice but to lie in the bed in pain. He drifted off to sleep again, only to awake a few minutes later. As he looked at the vines and flowers on the top of the curtains, they became similar to the thorns which the Romans placed on Christ's head. He lay in bed in agony for two hours. Then he miraculously began to feel better.

A passage from the book of Revelation came into David's mind: "I saw another powerful angel come down from heaven. This one was covered with a cloud, and a rainbow was over his head. His face was like the sun, his legs were like columns of fire, and with his hand he held a little scroll that had been unrolled. He stood there with his right foot on the sea and his left foot on the land. Then he shouted with a voice that sounded like a growling lion. Thunder roared seven times. After the thunder stopped, I was about to write what it had said. But a voice from heaven shouted, 'Keep it secret! Don't write these things.'" (Rev. 10:1-4)

His parents had not arrived yet. David was holding out for them because Ruth wanted to take him to the hospital. She and Naomi didn't share David's growing conviction that his physical symptoms were part of a religious experience. He began mentally rehearsing the presentation of his thesis to his father, General Lion. He needed to convince his dad of the truth of his conclusion that the U.S. was about to undergo an attack. David wanted to offer his father the opportunity to help him advise the president. David was nervous as he mentally rehearsed his presentation for his father. When his parents arrived, he told his dad what he had concluded.

David gave his paper to the general to read. The general read every line and said, "Good paper, Dave. I never knew that you wrote it! What do you want to do now?"

David responded, "I want to advise the president!" The general, still befuddled by the whole bizarre sequences of events, said, "But you have to realize the time in which it was written." David replied, "Many of the things in it have come to pass, except for the last part, and something bad is going to happen because we have not completed a defense system. I must advise the president."

"So you want to advise the president?" his father asked him affectionately, as if knowing that this would not be possible. He remembered meeting with then Vice President Bush, the current president's father, and then General Colin Powell to show them the Pershing II missile's accuracies. The president had called him, he hadn't called the president to set up the meeting! The general tried to distract David with his recollections of this meeting. "I even met with Cy Bush," he said. David didn't know who this was, and he really didn't care. All he knew was that time was running out. He had to talk to the president about how to prevent the holocaust he had envisioned just hours before.

David continued trying to convince all of them that his vision had been divinely inspired. He sat down at the table with his father and Ruth. As always, being the pragmatist that he was, he was bound and determined to prevent death and destruction from a missile attack. To put his vision into worldly terms was enormously difficult. Ruth asked him what the vision was like. David really didn't want to share all the grisly details of death and destruction. He wanted to stick to the ascension of the victims by putting it in a materialistic sense that she might understand. He replied to Ruth's question, "It was like

Disney World," to try to capture the joy that most people experience there. It was simplistic, but it was the best he could do.

He struggled to convince his family, during the time of this spiritual ordeal, that his paper, written years ago, might still be relevant.

The general was wearing a shirt with a logo of Mickey Mouse on it. Despite the fact that David never wore his matching shirt, today he had mysteriously picked it to wear. Disney World was an allusion to what heaven seemed to be like in the ascension part of his vision. The people who had been vaporized in the terrible blast of the building's implosion were as happy as people at Disney World as they ascended.

David had not told Ruth of the death and destruction part of the vision. He wanted to protect her from fear of evil, especially since he had seen her so close to the fire. Now to tie it all together, David pointed to his father's Mickey Mouse shirt, his Mickey Mouse shirt, and explained the allusion to Disney world. Then he pointed to the ceiling and said, "It's God." Ruth, her ever-agnostic self, replied, "That is weird."

David's family members were really concerned about him. They told him to go upstairs and get some rest. He was tired from not sleeping well, so he did what they suggested and rested for an hour. Meanwhile, they were plotting.

Doug MacArther, Naomi's father, was also there and had heard everything David said. (MacArther was a retired Army Colonel who had turned back the TET offensive in Vietnam). He said to General Lion, "He's your boy. What are you going to do about this?"

The general was under the squeeze now and wanted to work out a diplomatic solution. Ruth said, "You should have seen what we saw last night. It was like he was having seizures or something." There was a long pause before a suggestion was made. "You know, they have outpatient therapy." The general thought this might be a good middle ground. He didn't want to commit David to mental hospital. He just wanted to hold him off from having any more revelations, visions, or whatever he was having. Naomi really sided with her Mom, and with her psychology degree wanted to start exercising it on David.

After David's rest, they all agreed that they would visit the hospital. David thought they were going to the hospital for the great pain in his side. His family members wanted to take him there because of their concern about his mental state.

They arrived at the outpatient clinic in the late afternoon. It was the end of the day and the staff wanted to get things done quickly, so rather than interviewing David they told David to fill out their forms himself. David wrote down his premonition of an attack on the U.S. The psychiatrist was concerned, but he didn't have time to see David that day, so everyone agreed that David would come back in the morning. The whole family went home and went to bed.

In the middle of the night, David awoke with recurring thoughts that his vision, his paper, and all he had been through were connected to his relationship with Jesus Christ! This thought made him so excited that he couldn't sleep. His mind raced back to his college quest of the Olympics and his years skiing at Purgatory on runs named Upper and Lower Hades, the River Styx, and 666. He had overcome all of his past and now he wanted to help protect and save the United States. In return, he felt that God was going to return him to skiing in a big way at Sugarloaf Mountain. Sugarloaf was his reward for all those years of perseverance. He was so excited that he knocked on his parents' bedroom door to awaken them to the good news of Christ's redemption!

His bleary-eyed dad opened the door and let David in. They sat on adjacent beds. While his mother said the Rosary, David held his father's hands, much as Ruth had done the night before, hoping to transfer the positive energy. He relayed his entire mission of peace of twenty years ago to his father. He explained that every ski run had been a preparation for the 1984 Sarajevo Winter Games in order to spread diplomacy and peace and to try to avoid the conflict which might start World War III. He tried to impress on his father the spirituality of his vision. However, his dad failed to see things the way David saw them and just became more convinced his son was delusional.

It was 4 a.m. when David went back to his room and woke his wife. She was groggy from trying to sleep. He said, "I've got it all figured out." "What?" she asked. Then he told her his thought pattern of how Christ was enlightening him. She was convinced that he was crazy now, and she told him to go back to sleep. He was so full of "good news" though that he couldn't sleep. He awoke her again at 6 a.m., and he told her that his side was really hurting again. She said, "I think you're going to die!" He said, "Well, it's only a couple of hours now until we're planning to go to confession, so I'll just get ready, shower, and we'll go to breakfast at the Moons Café at 7:00. I'll go to confession at 8:00, and then we'll go to the hospital to have it checked out."

While David showered, he thought about how he could communicate his experience and revelation to his family. He called Doug, his father-in-law, and asked him to pick up his skis and his banners with gold medals won from ski races and bring them with him. David brought his paper to help him advise the president on how to protect the United States from the upcoming peril. When Doug arrived, David asked him if he had brought his stuff, and he had. Doug had arranged all the "pomp and circumstance" at many military ceremonies, so he seemed to be into this. David asked Doug, "Since you're the presentation man, how do you think I should present this?" Doug played right along and said, "You hold your skis, and we'll drape your banner on the table."

The skis were black with gold and white space-age lettering of "VR-17" boldly printed on them. The skis also sported a 25 year old fluorescent American flag sticker. David had bought them from a former World Cup racer and they had been his practice skis. They had helped him transition as a racer from being "good" to being "hot." Doug put them in the car so they could bring them to bring into the church later.

The breakfast restaurant was just down the street and was very Bohemian with a comic book shop in the front and a bunch of breakfast tables in the back. On the walls were paintings of super heroes like Wonder Woman, Batman, and Robin. The pancake platters were named accordingly. Although the sharp pain in his side had subsided, David wanted to be in the best shape for his physical at the hospital as possible in case they had to operate for the pain in his side. He suspected he might have some sort of blockage in the colon which could return at any time. Because he wanted to be in the best possible condition, he ordered the blueberry pancakes. He looked knowingly at everyone as he said, "Blueberries are the highest in antioxidants."

David looked at the clock. He didn't want to be late for his confession at Father Matthias's office in ten minutes. Doug paid the bill. On the way out, David saw a Captain America comic book showing the ending of World War II on the cover. He bought it. This would be useful for him in his presentation! The presentation was of his life's work and he didn't know if that pain in his side meant he might be dying. This presentation might be his last chance to say what he needed to say!

The Confession:
A Cleansing Before Becoming "Born Again"

David was certainly "pumped" now to share his vision of Jesus Christ's personal revelation with his family. But first he wanted to have a confession with his priest, Father Matthias. After all, Father Matthias had been the catalyst for his religious re-awakening, or birth again to Christ, and his renewal of a pursuit of world peace. His confession was to be a cleansing before becoming "born again."

Father Matthias always treated David as though he were the most important man on earth. Now, within the past 24 hours, David felt that his spiritual life was completely whole. He pictured his life as being a wheel with all the spokes of the wheel pointing to the center of his life, Christ.

As David walked into the office, he felt as though Father Matthias were responsible for this miracle. He considered the priest an impetus for the revelation he had experienced. With his military background, David pictured Christ's people as an army, and therefore Father Matthias was a general in his mind, a very holy man. Together, they would unleash the spirits in the George Washington Vision that would help the United States in the third and final woe of the attack against its inhabitants. He that thought Father Matthias would understand his experiences.

David wanted to make the confession quickly so he could share with his family everything that had been in his heart. He ushered his wife, mom, dad, and father-in-law into Father Matthias's tiny office where they could sit and wait for David and Father Matthias.

Father Matthias led David though the church to the confessional. They passed a dozen elderly gray-haired ladies fingering Rosary beads and praying to the Virgin Mary. "They're just like the children in Yugoslavia who saw the Virgin!" thought David. He followed the Father into a small room behind the altar, sat face to face with him, and began. "It's been twenty-five years since my last confession." Father Matthias seemed amazed and asked, "Do you know the Act of Contrition?" David was embarrassed that he had forgotten this prayer and asked the priest to help lead him through it. "Oh my God, I am heartily sorry..." David then asked for blanket immunity because in twenty-five years he had done a lot. Twenty-five years was too much to go into in detail. He blurted out that he wanted, "complete absolution for all my sins." "Yes, my son," said Father Matthias.

He also told Father Matthias that he was going to write a book about his vision and it was going to make his church so famous that people would flock to it because of the miracles that had occurred there. Once word got out, he would have to build a new church to hold all the people. David said he would commit a portion of the book proceeds to the building of that church. Father Matthias simply replied, "O.K." In his mind he was thinking, "Could this be true?" He had never been witness to "born agains" in the act of rebirth. It was simply not a part of the Catholic faith. The elder priest did not realize what had actually taken place. It was a transfer of the Holy Spirit days before at Father Mathias' fortieth anniversary of his ordination

The Presentation

David was totally pumped-up in Christ now! He was officially absolved of all his sins, and he was going to use the proceeds of his book to spread the miracle of His word. His experience might be a proven case of being "born again." He bounded through the church, following Father Matthias's into the tiny office where his family was waiting. The priest sat his desk and stared in bewilderment at the skis in the corner of the room.

David shut the door. Now he had to draw the connection for his whole family that his earlier Olympic quest at Sarajevo in 1984 was to gain a platform as a peace activist. Skiing was how he thought God would use him to prevent war. In fact, his skiing was a religious act of obedience for Jesus Christ! "Blessed are the peacemakers." He grabbed the skis from Doug and held them up in a victorious fashion like he was a winner on the Victory Stand. Then he put them back in the corner.

He got down on one knee and asked Doug for his daughter's hand in marriage again. A tear came to his eye, and he told Doug, "We'll have a glorious ten year renewal of our marriage vows at Sugarloaf Mountain Church and invite all the family!" Doug was moved to tears and said, "O.K."

Then David got up, moved close to his father, and said, "Here's to you, Dad, for with your inspiration. I wrote this paper through a sacred pact that George Washington made with God and the U.S. Army. It is the George Washington Vision, which I have come to understand, which will help prevent the United States from being annihilated." He shook his Dad's hand.

Next he moved to his mother who had been his inspiration in prayer. He said, "And lastly to you, Mom. You have prayed for me every day. Here's a tribute from your son, Captain America, who will help lead the United States through this perilous time." As he said this, he handed her the new comic book with Captain America on the cover overlooking battling army men. His mother, always praying, was praying "Hail Marys" to herself for help for her son. She put the comic book in her bag and still has it today.

Then David recalled part of George Washington's vision: "Instantly a light as of a thousand suns shone down from above me, and pierced and broke into fragments the dark cloud which enveloped America. At the same moment the angel upon whose head still shone the word Union, and who bore our national flag in one hand and a sword in the other, descended from the heavens attended by legions of white spirits. These immediately joined the inhabitants of America, who I perceived were well nigh overcome, but who immediately taking courage again, closed up their broken ranks and renewed the battle." He felt hopeful and inspired.

Father Mathias was literally speechless – although inspired – at what had transpired in his office. He got up and shook everyone's hand. All he could think of was Daniel in the lions' den as they left.

Jesus said, "Prophets are honored by everyone, except the people of their hometown and their own family."(Matthew 13:57) That was certainly true in David's case! David's presentation was all that it took to convince his family that he was in serious trouble! They immediately ushered David to the car and drove him to the Magog Medical Center.

OUT OF THE DEPTHS

The Sorceries of Ward P666

"Neither repented they of their murders, nor of their sorceries, nor of their fornication, nor of their thefts." (Rev. 9:21, KJV)

The English word "pharmacy" is derived from the Greek φαρμακεια (pharmakia) which literally means "sorcery" or "magic."

At Magog Medical Center on July 19, 2001, an admission clerk worked on David's chart. She wrote that the reason for David's admission was, "Patient claims war to begin!" A social worker came over and asked David to sign an admission authorization. David refused because thought the hospitalization wasn't going to be covered by his insurance. The social worker pressured David to sign anyway, and he told David he'd call the insurance company and come back if the admission wasn't covered.

David saw an old man standing there who was a guard, and he struck up a conversation with him about the Red Sox. The old man led David down the hall through a different wing of the hospital and into an examination room. David still assumed that he was at the hospital because of the tremendous pain in his side, so he consented to be examined. However, the examining doctor paid no attention to David's pain or to any of his physical symptoms. David was behind lock and key now at Magog Medical Center's infamous Ward P666. He had been declared mentally ill.

The process by which Magog Medical Center determined that David was mentally ill was very strange. At one meeting David asked his doctor, "Do you have any experience with enlightenments, Dr. Gogerrez?" The doctor looked at him like he had not even asked a question, and just kept writing out prescriptions.

Here is what the doctor wrote about David's condition:

Magog Medical Center
Medical Record Services
Psychiatric History and Evaluation

Patient was admitted with the complaint that war was to begin. His family brought him to the program, describing him as "out of control." Patient is affectionate and cordial. He speaks clearly, is mentally acute, and is physically fit. His emotions become heightened, though, when entering into delusions of grandeur. He continues to refer to the significance of a paper he wrote twenty years ago which he claims can cause world-wide nuclear disarmament. This claim, and his claims that he "skis for Jesus" indicate delusions of grandeur.

He appears to have sufficient impulse control and fair judgment. His relations with other patients and staff are exemplary. The nurses, however, have complained that he speaks right in people's faces, neglecting their social boundaries. He also seems easily excitable when discussing spiritual matters. This excitement seems to be controlled, though, as there are no violent outbursts. Again, the patient's religious delusions cause him to try to "save" others. His speech is at a normal rate. He looks individuals in the eye and grasps their hands firmly when shaking hands.

It took considerable coaxing to get him to take his medications. The drugs have calmed his excitement when discussing spiritual matters. However, his conversations continue to revolve around these themes. He appears to be no threat to society, although conversations with his family indicate he has emotional imbalances. Based on my observations he is hyper-manic. Prescriptions of Divalproex Sodium and Lorazepam have been introduced. CT scan, electrocardiogram, hemogram, and electrolyte results are still pending.

Signed: Dr. Joe Gogerrez

Although he was confined to a mental hospital, David knew that he was not only sane, but had a message of hope to share. God was not in Ward P666. The doctors did not believe in God, or HIS ability to cure the poor spirits there. David felt as though God had allowed him to be put on the psychiatric floor to be a help to the other patients. He surmised that many of the people on the floor were there because of suicide attempts. He wanted to talk them out of it. The nurses thought he was crazy, so he resorted to whispering to them. Here is what he said, as he brought each patient close to the barred window to look out: "Do you see how beautiful this place is? Look at the ocean! Do you want to get back out there?" The patient would nod "yes." David would continue, "Well, I just came through hell to get here, so listen carefully. Don't you see that you live in the most beautiful place in the world that God created? If you don't appreciate that and you kill yourself, God will send you to hell. Do you understand? So don't ever, ever, try to kill yourself again!" In every instance the patient would look at him with frightened eyes and nod their head "yes."

The nurses began telling David, "Stay away from the other patients!" "Don't talk to them!" "Shut UP!" One nurse came to David reinforced with heavy-duty dosages of drugs. David thought immediately of Nurse Ratched in the movie "One Flew Over the Cuckoo's Nest." He managed to hide some of the drugs under his tongue and then put them under his mattress when the nurse left. She came back, found the medication and made him take it as she watched.

The whole object of treatment in Ward P666 was to get you to "behave" and to fall asleep. David had trouble sleeping. They gave David earplugs to wear because inevitably in the middle of the night someone would start screaming or crying at the top of their lungs. Orderlies would run down the hall and strap him to a rolling bed and cart him away. Where? Maybe to get a lobotomy like at the end of "Cuckoo's Nest." "Better be a good boy and stay in your room, so it doesn't happen to you!" David thought.

However, that thought didn't stop him from looking around for a big "Indian Chief" who could throw a sink through a wall to help them escape. Although he was imprisoned for religious thoughts, he reasoned the best way to get out was to submit to the "drug-pusher," Dr. Gogerrez.

David had studied Shinto monks and learned about their ability to reach a higher spiritual plane through communion with nature and their environment. His trip to Sugarloaf was such an experience. The rediscovery of his prophetic paper and re-birth to God through a crucifixion with our Lord Jesus Christ gave him extreme insight. He believed that he was part of the George Washington Vision and hoped to warn the president within enough time to prevent an attack that he felt was coming. The only reason that he had this ability was because of his conviction in our Lord and because he wanted to live his life for God's purpose. He used his subjective mind to perceive by intuition. Current American psychiatric principles have no idea how to address this situation!

David was belittled and misdiagnosed by the psychiatric community. He accepted his vision with faith and prayer in his God, Jesus, and the U.S. Constitution. His belief in the George Washington Vision was to be put to the test. David had reached the apex of his full potential.

Dr. Gogerrez carelessly labeled David as bipolar. David knew he was not mentally ill. He argued with Gogerrez for a while, but he soon realized that the "zoo keeper" would not let him free until he took drugs, lots of them. David fought them with the energy of his eternal unconscious – his spirit. During this period of time, he doubted himself, doubted the "doctors," but at no time did he ever doubt his Lord and God.

He didn't want to stir up trouble because he was afraid they might give him a drug to take away his mind altogether. Although he was admitted because of a spiritual experience, they didn't have him speak to the hospital chaplain or participate in religion. It appeared that they were trying to drug the spirit out of him. The wanted to erase his mind of the communion with his Lord which had been such a beautiful experience. They were trying to make his experience dirty. A mental illness, the called it. They were guilty of rape. Mind rape. Character assassination.

David knew he would sort things out once he got out of this mental prison. But right now he was more concerned about his vision and figuring it out. As the spirit was being drugged out of him, David started writing a book in order to keep mentally alert. He fought the powerful mind-erasing and body-energy-sapping drugs. To keep his mental balance, he just wrote and wrote and began writing his book. It was about his family, his Olympic quest, and his life. He wanted to trace all the steps back to figure things out. What was the spiritual world trying to show him? In order to analyze it, he had to maintain his identity and unique self at a time when the psychiatrists were trying to kill his uniqueness with drugs. However they interpreted his prayers and his relationship with God, he was committed to remaining faithful.

Faith in God vs. the Sorceries

"We cannot change anything until we accept it."

Modern psychiatrists do not care about talking to their patients or about understanding the circumstances and the human interaction which brought the patient before them. Their training is to explain things on a chemical basis so that the chemicals they inject into the body of a patient will create calmness. As such, they have become agents of the pharmaceutical industry, netting billions of dollars and hundreds of thousands of jobs.

Pharmaceuticals are at the root of many of America's problems, and the drug companies are big business. The latest surge in the stock market has been due largely to stocks in the pharmaceutical group. The coming crisis in America will be ushered in because children have been drugged from a very young age instead of being understood. This will create young adults who feel inferior unless they take a powerful combination of drugs.

How many children do you know who have been diagnosed with ADD (Attention Deficit Disorder)? They are labeled medically, and when they grow up they will be discriminated against for jobs and for medical and life insurance. They will be made to feel guilty for any spiritual thoughts or insights. If they tell their doctor about their insights, he will increase the dosage of their drugs. This leaves the patient addicted to drugs more powerful than illegal narcotics.

Millions of mentally challenged individuals will find their futures in hospitals separated from loved ones. The patient will face a detachment from God, church, family, and his or her community. These institutions traditionally have been what have held the United States of America and its citizens together in times of tribulation. The evil attack is upon us from within: If one's mind and spirit are destroyed, where is the person's indignance to what is wrong, much less the ability to question, argue or fight the wrong? What if the United States were attacked and we did not have a simple majority left that thought it wrong? A large portion of our families are being attacked right now, legally and with our consent, by the medical establishment and the drug companies.

At the end of the week of David's false imprisonment at Magog Medical Center, he was sent home to face dark and difficult days. The medications made him unable to work, and he still wrestled with the same spiritual dilemmas as before.

He was released to outpatient care under Dr. Thomas Doubtus. Instead of giving support, his family had been convinced by Dr. Doubtus that medicine was the cure. At any attempt at communication or cry for help by David, his family would call the doctors for an adjustment to his meds. David's friends, though, who were aware of his family tension, knew instinctively that what had happened was an act of God and sent him cards and letters with various spiritual messages such as these.

Saint Clare of Assisi
(1193-1253)

May Almighty God
bless you.
May He look upon you
with the eyes of His mercy
And give you His peace.
✟
Here below may He pour
forth His graces on
you abundantly
And in heaven may He
place you among His saints.
Amen.

St. Michael the Archangel

Saint Michael the Archangel,
Defend us in battle
Be our protection against the
wickedness and snares of the
devil;
May God rebuke him, we humbly pray;
And do thou, O Prince of the
heavenly host,
By the power of God, thrust into
hell
Satan and all evil spirits
Who wander through the world
For the ruin of souls. Amen

David secretly stopped taking his medications within two weeks of his release and began to review the doctors' notes written during his incarceration. He found renewed energy to fight against their unethical and damaging treatment when they sent him a bill for $7500, which they had earlier claimed would be covered by his insurance. Another injustice!

The fathers of psychiatry all accepted the spiritual world and included its existence in their practices. Thomas Hudson, Abraham Maslow, and Carl Jung all were aware of the elements of bipolar disorder, or manic-depression, in which the mind is divided into the subjective and the objective. In order to function in this world, both parts of the mind are essential for proper thinking. Bipolar people and manic-depressives think only with the subjective part of their minds, and therefore their thoughts and actions are unrelated to the real world around them. Or do these people have a higher ability with which makes them able to think more instinctively? For example, there are patients who believe they see and talk to spirits despite no clear proof. Unfortunately, modern psychiatry has removed the spiritual element from their practice. Instead, they have opted to prescribe medications which can easily cost the patient hundreds of dollars every month! This has been enormously profitable for the psychiatrist and the pharmaceutical companies.

Religion is free. The person who experiences a revelation of prophecy, a life altering spiritual vision, or a re-birth to the Savior and relates it to a modern psychiatrist will be placed in the bipolar category and prescribed powerful drugs until he can see spiritual visions no more. Are we persecuting them because we lack of their abilities to visit the spiritual realm? Does labeling them as "crazy" make us "normal" people feel more comfortable?

The persecution of those who have religious visions and our country's dependence on drugs to solve such "problems" is part of the final attack on the United States of America. The intent of the psychiatrists and drug companies is to separate our country's inhabitants from God. If the final battle is a spiritual one, how will we fare? What will the outcome be if we have allowed the sorcerers to drug the spirit from us?

Samuel Adams: Thunder and Lightning

"I saw a windstorm blowing in from the north. Lightning flashed
from a huge cloud and lit up the whole sky with a dazzling
brightness." (Ezekiel 1:2)

A little less than two weeks had passed since David's release
from Magog Medical Center. David was so convinced of the vision
of destruction that he wanted to see the historical sites related to the
George Washington Vision. When he traveled to Boston with his
sons James "Hawk" and John "Eagle" to pick up his daughter Ava
at Logan Airport, they stayed an extra day to go on the harbor boats
touring Boston Harbor. David wanted to see the site of the Boston
Tea Party.

The day before he left on his trip he read the story of Washington
waiting a year, all the way through 1775, until the Continental Army
was strong enough to liberate Boston and Dorchester Heights. The
liberation occurred on St. Patrick's Day in 1776.

In Boston David looked south to the John F. Kennedy Memorial
Library from the sun-drenched deck of the tour boat. He felt a
patriotic power surge rush within him. "I am right!" David thought.
"My vision is of the third woe of the George Washington Vision.
The USA is going to come under attack."

The tour boat circled around the U.S.S. Constitution, "Old
Ironsides." It was so named because cannonballs would bounce off
its sides. It is one of the oldest warships in the U.S. Navy. David
had built a model of it when he was very young.

The tour boat docked. The weather was hot, almost one hundred degrees.

David and his children walked the Freedom Trail. They walked past the graves of Samuel Adams, Benjamin Franklin's parents, and other founding fathers on their way to the Old North Church. They went up into Paul Revere's house. In his bedroom, a young tour guide of 19 or 20 years old told them that Wadsworth's poem "The Midnight Ride of Paul Revere" was wrong. He said that Paul had no partner to put the lanterns in the steeple. It was he, working alone, who led his steed to the church and climbed the stairs to the belfry tower for insurance. He did this in case he should he be stopped by the British sentries. Then he went on his famous ride.

Outside the Old North Church, David bought them all Red Sox hats. Then they went into the church. They walked down the red carpeted aisle and looked at the brass plates on the doors of the pew boxes. The plates named the families that had sat there on Sunday mornings in the late 1700's. Finally, on the left side of the church, they saw the box that said "Revere." They all sat down in the pew box that Paul Revere had sat in. "So this is what it would have been like," said David. "The seats are so uncomfortable," returned Ava. David looked up, and he saw General George Washington!

He left the pew box and walked up to the altar, and there on a pedestal was a marble bust, carved in 1789, of the father of our country. The eyes on the bust were the strangest eyes he had ever seen. They had no pupils but were all white and stared through you into eternity. On a column off to the side was a brass plate which bore the quote from the Marquis de Lafayette which said, "No place else had I ever seen a likeness of George Washington that was truer to the man himself." David looked back into the hollow stare. What more could he do for his country? He would pray right there for inspiration. The George Washington prophecy came back to him. He must warn the president!

As they all made their way back through the cobblestones of Boston, it began to rain. "We'd better run for it," David said. They had to stop right in front of the huge statue of Samuel Adams in front of Faneuil Hall. James asked David who "that guy was." David responded, "He was the leader of the Massachusetts Delegation to the 1776 Continental Congress."

David had forgotten that he had played the part of Samuel Adams when he was in eighth grade in Mr. Granucci's re-creation of American history. It came back to him now. Samuel Adams had been the force behind the American Revolution!

A red traffic light forced David and his children to wait in front of Samuel Adams' twenty foot likeness in the pouring rain. Then, out of nowhere, a giant lightning bolt exploded directly above at high noon, splitting in bright arteries to the north and south. People next to them crouched down. David felt grit from the bricks of Faneuil Hall blow onto the skin of his face. He closed his eyes and he could still see the flash. Then came the "boom" of the thunder. David was about to tell the kids to hit the deck, but the light changed. They crossed the street and ran up three flights of stairs as fast as they could. At the top of the stairs, David looked back at Samuel Adams, standing tall, and thought, "Wow! God and Samuel Adams want me to get out my message."

Salem

On the way home from Boston, David and his kids stopped in Salem, Massachusetts, at the site of the Salem witch trials. What the learned there astonished them. They found out that Salem was a veritable hub of commerce. It was actually the most profitable settlement in the New World in the early 1600's. Many different kinds of cultures – from the West Indies to China – came together in trade at Salem. The first trade between the American colonies and China was established in Salem. The first American to become millionaire made his fortune in Salem.

Salem was a modern, progressive place until the Indian wars. Fear of very horrible deaths at the hands of the Indians caused the people of Salem to maintain close quarters and become mistrustful of the outside influences. Titchiba, the accused "witch" from the West Indies, was merely practicing her own religion when she was brought under suspicion in Salem.

What ultimately occurred in the Salem witch trials was the most blatant denial of the religious or individual rights of individuals in the American colonies. The witch trials led to the ultimate wrong of a gruesome death for the accused witches. "I am wronged. It is a shameful thing that you should mind these folks that are out of their wits," said Martha Carrier before she was hanged for witchcraft on August 19, 1692.

David realized that tremendous acts of evil had happened in Salem during the year of the witch trials. 156 innocent people were accused, and 20 were convicted and killed. The evil was in the accusers. Now, in 21ˢᵗ century America, with all of our purported religious and individual rights, could something like this happen again?

There are strong parallels between the Salem witch trials and the more modern examples of treatment by the psychiatric community. The tremendous profitability of the powerful pharmaceutical industry leads to a similar denial of individual rights of religious expression. This had happened in David's case, except without the hanging. However, the drugging of the spirit was a hanging of the mind.

As a purveyor of the George Washington Vision, David was demeaned, belittled, labeled, ostracized, analyzed, drugged, and imprisoned. His conviction and belief in God beat these sorceries, mind control, and attempts to lead him into drug addiction. The pharmaceutical industry has high stakes in this "witch hunt" as it rakes in billions of dollars a year in revenues from people who could be spiritually healed through faith and prayer for free. David's prescribed medications cost over $300 a month! One wonders if the George Washington Vision would have died long ago if George himself had told it to a drug-pushing psychiatrist. David threw all his prescription medications in the woods that day and has not taken any medications since then.

When David returned from Boston, he knew he needed to get his old paper to the president, the secretary of state, and the secretary of defense. He had to do something to help prevent the terrible vision from happening! As he re-read the paper he'd written twenty years previously, he realized that his vision of buildings imploding from the inside out had to be a missile attack! The fact that the U.S. had failed to build the missile defense system was going to allow a missile to get through and hit a major American city! He must warn the leaders!

On August 11, 2001, he set about photocopying his old paper, writing personal cover letters, and shipping them by overnight carrier to the national leaders. He hoped that they would read them. David did all of this in secret because his wife thought that he was crazy. She had even arranged an appointment with another psychiatrist.

Warning the Leaders

David felt a strong premonition of the 9/11 missile attack coming, but from the vision of the buildings imploding believed the attack would be a nuclear blast. He hoped that perhaps a missile defense system might have been built as a top secret project and might be ready to prevent such an attack. He believed the prophecy of his paper might convince the national leaders of the urgency of the situation. Only the top leaders would be able to implement such a plan if it was ready.

David became inspired to draw a sketch of a peace-ball – a killer satellite which would work in teams of four, circling around our 600 defense satellites to protect them from enemy missile or satellite attack. He envisioned peace-balls orbiting the defense satellite and then attaching themselves to an enemy missile. The peace-ball would then fire its engines and remove the enemy missile from the space battlefield. It would detonate away from the area. A spinning battlefield vacuum satellite would follow and vacuum up the debris.

David firmly believed that all Americans should take advantage of their privileges as citizens in democracy by writing to their leaders. On August 11, 2001, he sat down and wrote a cover letter and an addendum to President George Bush, Secretary of State Colin Powell, and Secretary of Defense Donald Rumsfeld. He sent these letters with copies of his twenty-year-old paper, "Averting the Holocaust," along with drawings illustrating his peace-ball and other ideas for defense. As he dropped his Airborne Express package to

Secretary of Defense Donald Rumsfeld in the pick-up box, he said to himself, "I hope he reads this."

Here is David's letter to President Bush:

To: President George W. Bush
From: David Lion
Date: August 11, 2001
Re: Satellite Defense Initiative

Mr. President,

Enclosed please find a paper I wrote in 1981. Many of its predictions have been fulfilled. As Ike said, "Only an alert and knowledgeable citizenry can compel the proper meshing of the huge industrial and military defense complex with our peaceful methods and goals, so that security and liberty may prosper together."

A part of the "citizenry" Ike mentioned, I hope I will be able to help you with the defense of our county. Please pay close attention to my recommendations made in 1981. In the other enclosed materials I have repeated these recommendations in today's context. I don't know why it has happened now, but a premonition has increased my fear of our enemies using nuclear extortion or even a missile attack in the near future. Please do all you can to get the satellite missile defense system to a flawless state and demonstrate it before our enemies launch a missile.

Thank you very much.

Sincerely,
David Lion

He also sent a letter and his paper to Greg Smith, the curator of the Smithsonian Institution. Later in that week in August, 2001 Mr. Smith called David and told him that his paper was "prophetic" and that it would be included in the papers in the Smithsonian Institution.

(To see the rest of the letters David wrote to the national leaders in August, 2001 and his letter to Mr. Smith, turn to Appendix B at the end of this book. To see the drawings of the peace-ball and other defense ideas, turn to Appendix C).

David hoped that his words and papers would provide some inspiration to his leaders. Debate over need for a missile defense system caused twenty years of stalling. Although David did not realize it, the timetable for implementation of such a plan was falling farther and farther behind.

It was the eighteenth anniversary of the President Reagan's Star Wars speech, and it had been twenty years since he had written his paper. The George Washington Vision and his own vision had awakened him to his sense of duty. While others were walking around with signs of protest, he was actually faxing his support and advice to the most powerful Americans in the world. They are the standard bearers of the flag which says "Union" on it. Would they listen to the George Washington Vision?

David envisioned the day of demonstration of a "Star Wars" system as one of pride for all Americans similar to the day Americans landed on the moon. It would be a great day for mankind too, because they would no longer be subject to missile extortion from any country. Nuclear weapons would become obsolete and would ultimately be removed.

The Fraud of the Sorcerers

On September 5, 2001, David had an appointment with his outpatient psychiatrist, Dr. Thomas Doubtus. He decided to go all out and tell him the whole story of how he had the vision of an attack on the USA, been incarcerated at the Magog Medical Center, and since his release had written to the top leaders of the land about his fear of a missile attack. Doubtus was very clinical. He barely talked to David, but continually wrote on paper on his clip-board. David wondered what the heck he was writing.

David had brought some of the religious items that friends had sent him recently along to his appointment. He put them around the doctor on the chair. There was Dr. Doubtus, sitting next to pictures of saints, angels, and Jesus. The doctor reacted in a frightened manner, like David had "cooties" or something. David could tell that Dr. Doubtus didn't understand what he was saying and that he was "losing him." He got scared for this poor lost soul.

The doctor said, "I know how you religious guys are." He said this in a very demeaning manner.

"This guy is going to hell," David thought.

David stood up. He was getting nowhere with this guy. The "doctor" sat at his desk and began writing out powerful prescriptions. He handed the slip of paper to David and dismissed him. David was so mad that he was shaking when he left the office. He wanted to go back to the doctor's inner office door, knock on it, and tell the guy off. However, he decided that Dr. Doubtus was probably going to hell of his own volition, so he would just let him.

He got in his car and drove down the beautiful coast. As he drove, he watched glimmers of the sunlight off the ocean. When he arrived at home, his wife was holding the phone. Doubtus had called her and said, "David isn't taking his medications." Naturally, this apparent attempt of Doubtus to control David's life, spirit, wife, and family was too much. In that instant, David told his wife, "Too bad he's fired." (The next day he changed doctors).

That evening, David made some notes about his doctor's appointment. He wrote, "Thomas Doubtus just wanted to increase my medication to include Respirdol and other drugs. I told him that this synergy was not good. Furthermore, I told about how fast I ride my bike downhill and my powerful stand up riding lawnmower. I told him that the level of Divalproex Sodium I am currently on leaves me too impaired to ride my bike and cut the lawn safely. I told him I felt that the combination of his drugs and my normal occupations was dangerous.

"Also, he and other doctors have breached the confidentiality agreement that should exist between a psychiatrist and patient in several ways: 1) by obtaining my signature by fraud, essentially without my consent, 2) by rendering a medical opinion on the insurance form without even having my records or a thorough knowledge of my condition, and 3) by basing his opinion on hearsay, which seems to be his standard method of operation.

"I had only one hour to explain to him how my religious faith had caused the vision and contributed to my condition. He would not believe me, and he was very adamant about his already misdirected medical opinions. He also admitted that there was no way to ascertain that I had a chemical imbalance at all. He seemed to imply that I would need a five year treatment program. He seems more intent on making a profit and pushing drugs on than listening to me.

"He has rushed into a diagnosis based on two appointments and hearsay. He is not very open-minded. I told him that I was seeking a second opinion and he was very intent on finding out who I planned to consult. When I would not tell him, he became agitated."

Dr. Doubtus was also thinking about David that evening. He had smelled money and had worked to send in an insurance claim.

He wasn't ready to let David and his money go yet, and he thought he might have any ally in Naomi.

Naomi was concerned about David the week after he was released from the hospital and had called Dr. Doubtus. She told him, "He can't work." It was true. He was still taking the powerful drugs recommended by Dr. Gogerrez upon his release, Respirdol and Valproic Acid, in dosages of 2000 mg per day. He hardly knew who or where he was, but it wasn't because of the alleged "bipolar disorder." It was because of the powerful combination of drugs.

In response to Naomi's call, Doubtus filed a claim stating that David could not work because, "Patient was hospitalized with hypomania that involved grandiosity, impaired judgment, and impaired thoughts." David had a very large disability policy that would pay him if he were so impaired as to not be able to work, and in return, the doctor would get his fee. It seemed air-tight – except that David thought it was fraud. Doubtus sent David a bill. Little did he know that David would not sign the insurance claim form and had decided to fight for his rights.

Here is the response David sent to Dr. Doubtus in response to the bill:

To: Dr. Thomas Doubtus
From: David Lion

Dear Sir:

I personally never signed a letter authorizing you access to my Magog medical records. (See the attached letter dated 7/31/01). On 8/1/01 we had a meeting in which you made a diagnostic interview. We did not discuss anything specific. I wanted you to formulate your own opinion. After the meeting, my wife called you and told you essentially what to say in your writing. You did not have my best interests in mind when you wrote your opinion. Since you were unauthorized to receive the Magog medical records, your opinion was totally based on hearsay.

At our second meeting on September 5, 2001, I showed you my letters to President Bush, Colin Powell, *et al.* of August 11, 2001. I told you of my premonition that the United States was under threat of a missile attack. You branded this grandiosity. Please find evidence that you were wrong by reviewing the enclosed copy of a letter from Secretary of State Collin Powell (dated September 7, 2001) acknowledging my "old and new insights."

I also told you that the Divalproex Sodium medication was upsetting my stomach in the dosage you prescribed. You seemed unconcerned about this, and went about prescribing even more different medications, with unknown synergistic effects on my body. I feel as though this is malpractice.

I also requested confidentiality because of what I perceived to be errors in your judgment based on past correspondence with others.

After that, you proceeded to breach the Hippocratic Oath. A copy of it is enclosed so that you may reread it.

Your involvement in my medical care has actually caused me detriment, and as such I cannot in good conscience pay you. You are no longer appointed as my doctor. If you have corresponded with anyone or any organization regarding my case, you run the risk of legal action.

Sincerely,

David Lion

SECRETARY OF STATE   1 Sep 01

Dear Mr. Lion,

Thanks for your note and for your "old and new" insights,

And thanks for coaching Bryan.

Sincerely,

COLIN POWELL

THE SECRETARY OF STATE
WASHINGTON, D.C. 20520

U.S. OFFICIAL MAIL
PENALTY FOR PRIVATE USE $300
≡ 0.34 ≡
PB METER
U.S. POSTAGE

SEP 10'01

Mr. Daniel L. Lion

ME

POSTMARKED THE
DAY BEFORE 9.11!

The Hippocratic Oath

"I swear by Apollo the physician, by Aesculapius, and Health, and All-heal, and all the gods and goddesses, that according to my ability and my judgment, I will keep this oath and this stipulation - to reckon him who taught me this Art equally dear to me as my parents, to share my substance with him, and relieve his necessities if required; to look upon his offspring in the same footing as my own brothers, and to teach them this Art, if they wish to learn it, without fee or stipulation; and that by precept, lecture, and every mode of instruction, I will impart a knowledge of the Art to my own sons, and of my teachers, and to disciples bound by a stipulation and oath according to the law of medicine, but to none others.

"I will follow that system or regimen which, according to my ability and judgment, I consider for the benefit of my patients, and abstain from whatever is deleterious and mischievous.

"I will give no deadly medicine to any one if asked, or suggest any such counsel; and in like manner I will not give to a woman a pessary to produce abortion.

"With purity and with holiness I will pass my life and practice my Art. I will not cut persons laboring under the stone, but will leave this to be done by men who are practitioners of this work. Into whatever houses I enter, I will go into them for the benefit of the sick, and will abstain from every voluntary act of mischief and corruption; and, further, from the seduction of females or males, of freemen and slaves.

"Whatever, in connection with my professional service, or not in connection with it, I see or hear, in the life of men, which ought not to be spoken of abroad, I will not divulge, as reckoning that all such should be kept secret.

"While I continue to keep this Oath unviolated, may it be granted to me to enjoy life and the practice of the Art, respected by all men, in all times. But should I trespass and violate this Oath, may the reverse by my lot."

How many doctors have you known who have violated the Hippocratic oath?

That was the end of David's relationship with Dr. Doubtus. It was a positive change for David.

A Page from David's Paper
Twenty Years Later

When you read the newspaper at that time, it looked more and more like David's paper was coming true.

Here are some articles that appeared in *Nation's Newspaper* in the late summer and early fall of 2001. The first article appeared on July 31, 2001.

Statement by the Foreign Affairs Ministry of
the Russian Federation on the Occasion of
the Tenth Anniversary of the Signing of START Treaty

This date marks the tenth anniversary of the singing of the Treaty on the Reduction and Limitation of Strategic Offensive Arms (START Treaty) to which Russia, Byelorussia, Kazakhstan and Ukraine – the states that are the former Soviet Union – and the United States of America are parties. It was signed in Moscow and came into force on December 5, 1994.

The START Treaty is at present the only international treaty under which real cuts of strategic offensive weapons are being made. Throughout the ten-year period it has played and continues to play an important role in strengthening strategic stability and international security.

In the course of compliance with the Treaty, all the strategic nuclear weapons of the former USSR have been removed to the territory of Russia. Byelorussia, Kazakhstan and Ukraine as non-nuclear states have become parties to the Nuclear Non-Proliferation Treaty.

The START Treaty envisages that by the end of this year, that is, upon the completion of the third and final stage of reductions, Russia and the U.S. will have reduced the number of their strategic carriers to 1,600 and the warheads on them to 6,000 on each side.

A key factor and condition for the implementation of the START Treaty has been the existence of and compliance by the parties with the 1972 ABM Treaty. The parties to the START Treaty have carried out a large amount of work to liquidate strategic offensive weapons, to monitor compliance therewith, including by large-scale inspection activities and resolving the questions arising within the mechanism envisaged by the Treaty, the Joint Compliance and Inspection Commission.

Taking into account the experience accumulated during the past decade, Russia comes out for further radical cuts of strategic weapons to 1,500 warheads for the Russian Federation and the United States of America by 2008. The corresponding initiatives and other measures to strengthen strategic stability and its legal-treaty basis were set forth in the Statement of the Russian President of November 13, 2000.

When David read the newspaper on August 21, 2001, he saw a sign that President Bush had read his letter and paper and was following David's advice. The newspaper said that Bush had appointed General Richard Myers as Chairman of the Joint Chiefs. Myers had been the Air Force's top man in charge of space command. This was only a week after David had sent the president his paper, so David was happy about the decision. He saw it as a sign that the missile defense system would be completed.

The next day, there was more good news. David read the following article on August 22, 2001.

China Will Get Info on Shield

WASHINGTON - China will receive an update on U.S. missile defense plans before President Bush visits Beijing in September as the United States tries to show other countries that the proposed missile shield is not a threat.

"This is part of the administration's outreach to China and other nations such as Russia to discuss with them the reason why we are developing a missile defense system and how it is designed to protect us from rogue nations or accidental launches," White House spokesman Ari Fleischer said in a telephone interview.

"It is something we are hoping they will support because it is not aimed at China," he said. "The president thinks it is important to consult with our allies and other nations."

The next week David was pleased to see another newspaper article that showed the president acting on his letter and paper. Here is that article, which appeared in *Nation's Newspaper* on September 6, 2001.

U.S. - Russian Arms Negotiation on Missile Defense

A senior U.S. diplomat held arms talks with a Russian envoy in Moscow, keeping up a brisk diplomatic pace forced by an approaching showdown over the ongoing U.S. missile defense program. But both sides kept hopes muted, pending a Pentagon review that will put firm numbers forward. Washington wants Moscow to agree to scrap the 1972 ABM Treaty banning a missile defense shield Bush wants to build. Moscow is opposed to such a move.

David could see direct evidence that the president was taking steps in the right direction but he hoped it would be in time. Time was running out! Little did David know that the enemy had already boarded the missiles.

September 11th

"We have not escaped any of the terrible curses written by Moses, and yet we have refused to beg you for mercy and to remind ourselves of how faithful you have always been." (Daniel 9:13-14)

"The most fearful is the third, but in this greatest conflict the whole world united shall not prevail against her." (George Washington's Vision)

Everyone certainly will remember where they were when they first learned about or watched the explosions and fall of the World Trade Center towers in New York City on September 11, 2001.

There was a big screen TV upstairs in the office at David's home. David heard Naomi screaming for him to come upstairs. As he entered the hallway he could see the first tower in flames at the top. Then the second airliner flew into the second tower like a missile. The first tower collapsed, and the second likewise would follow. Buildings were imploding like in his horrific vision! He hoped that there was no nuclear device on board the planes to spread radioactivity through all of New York. In one sense David felt a sense of relief that he was not crazy, but he also felt extreme sorrow for all those harmed by the attack. He grieved inwardly for the injured, those who died, and the families they left behind. He was angry at those who carried out the attack.

The frightening premonition he had of missile attack was real. He thanked God that there were no nuclear devices on board any of the 9/11 airliners.

The next morning, the newspapers showed a photo of Mohammed Atta passing right through the security at Portland Airport, only minutes from David's house. Within a week Ruth called from New York and told them that while traveling through Maine, the terrorists had stopped at the house next to her sister's house to ask for directions to Portland. David's premonition of his mother-in-law being close to the buildings imploding had been right!

War had begun. Damn it! Damn it! Damn it! He had tried his best to put his finger on it and stop it in the only way he knew how, but his prayer had been interrupted by the drug pushers. He had let the psychiatric community document in writing his premonition and his religion. They had belittled and slandered him. He had been persecuted for the proof of his theory of Christ's interaction as Savior for people that believe in Him without a shadow of a doubt.

Then came more evidence that supported David's vision and theory. Another plane was hijacked with its target being the White House or the Capitol building in Washington, D.C. However, the passengers forced it down in a Pennsylvania field. Their rallying cry was Todd Beamer's last Lord's Prayer which was transmitted from the airways via cell-phone and the telephone operator. "Whenever two or more of you are gathered in my name, I am there," saith the Lord.

Further evidence began to emerge as a French video team filmed Fire Chief Father Judge of Fire Company #1 walking in the lobby of the World Trade Center with rapidly wavering lips of fear: he was praying to our Lord. Soon, the danger was near, and they all had to rush down the escalator to the basement. The tower collapsed. Rubble was all around. They used the light of the camera to identify where everyone was. They turned the priest over and he was dead. His death certificate is listed as #0001 of the disaster. They took his body to the altar of St. Paul's Cathedral where his blood flowed down the steps. He was a martyr for Jesus and he had been holding back the evil.

The next days were tough for the whole country. On Thursday, September 13th, David went to his mailbox and found a letter from the Secretary of State, Colin Powell. It was dated September 7th and postmarked Sept. 10th. It said, "Thank you for your insights, 'old and new.'" He had gotten his message to the highest offices of the land and they had listened. Now was the time of war that he had foreseen. He went to see Father Matthias who urged him to keep trying to promote peaceful means and creative defense in a time of war.

David's cousin's husband, Frank, died of cancer shortly after September 11th. He was a retired colonel who had worked as a missile officer in Turkey. He later worked in the Pentagon in the very area that the terrorists had hit. He was retired, so he hadn't been in the building when the attack occurred. They cremated him and held the funeral in late October. David flew down to Washington to do the readings for the funeral Mass. He still felt a spiritual elevation from the events of just weeks before, and he wanted to give Frank a good "send-off" to heaven. Family and friends gathered at his cousin Janice's house after the funeral to grieve together. Career Washington civil servants were sitting around prognosticating about the extent of the war we had just entered. Janice said, "People don't realize how serious this is!" David knew that better than anyone, but he just kept his mouth shut on the matter of his premonition, vision, and hospitalization.

That night David's dad asked him about the medication he was taking. Not wanting his dad to get upset, David said, "It's O.K." He didn't want to tell his dad that he had weaned himself off of it after only two weeks of taking it. He had decided to quit when he had another premonition in the Old North Church in front of General Washington's statue. He thought the medicine was B.S. and had started putting his pills in his fishing tackle box or throwing them in the woods daily. That way the number of pills in the bottles would gradually diminish in case his wife was checking the bottles.

Hospitalization Aftermath

Magog Medical Center had played like a drum the division within David's family over his prophetic vision. The hospital had extended what should have been an outpatient visit followed by a quick release into a week-long hospital stay. This inflated the hospital bill to well over $7500. David had no insurance that would pay for it, and he knew that the whole stay was actually a violation of his First Amendment rights under the Constitution. Also, state law prohibited how he had been treated by the hospital. The law of Maine says that no hospital facility can restrict freedom of religion. This law applies specifically to patients hospitalized for mental illness.

During David's hospital stay, he had told Dr. Gogerrez about his religious experience. Dr. Gogerrez wrote "Patient experiencing religious delusions" in David's chart. But at no time did Dr. Gogerrez ever try to explore this. In fact he showed a prejudice against people of faith when he told David's family, "Bipolars are always walking around talking to God." At no time during his hospital stay was David allowed to study the Bible or to visit the chapel. At this time of national crisis and personal crisis for David, there were no Bibles, no kneelers, no church and no Jesus.

Magog Medical Center continued to send David billing and collection notices. David did his best to fend them off with letters. But their bills and notices forced him to continuously relive his hospital experience and to recant it. This became very painful.

The hospital would do nothing to admit or deny wrongdoing. They continued their billing process through collection agencies. David had to find a lawyer. He talked to numerous lawyers about the case. None wanted to take on the case because of the Scopes-Monkey trial-like atmosphere which it would present. Some who might have taken the case wanted a $10,000 retainer before doing anything. Other lawyers just told him to pay the bill or to pay half of it. David was indignant.

One day, while reading the liberal writer's column in the local newspaper, he saw a story about the case of another "mental patient." His lawyer who had won a case against the state on behalf of mental inmates so they could continue having visits from religious volunteers who brought them pies. The state had stopped the visits for security reasons. Perhaps the pies might contain flat files which could be used to file the bars of the jail! This lawyer argued successfully on the grounds of "freedom of religion," and the visits were allowed to continue. "Wow! That's my man!" thought David. A true believer in the Constitution – Mr. Andrew Christian.

David called Mr. Christian and arranged a meeting. The lawyer lived all the way up in Walden, and so David drove about an hour by the lakes and ponds of Maine to meet him. When he stepped into the office, he knew he had found the right man. The first thing David saw was a crooked, antique picture frame on the wall. In the frame was the famous picture on the back of every $2 bill, the founding fathers signing the Declaration of Independence. David was energized!

David's meeting with Mr. Christian was July 19, 2002, exactly one year since his religious persecution and false imprisonment and drugging at the hands of Magog Medical Center. Mr. Christian listened very intently. He interjected that he had once defended a fellow who allegedly had painted "666" on all the Catholic churches within the area. His client had done this because he had the revelation about the Beast in the book of Revelation.

"Interesting fellow," David thought. Even more impressive was the lawyer's total conviction of the freedoms of the Constitution. "There is little religious consideration in mental health care," said Andrew. "I'll take your case. There will be a small retainer fee. Send me a check." David left and felt overjoyed that a member of the legal profession was pure and true.

He heard nothing from the Magog Medical Center for the next three months. Then the collection agency sent him another notice. David called Andrew and Andrew fired off the following letter:

Christian Law Offices
Andrew Christian, Esq.
November 7, 2002

To: Vance Colic
Magog Medical Center
Re: David Lion vs. Magog Medical Center, Vance Colic, Dr. Joe Gogerrez

Dear Mr. Colic:

The situation presented by the October 24, 2002 letter from your collection agency cannot be allowed to continue. I have not addressed Dr. Gogerrez directly at this point because I have not yet initiated a legal dispute. I do not wish to put my client through any more is necessary; I do no want to scratch the scar of what for Mr. Lion remains an unhealed wound.

Neither I nor Mr. Lion wish to trigger the medical malpractice mechanisms unless this is surely a matter which cannot be promptly and fully resolved. However, given this billing practice and what we foresee, my client is simply not able to tolerate the continued aggravation augured for himself, his family life, and his ability to earn a living that this unfair billing and reminder of a most unfortunate time and experience in his life creates.

This firm represents David Lion with respect to the above claim and the collection agency letter of October 24, 2002. Please be advised that Mr. Lion holds the collection agency, yourself (to whom he has been attempting repeatedly to communicate his concerns) as well as Magog Medical Center and Dr. Gogerrez responsible for all injuries and damages arising out of the abusive collection processes this letter continues. Continued harassment by the collection agency is an aggravation of the damages and injuries already caused to Mr. Lion by Magog.

Mr. Lion contends that his admission was coerced in gross deviations from the standard of care. On 7/19/01, Mr. Lion was admitted to Magog for the following reason: "Patient's compliant: War to begin." In particular, he anticipated a missile attack. Mr. Lion had a premonition which was correct. On September 11, 2001, the World Trade Center was attacked. Subsequently we went to war in Afghanistan, and now we are about to go to war with Iraq.

Although no one can tell the future, the psychological reality of precognition is no reason to commit a person. This quality indeed was attributed to one of the fathers of modern psychology, Carl Jung, in 1914. However, Dr. Gogerrez (acting for Magog) equated this attribute in Mr. Lion's case with "grandiose delusion" and diagnosed a hypo-manic episode.

Mr. Lion was admitted directly from a church service at which he had been taken from a deep state of prayer, straight to Magog. On admission to Magog, Mr. Lion was told he would simply be given a physical. He had no insurance to cover admission, and consented only on a limited basis for that exam alone. You will find the fact of his lack of insurance recorded in the social services work up. You will also find in the notes about his psychiatric exam that his actual chief complaint was, "I was pushed to come here." That is, he was coerced.

Records indicated that Mr. Lion was medicated, as well as incarcerated, without his consent. He was given a powerful combination of anti-psychotic drugs and Divalproex Sodium, and he was held on the psychiatric ward for a week. The records benignly indicate he was "coaxed" to take this combination of powerful drugs. That is, he was "coerced."

DSM IV clearly indicates that religious experiences are not to be treated in the same manner as delusional psychiatric conditions. Mr. Lion was diagnosed as being in a "hypo-manic" episode. He experienced Magog's treatment as an attempt to reduce the spiritual and religious aspects of his life and life experience to a level of non-belief. Mr. Lion's basic right to attend mass and to see a chaplain or representative of his faith, fundamental under the Code of the Rights of Recipients of Mental Health Services, was also not honored.

Mr. Lion, who had to live through this experience, has a much more intense and detailed recollection of these events. However, this brief summary should be more than sufficient to indicate why the bill is challenged. More significantly, it presents the basis of his claim. The question now is presented: what is to be done?

Under the circumstances, for a full settlement of all claims and demands, Mr. Lion demands as follows:

1) That his medical records be corrected to reflect that what he experienced was a case of Jungian precognition. This is now quite apparent in hindsight! There is an element of libel in leaving his records uncorrected considering the events that in reality have transpired.

2) That he be absolved of any claim by Magog Medical Center.

If this is not satisfactory, Mr. Lion is prepared to seek damages. This involves going to the initial expense of obtaining an expert opinion. This should not be hard to find, given the treatment Mr. Lion received. Mr. Lion has *bona fide* claims for false imprisonment, medical malpractice, intentional or negligent infliction of mental distress, and violation of his civil rights, as well as unfair collection and trade practices.

It is my contention, on Mr. Lion's behalf, that the hospitalization was, at best, unnecessary, and at worst, a degradation of his legitimate rights as a rational person with a belief in eternal life. The discharge left these matters unresolved. Based on the knowledge of the facts, my client has received improper treatment, to say the least. However, instead of seeking all his legal remedies, at this time Mr. Lion is still open to intelligent, amicable and civilized resolution of the dispute. Given the short limitations period, time is, however, of the essence.

We would like to resolve this matter at your earliest convenience. The collection letter makes it essential, from the perspective of my client, that he either bring action in relatively short order or that this bill be forgiven promptly. The above statements are not, in this respect, simply an attempt to get out of a bill, but are assertions deeply felt by my client, which is reopened by the collection agency's and

Magog's efforts to collect an uninsured claim, the origins of which are out of the ordinary course.

Thank you for your attention.

Sincerely,

Andrew Christian

To date, neither David nor Mr. Christian has heard back from the lawyers from Magog. There seem to be no takers on battling the George Washington Vision or the United States Constitution. David is prepared to take his case to the Supreme Court.

THE PRESENT

Post 9 / 11: Inspiring Our Leaders With the George Washington Vision

Peace. That's what life was all about for David. His major goal since his youth was promoting peace for his country. Life had forced him to take some detours from his goal, but now he was determined to work on it as well as he could. The two things he could do were pray and write, so that is what he did.

David put a lot of time and energy into his writing. He read newspapers voraciously and wrote letters for their editorial columns. He also wrote letters to the national leaders telling them his many ideas for promoting peace. Some of those letters are included here. If you wish see all of David's letters, turn to Appendix B at the end of this book. If you prefer action to political writing, feel free to jump over this section and turn to the next part of this book, "The Future."

Here is an editorial that David wrote for *Nation's Newspaper* in July, 2002:

I read with great interest Mr. Daniel's column, "ABM Treaty Ends," which appeared in the June 17th edition of your newspaper. This article made many good points regarding defending our cities. It "hit the nail on the head" about America's vulnerabilities.

In 1981, I wrote a political science thesis called "Averting the Holocaust" which recommended removing both the Pershing II and the Soviet equivalent. My conclusion was that the only way to end nuclear war was to make nuclear weapons obsolete by the implementation of a space-based system using the space shuttle, satellites and laser beam weaponry. My paper and other items are in an exhibit at the Smithsonian Institution's Air and Space Museum called "Ending the Cold War."

As it turned out, the Pershing II was so accurate that the Soviets could not compete with it. Later, President Reagan was able to bargain using the Pershing II, and he laid the framework for peace and the START Treaty.

In 1983, Reagan gave his "Star Wars" speech. The Berlin Wall came down. Now just imagine what might have happened instead if American technology had not provided the President with tools and the options he needed for bargaining. We might not now be free and able to state our opinions on this matter.

Right now, we are involved in war in a dangerous world. Many countries are ruled by dictators who have the ability to start nuclear war. Every aspect of the lives of every person on this planet could be altered in a moment if a nuclear weapon were used. It would be like 9/11 to the nth power.

Peace can only be maintained through our ability to achieve a higher level of technical and economic superiority. We need to give our leaders the money and the best tools to protect our freedoms and save lives.

David Lion

David feared that the president was going to go to war with Iraq. As a descendent of Daniel Lion I, one of the nation's first prisoners of war, David felt that war could be avoided through non-violent means.

David wrote many letters to Secretary of State Colin Powell. He felt that the similarities between Powell and George Washington were uncanny. He also wrote to Powell because he knew that Powell remembered the efforts of his father, General David Lion Sr., to end the cold war. The secretary of state had also recognized the value of peacetime deployment of the missile defense system. David decided that maybe he could help advise Powell. Moreover, the note that Mr. Powell had written back to David before 9/11 verified in writing the fact that David had a precognition of an attack on the United States.

Here is some of the information David shared with Mr. Powell about George Washington:

George Washington was very upset. He didn't want this new job. He felt that he had done enough. He was fifty-six years old now. His hair was white and he couldn't see very well without glasses. He had to wear a set of wooden false teeth that pinched his mouth. The Revolutionary War had made him feel even older than his age. He felt that now he had a right to stay at Mount Vernon and be a planter again. He had a right to rest.

However, many people felt Washington was the only man who could unify the United States and keep the states working together in harmony. Washington was not sure this was true. Finally, he gave in and took the job. He became the first President of the United States.

As he prepared to leave home again, Washington turned to his wife Martha and asked, "Why?" He wondered, "Why do all the roads lead *away* from Mount Vernon?" George Washington was riding off to his last adventure – the adventure he did not want.

David had some very creative ideas for promoting peace in the Middle East. On April 5, 2002 David Lion faxed the following idea to Secretary of State Colin Powell:

Balls Instead of Bullets

Soccer balls, goal posts, and other sports equipment should be provided to each settlement town. Americans will donate them, mailing the equipment directly to the Middle East if proper addresses are provided. Even the Israeli Army could field teams. There could be young Palestinian teams and Jewish settlers' teams. Business construction co-ops hopefully would be willing to build great fields to help promote peace. Soon integrated teams would appear. Hopefully there would be many teams. The world loves soccer – it's the #1 sport. The U.N. could carry out and administer this program. The desire to kill would dissipate on the soccer field of friendly strife.

Another alternative would be whiffleball. No one could get hurt because the whiffleball is light and dependable. This game could be played in the streets of Palestine or on the fields of the settlements. It is cheap and American. Imagine an Israeli soldier holding a yellow bat instead of an Uzi, or a Palestinian boy throwing a "knuckle curve ball" instead of a rock.

David Lion

The period in David's life after 9/11 was one of thoughts and prayers for our leaders. He still hoped that perhaps the war in Iraq could be avoided, although war was what he had seen in his terrifying vision in July 2001. He continued to advise the leaders about other non-violent and less costly alternatives in terms of lives and money. He truly believed that the president was going to go to war, but war could be avoided through psychological means.

Here are two inspiring letters that David sent to President Bush and the reply which the White House sent David:

To: President George W. Bush
From: David Lion
Date: February, 2003
Subject: Lion's Prayer

Mr. President,

In the Bible, Jesus says, "I promise that when any two of you on earth agree about something you are praying for, my Father in heaven will do it for you. Whenever two or three of you come together in my name, I am there with you."
(Matt. 18:20)
George Washington prayed a prayer at Valley Forge. It was answered. George Patton prayed a "snow" prayer. It was answered also. I feel that you, George W. Bush, should have a prayer also after you have done all the preparation that you can possibly do.
My prayer for you is this:
God our Father, please bring Osama Bin Laden and Saddam Hussein to you now by natural causes, to await your judgment, so that we may offer the peoples of their countries freedom from the pain they have caused. Amen.

God bless you,

David Lion

To: President George W. Bush
From: Mr. David Lion
Subject: A Supporting Comment on National Security in the Middle East

Dear Mr. President:

Here is a poem that I hope will be an inspiration for you:
No one but the Father knows the hour of the return of the Son,

It is folly to think that the job has been done,
That the Battle and War are completely won.
We can't make the return happen of our own deeds.
But we'll be able to say at our end we planted the seeds.
Now must come a time, a longing for Peace.
In the place of His birth, the Middle East.
Gather them together, but exclude the beast.
That the USA is a part of this we both know,
In our Flag, proof below doth show.

With this poem you will see an amazing picture of an American flag with the sunlight reflecting through the blue star background casting the exact image of a cross in the stars of the flag!

Sincerely,

David Lion

The national leaders were listening. David was very pleased to receive this reply from the White House:

THE WHITE HOUSE
WASHINGTON, D.C.
June 16, 2004

Mr. Daniel Lion
Post Office Box 581
Wildwood, Maine 04222

Dear Mr. Lion:

On behalf of President Bush, thank you for your message about conflict in the Middle East.

On June 24, 2002, President Bush outlined a roadmap for the Middle East based on a vision of two states, Israel and Palestine, living side by side in peace and security. He called upon leaders in the Middle East to abandon old hatreds, fight against terror, and meet their responsibilities for building a peaceful and prosperous region. The President firmly believes that all parties – Israelis, Palestinians, and the neighboring Arab states – have an obligation to make progress toward security and peace for Israel, a viable and democratic Palestinian state, and a just, comprehensive peace for the entire region.

The President's efforts are guided by two clear principles: all people in the Middle East deserve to live under free and honest governments, and people who live in freedom are more likely to reject bitterness and terror and to embrace reconciliation, reform, and economic development. In his State of the Union Address on January 20, 2004, President Bush proposed to double the budget of the National Endowment for Democracy and to focus its new work on the development of free elections, free markets, free press, and free labor unions in the Middle East. He has pledged that America will be the active partner of every party that seeks true peace.

Thank you again for writing, and best wishes.

Sincerely,

Heidi Marquez

Special Assistant to the President
and Director of Presidential Correspondence

David was still hoping we would not go to war in Iraq. He felt that democracy, capitalism, and Islam should be able to co-exist in "enterprise work zones" where students in the Middle East are taught business and trade skills and learn to become productive and contributive.

David felt that the true Muslim faith was non-violent. Like Patton said, "I read that book too." He hoped there would be some way to teach terrorists the truth of their faith and make them practice the real Islamic verses from the Koran. He wrote to Collin Powell about these ideas on April 17, 2003

To: Secretary of State Colin Powell
From: David Lion
Date: April 17, 2003
Subject: Return Islam to Allah

Dear Mr. Powell,

As a young boy, I often wondered how suicide bombers thought they were going to heaven. I've seen a picture of kindergarten graduates on the West Bank dressed in white with hoods and bomb-belts. It appears as though the "purse" of terrorists has funded violence.

The U.S. should use its "purse" to return Islam to Allah. Faith based initiatives of Muslim clerics who support strong community values should be rewarded financially. This will protect non-militant, true faith and help it to grow. Separation of the virulent violence virus that has attached itself to Islam will take diplomatic surgical precision, but this process could start with re-education in the truth through airdropped Koran verses. This is applicable not only to Iraq but also to the West Bank and Palestinians. Catch phrases and Koran verses could be translated and airdropped to return the children of Islam to Allah.

Sincerely,

David Lion

As David considered the situation in Iraq, he realized that every country needs a founding father like George Washington, a man who will bring faith, strong character, and a vision to his nation. Therefore, he wrote this letter to Donald Rumsfeld:

To: Mr. Donald Rumsfeld
From: David Lion
Date: April 23, 2003

Dear Sir,

When our country was first founded, the new central government needed a leader who could unite our fledgling country and lead her into the future. That man was George Washington.

Iraq needs a leader like Washington. I urge you to find the "George Washington" of the Iraqis. Help him assume leadership. He should not be a radical, but a more centered person, like Confucius. This was said of Confucius: "Though his theories were at odds with the reality around him, they worked," and, "While he ruled crime virtually disappeared, streets were safe and merchants no longer cheated their customers." Confucius once wrote, "If you use laws to direct people and punishments to control them, they will merely try to evade the laws, and they will have no sense of shame. But if by virtue you guide them, there will be a sense of shame and the right."

Once the Iraqis install their "George Washington" their nation will be able to heal. He will give them hope for the future, as George Washington's vision gives hope for America.

Sincerely,

David Lion

David Studies Islam:
The Mahdi vs. Ad-Dajjal

David became aware that the fundamental problems behind the 9/11 attack and the wars in Afghanistan and Iraq were religious. Militant Muslims misunderstand both their own faith and what the United States of America stands for. He realized that we need to teach the radical Muslims that the man they are following, Osama bin Laden, is not the *Mahdi,* or the one to assist Christ, but rather the *Dajjal,* the deceiver. Here are some of the things which David learned from his research on Islam and presented to our national leaders.

The Mahdi: The Arabic term *"mahdi"* is best translated as "divinely guided one." Muslims believe he will come down in the Damascus Mosque in Syria.

There are several different interpretations about this savior figure in Islam. In Sunni Islam, and in one dominant interpretation in Shi'I Islam, the Mahdi is just one of several important figures. However, the Mahdi of most of Shi'I Islam has real eschatological importance. In the future, he is the most important figure for Islam as well as the world.

The main principle of the Mahdi is that he is a figure that is absolutely guided by God. This guidance is a stronger form of guidance than normal guidance. In the Islamic faith, normal guidance usually involves a human being willfully acting according to the guidance of God. The Mahdi on the other hand, has nothing of this human element, and does the will of God directly.

There are several reasons why Osama bin Laden cannot be the Mahdi. The Mahdi must be born in Medina. Bin Laden was born in Yemen.

Mahdism is a mass gathering of jihad warriors in the cities of the twin Holy Mosques of Mecca and Medina. This will happen when a divine signal is given. The signal is when three celestial stars will be aligned on one axis.

Ad-Dajjal: The word *"Dajjal"* comes from the Arabic word meaning "to deceive." Ad-Dajjal is described in Islamic writings in the sections which are concerned with the "the last days," the period of time immediately preceding the end of the world. Ad-Dajjal also is described in many other compilations of Hadith such as Al-Mishkat Al-Masabih. A new star, never seen before, will be in plain sight to all humanity when he appears.

Ad-Dajjal is an Islamic version of the Anti-Christ. He is an individual who resembles a young man who is blind in the right eye and has some deformity in his legs, causing him to limp. In Arabic, his name is Al-Masih Ad-Dajjal. He will rise in his final manifestation east of Saudi Arabia, spreading deception and destruction. He has supernatural powers and can cause seemingly miraculous signs to appear to the world. This is a false proof that he is God. Many will be led astray by him.

The prophet Mohammad used the name "the liar" or in Arabic Al-Masih Ad-Dajjal for him. This literally means "the imposter messiah." He will bring with him what will resemble hell and paradise. However, what is called paradise will actually be hell. Therefore, be warned against him.

Osama bin Laden thinks that he is God's disciple to overturn what was the Dajjal (Anti-Christ) system of Christianity. He thinks Christianity has gone astray from the teachings of Christ to follow the writings of the Apostle Paul.

Islamic writings say that this imposter appears within the Ummah to turn Muslims against one another just as the Taliban did. It says, "Since the birth of Adam till the advent of Qiyamah there is no fitnah (evil, test) much greater than of Dajjal."

Muslim radical clerics still cling to the belief that the USA is the Dajjal.

Their scripture says, "Let there arise out of you a band of people inviting to all that is good, enjoining what is right, and forbidding what is wrong: and these it is that shall be successful." (Qur'an, Sura 3:104)

The reason the radical, fundamental Muslims think the United States is the Dajjal is our decadence and immorality. They believe that they can challenge the USA with an ideology or a movement that is both physically and morally strong. Their goal is to do battle against the forces of evil (the USA) that they feel are destroying the earth and all life upon it. This is why there is continued to resistance within Iraq. They believe in a form of utopian ideal such as Rousseau had, or perhaps a pure religious Islamic idealistic communism, regulated by a strict interpretation of the Koran. This utopia cannot be bought, nor can it be led astray by temptation.

Part of their problem with the USA is the excesses that oil money brought to the princes of Arabia. Oil money led them into extreme drunkenness, lustfulness and violence. The fundamentalist Muslim clerics seek a movement free of vices that sedate the mind and weaken the body. They want with a system that is pure and righteous and that judges all things by one standard and emphasizes personal responsibility and accountability above all else. Their primary objection is not to democracy but to capitalism. They view democracy as a tool of capitalism. They feel that capitalism exploits resources and people "as the steel teeth of the machine chewed up and spit out people."

The fundamentalist Muslim clerics want to live at one with the Law of Allah and the Shariah of Islam. They scorn the desire of pleasure, including homosexual acts, abortion, and drug and alcohol use. In addition, they felt that they must spread their religion to others. They want to evangelize the world to free it from its sins. In some cases they want to administer punishments. This desire to punish is why fanatical Muslims had no problem beheading foreigners in Iraq. They believed they were being led by Mohammad in sacred scriptures and traditions to reveal a truth and usher in an era of messianic consciousness. Fundamentalist Muslim clerics believe that they will usher in the time of the Mahdi by doing whatever is necessary to fight the forces of evil. These forces include capitalism and the United States, and their fighting is "jihad" and includes attacks like the 9/11 attacks. Only then will the forces of evil be beaten back enough so that a spiritual awakening will happen. This is necessary so that the Mahdi will return.

They believe that the United States is "mystery Babylon" as was foretold in the Bible in the Book of Revelations.

Of all the issues pertaining to Islamic eschatology, none is more popularly discussed than that of the rise of the Imam al Mahdi. Shi'a and non-Shi'a alike are in agreement in the belief that at the end of the age the Mahdi will emerge and fill the Earth with justice just as it has previously been filled with oppression.

The fundamentalist Muslim clerics also believe that the USA is the anti-Christ or great Satan. Dajjal is a person with "one eye." This means "new world order" to them. This concept was initiated by former President George Bush Sr. during war against Iraq. This concept works only in one direction. For example, whatever the United States says is the law. No question, no argument. Hence this is considered the "one eye order."

David passed on what he had learned about Islam to our national leaders. Here is what he wrote to Powell and Rumsfeld:

To: Secretary of State Colin Powell
From: David Lion
Date: Memorial Day, 2004
Re: The single eye on the top of the pyramid on the back of the $1 bill

Dear Mr. Powell,

We should educate militant Muslims about the eye on the top of the pyramid on the back of our $1 bill. They say the eye means "one world order" and circulate the false information that this is the one eye of Dajjal. This is what we need to do:

1. Educate them regarding our great seal and what it really means.

2. Every time we capture one of their leaders, present some evidence that they could be the Dajjal.
3. Soften resistance by continuing to bombard the fighters and followers with truth flyers and internet web sites saying that their specific radical cleric is the Dajjal.
4. Create doubt that they are following the right cause and not the Dajjal.

Remember what George Patton said – "I read that book too."

David

To: Secretary Donald Rumsfeld
From: David Lion
Date: Memorial Day, 2004
Re: Operation "Fooled Ya" Truth Flyers

Dear Mr. Rumsfeld.

I would like to share with you some of my insights about the fall of Fallujah/Najif. It appears as though Al-Sadr and a great many other Muslim clerics think they are connected to the Mahdi, or the one to assist Christ. This is why he named his militia "Mehdi." There is evidence that Osama bin Laden also believes himself to be the Mahdi.

However, I believe them to be the Dajjal (the deceiver) or the Anti-Christ. Support for militant clerics would be eroded if we drop truth flyers written in Arabic which say, in effect, "If your cleric were the Mahdi, where is Jesus, and where is Mohammed? You've been deceived! Your cleric is the Dajjal, and you will perish in hell."

At the same time, perhaps we could offer the clerics a reward for turning in weapons, with the prize being a seat in the Iraqi government. A point system would be a good way to determine the prize winners. For example, they would get 10 points for an RPG launcher, 5 for a grenade, 2 for a roadside bomb, 1 for AK47. For the common man, use the existing system of pay equal to black market prices. Set an extra bonus for WMD.

Take care,

David

David's study of Islam brought him no peace. He knew that still worse things were being planned by enemies of the United States of America.

THE FUTURE

The Code

Since his enlightenment during the summer of 2001, David sometimes became preoccupied with the code discovered by Isaac Newton. Naomi became jealous of his love and quest to serve his God and Lord Jesus Christ. But to her credit, she stayed with David.

David had married Naomi to produce children who would be strong enough to defend our country if they had to. This was in the DNA he had inherited from Colonel Daniel Lion I, the valiant soldier of the 14th Virginia regiment who had shared the vision of General George Washington at Valley Forge.

David Lion was deeply dependent on his religion which had been imbued in him since the beginning of time. He knew that God had pre-programmed his DNA so that he would be able to interpret the signs that the prophets had laid down before the time of Christ. He was a descendent of the Revolutionary War soldier who had fought side by side with General George Washington so closely that he had seen two horses shot out from under Washington in battle. David knew instinctively that the U.S. Army would be part of the final battle at the end of time, the battle which would usher in the new age. He felt that the United States would hold off the forces of evil and Satan until the arrival of overwhelming numbers of good spirits who would defeat evil completely.

He began his study of the code by reading the Book of Daniel. The Book of Daniel is so important to the puzzle of what will happen at the end of time that Sir Isaac Newton devoted much of his life to the study of it. Certainly Newton would not be wrong. He was a man who could see so deeply into the universe that he tied natural phenomena to mathematical equations which we are still proving today. Newton's belief that the Bible was 100% accurate would not be wrong.

David stayed up late at night studying the Bible, trying to find correlations, and researching the links between the prophecies. David Lion personally experienced a prophecy from the book of Daniel when he swallowed a little scroll, which was bitter in his stomach, during his premonition of the attack of 9/11. The intense pain in his side, which he felt as the Roman Soldier pulled out the spear, was due to the bitter scroll of his paper which he had eaten.

David's vision of the lady leading children up to heaven followed by starburst was an actual event also. What it represented was the aurora borealis covering the entire country in July of 2001. Carl Jung had similar experiences which led to his theory of precognitive thought. In Jung's experience, he saw masses of people swimming in their own blood. A similar event happened in 1917 at Fatima at the beginning of World War I. On January 25, 1938 the event occurred all over Europe, and then Hitler began World War II.

David was still haunted by the fact he had been on the verge of knowing the future through his religious experience, yet he had been unable to figure out the code that he had witnessed during his vision. The powerful drugs that had been prescribed to him by Drs. Gogerrez and Doubtus had wiped the entire vision clean. It was particularly hard for him to remember the code because of the agnosticism of his family, and especially because the message had flowed so fast through his brain that is was like numbers flowing around on the inside of a computer.

David continued to get inspiration from Sugarloaf Mountain. He returned there frequently to ski, and he skied as fast as his aging and aching body would allow him. While on the chairlift ride, he would say "Our Fathers" for the cause of peace in the world. During the period of the Iraq War from 2003 to 2004, he remained quite active in advising the president, secretary of state, and secretary of defense about the future of Iraq and of the Middle East in general.

He knew that this was a critical time because of Biblical prophecies of the evil leader who would arise to deceive the whole world. This evil leader would declare himself Christ on earth and arrange a throne in Jerusalem. The restoration of Iraq was key in the events of the end time because, in the Book of Revelations, Iraq was named as "Babylon the Great" and "It Has Fallen." He wasn't sure how long it would take, but he was sure that Christ would prevail as the Bible says.

Then one evening while sitting in his den, David noticed that years had worn the frame around an old painting of General George Washington and his forefather Colonel Daniel Lion I. The worn area revealed something barely showing behind the bottom corner of the painting. David decided it might be time to reframe it, so he carefully removed the frame. There, behind the matting, was the 350 year old parchment on which Isaac Newton had written the code. He had given this parchment to Peter Lion before his death, and it had been passed down through the generations of Lions in its hiding place behind the painting.

David studied the parchment thoroughly. He saw specific characters, such as Δ and Ω, and he sought to find out what they were. He believed them to be part of an ancient code of some kind. Shortly after finding the parchment he was invited to a friend's child's Bat Mitzvah. There he began looking at the Torah and though he might have the answer. However, he knew the characters in the Torah were not exactly what he had seen. Besides, his vision he ended with a revelation of Jesus Christ. This made him think that the characters were probably from the language of the New Testament, Greek.

As he scanned the parchment more closely, he saw the code. What was it? It was the same code he had read a portion of in July 2001. At that time he had thought he was reading missile launch codes.

Why had he failed in warning the president about the 9/11 attach being jetliners? Had he been selfish? Was it because of his sinfulness? He had some Catholic guilt about his failure to warn the president.

If he had made his usual trip up Route 302 to Ruth's sister's house in Maine the summer of 2001 instead of playing mental games with the psychiatrists at Magog Medical Center, would he have crossed paths with the terrorists responsible for the planning and attacks of 9/11? Would he have been able to "look them back" like an infielder third baseman trying to get an out at first with a man on third trying to score? Was that the reason God had called him to Maine and he had failed? Had he failed his ancestors and George Washington by not manning his outpost?

Naomi didn't help him at all. Whenever they would get into an argument of any magnitude, she would call him the Anti-Christ. But David remained devoted to her because he knew that they had produced wonderful kids who would carry the George Washington Vision into the next generation.

God didn't leave David without support, in spite of Naomi. People from around the world had written him letters of encouragement. One such letter follows:

Science of Mind

A philosophy, a faith, a way of life

David Lion
P.O. Box 868
Wildwood, ME 04222
Dear David,

World Ministry of Prayer

We appreciate the opportunity to pray affirmatively with you for your focus, centeredness in God, and continued creativity.

3251 West Sixth Street
P.O. Box 75127
Los Angeles, CA 90075

Affirmative prayer is a powerful tool for realigning ourselves with the Spirit of all life. It turns our focus from our problem to God, in who lies our perfect answers.

At World Ministry of Prayer, we know the Presence is firmly established in your life and the lives of those you care about, and that all that is necessary for the highest good to come forth for you is already a part of your being. Rest in the assurance that the Presence and Power of God works through you to bring about a greater sense of peace, love, joy, harmony and wholeness. Open your heart and your mind to receive the blessings you desire. They are yours.

Know that you and your loved ones are enfolded in prayer and let us know of your progress.

In God's love,

Your friends at
World Ministry of Prayer

The Senator

David Lion became a celebrity once people began to discover that he had a vision of the 9/11 attacks before they happened. He garnered so much popularity that political forces pushed him to run for Senate in the year 2008. Amazingly, he won the election!

His common sense approach to everyday problems made him a very key member of many committees, one of which was the armed services committee. As always, he carefully monitored the progress of the missile defense programs because he considered them vital to repelling what the biggest threat to homeland security. Since he was still unable to crack the code, he took the code to the president, who referred him to the top secret code specialists in the Pentagon.

The code turned out to be a complex matrix which was in the Bible. When they applied the code to biblical text in Greek, it formed a completed matrix. The matrix was a three dimensional hologram with the outside layers being the biblical text and the inside layers containing hidden texts.

THE PROPHETS IN THE BIBLE HAD FORETOLD THE EVENTS OF THE CURRENT YEARS BEFORE THE BEGINNING OF THIS AGE!

The United States Department of Defense converted this complex code into a defensive computer plan to protect the country.

The Next Generation:
The Hawk and the Eagle

In the year 2016, David still skied. He had taught his sons James "Hawk" and John "Eagle" how to be top ski racers. He also passed the George Washington Vision on to them, teaching them their family history, American history, and the story of the Constitution. He instilled in them a trueness of heart to God and country and taught them to carry the vision on. They still went church together as a family when the boys were in town and they prayed together for world peace and for freedom. They also prayed that we would elect leaders who are true to the pact with God that George Washington made for the direction of the United States.

David had always let his children formulate their own political and religious thoughts and convictions. However, in recent years David's contemplation of the George Washington Vision had led him to believe that since their forefather, Daniel Lion I, had been a witness to the same vision, and George Washington had fathered no male heirs, that the last and final part of the vision, the destiny of the United States, was entrusted to the Lion family. It was the spirits of the Lions that would help the United States in the third and most fearful conflict in which "the whole world united shall not prevail against her." (George Washington's vision)

James was a very successful space fighter pilot. His mind sometimes drifted to a simpler time, back when he and his brother John would hurl themselves down Sugarloaf Mountain on skis just as fast as they could. John was always the fastest. He ended up on the U.S. Olympic Team. James applied the razor-sharp reactions he learned on skis to defending space for the United States.

James, like his grandfather, believed in the family military tradition of "might makes right" or "peace through strength." John was always repulsed by that philosophy and believed in peace through diplomacy. He lived his life as an extension of this belief. John's ability at downhill skiing was an expression for the whole world to see – a testament to his belief in peace. John Lion had skied the previous year on the World Cup circuit and had racked up more points to date than any male American skier since Bode Miller, winning the overall championship. Like his father, his specialties were the speed events, downhill skiing and the Super Giant Slalom. He skied as fast as he could in these events for God and country.

John Lion first learned to ski when he was four years old. His father taught him using food analogies. In John's ski training "French fries" meant to turn his skis straight down the hill, and to slow down the wedge was a "piece of pizza." On his first day of skiing, the little boy told his father, "I just want to make French fries!" David Lion laughed as he watched his son bomb down the mountain. He thought, "I'd better buy this little downhill racer a helmet!"

For the next few years Sugarloaf skiers watched from the chairlift as the old man in his 40's with international F.I.S. racing form skied down the mountain with a little protégé following right behind him. On one occasion John boldly told his father, "I want to ski over the top of the mountain to the snowfields and the backside!" On that day, he ended up out of bounds, skiing in powder over his head to get back between trees that were only six inches to one foot apart. On another occasion, at about age 7, he told his dad to take him to the top of White Nitro, a double black diamond super expert run, which is so icy and steep that if you fall down, you'll likely fall all the way, 1,000 feet down the mountain. David was amazed as the boy created perfect turns using linked edge-sets of the downhill and uphill skis, making it all the way down this steep windblown icy trail.

David's fellow Sugarloaf skier and friend Mike Jacobson told David, "I've got to teach you guys how to ski with a group." The

Lions smoked down the mountain – just the two of them – in response! Mike later said, "My girls and I don't like to ski so fast!"

Mike told David that he had really put John through a great training program already, but that he should enroll John in the SCVA racing program for kids. David decided that if John were ever to have a chance beyond what his father had given him, he needed to scrape up the $825 and enroll him. So he did it.

The SCVA racing program coaches couldn't believe it as they set up giant slalom courses that just couldn't contain this kid. They started making the turns bigger, faster, and closer to super giant slalom or downhill. One of his coaches said, "He flies down the mountain like an eagle," and the name stuck.

When David was not skiing with his children and winning races, he was at the dinner table with his family, busily teaching all of his kids about George Washington, John and Samuel Adams, Thomas Jefferson, and other great people of history. It seemed as though the George Washington Vision was about to pass to the next generation.

The Final Vision

James (Hawk) Lion enjoyed skiing with his brother John (Eagle), but from a young age Hawk was more devoted to becoming a U.S. space fighter pilot. However, he still liked to ski with his brother on special occasions.

One the day of Christmas Eve, David's sons went skiing at Sugarloaf Mountain. Late in the afternoon the whole mountain became enveloped in one large fog cloud. (This is classically known as a "white out"). The boys were skiing in the trees and became lost. As they sat down on a fallen tree, both boys thought they might have to spend the night there and could possibly freeze to death. John started saying "Our Father, who art in heaven." James joined in with, "whenever two of you are gathered in his name." Then they both witnessed a cloud and mist swirling around them. As they knelt in the snow, they saw a white haired general in the blue overcoat of the continental army of the United States. It was George Washington!

Washington said to them, "Sons of the Republic, look and learn!" With that, he held his hand out as though introducing a scene from a movie. Behind him was a vision of a red light from which came armies from Europe, Asia, and Africa to attack America. Then the boys saw the inhabitants of the cities and towns of America engaging in battles with the invaders. The Americans were losing. The heavens opened up and the boys could see a bright snow covered mountain. Then from the heavens above they saw something that looked like lightening except it was so bright that it left them blinded. Next they saw an army of white riders led by a leader on a white horse. The leader was so bright they could not even look at him. Then they heard the voice of General Washington say, "Your forefathers have shed blood with me, and you will help carry out the destiny of the United States."

With that, the vision was gone. The cloud lifted from the mountain, and they could clearly see the sun setting across the western slope. Neither boy spoke as they looked at each other. They hugged and knew that what they had seen was real. The carefully skied to the top of the King Pine chairlift, then down a run called Ramdown, and then to pole-line and to the parking lot below the chapel.

Both boys got into their car and neither one said a word. They were still trying to soak in the experience of what had happened. Strangely though, each was interpreting the vision within his own perspective, and the fulfillment of the vision was going to be according to their individual capabilities. James (Hawk), for example, saw the vision as part of his family's long line of military tradition and his dream of being a U.S. Space Force fighter pilot. He wanted to protect the United States from foreign attacks from the skies above. John (Eagle), the nature loving, fast downhill skier, saw his talents being used as a peacemaker through the Olympics. He hoped that the U.S. would not have to use its nuclear, neutron, electron, or biological weapons and thus render the earth uninhabitable. He pictured himself winning the gold medal and standing on the medals stand. When the TV reporters came interview him, he would make statements to warn the people of the world that no country should try to attack the United States because it might trigger the most devastating war in history. In order to prevent this, peaceful negotiations would have to continue perpetually.

In a sense, David Lion had split his hopes and dreams into two parts. These two dreams were embodied in his two sons. He had fed them on these dreams and kept them patriotic with a vision of one nation under God. The boys never told their dad about receiving the George Washington Vision because they thought he might say they were "on something." What they did not know was that he would have understood their psychic phenomenon completely. In fact, because of their commitment to their individual personal goals, not only did he see a piece of himself in each of them, but he also knew that each of them must have had a personal revelation. Had he known that it was a shared vision, he would have been even more amazed and committed to the fulfillment of their dreams.

The Eagle Competes

John "the Eagle" loved skiing so much that at the end of the summer months he would start dreaming that it would begin to snow soon. In his dreams, great big white puffy flakes would be coming down all around, so numerous that you really couldn't see but a few feet in front of you. He dreamt of deep powdery snow being rolled flat by the snow cats on the mountain at night. Such a scene helped him endure the heat and made his Olympic ski race training more bearable. He became a great mountain biker in the summer, taking trips with his father up to Sunday River Ski Resort where riders could take the chairlifts up to the top of the mountain and ride down the ski trails as fast as they could.

The Eagle loved to run in the rain during the summer, going for long runs which would cool him off but also soaked every stitch of his clothing and caused his feet to get water-logged and wrinkled. He would run for miles and miles along the country roads of Maine, flanked by millions of blue, pink, yellow and white wildflowers. From the top of hills, he could spy the mountains to the Northwest. In winter those mountains would become a white wonderland and be essence of his existence.

The average American who sits on the couch and gets fat watching TV does not realize the physical requirements of a ski racer. An alpine ski racer must pass athletic standards that far exceed those required of athletes in most of the professional sports like baseball and football. These high standards were not hard for John because he had learned cross-training form his father, David, and David had a reputation for being so intense about his cross-training that he was considered wild.

When David was young, the kids from Aspen (not known to be tame themselves) called him "the wild man from Wildcat." This nickname referred to his downhill mountain running. When he ran down steep ravines and crevices etched in eroded Rocky Mountain passes, he ran straight down the way water had carved them. His only protection was the running shoes on his feet and the old ski gloves on his hands. The gloves prevent scraping the skin right off his hands if he fell.

John needed to be a top athlete in so many areas of strength, endurance, balance, quickness, and hand-foot-eye coordination. In addition to running, he trained by just staying in his tuck for two minutes, bent over like an egg. Now imagine doing that at 90 mph! He needed to be ready for winter; the snow would be coming soon enough. Weightlifting was a powerful addition to his regimen. He did squats in sets of 10 with 540 pounds on a bar on his back. He watched videos showing the latest giant slalom, super G, and downhill techniques. These helped the Eagle integrate what he saw into his form, as there is no greater teacher than imitation.

David remembered his college years when he had the discipline to train three to four hours per day in addition to carrying a full course load of college studies while holding down a job. Doing all of that was very difficult and eventually broke him. So that Eagle would never have to live through that same experience, David worked nights writing books to pay for skiing equipment, season passes, coaches, and training. David still believed that if it had not been for the financial pressures to make it on his own, he would have made the U.S. Ski Team. (In fact, if you watch David ski now at Sugarloaf Mountain, you would think that you were watching an F.I.S. racer coming down under the chairlift instead of a 60 year old man. He stays in shape by doing over 200 sit-ups daily, biking, mountain running and weightlifting). The Eagle naturally adopted the discipline his dad had, and it paid off.

John first made the U.S. Ski Team in 2015 at the age of 21, climbing up the ranks by winning the Giant Slalom at Val d'Isere, France in December of that year. He finished with a silver medal in the Super Giant Slalom at the world championships at St. Moritz, Switzerland in February of 2016. He was very disappointed that he missed the gold medal by one hundredth of a second. He called his dad, and this is how their conversation went:

David: "Hello."

Eagle: "Dad."

David: "Hey, buddy. I watched the race on TV and you did great!"

Eagle: "No I didn't!"

David: "Why?"

Eagle: "I didn't win, so I lost."

David: "John – remember – better, farther, faster!"

During the next two years, the Eagle took flight and didn't land. He won a record number of super giant slalom races for any male skier, let alone an American. The Olympics were to be at Lake Tahoe, California in February 2018, and he was "flying" into them at the peak of his form and career. In January, he won the Lauberhorn Downhill course in Switzerland at the bottom of the Hundschopf jump as a radar gun clocked him at a record 100 mph.

The U.S. Space Force

Captain James Lion had wanted to be an astronaut ever since he was a little boy. On his sixth birthday, he remembered getting a space shuttle set-up which had all the details: the NASA logo, the United States flag on a white tile background, the black underbelly, and the solid rocket boosters. When his grandfather, General David Lion Sr., came over from the Pentagon, they would practice launches together, counting down backwards. "10, 9, 8, 7, ..." "Stop the countdown! There's an external tank leak!" General David Lion would shout, and James would know exactly what to do. He had to stop the whole process, run through a complete inspection of the SRB's (solid rocket boosters), and then declare, "All system, go, Houston!" The launch code would continue until liftoff when Hawk would lift the toy shuttle as high as his little arm would stretch, while the general would proclaim, "She's three miles downrange now, approaching escape velocity."

General David Lion had been instrumental in the deployment of the Hyper-X missile in the year 2001. At his retirement he was considered "The Father of the Hyper-X." He had taken a failing program, worked out the kinks, and turned it into one of the mainstays of America's defense shield. By the time he retired as a four star General in the Air Force, he was a logical choice to become the Chief of Staff. "Peace through strength" was always his motto. He believed that if the United States had superiority in scientific development of weaponry, then no country or group of countries would threaten U.S. or global freedom. He gave Rev Con (Revolutionary Concepts in

Aeronautics) a blank checkbook to get its projects completed. With this funding, breakthroughs were made in revolutionary departures from the standard thinking about spacecraft. The Hyper-X-43 was the chief benefactor of this funding.

Hyper-X missiles are 12 feet long with a wingspan of 5 feet. They were the first air-breathing missiles to achieve supersonic flight, flying at speeds of Mach 7 and 10 (or at 7,200 mph) at an altitude of 95,000 feet above the earth. From that position, they were able to use satellite guidance and geo-positioning to ram their warheads into incoming missiles, enemy satellites, or enemy satellite destroyers.

The early Hyper-X program was marked with failure as continual attempts were made to launch them from modified B-52 Strato-fortresses. In June 2001, failure occurred and the very expensive missile had to be destroyed.

After more failures threatened the program, General Lion got the idea to launch the Hyper-X from much higher altitudes. His basic theory was that Air Force teams were trying to launch the missile up, but all matter travels faster going downward with the aid of gravity. So why not launch the Hyper-X from a descending space fighter plane, the X44? The general's idea worked much better than expected. Unlike the space shuttle which requires re-entry, the new top secret X44 fighter planes have super heat shields. (These shields came out of the technology that was developed after the Columbia disaster). The heat shields allow the plane to "helios-plane," which is a process of high speed friction skipping off the particles in the upper atmosphere (exosphere). The plane starts its descent, but pulls up at a rapid speed, skipping along the upper atmosphere. Hyper-X missiles were launched above the target from five open slot-retractable bay doors for each missile. Each X44 carries 10 armed Hyper-X's. Five Hyper-X missiles may be fired simultaneously. The accuracy of the missile was a 90% hit ratio.

Not only was Captain James Lion was the beneficiary of his grandfather's good name, but also of the mastery of space weaponry. He had been picked from an elite core of U.S. Air Force Academy graduates whose Department of Defense files became top secret as they transitioned to become space cadets. They were sent to the

Space Warfare School, which was part of the 76th Space Control Squadron at Patterson AFB, California. These men were in the top 90% of their class and had to have 20/15 vision, have no more than 5% body fat, and be of normal height and weight for the pilot space flight suits. But above all they had to have had top scores on all flight training and target exercises. Their purpose was to win the next war from and in space.

Hawk's name was already well known by the time he arrived at the Space Warfare School in the fall of 2007. Although he had done very well at the Air Force Academy, he was mostly known because of his grandfather's reputation. However, soon after he arrived at the school, he became well know for other reasons. As officers watched from inside Cheyenne Mountain, Colorado, the young lieutenant literally had a hit ratio of 100% in a simulated war in space exercise. This exercise was against a mock enemy, the 527th Space Aggressor Squadron, based at Schriver Air Force Base. The 527th had deployed micro-satellites – miniature, elusive, and with the purpose of jamming signals.

The secretary of defense decided at that time that Hawk might be the next Chuck Yeager for his top secret X-44 space fighter plane. Hawk's reaction skills were faster than any other pilot's, and his accuracy was the best. There was no room for error at this speed and with the high-stakes cost. At first, only one prototype plane existed and only one pilot. Hawk was chosen for the retina-vectoring. (Retina-vectoring was an extension of the vectoring usually used by these fighter planes. Top engineers use retina scanning within the space helmet to hook up with the onboard computers so that an instantaneous plane reaction could occur in response to the pilot's vision).

The Aries 12 Project had developed a super satellite." Its code name was "peace-ball." Approximately ten feet in diameter, it was a virtual killer satellite designed to orbit defense satellites in groups of four, similar to a defensive backfield in football. Two peace-balls orbited in a one mile outer ring of spherical orbit, and two more were positioned in inner elliptical paths of one-half mile, forming the core defense.

The peace-balls had four main thrusters evenly spaced on north, south, east, and west positions. These thrusters enabled the peace-balls to travel in any direction. They were heavily armed with eight laser cannons each and were EMP (electromagnetic pulse) capable. If they failed to shoot the enemy out of the sky, the magnetic siding on their flattened sides would attach them to enemy satellites and missiles during intercept. Small retro-rockets corrected the course of exact intercept with guidance from a camera eye's telemetry. Azimuth repositioning would make sure that the peace-ball would redirect the enemy away from the earth. Once the peace-ball was attached to the enemy, the main thruster on the downward earth side could fired by mission control, with the ignition lasting long enough to expel the enemy from the earth's atmosphere. There, the peace-ball would become a virtual space mine. Each peace-ball was packed with ¼ ton of C-4 explosive. After the peace-ball and the attached enemy missile were at a safe distance from anything else, the explosive could be detonated remotely.

SBADS (Space Battlefield Debris Satellites) followed the peace-balls around and could spin and vacuum an area of space debris. SBADS were spherical in shape, with octagonal outside panels. They had a recess going down to a screened-over vacuum sucker porthole. This porthole leads to a tube which would carry debris down to the central collection bay. Inside the central collection bay, debris would be compacted into brick form. These bricks could be jettisoned to be burnt up on atmosphere re-entry. SBADs became an important part of the satellite defense system because of their ability to reduce the confusion of trying to tell important objects from of decoys and debris in space.

Once developed, peace-balls and SBADS were deployed by astronauts in groups of four in the space shuttle bay. Also, multiple stage rocket deployment was used to put peace-balls and SBADS into permanent orbit around each of our 600 defense satellites. This was similar to the satellite being the Earth and the peace-balls being like four little moons.

Area 51

When James "Hawk" Lion completed his U.S. Space Force training, he was assigned to the super secret USAF facility in Nevada named Area 51. Area 51 is in a very desolate area of the Nevada desert about 130 miles north of Las Vegas past Tikaboo Valley in the Nellis Range of the mountains.

Through the years, this facility at Groom Lake, Nevada had been linked to original UFO sightings, conspiracy theories, rumors, and information. There are warning signs threatening fines and imprisonment on the road into Groom Lake. Top-secret USAF patrols in Ford F150 pickups are alerted to presence of cars on Groom Lake Road by a pulse wire running under the road.

In spite of the UFO issues, the Groom Lake facility is the birthplace of some of America's best weaponry. It was here that the stealth bomber and fighters were tested and perfected. At the main base, the longest runway in the world makes it possible to land the newest and fastest space planes. The facility has several hundred buildings where scientists and engineers from all of the top defense contractors pore over advanced theories and concepts and work on perfecting new secret projects. Outside these buildings there is a huge dish pointed to the heavens. This dish is part of the dynamic coherent measurement system (dycoms) which measures radar in dissected cross sections. The dycoms is part of the radar quick kill system.

Hawk was on his way to Area 51. He was so excited! He had been chosen from a handful of the top space fighter pilots in the world to be a test pilot in the re-engineering of a top secret spacecraft. He hopped a plane from Las Vegas on EG&G and flew over Area 51 in the Nevada desert. Hawk was flown to the base in a small white Boeing 737 plane. He wore civilian clothes. They flew over the middle of the base which encompasses three million acres. The plane touched down at the northern edge of the base where there is an ultra-secret area known as Area 19. Hawk landed in the no man's land at the northern point of the test site, just north of Area 19, in the vicinity of the dead horse flat. Here was the heart of America's space defense.

It was a routine flight. As he peered out the window during the descent, he couldn't see a runway, only desert scenery. "Holy smokes! We're going to crash!" thought Hawk as he almost got out of his seat. With his eyes still riveted on the desert, to his surprise he suddenly saw sprinklers within a runway which were turned on it make it visible!

As soon as the plane landed, Hawk was met by an Air Force colonel whose black nameplate read "Fishburne." They walked towards a hill that appeared to be just sand and cacti. Actually, it was a building which had been camouflaged to look like a hill. Once inside, Colonel Fishburne led him into a small capsule like a car in a monorail, and they sped off through a tunnel. When they came to a stop, they exited and walked up a stairway, through a door, and into a very large aircraft hangar.

When Hawk entered Hangar 18, he saw the sleekest, stealthiest looking plane that he had ever seen. It was very similar to the 117A Stealth Fighter plane, but it was white and was labeled the X44. As Colonel Fishburne was showing him around he said, "Now watch this!" He waved his hand in the air and the plane disappeared!

Hawk, like his father and grandfather before him, was not easily taken in because he was always up on the futuristic technology before it became reality. "Electro-chromatic panels!" he said nonchalantly, even though he was so excited he almost had to go to the men's room. As young boys at their mountain cabin, he and his brother had sat around late at night looking up at the stars through the skylights in the roof above their beds and imagining electro-chromatic panels before they fell asleep. These panels are comprised of tiny sensors that are like mirrors on each side, and they transmit the picture to the sensors on the other side.

During World War II, the underbody of the British Spitfire aircraft were painted gray so that the Nazi gunners shooting at them on the ground saw only what looked like sky. Similarly, the tops of the plane were painted a blend of brown and green that looked like trees and foliage below. That way the Messerschmitt planes shooting at them from above would have a hard time seeing them, not "seeing the forest for the trees."

Near Groom Lake many science fiction buffs thought that the UFO's that they saw were alien crafts or alien technology that the U.S. had gained from the Roswell crash in 1947. However, the flying objects they saw were just the result of good old American ingenuity that took camouflage to the next evolutionary level, that of using electro-chromatic panels.

Electro-chromatic panels transfer the mirror image of the background to the other side so that the object is virtually transparent, except for motion wave lines, which are like a blur in the focus of vision because the aircraft is traveling so fast (Mach 7 to10). The motion waves are what people had been seeing when they reported UFO's.

The skin of the space planes in Groom Lake was made of electro-magnetically conductive polyaniline-based radar-absorbent composite material. The planes had photo sensitive receptors interpreted by their onboard computer. The computer transmitted the images from one side of the plane to the other side like a computer monitor. This made the planes appear invisible.

Colonel Fishburne was impressed that Hawk recognized the electro-magnetic panels. "Well, well, Mr. Smarty Pants, how can you fly something you can't see?" he queried.

Hawk had remembered the precise location of the plane, so he walked over to it and started knocking on it. "Let me in!" he said. "Not so fast, Flash Gordon," said the colonel. "We need to fit you up." Hawk followed the colonel to a fitting room where there were helmets hanging on racks. Technicians were waiting for him and already had a helmet sized up and waiting for him. After he sat down, his technician took some leads like those on an EKG or

EEG monitor out of the inside of the helmet and attached them to the points on James' head right above the area of the brain which controls motion and motor function. "What the...?" said Hawk.

The colonel returned, "This plane is gonna read your mind!" Next the technician put the helmet on Hawk and pulled down a visor over his eyes. He said to Hawk, "You're going to see bright lights now and it is entirely normal." Then Hawk saw a laser beam entering into his eye and bouncing back onto the inside of the visor. This created a virtual screen on the inside of the visor. "All right birdman, now it's time to become one with your body," joked Fishburne.

Hawk stood up and walked over to a flight simulator which was just like the cockpit of the X44 space plane. As soon as he sat down, the inside was illuminated because it was receiving remote signals from the inside of his helmet. "Too bright.," Lion thought. Instantaneously with that thought, the cockpit lights dimmed to his exact preference!

He slipped on his sensor gloves, which he would use instead of a joystick. There were sensor keypads which would control the entire plane. The screen in front of him became illuminated with the image of what looked like a giant manta ray with a slight fuselage in the middle. It was a schematic of the X44 plane. As he moved his left glove across the touch-pad, the wing gently flapped!

Oh Holy Night

David and Father Mathias had remained very close friends in the years since his vision. David had a long talk with Father Mathias shortly before Christmas 2017. Then on Christmas Eve, David had another experience similar to his premonition before the 9/11 attacks. When he went outside shortly after dark, he looked to the eastern sky. There he saw illuminations of red lights stretching across the upper atmosphere. As he was about to go into the house, he saw something more astonishing! It appeared to be a beautiful woman wearing a veil on her head and flowing robes that reached down to her slippers. Her beauty was indescribable, but she was crying and beckoning him to come to her. David listened to her. Then went inside and didn't tell a soul about what he had seen.

This experience with the spiritual world led David back to the counsel of Father Matthias. The elderly priest certainly had seen the Holy Spirit work through David in the premonition of the 9/11 attacks and his single-minded attempts to stop the attacks. The priest was just as intrigued, however, by the patriotic genetic make-up of this fellow sitting in his office.

David was sure that his original vision had come from his deep belief in George Washington and Christ. There are many similarities between Washington and Christ, the chief of which is their self-sacrifice for the future of mankind. Moreover, both the scripture about the biblical accounts of the return of Christ and the third and final woe of the George Washington Vision deal with a final attack on the United States and with the country being assisted by spirits.

There are amazing similarities between the prophecies of the Bible and George Washington's vision.

Now David Lion was sitting before Father Matthias. The priest asked, "What can I help you with, David?"

David replied, "I've been having premonitions again."

"What about?" questioned the elderly priest.

"The United States is going to come under attack" said David.

"Wow!" said the priest.

"Father, I've had a vision where the Virgin Mary has come to me!" exclaimed David.

"I see," said the priest, remembering the last time David had visions. They had ended up being a premonition of 9/11 attack.

Proceeding carefully, Father Mathias asked, "And what did she show or tell you?"

David answered the question quickly and in all honesty, "That the North Koreans are going to launch a nuclear missile at San Francisco!"

Father Mathias thoughtfully leaned forward in his chair and asked, "And what next?"

David replied, "My vision ended before any conclusion."

This was troubling news indeed. But both men remembered the last time David went about prophesizing, so they decided to keep it quiet and ended the session in prayer.

As David stood up to leave, Father Mathias reminded him, "Remember, not even Jesus knew the time of his return, only God the Father."

"Amen," David said as they parted.

The priest urged him not to dwell upon it. Secretly he was worried. David had been right before.

A few days later, near the end December of 2017 when all the Lion children were coming home for a belated Christmas dinner, David learned secret intelligence at a Senate hearing. He heard that the Chinese had heightened activity around their space launch facility. This troubled him so deeply that at the family gathering his daughter Angel came up to him and confronted him about his sour mood. She had some of the clairvoyance that her father and brother Hawk had, but with a woman's intuition.

"Dad," she said, "what's wrong?"

Not one to mince words, the elder man returned, "We're going to be attacked!"

Practical but stern, Angel replied, "How can I help?"

"A sleeper cell of Chinese agents is infiltrating the country, both in cyberspace and physically, to be the precursor on setting up operations for attack. What I need you to do is protect your brother, John."

"How?" replied the dutiful daughter.

"I will contact you when the time arrives." replied the Senator.

After she left the room, Senator David Lion picked up the phone and called Rusty Redson, a former secret service agent who had guarded presidential family members and was well versed in homeland security matters. "Russ, this is Senator Lion. How've you been? How's Patty?" I've got a job for you. I'll meet you at the Globe and Laurel restaurant tomorrow at noon for lunch. O.K.? Fine."

The next day Senator Lion met Rusty for lunch. The former secret service man was now the head of his own private investigation firm. David said, "Russ, intelligence has told us that Chinese and North Korean agents have infiltrated the coast of California. They have set up operatives there with certain objectives that compromise homeland security. We haven't seen this level of chatter since the 9/11 attacks."

"Where do you want me to go?" asked Russ.

David replied, "To the West Coast."

Hacker Attacker:
The Kujinator

By 2017, terrorists had taken to the Internet to pursue campaigns of disruption instead of destruction. A "'net war" consists of nonmilitary attacks perpetrated by individuals rather than by countries. Whereas cyber war usually pits formal military forces against each other, 'net war is more likely to involve non-state, paramilitary, and irregular forces.

The Internet – and the window to it, the computer terminal – became two of the most important pieces of equipment in the extremists' arsenals, not only allowing them to build membership and improve organization, but also to strike alliances with people and groups that even a decade ago that they might never have known about or been able to easily communicate with.

"Cyber terror" may have marshaled a world-class offensive info war capability.

The North Koreans, whatever their limitations, have a capacity to think deeply and innovatively about military affairs, and they devoted considerable attention to cyber war. Their top operative in the world was known as the Kujinator.

The Kujinator was in Honolulu, living under an assumed name. He had his own server with firewalls protecting his identity, and he was hacking into the United States Air Force computers. He was specifically targeting the computers that controlled and coordinated the U.S. Missile Defense System.

This system had been installed in Alaska as a ground based system around the year 2010. The North Koreans had put much emphasis on hacking into the defense system because they believed that if they could get a missile through the system and hit a California city, it would kill millions and shut down the entire economy of the West Coast. This would support other attacks on the East Coast. There attacks on financial, military and political centers would combine to lead to the financial collapse of the United States.

Unbeknownst to the Koreans, the ground-based defense system was never intended to be the top rack of missile defense despite the fact that it had been presented to Congress and the public as such. The real defense system was built under secret cover in outer space. The North Koreans took the bait and wasted most of their resources on preventing the ground-based system from working.

North Korea threatened to "bathe Seoul with fire" using its nuclear weapons and ballistic missiles. In the meantime, it was using its private website Heavens-above.com to track U.S. spy satellites and hide all of its missile placements. Also, the computer hacker named the Kujinator was busy obtaining missile codes for the U.S. arsenal. He successfully hacked into the U.S. Air Force computers using access through the South Korean Atomic Energy Commission. From his firewall-protected computers in Hawaii, the Kujinator was able to obtain U.S. defense-crippling codes.

Kuji (as the Kujinator was called) walked down Waikiki Beach towards the towering volcano of Diamond Head. He was to meet his contact person at Duke's Restaurant, which was named after a great Hawaiian surfer and statesman. As he sat down at the bar, he marveled at the tiny men in a picture on the wall. They were holding up surfboards that were fifteen feet long. What courage to surf on those giant boards! He respected that.

In the next couple of days he would have to summon every bit of courage that he could in order to carry out his mission. Of course, that would be if he were given the go ahead by his contact. He was positive that he would be told to proceed, as this was the only time since he had been on Waikiki that he had ever met with anyone. He was about to meet a high-ranking contact of Kim Jong Il of North Korea.

Mr. So, his contact, showed up and sat down next to him. He was a squat man, a North Korean like Kuji, but dressed in a Hawaiian shirt, he looked more like Chin Ho from Hawaii Five-O. This meeting had been arranged so that no one who might have been following Kuji on the Internet would be able to trace that he had been given orders. Mr. So looked at him and said, "Order the kimchee." He made sure that Kuji had understood what he had said, and then got up and walked away.

Kuji got up and left some money on the bar for his drink and hurried back to his apartment. His entire life's work was about to come to culmination with the codeword "kimchee." The order had come from Kim Jong Il leader of North Korea. It meant that the Kujinator was to disrupt all the missile defense codes within the USAF computers. This would cause the computers to malfunction all at once and allow a Chinese nuclear missile to strike the California city of Lake Tahoe! He was filled with an evil sense of glee as he entered in a virus code, which would cripple the U.S. Missile Defense System. He felt secure behind the massive system of computers and firewalls that he had spent almost thirty years building. Now that the viruses had been launched, he could sit back and watch the United States fall to its knees.

The Red Peril

Generals Qio Liang and Wang Xiangsui had risen to the top of the PLA (People's Liberation Army) largely because of their fame related to the 9-11-2001 attacks on the United States. In the wake of September 11th it came to light that they had together authored a book called *Unrestricted Warfare* three years before the attacks. In the book, they had suggested that bin Laden carry out an explosive detonation of the World Trade Center. Additionally, they suggested harming the United States by using a small army of computer hackers, disrupting the stock and bond markets, dividing the United States Congress, infiltrating the news media, smuggling illegal immigrants, and using weapons of mass destruction. President Jiang Zemin noticed the value of their advice and strategy with the success of 9/11. He gleefully replayed videos of the aircraft crashing into the twin towers.

After the president noticed them, they both rose rapidly through the ranks, earning promotions much faster than perhaps more deserving peers. With promotions came assignments and commands with higher importance and power.

On the other side of the world, David Lion still remained active in sharing his insights with the Secretary of Defense. He hoped this could help prevent future events that might be worse than 9/11. He was still haunted by the fact his premonition had been so real and close to the outcome on 9/11 and yet he had not been able to prevent the attacks. He faxed whatever he found as evidence of continued efforts or strategies of enemies of the United States directly to the secretary's desk.

One such memorandum said:

In the book *Unrestricted Warfare*, two Chinese colonels recommend that Osama bin Laden orchestrate a major explosion at the World Trade Center or a bombing attack. They recommended these actions because they greatly exceed the "frequency bandwidth" understood by the American military..."

Other disturbing information from North Korea includes:

1. After 9/11, Zemin obsessively and gleefully watched and re-watched a videotape of the aircraft crashing into the World Trade Center.

2. The book was full of plans and strategies, from using computers, to smuggling in illegal immigrants, to manipulating the stock markets, to influencing the U.S. media, to using weapons of mass destruction. These plans were all aimed at destroying the USA.

3. Recent press reports indicate that China has assisted and continues to assist militarily and economically the Taliban and al-Qaeda even after September 11.

4. *Unrestricted Warfare* reveals China's game plan in its coming war with America. China thinks it can destroy America by using these tactics.

David was still hard at work, writing to try to protect his country.

Hawk and Databyte Cowgirl

Hawk was at a secret debriefing when he saw the long flowing locks of blonde hair falling down around the most beautiful shoulders he had ever seen. As he peered down the row of desks, he saw the back of the most elegantly curved figure in the world.

Space pilots have the reputation of being good in bed because of the superior reflexes required to perform their duties. However, Hawk had never been with a woman. He had chosen to wait for the woman of his dreams. He wanted to come to her in marriage and to be chaste, holy and true to her. He really thought that he had found her this time.

Databyte Cowgirl was a member of the Hong Kong Blondes, a group of computer hackers who hated the Chinese government and the oppression of communism in general. Early in the year 2010, she had been contacted by a U.S. Air Force general who proposed that she work undercover for the cause of freedom. Her mission was to mirror the actions of one North Korean hacker named the Kujinator. Once successful, she was to hack into his computers and create viruses within his programs which would show false access. This would create a reverse indicator back to the Kujinator showing that his viruses were working, when in fact they were being routed to a separate Air Force computer where they were captured and terminated.

She was beautiful, with long blonde hair and translucent blue eyes. Standing five feet, ten inches tall, her long thin legs appeared to come halfway up her body. Smart too, with a 140 IQ. She had taken to computers at the early age of four years old under the tutelage of her father who had been a computer "geek" all his life. Raised in the insulation of Silicon Valley, she had always wanted the intriguing of the life of a spy.

Hawk knew that he must find out more about her. Not only did he want to know, but he knew he would have to answer "twenty questions" when his mother and sister found out about her. He just couldn't wait this time. As the meeting ended, he practically ran up the row to her seat. In his rush, he lightly brushed her butt with his hand. "Oh, excuse me," he blurted out. She smiled at the handsome face looking into hers.

Was it love at first sight? As she looked into his purple-blue eyes, she felt a maternal instinct rising within her. She wanted to replicate him for future generations by having his baby. With his short-cropped Air Force-cut blonde hair, high cheek bones, and broad shoulders set atop a body of only muscle, Hawk was perhaps the most handsome man she had ever seen.

Little did either of them know, but they had been made for each other a long time ago. Both of them seemed to feel it. "So what are you doing tonight?" blurted out Hawk.

"Nothing" she replied and implied "until now" with her eyes and her body language. "What did you have in mind?"

"Oh, maybe we could meet up with my brother and sister for a little dinner a few drinks and watch them to get wild," replied Hawk.

"That sounds fun," she said, hiding her disappointment. She was hoping for a quiet one-on-one romantic dinner after which she could take him home and jump his bones.

"How about if I pick you up at 7 o'clock?" he said.

"Fine," she replied.

"Where do you live?"

"Behind Harrah's, in Tahoe."

"Right," said Hawk. I'll call you on my cell phone when I get close to get better directions. What's your number?"

"415-878-6520." Databyte usually didn't give out her phone number that easily, but she gave it to Hawk in an instant.

"Great," said Hawk. "I'll call you at 6:45."

Both of them were excited as they began their first love.

True Love

Both Hawk and Databyte Cowgirl hated the oppression of communism. They were both also romantics living in a world of cold, cruel realities. Hawk had dreamed of a beautiful, Gwinevere-like princess as a young boy. Cowgirl had dreamed of a knightly champion of free-world values, with chivalry like Sir Lancelot's or King Arthur's. Hawk was handsome, over six feet tall, and had a chiseled face and sculptured body from years of athletic competition. He had blonde hair and deep blue eyes that seemed to penetrate her soul. Cowgirl had an almost perfect 36-24-36 model's figure with soft white skin and sumptuous full lips.

They met for dinner. He had a t-bone steak, his favorite cut. She had the fish. As they stared at each other over the candlelight, small talk became lost in the fog of their desire for each other. Hawk poured another glass of red wine, Pinot Noir, from California's Napa Valley, and it merely increased the focus that each had on the eyes of the other. He dismissed the waiter and paid the bill as though the man didn't even exist. As soon as they left the restaurant, he took her hand in his. Her touch was warm and inviting. They walked hand in hand to his silver sports car. The magnetism among the celestial bodies was too great to unlock her car door as he stuck the in key. Her warmth drew him closer to an embrace. His lips met the lusciousness of the fullness of hers, wet with passion.

Hawk broke the embrace and stood erect. He seated her in his car. He got in and started it up. "Where are we going?" she asked. "To the most beautiful place on earth," Hawk replied.

He drove up the mountain road. At the top of the mountain was a small chapel with huge glass windows that formed a peak with a view to the west. Remarkably, the doors were open so they went in and sat in the front row. The windows looked past the altar to the snow-capped mountains beyond. Stars dotted the clear black sky, and in the town below, lights flickered in the windows of the houses. Hawk knelt in prayer, saying a quick "Our Father," and when he finished Cowgirl was kneeling too .

Impulsively, he softly whispered, "Will you marry me?" She couldn't believe what she'd heard, so she wanted to hear him say it again. She asked him and he repeated it with the caveat.... "someday." She didn't know how to respond. But she felt the magnetism again and kissed him softly. They embraced and sat down, overwhelmed by each other. "Come on," Hawk said, leading her out of the Chapel and around to the front of the windows. They sat on a small bench there and reveled in the same panorama as before except in the clear, crisp mountain air.

The warmth of her body was irresistible. Hawk began kissing her, and she kissed him back hard. He knew he had to have her, but he also knew he couldn't do it without being married. He asked her again, "Will you marry me?" and she said, "Yes." It was getting cold, so they decided to go back inside. The door was still open, and there was a priest at the back of the church. "Let's not wait," suggested Hawk. They talked to the priest, and he agreed to marry them right then and there.

Hawk drove her home. They went inside and started kissing. They fell on her padded, deep carpet locked in a tight, natural embrace. All their body parts seemed to mesh exactly; there were no clumsy motions at all. They awoke on the floor in the middle of the night. She led him up to her bedroom and undressed herself, then carefully undressed him. He rewarded her by kissing her entire body, inch by inch until they fell into bed exhausted. He slid into the warm softness effortlessly as if he had been born there. She continued to kiss him hard. Their eruptions were like gigantic volcanoes, over and over until they both passed out.

Hawk awoke to the alarm at 6 a.m. Holy Smokes!

Hawk couldn't believe what had happened the night before! He had married Databyte Cowgirl without even answering his mom's twenty questions! "I better call Dad," he thought. David was surprised at the news, but he was very happy for Hawk. Naomi felt like she'd been left out of a special family occasion, so the newlyweds decided to have a wedding with their families also. They went back to the priest that morning and set a date for an "official" wedding the next weekend to give their families time to travel to Nevada. The next Saturday they had a small family wedding in the chapel they had visited on the day they met.

The Wahhabis

The average American does not realize that his country was founded by men who formed a pact with God to do righteous works in order to spread Christianity. Most Americans also do not know that radical Islam produces what is known as the Dajjal, or the Anti-Christ. By being diametrically opposed to Christianity, the Muslims created a culture which produced him.

The Wahhabi sect hatched the Dajjal from the discord seed which they had planted centuries ago. Here is the story:

On the first Wahhabi mission, Abd al-'Aziz ibn Muhammad ruthlessly massacred Muslims in order to disseminate Wahhabism,. He then sent three Wahhabis to Mecca in 1210 A.H. (1795). They wrote and signed a long declaration which stated that Ahl as-Sunnat was right and that they themselves were on a wrong, aberrant path. The three Wahhabis put forward twenty points to convince Meccan Muslims of what they had written.

Do you think that this cursed sect has been exterminated? Absolutely not! Some of them are still in the womb of their mothers and others are in the sperm of their fathers. When one of these groups will be exterminated the other will rise with the *Fitna* and this will continue until from the last group will emerge the cursed Dajjal!

This is the very sect that will emerge in the future with different names and disguises. Now, in this last period of time the very same cult emerged as "Reformers of Deen" and called themselves Wahhabis. All the signs about this group were foretold in the Sahih

Ahadith Shareef. These signs are found exactly in the present Wahhabi followers.

How true are the prophecies of Sayyaduna Rasoolullah (Sallalahu Alaihi Wasallam) of over 1,400 years ago. At the time Ibn 'Abdul-Wahhab and his assistants initiated their treacherous ideology by which they called the Muslims blasphemers, they were gaining control of eastern Arabia, one tribe after another.

Initially, the Wahhabis sent some of their members to Makkah (Mecca) and al-Madinah (Medina) with the hope that they would be able to corrupt the beliefs of the scholars there through misconstruing prophecy. However, when these Wahhabis declared their beliefs, the scholars of Makkah and al-Madinah refuted them and established the Islamic evidence against them. The Wahhabis could not refute the evidence of the scholars. The scholars were certain about the Wahhabis' ignorance and misguidance and found them absurd and thoughtless.

After thoroughly evaluating the Wahhabis' beliefs, the scholars found that they contained many types of blasphemy and wrote an attestation against the Wahhabiyyah to the Head Judge of Makkah confirming the Wahhabis as blasphemous. The aim of the scholars was to eradicate the Wahhabis interpretations and make the errors of the Wahhabis' beliefs known to Muslims near and far.

Some Wahhabis managed to escape imprisonment. They went to ad-Dar'iyyah and spoke about what they encountered in Makkah. This made the Wahhabis more determined and they started attacking the tribes which were loyal to the prince of Makkah. After fighting in Makkah, the Wahhabis became involved with fighting many of the tribes. In 1220 A.H. they lay siege to Makkah and surrounded it from all directions to tighten the noose.

The tribulations inflicted by the Wahhabis were a calamity for the Muslims. The Wahhabis shed a great deal of blood and stole a great deal of money; their harm was prevalent and their evil spread. Many of the hadiths of the Nabi, sallallahu 'alayhi wa sallam, spoke explicitly about this tribulation. One narration said:

"There will be people who come from the eastern side of Arabia who will recite Qur'an, but their recitation will not pass beyond their collarbones. They will go out of Islam as swiftly as the arrow goes through the prey. Their sign is shaving their heads."

Saudi Arabia's ruler, Crown Prince Abdullah, faced a similar loss of the power of the ruling elite. This was not unexpected because there were only a few thousand princes the millions of common people making up the masses of the Muslim population.

However, early on in these problems David Lion had faxed Secretary of Defense Donald Rumsfeld a paper called "Wahhabi Wannabees" in which he urged Special Forces to develop undercover clerics who could infiltrate radical sects, gain the trust of the people, and rise to high positions in the clerical order, or at least be within the inner circles.

The transcript of David's letter to Secretary Rumsfeld follows:

Memorial Day, 2003
To: Secretary Donald Rumsfeld
From: David Lion

Dear Sir,

I believe an outstanding unit of the Special Forces called the "Wahhabi Wannabees" could be established to infiltrate this organization. The long-term objective would be to get to the inner circle of radical clerics and chart their every move from the inside. The pool of applicants would probably be very, very narrow. I am not sure if Americans of Muslim descent would be able to do the job. Perhaps we would have to use homegrown Saudis with proper training.

Every detail should be adhered to carefully for our "Wahhabi Wannabees" to be able to pass as true clerics. They will have to follow tribal customs and have proper dress, dialect, sect and family. This assignment would be long term; the ultimate goal would to become a prominent cleric, or at least a right-hand man. Only young, single, Islamic, American men need apply. Then, in 10 to15 years we would have undercover clerics that would be able to moderate extremism or arrange for elimination of elements of violence.

The U.S. made costly foreign policy mistakes in the 70's and 80's by backing bin Laden vs. the Soviets and Saddam vs. Iran, only to have them turn sinister. To stop the Wahhabi movement from within would help restore peace in the region and save American lives and billions of dollars.

Godspeed,

David Lion
Citizen/Patriot

More Study of Islam and the News: Saudi Arabia

Senator David Lion continued to advise the national leaders about the situation in the Middle East and American security. Not all of his insights came from visions, however. A lot of them came the old-fashioned way – from keeping up on the news and spending time thinking. David continued to study Islam and the situation in the Middle East. (Note to the reader: If you're reading strictly for "action" and are not interested in this information, you might want to skip ahead two or three chapters).

Here are some of the things that David learned, beginning with some background information on Saudi Arabia:

The most important of the early ancestors of the Al Saud family was Muhammad Ibn Saud, who was born in 1710. He was a local ruler in Ad-Dar'ia. In 1744 he forged a political and family alliance with the Muslim scholar and reformer Muhammad ibn Abd al Wahhab. Muhammad Ibn Saud agreed with the Imam's burning desire to revive a purer Islam in its simplest and original form. The two men took an oath in 1744 that they would work together to achieve this. Muhammad ibn Suad's son, Abdul Aziz, married the daughter of Imam Muhammad. The pact sealed between the families has lasted to the present day.

However, the royal family's devotion to "pure Islam" has not lasted to the present. The ruling class of about 1,500 princes lives in extreme opulence on the money they make from oil while the average citizen lives in poverty. Also, the princes live in decadent defiance to Muslim principles. This has created a detachment of the royal class from most of the population. This makes Saudi Arabia ripe for a civil war.

Americans are deeply involved in Saudi Arabia. The Bush family has close ties with the Saudi royal family due to oil. During the Persian Gulf War, President George Bush Sr. maintained involvement with the Saudis in order to finance their oil companies in spite of the specter of adverse American press regarding protection of Saudi oil interests during the first Gulf War. Bush felt it was safer to try to destroy Saddam's oppressive regime than to enter a Saudi civil war. As the war played itself out, the US military ended up securely in control of Iraqi oil interests. The total oil reserve was not nearly as large as the Saudis' reserve, but it was at least a close second. Gaining control of Iraqi oil was also necessary because the foolish United States Congress refused to develop the Alaskan oil reserves in deference to environmental concerns. Thus, a combination of factors led to the involvement of U.S. military forces in order to assure enough free flow of oil to keep the economy of the world from slipping into a global depression.

There is another American "tie" to Saudi Arabia, and that is the 9/11 attacks. Almost all of the 9/11 terrorists were Saudis, and their leader was Osama bin Laden who was also a Saudi. Some say that bin Laden thinks he may be the Mahdi. There is a video clip of bin Laden in which he stands before a dry-erase board with an Arabic phrase written upon it, "awaited enlightened one." Interestingly, since the end of 2001, bin Laden has been signing his name "Osama bin Muhammad bin Laden," rather just Osama bin Laden. This is significant because it gives the al-Qaida leader an apocalyptic dimension.

Here is some of the information Senator Lion presented to the president about Saudi Arabia:

Presidential Daily Briefing: December 1, 2017
Re: Kingdom of Saudi Arabia.

1   Saudi oil reserves account for a quarter of the total oil in the world. This gives the country a special, and sometimes stressful, global significance. It is a key to global energy markets.
2   As the custodian of the Two Holy Mosques, of Makkah and Madinah, the Saudi king is the protector of the two holiest sites in Islam.
3   The threat to the royal family has mobilized security forces.
4   Terrorist bombings have shocked the Saudi public in their scale and volume.
5   Saudi funds organizations and charities connected to terrorist groups: Hamas and Hezbollah.
6   The target is stability itself in the oil-producing kingdom as well as the House of Saud.
7   There is evidence that the royal family is in danger.
8   There are hard feelings against the monarchy and against the government.
9   There have been mass demonstrations against the royal family.

Presidential Daily Briefing: December 25, 2017
Re: Jihadists in global frenzy over coming of prophesied Mahdi

See the communication "Dangerous Islamic Messianic Black Hole" which features a number of prophecies culminating in the coming of the Mahdi and makes several predictions about world events pointing to the coming of the Mahdi. The Mahdi is a messianic figure Muslims expect to come and lead them in victory against the infidels in the last days. These are the events predicted:
1   Two European countries will be attacked.
2   Another attack is planned against the U.S.

3   There will be an assassination attempt against a high-ranking Egyptian official.

4   A mass gathering of jihad warriors is expected in the cities of the twin holy mosques Mecca and Medina.

5   The Vatican will be subjected to constant verbal attacks on the pope as an enemy of Islam and there will be rejection of Christian missionary movements in Africa and the Middle East.

The communication includes other apocalyptic predictions such as the march of Islam through Russia, the return of Islam to Andalusia, and a victory parade in Jerusalem with a liberated Saddam Hussein at the lead. This will follow after a war in Syria and the assassination of King Abdullah of Jordan.

The Internet is now the most important tool used by the jihadi propagandists. Some of the material is clearly a warning to Muslims to distance themselves from possible target areas.

Experts say the latest Ramadan saw, according to Muslim scholars, three aligned starts. But, the Hadith, a collection of Islamic holy writings that supplement the Qur'an, predicts the messianic figure will arise in the last days of history. This "Mahdi," along with the "Prophet Jesus," will lead the believers to victory over the infidels. He will bring peace and justice to the world, rule over the Arabs, and lead a prayer in Mecca at which Jesus will be present, according to Islamic scholars.

Muslims Victories before the Dajjal's Appearance

Then, you will invade Ar-Rum and Allah will grant it (to you).
Then, you will invade the Dajjal and Allah will grant him (to you).
"Nafi said to Jabir, "O Jabir! We do not believe the Dajjal will
appear until Ar-Rum is conquered." (No. 2028)
The land of Ar-Rum is Europe and Rome is its heart. The
Messenger of Allah gave us the good tidings that we will conquer
Rome.

Osama bin Laden believed himself to be the Mahdi, which in Arabic means "he who is divinely guided" as the restorer of faith. The Mahdi will be preceded the appearance by Al-Dajjal, a Muslim antichrist, who will be slain by Jesus. The Mahdi will restore justice on earth and universal Islam. He will be tall, have a fair complexion, a broad forehead, and a high nose. He will receive his knowledge from God. U.S. military planners became aware of bin Laden's belief that he was the Mahdi when they noticed that he began linking himself with Mohammed by using Mohammed as his middle name.

Bin Laden's desire to drive the modern crusaders (i.e. the Americans) from Muslim holy lands was a result of the belief that he is the Mahdi. The United States Departments of Defense and State realized this and started a campaign of disinformation. This campaign dealt with any self-proclaimed Mahdi by the United States. Its Muslim scholars (preferably practicing Muslims themselves) tried to disprove Mahdist claims by portraying of superstitions and by pointing out incompatibilities between the Mahdist claimant and the hadiths.

Many fundamentalist Christians in the United States believed in the prophecy that an antichrist would appear on earth to deceive the millions of masses before the return of Christ. What they did not know however, was that Muslims were expecting an antichrist too. His name was Dajjal, and he was to appear before the time of a good prophet or Mahdi, who was to return to help Jesus Christ. This is why so many of the Muslim leaders presented themselves under the name of the leader of an army of Mehdi or Mahdi.

Rather than considering a person to be the Dajjal, many Muslim leaders consider the United States to be the Dajjal. They think this because of our decadence and materialism but primarily because of the one eye on the back of the one-dollar bill. They expect us to lead to a one-world order of an economic system through which the antichrist could exercise control.

There are many specifications about the Dajjal from the Hadiths of the Koran. The United States hoped for a reversal to show that bin Laden was actually Dajjal so that it would cause self-doubt within his followers leading to a massive surrender by the forces of radical Islam.

The Kaaba and
the Capture of Osama bin Laden

In the Islamic religion, the Kaaba, or the "House of Allah," is the central shrine of Islam. The Kaaba is an ancient stone building in Mecca, Saudi Arabia, and it is considered the holiest place in Islam. It measures 45 feet high, 33 feet wide, and 50 feet long. It has a gold-colored cover that is replaced every single year. The Kaaba is housed within the Masjid, which can hold a total of 1,000,000 worshippers under one roof. The current Kaaba is actually a rebuilt version of the original one. However, even this rebuilt version is incredibly old. The original Kaaba became decayed so it was torn down. The materials used in the construction of the new Kaaba were salvaged from a ship which traveled all around the Red Sea, taking materials to many places en route.

The Kaaba was the most important sanctuary in pre-Muslim times in Arabia. It is a cube-like building constructed of Meccan granite. It has a single door facing to the northeast and no windows. On the infrequent occasion when the Kaaba is opened, mobile stairs give access to the interior. Its interior includes gold and silver lamps suspended from the ceiling. There are three wooden pillars supporting the ceiling, which have been recently replaced. Members of the U.S. Special Forces Wahhabi Wannabees infiltrated the temple guards and became guards in the Kaaba.

The Koran confirms the traditional belief that the Kaaba was built by Abraham and Ishmael, from whom the Muslim peoples trace their heritage. The historical background of the Kaaba is not known for sure, but it undoubtedly existed for centuries before the birth of Mohammed in 570 CE. Historically, the Kaaba has involved multiple groups of peoples. It was used by Arab pagans until the Muslim forces took control of Mecca and cleansed it of all its false idols. At that point the Muslim people claimed historical identity.

The Black Stone, or the Kaaba stone, is set on the outside of one corner of the Kaaba and is kissed by all pilgrims who can gain access to it. It is a dark red-brown color, and is now encased in a massive silver band. It is presumed to be of pre-Islamic origin, possibly meteoric. Myths claim that it fell from heaven or perhaps that it was brought to earth by angels as a white stone in order to provide the cornerstone of the original Kaaba. It tuned black due to the impure touch of humans across the millennium. It is lovingly referred to as "the cornerstone of the house" or "the right hand of God on earth." This stone was presented by Gabriel for the Kaaba and the people who worshipped within it. Muslims, in general, try to kiss, touch, or point to the Kaaba Stone, and often make circumbulations (tawaf) around it. During the pilgrimage season such circumbulations form an integral part of the pilgrimage performance. This circumbulation is performed in the vicinity of the Kaaba, on the polished granite called the mataf. There is a place between the Black Stone and a raised door where pilgrims press their bodies in order to receive the blessings and powers that are associated with the holy house. Muslim peoples claim that the Black Stone is not an idol to be worshipped, but that instead it is a special place from which to send prayers. The Arabic name for the Kaaba Stone is the Al-Hajarul Aswad.

Members of the US Special Forces Wahhabi Wannabees guarded the shrine as fully accepted Muslim leaders. They watched a small group of ten hooded men entered the shrine and walked to the Kaaba stone. One of them separated himself from the group and went to kneel down before the stone. As he was preparing to kiss it, he went into a kind of wild prayer that declared himself the Mahdi. As he removed his hood, they saw that he looked like the number one terrorist in the world. The Wannabee leader, Colonel Awad, gave the hand signal. Simultaneously, the men surrounded the group and used powerful taser guns to freeze the worshippers in their tracks. The leader's hood was removed. He was gaunt, thin, pale, war weary, and his right eye looked damaged, like a floating white cloudy storm. It was none other than Osama bin Laden.

Arrangements were made to bring him back to New York City in the United States. Evidence was gathered to show radical Muslims that their self-proclaimed Mahdi was actually quite the opposite, the Dajjal. Jag officers and attorneys from the State Department prepared the case from the standpoint of proving not only that bin Laden had ordered the 9/11 attacks that had killed over 3,000 Americans, but also from the religious perspective that he was "the deceiver" or in Muslim the Dajjal. The following are some of the information and the Hadith's that were prepared to prove the case to the radical Muslims of the world:

For bin Laden to reveal himself as the "Rightly-guided One," ulema and muftis could draft and disseminate official opinions challenging his Mahdist claims by noting that: 1) the Mahdi must be born in Medina, but bin Laden was born in Yemen; 2) the Mahdi must not kill other Muslims as bin Laden and al-Qa'ida have done in New York and Afghanistan; 3) the appearance of the Mahdi is to be preceded by not only the Muslim antichrist, the Dajjal, but also by Jesus, neither of whom is know to be present on earth now.

"When Al-Dajjal appears, he will have fire and water with him. What the people will consider as cold water, will be fire that will burn (things). So, if anyone of you comes across this, he should fall in the thing which will appear to him as fire, for in reality, it will be fresh cold water."

"The last day is coming soon! It has been foretold in all major religions. The Dajjal (Anti-Christ) will mislead people and bring an end to righteousness. Prophet Jesus (peace be upon him) will descend from heaven and vanquish the Dajjal."

As God revealed in another verse, "The devil wants to stir up trouble between them: to destroy feelings of friendship, love, compassion, forgiveness, peace, and trust between people, and to incite them towards violence. These are the objectives of the Devil." (Qur'an, 17:53)

"Those who hear about Dajjal should stay far from him. By Allah! A person will approach him thinking him to be a believer, but on seeing his amazing feats he will become his follower."

"The Dajjal has taken your place among your families. They will then come out, but it will be of no avail. When they reach Syria, he will come out while they are still preparing themselves for battle, drawing up the ranks. Certainly, the time of prayer will come and then Jesus (peace be upon him), son of Mary, will descend and will lead them into prayer."

"Allah's Apostle said: The Last Hour will not come until the Romans land at al-A'maq or in Dabiq (Syria). An army consisting of the best (soldiers) of the people on Earth at that time will come from Medina (to oppose them). When they arrange themselves in ranks, the Romans will say: Do not stand between us and those (Muslims) who took prisoners from among us. Let us fight them. They will then fight a third (part) of the army, whom Allah will never forgive, will run away. A third (part of the army), which will be constituted of excellent martyrs in Allahs's eyes, would be killed. The third who will never be put on trial will win and they will be the conquerors of Constantinople. As they are busy in distributing the spoils of war (amongst themselves) after hanging their swords by the olive trees, Satan will cry: The Dajjal has taken your place among your families. They will then come out, but it will be of no avail. When they reach Syria, he will come out while they are still preparing themselves for battle, drawing up the ranks. Certainly, the time of prayer will come and then Jesus."

"He will be a Saudi and cause Saudi Civil war. Why are you killing Christians who are true to Jesus Christ? Who in the holy book of the Koran believers in the Christ who is to assist the Mahdi? Therefore, whoever teaches this is anti-Mahdi or anti-Allah, or a servant of Dajjal."

At this time terrorism, murder and violence had become a part of normal, everyday life. It was Osama Bin Laden who began this terrible period of war and terrorism. Many people attach little importance to that power bin Laden had, known as the Anti-Christ (Dajjal). That is because most people either have little knowledge of the matter or have never heard of it at all. However, the subject of the Anti-Christ is very prominent in the Prophet's hadith.

The wars, conflicts, acts of brutal terrorism, slaughter, and acts of genocide that still go on in various parts of the world today are the work of the Anti-Christ, the principle devilish power in the run-up to the last day. The main aim of the system of the Anti-Christ is to turn people away from religious belief, proper morality, spiritual depth, love, and all human values, and to turn them into uncompassionate and aggressive creatures who take pleasure in savagery and violence, and thus to turn the whole world into a battleground. However, it must never be forgotten that this plan will not succeed and that the system of the Anti-Christ is doomed to annihilation. Whatever the degree of strife and chaos it creates, the ideological system of the Anti-Christ is doomed, under the law of God, to ultimate defeat and destruction. By the will of God, that defeat will come about through a war of ideas waged by those who turn to Him with true sincerity and who strive to spread belief and proper morality all over the world.

Meanwhile many Muslims believed that the United States was the Dajjal. That's where they got the idea of the U.S. being the "Great Satan." However, right before his capture, the true Dajjal Osama bin Laden, still convinced he was the Mahdi and destined by the Koran to conquer Rome, released his fury. His last order was that of assassination. Communications were made through many middlemen until the message finally reached Rome.

Son of Atta

Abdul Mohammed was actually born Chance Miller in Portland, Maine. He was always darker-skinned than all the other children in the whitest state in the union, and in school he certainly stuck out. But no one ever checked his DNA. If they had they would have found that half of his DNA matched that of Mohammad Atta, one of the terrorists who carried out the 9/11 attacks. Atta had met Chance's mother years before he had perpetrated the most deadly attack on American soil, and Chance was a product of a one night stand at the Comfort Inn in Portland.

Children can be cruel, ostracizing those who are different, especially children of color with a white single mother. (This was true in the Columbine High School killings, when the outcasts decided to get revenge). Chance always felt ostracized. By the time he was in high school he had a huge, burning desire for justice for all the cruelty he had been subjected to. The largest mass murderer in history of the United States was his father, so he had the genetic predisposition toward revenge. Rather than kill high school kids, he felt that he could affect change on a global scale by attacking a society he felt was pure evil. In his mind, the society of the USA was responsible for spawning attitudes of non-inclusion, which he viewed as taught by the ruling class of capitalism against those different or less fortunate in order to exploit them. He had a natural predisposition to become a radical Muslim.

Since his father was responsible as the central figure in the September 11, 2001 World Trade Center bombing, Chance was whisked into hiding at the age of fifteen by the top members of the Hamas organization. His father was considered a martyr for the Muslim cause against American hegemony and Zionism. Chance was sent to school and then trained at a secret PLO camp north of Haifa, to the west of Golan Heights.

Conditions at the PLO camp were harsh. There was barely any food to eat except for a stable diet of flat bread and water. The rigorous demands of mountain running with an AK47 over one shoulder and a rocket-propelled grenade launcher in both hands taxed him to the physical and mental limits.

At one point during training, he experienced severe dehydration and seemed to fall into a hallucinative state. However, he thought he had experienced a true vision of Mohammed coming down from heaven with his father and escorting him up to the clouds. He believed that this delusion was real and built it into a central theme for living his life. To him it meant that he should fulfill his destiny by carrying out terrorism against the infidels. He was Allah's instrument, His tool to carry out His plan for the world.

As an American, Chance had many opportunities that his Arab brothers did not. One such ability was that of travel. Many times he had been wired money by unknown relatives, and always it was for the purpose of traveling to Rome. He was to get to know the city, for he would live there one day. While he traveled, he was instructed to wear a pair of special shoes which had thick soles.

The first few times that he traveled, he did not know what the soles contained. However, on a subsequent trip to Rome, a dark character came to his room and instructed him to remove the shoes. Quickly the man tapped the heel at its end three times, and then twisted the whole sole to reveal something black, smooth and shiny. It was a blade made of polished obsidian stone, sharp as a razor! The Aztec priests had used similar blades to cut through people's chests and rip out their hearts. They then held these hearts up to their sun god and thus keep the sun in the sky!

(Obsidian is dense volcanic glass, usually rhyolite in composition and typically black in color. Compared with window glass, obsidian is rich in iron and magnesium; tiny crystals of iron oxide within the glass cause its dark color. Obsidian is often formed in rhyolite lava flows where the lava cools so fast that crystals do not have time to grow. Glass, unlike crystals, has no regular structure and therefore fractures in smooth conchoidal (curved) shapes. The intersection of these fractures can form edges sharper than the finest steel blades. For this reason, obsidian was used by many native cultures to make arrowheads and blades).

The dark man who visited Chance and demanded his shoe looked at him and said, "You will wield this knife for Allah someday!" Then he left as suddenly as he came. Chance could not sleep that night. He suddenly felt that Allah had chosen him for the most sacred mission of all time. Soon his mission would take him to the presidential palace in Rome.

The year 2010 brought many changes in several parts of the world. The American economy crashed due to the U. S. Congress hiding social security shortfalls and pension fund fraud in major corporations. The U.S. Army had shrunk to a force just adequate enough to defend the oil fields in Iraq that President G.W. Bush had opened up to the land bridge off the Mediterranean Sea of Israel.

The European community of ten member nations had united to form a super state. Earlier conversion to a common currency, the Euro, had laid the groundwork for the merger of the ten European nations. The government and presidency were based in Rome.

In the year 2017, the president of the European Union was Gustav Caesar who believed that he was a direct descent of the line of Caesars who ruled the ancient Roman Empire. He had German roots also. He had rebuilt the European combined army to one million men. Caesar thought, "Israel, ah yes. If only I could rule from Jerusalem, I would be king of the world." He knew that many of the munitions brokers and bankers who had brought him to power would love for him to do this so that their wealth would multiply infinitely.

The economy of the European Union had collapsed in 2010, brought down by the collapse of the American economy. Banks and stores closed; no one was able to use credit cards or cash a check. Cash was king, but it would only last most people a day or so because that was all the money they had. Americans of this generation have never known this lack of liquidity. The only time like it before was the Great Depression, and all the people who lived during the depression were dead. Caesar knew that economics determines everything and would be the way to gain ultimate control of people's lives.

Caesar saw what had happened in America and seized the day. Behind the scenes, Caesar's bankers had restored the information about all of people's accounts on a master computer in Brussels, Belgium. It had a database of every person in the world and all of their accounts. This database was so large, in fact, that it was called the "Beast." In the event of economic collapse, the only way to re-create all the banking records would be to go to the top-secret "Beast" supercomputer in Brussels to call up data. For speed and efficiency, and also so that no one would be able to commit fraud, every person would have one magnetic strip like those on the back of a credit card containing all their up-to-date bank account balances inserted in their right hand or on their forehead.

Initial public reaction to these "personal barcodes" was amazement. Then as the magnetic strips were inserted into their right hands to be quickly scanned over laser scanners, they realized that the new system was very convenient. No one was required to carry a wallet or money any longer. Similarly, medical records were encrypted so that every thing about the individual had been implanted into their right hand. Some right-handed people objected to having the strips inserted into their hands because it made it more difficult to play certain sports, so they were given the option of having the strip inserted in their forehead.

What the unsuspecting populace did not realize was that their freedoms had eroded to the point that they had become slaves of the Beast. The magnetic strip implants also contained a GPS tracking device. Although the system was sold to the populace as a way of locating an individual in the event of kidnapping or other evil, this was the mask of control. Any rebels against the system could be rapidly hunted down and eliminated. Additionally, the magnetic strip was encrypted with the master code: Gustav Hister Caesar, numerically six letters in the first name, six letters in the middle name, and six in the last, 666.

Little did Chance know that one day his path would meet that of Gustav Caesar.

The Mortal Head Wound

Chance awoke to the beep of his phone. "It is time," the voice said before he heard the inevitable hang-up. He knew what the message meant, and he dressed and put on his specially soled shoes.

He made his way to the Vatican where the Pope was meeting with President Gustav Caesar. Once inside St. Peter's Basilica, he donned the robes of priestly vestments. No one took notice because he had been walking around for months under an assumed identity as a priest from Calcutta and had blended in so well as to become part of the tapestry. The Mass and reception were scheduled to begin at noon. He was to be on the right side of the Pope. "Allah the great" he kept repeating to himself.

Around 11 a.m., as he was lighting candles in the chapel, the president's own guards came in and waved wands of metal detectors over him. Beep...Beep....Beep. Chance's heart jumped into his throat. The guards made him remove his vestments and passed the want over him again. The wands beeped when they came to his belt buckle. "He's fine," they snorted as they left. Chance's heartbeat returned to normal as he put his vestments back on. "Praise Allah" he thought to himself. What a genius to have crafted the fine obsidian blade that could pass through any metal detector!

The Pope soon entered the rectory. Chance took the Pope's hand, and dropping to his knee, kissed it. He picked up an incense urn on a chain and followed the Pope out the door, clanking up on the chain, spewing incense high above the altar. The pope then sat in his chair in front of the church which was now packed to capacity. In the front row was President Caesar.

The president held his head up in an arrogance that seemed like a slap in the face of God. He walked forward, went up the steps of the altar, and bent in front of the Pope's ring. Not a soul's eye had caught a glimpse of Chance as he clicked the heel of his shoe on the marble and reached down to exculpate the knife. As he had practiced before, his hand came windmilling up and over his head. With one stroke he struck President Caesar in the left temple. The obsidian blade lodged in the leader's head. He let out a spine-chilling guttural scream as he fell to the floor with blood gushing from the wound. As if in slow motion, the European Union's secret service agents' glock pistols were drawn and began firing rounds into Chance as he yelled, "Allah is great." Within minutes, his lifeless body lay splattered in blood and full of many holes. His blood ran down the steps of the altar, combining with that of the fallen leader.

The Whole World Was Amazed

"Gustav Caesar has been wounded in the head by a short sword, and there is no brain activity," was the report people across the world heard on the nightly news that day. Not since the assassination of John F. Kennedy over fifty years previously had a president of a major superpower country been mortally wounded in the head. On TV, doctors showed diagrams of his brain and the area where the knife had entered it. The doctors went on to explain how they had put clamps on the cranium to reduce the pressure and swelling on the leader's brain. The reporters asked, "Will he ever recover?" Doubtful. "Is he dead?" Not yet, but he really was for all intents and purposes. "Was there any EEG activity?" No. Gustav Caesar was dead. He was only being kept alive by a respirator, a breathing machine for air, and an IV tube for feeding. As soon as these were disconnected, he would die.

Weeks went by, then a month, then two, and ultimately three. Who was going to pull the plug? No one apparently had the authority. The vice president was in charge of the European Union and, strangely, the world was full of calm during this period of time.

Inside Gustav Caesar's head, undetected by the EEG monitor, a storm was going on. The nightmares never ended. All was red, like everything was on fire. Smoke billowed up from the abyss. He was in constant throbbing, dull pain as if he were in some sort of torture from the medieval or the Inquisition period. Three months of torture passed and suddenly an angel flew out of the abyss. He was the most beautiful and perfect angel of them all. In the dream, Caesar

204

asked the angel, "Who are you?" The angel replied, "I am no one!" The leader took that to mean that this was the lord of the earth, and as such he must worship him and his ways. Like a wraith, the leader flew side by side with the angel over the capitals of the kingdoms of the earth. The angel told Caesar, "These are the same kingdoms of the earth that I offered the King of the Jews as he fasted in the desert. But he refused and his penalty on earth was death." Caesar became seized with fear, a primordial fear that if he did not accept the offer of this powerful being he would die and be cast alive into a lake of fire forever. Out of this fear, he accepted.

A nurse came into the president's hospital room to perform the routine task of checking on the leader's monitors and respirator. As she entered the dark room, she could hear the beep, beep, beep from the machine. Illuminated on the EEG monitor screen were bouncing waves, indicating normal brain function. She thought, "This must be a mechanical malfunction," and leaned over the leader to get a closer look. While she was about an inch away from his face, his eyelids popped open! His eyes were blood red! She felt a primal fear that told her to run. However, before she could move an inch, his hand came up and grabbed her by the throat. After several seconds, Caesar released his grip and the nurse ran away screaming. He sat up in bed and pulled the needles and tubes out of his body. It was not thirty seconds before a team of doctors and nurses came into the room to examine him. Their mouths hung open in bewilderment. He was alive. He had survived a mortal head wound. He was their leader. He must get back to the presidential palace to lead.

The nightly news had let the story of Caesar's medical condition slip into the mundane, but that night the excitement reached fever pitch worldwide with the headlines, "European Union Leader Comes Back from the Dead." There were cable and satellite broadcasts of the leader sitting up in his hospital bed. His medical records were set up for viewing on-line so the doctors of the world could try to figure out how this had happened. Though many people did not ask it out loud, they assuredly were thinking, "Could this man be Jesus Christ? He has suffered a mortal wound to the head, appeared to have died, and yet came back to life. Is this the time of the Resurrection?"

Moreover, the entire world seemed to pause momentarily from violence and wars and take note of what had happened to Caesar.

Gustav Caesar was checked out by teams of doctors. It was found on IQ tests that his intelligence scores were higher than before his assassination! This information was puzzling, yet it proved that he indeed was fit to rule the European Union once again. Within weeks he was back in that role as president. With the idea to fully capitalize on the situation, he arranged for a meeting between the prime minister of Israel and the Palestinian leader to sit down in Jerusalem to sign a peace treaty. In order to assure the peace, it was agreed that Gustav Caesar would move his office to Jerusalem. He would take with him 100,000 peacekeeping troops with tanks to integrate within tension areas between Jews and Arabs. He expected some opposition to his plans for peace. However, the whole world was amazed when the papers were happily signed by all parties with little or no opposition.

Years previously, the United States President George W. Bush had sensed that worldwide coalition would bring a loss of freedom to people and had therefore de-coupled the American dollar from world markets. As a consequence, the dollar collapsed and the Euro became the dominant world currency, replacing the dollar. Outside of the U.S., it was a totally cashless society. Evangelical Christians within the U.S. remained there and hoarded gold, silver, and guns, fully anticipating the imminent announcement by President Glendon Rush that the Congress had voted through full participation with the seven major nations out of the group of ten European nations. But it did not happen, and as a result the U.S. pursued a period of isolationism. This isolationism was made possible largely as a result of a direct link to cheap, high grade Middle Eastern crude oil. This link was the result of securing the oil fields of Iraq in 2005. Full control was secretly held in the interest of the United States.

The U.S. oil oligarchy had effectively used the U.S. military to secure pipelines that ran from the Caspian Sea all the way to the Persian Gulf. When one observes a map, it shows the extreme foresight demonstrated the administration of George W. Bush, along with Secretary of State Colin Powell and Defense Secretary Donald Rumsfeld. The United States had secured land bridges of

Afghanistan to deter the Chinese from the North and secured Iraq to be a buffer from Russian advances. All in all, it was a lot like the old game of "Risk" in which players fight for world domination.

World domination was precisely what President Gustav Caesar had in mind ever since his miraculous recovery from the apparently mortal head wound. Every day a piece of the puzzle would fall into place. During the military build-up, top military officers had been appointed to political power. (This was similar to the system the Nazis employed before and during World War II). Christians in Europe who refused to join the economic system were forced to immigrate to the U.S.; otherwise they would not be able to buy or sell anything. In some instances, there was persecution was similar to the persecution of the Jews during the Holocaust, but it was a modern, more acceptable form of persecution – one of total exclusion from the economy, meaning poverty, starvation and death.

Of course, none of this made the nightly news, as it was overwhelmingly flooded with the "good" news of the leader's continual achievements in areas of world peace. In the USA., people were more concerned about just hanging on and remained suspicious of the world events unfolding. Many of the stars in Hollywood, however, moved to France and accepted the economic system, as that country became a center of filmmaking.

Late in the year 2017 Major General Hermann von Rommel went to President Gustav Caesar and proposed shifting the main armor units of the unified European Army to Middle East. More specifically, he suggested putting them just south of Nazareth, in Israel. Caesar knew exactly that this was the coming of age of his military forces. It was Rommel's grandfather Field Marshall Irwin von Rommel who fought allied forces at El Alamein in World War II. Von Rommel's idea was brilliant. It meant that Caesar's army could defend his now international seat of government in Jerusalem from the north. This would be needed because it appeared that the Russians were going to attack Israel to punish the Israelis for bankrupting their country by privatizing the oil companies and funneling the money to Israel. Also, the American occupation of and alliance with the new Iraq forced their hand towards Syria, which had formed a pact with the Russians. Allied in their common hatred of Israel, Russia and Syria had become a major threat to world peace if they sought retribution for their losses. From Nazareth, amphibious assault landings could be turned back, as the most likely landing point would be Haifa on the coast, or slightly between Haifa and Acco. Brilliant! Also, it would solidify Caesar's place in the center of world politics, economy, and power if he had a legitimate army nearby to enforce his accords.

Von Rommel was dispatched with five armored divisions to surround the city of Jerusalem and carry out his plans for repositioning the military south of Nazareth.

Then an even stranger thing happened. A descendent of the famous Italian sculptor Michelangelo came forward to make a sculpture of the leader. However, this was to be a sculpture like no other in existence. It was to be stationary, but fully robotic and computerized with artificial intelligence so that it would look like stone or a graven image of the leader. It would have blood red eyes and could talk, think, and issue bold proclamations.

When the sculpture was finished, over five million people flocked to Jerusalem to get a first glimpse of the image that had life breathed into it. The leader felt much better about the security issues when the crowds who came for the unveiling of the sculpture left, because people were beginning to act very strangely. Two American men, clothed in sackcloth, had come to Jerusalem and were preaching about the end of the world or some such nonsense.

After a year or so, Caesar found the preaching of the Americans so disruptive that he plotted to have them killed. However, something strange always happened. Every assassin that he sent out to kill them somehow ended up being burnt to death. What was even more maddening was that the circumstances were never the same. One assassin's high-powered rifle exploded in his face. Another was lighting a cigarette and became immersed in flames. Still another had practiced for months, only to become intermingled with a busload targeted by a Hamas militant suicide bomber while on the mission. TV cameras actually caught this man emerging from the bus totally immersed in flames, running with his arms outstretched in a sign of a cross. He floundered helplessly, trying to extinguish the flames that engulfed him, until he finally toppled to the ground and his lifeless burnt corpse stopped moving. After this run of "bad luck," the leader decided it wasn't worth it to pursue assassinating the two Americans. The same fate might befall him. In fact, after viewing his last assassin's death on TV, he began having a recurring nightmare about being thrown into a lake of fire. Each time he had the nightmare he would wake up in a cold sweat and not be able to return to sleep.

Worldwide, there had been a tremendous drought. Conditions in the western and midwestern United States had turned many former lush green farmlands into the same dust bowl conditions which occurred during the Great Depression. Not only were crops dying worldwide, but so were the livestock. The animals went to the riverbeds to die, and the trickles of water running down the former riverbeds flowed with the blood of these animals. Insects feasted on the carcasses and became so large and bothersome that stronger and stronger insecticides were used against them. They became immune to the pesticides and began to land on people to sting them and inject some of the pesticide poisons stored in their bodies.

The conditions that resulted from the drought became so worrisome that the majority of the people on earth blamed the drought on the two American prophets preaching in Israel. Caesar decided to revitalize his plan to kill them, so he recruited volunteers from his Special Forces units and assembled a group who finally did the evil deed. To make sure that everyone on earth saw their dead bodies, the corpses of the American prophets laid untouched for three days. During this time, Caesar's press secretary encouraged TV news cameras to reaffirm that they were dead so the people of the earth would rejoice.

And that they did. It was just like winning a Super Bowl, World Series, or a World Cup, people were drinking and reveling in the streets across the world. By the fourth day, the bodies of the Americans were gone. No one knew where they had gone.

The death of these two prophets was especially significant because during this time millions of people in the European community experienced sores around the magnetic strips that had been implanted in their hands for the economic system. The sores were a natural body reaction, but they smelled like rotting flesh. In addition, the ozone layer had been so depleted by hydrocarbons being burned that every year the sun became more intense. Just being out in the daylight for a short period of time could give people a wicked sunburn. The skin near the implant areas was especially sensitive. These sunburns approached third degree burns on the areas of the magnetic implants.

The corps of engineers had built several new damns and hydroelectric projects along the Euphrates River. The combination of the dams and the increase in the intensity of the sunlight due to ozone depletion completely dried up the river. The reasons for building the dams and hydroelectric projects were complex, but after Operation Iraqi Freedom, locks, dams and hydroelectric facilities harnessed the power of the river. The result was that Baghdad renewed its vigor and stood out on the horizon like a modern Las Vegas across the desert landscape. However, Muslim clerics were not pleased at the change in Baghdad. They were upset about the international trade that came through Baghdad International Airport and brought the unsavory elements of prostitution and gambling. The new government of Iraq, a pro-western modern democracy, allowed these developments as generations of a morally oppressed people swung the pendulum toward excess. World leaders were not unhappy to see this as a new and exciting center of commerce. Iraq is the very place of "Babylon the Great" which is named in the Book of Revelation. The water table became taxed to capacity however, and the intense sun and prolonged lack of rain combined to make the Euphrates River dry up.

At about the same time as the death of the two Americans in Jerusalem, a tremendous earthquake ripped through the Middle East. Its epicenter was in Baghdad and the ripple effect was felt all the way to Jerusalem. Its magnitude was off the Richter scale at 12.0. (For comparison, the earthquake in the San Francisco Bay area during the World Series of 1989 was about 7.3 on the Richter scale). The tremendous quake left the city split in three parts. Most of the construction in Baghdad was not strong enough to withstand an earthquake so much of the city crumbled and caught on fire. At least 100,000 people died in the initial quake and many more remained trapped in fallen buildings and dying. Rescue equipment and teams responded from around the world to assist the victims. The earthquake caused property loss in the quadrillions of dollars.

The earthquake and devastation that followed it caused a "domino effect" economic collapse. This was due in part to the tremendous investment in Iraq by the U.S. and world economy which had occurred in the previous decade. Caesar knew that he must do something. What had revitalized economies over the century? War! War would consolidate his power and unify the world. Whom would he target? Answer: Christians! Why? They had brought all of this trouble upon the earth by belief in God and a Bible which had predicted this from long ago. They were the ones to blame!

King of the South

The Hosni Mubarak government had formed a natural alliance with Russia when an assassination attempt on the president of the European Union failed to kill him. Muslim extremist factions were threatening a revolt. Revolt seemed particularly likely in the military, as children who were inspired by Osama bin Laden and sympathized with the Palestinian cause spread their feelings upward to their fathers in the ranks.

The unwillingness of the United States to fully arm an Arab neighbor of Israel had roots stemming from back to the Six Day War in 1967. Since they knew the U.S wouldn't help them, as a matter of self-preservation, the ruling elite of Egypt turned to Russia for help. With Egypt, the "king of the south," added to the alliance of Arab nations, the circle of the pincher jaws upon Israel would be complete. In addition, the U.S. Navy would be blockaded out of both ends of the Suez Canal.

The top military officers in Russia knew that they needed allies in their efforts to make peace with the Israelis but had thought that they would have to wait until a transition of power happened in Egypt. Or would they? Why not arrange for an assassination like in the "good old days?" They did not have to look very far for an assassin since Mubarak's regime had used torture, imprisonment, and death sentences to quash the two most prominent militant Muslim groups, Al-Jihad and Al Gamma's Al-iscamiyya. Egypt is the most populous Muslim country, and by suppressing the militant factions of Islam, it added stability to the region, which was in the interest of Israel and the United States.

Money was funneled to a young radical, Hasan Al-Banna, who was named after the founder of the Muslim brotherhood. He had begun studying the writings of Sheikh Omar ABD El-Rahman, who was associated with the 1993 bombing of the World Trade Center. He was a graduate of the University of Al-Azhar, a government sponsored center for higher religious education, but had concealed his true views about how Egypt would become an Islamic state from everyone. After college he was unemployed and joined Al Gamma's Al-Islamiyya, a radical group that tried to assassinate President Mubarak in 1995 but failed.

The Russians had found their man to eliminate Mubarak, but their promise of helping an Islamic state grow thereafter was a false one. After Mubarak's assassination, the army would stage a coup de tat and appoint a leader who would then track down Al-banna the killer and imprison him. Russian amphibious ships made their way up the Suez Canal.

The Oilfields

President George W. Bush knew, as oilmen do, that oil runs the world. As an oilman, after the events of 9/11, the foremost thought in his mind was that most of the world's oil comes from the Persian Gulf area of the Middle East. The decision to invade Iraq became one of long-term strategy. President Bush was a man who knew about the Biblical matrix which would unlock the key to Armageddon and the eventual return of Jesus Christ. The allegiance which George Bush had with God clearly predetermined that Russia (Gog) and China (kings of the east) would not be able to overrun the oil-rich region of the Middle East militarily in order to provide economic prosperity to their countries. Invading Iraq was brilliant move, which isolated Iran between the two U.S. allied newly democratic countries of Afghanistan and Iraq. In Afghanistan, the land bridge China might have used to move large invasion forces of infantry troops was blocked by the presence of U.S. Army troops.

Russian military planners of a large-scale armor blitzkreig were now miffed by the huge number of U.S. armored and tank divisions in Iraq. However, the U.S. Forces had been stretched so thin from the Bosnian/Serb conflict through the areas of the Middle East that they could not withstand an "Axis of Evil" type alliance. United, China, Russia, and North Korea could make a credible and formidable attempt at taking and splitting the oilfields in a divide-and-conquer strategy. Thus they were using the American ideal of United States, United Nations, and NATO in mirror ideology against her.

Little did they know that the George Washington Vision had predicted "the whole world against her" and "the red light of vast armies." Astonishing as it was, the George Washington vision had accurately denoted the communist red flags of Russia, China and North Korea almost two hundred and fifty years previously. Also, the complete Biblical matrix code which Isaac Newton had calculated gave the United States the complete planetary protective shield and the precise year. This information would be needed by, and was the driving force behind, American military planners. In effect they were carrying out the original plans of their original commander-in chief, George Washington, on a daily basis through their cohesive efforts to secure the Middle East.

Clearly, the reference to the peoples of the Bible who went north and settled in Russia would be Gog, of the Land of Magog, the chief prince of Meshech. Notice how closely the word Meshech word resembles Moscow, the capital of Russia. Here is the Biblical prophecy against Gog:

"The word of the LORD came to me: 'Son of man, set your face against Gog, of the land of Magog, the chief prince of Meshech and Tubal; prophecy against him and say: "This is what the Sovereign LORD says: I am against you, O Gog, chief prince of Meshech and Tubal. I will turn you around, put hooks in your jaws and bring you out with your whole army – your horses, your horsemen fully armed, and a great horde with large and small shields, all of them brandishing their swords. Perisa, Cush and Put will be with them, all with shields and helmets, also Gomer with all its troops, and Beth Togarmah from the far north with all its troops – the many nations with you.

"'Therefore, son of man, prophesy and say to Gog: "This is what the Sovereign LORD says: In that day, when my people Israel are living in safety, will you not take notice of it? You will come from your place in the far north, you and many nations with you, all of them riding on horses, a great horde, a mighty army. You will advance against my people Israel like a cloud that covers the land. In days to come, O Gog, I will bring you against my land, so that the nations may know me when I show myself holy through you before their eyes.""""

.Gog and Magog are two ancient tribes or nations mentioned in both the Bible and in the Holy Qur'an, and both books contain prophecies about their resurgence in the latter days. As this resurgence is linked to the coming of the Messiah, Hazrat Mirza explained that Gog and Magog in the prophecies represent the two dominant European races of modern times, which are the Eastern European Slavonic peoples and the Western European Teutonic peoples.

The Russian Equation

"And many will go out to deceive the nations which are in the four corners of the earth, Gog and Magog, to gather them to together to battle, whose number is as the sand of the sea. They went up on the breadth of the earth and surrounded the camp of the saints and the beloved city. And fire came down from God out of heaven and devoured them."
(The Book of Revelation)

General Mikhail Bolshvouy had seen a different time in Russia, one of leadership, one of pride, one of respect, one as a world superpower. Since the fall of the Berlin Wall in 1989, it was like his persona was frozen in time. He had seen his officers living on the top of the social strata and financially reaping their reward of service to Mother Russia. In the years that followed 1989, however, there had been an erosion of the stature of his officers to the point that many had taken on second jobs. They "moonlighted" as security guards and had other jobs that seemed to represent the protection of capitalist motives such as greed and profit that the Russian ruling elite had come to espouse. Bolshvouy hated it. It seemed like great prostitutes had sold the body and soul of his country. He had waited patiently and survived many years to witness the rebirth of Mother Russia's military glory, and now that time had come.

President Gog had chosen Bolshvouy to be the military chief of operations because of his absolute loyalty and his flawless patriotic fervor. Bolshvouy's experience as the commander of the SS20 missile deployment had given him much knowledge of ballistic missile technology as well as the strategy needed to seize the higher ground. In his opinion, the Cold War had been lost because Kremlin leadership had failed to allocate the necessary resources to fund technology in the areas of satellite deployment and control of space. The United States had seized those initiatives, and hence had revolutionized the way wars were fought by controlling the entire battlefield from outer space. He had realized long ago that it would be an uphill battle to regain equality for superiority of Russian forces. It was just like trying to knock the enemy off the top of a well-fortified mountain.

Russian military planning had not changed significantly since the cold war when they used massive armored columns in a "blitzkrieg" type of strike with T-72 tanks supporting the armored personnel carriers. High altitude support would be provided by the newest jet fighter, the Mig 30. Technologically superior to the U.S. Air Force's F-15's and F-16's, their job would be to keep the Americans from bombing the infantry on the ground by knocking them out of the sky. At lower altitudes, the Americans had very successfully employed the F-10 Warthog planes in both the Gulf Wars and these planes earned the name "tank killers." To counter that threat the Russians had armed new supersonic Hind G Helicopters with the P270 Moskit missile. This is the most feared and advanced missile in the world, aptly nicknamed the "sunburn." It literally scorched human flesh right to the bone and melted eyes in their sockets within thousands of yards from a blast.

The Russian economy was crippled by the collapse of YUKOS, the giant oil and gas conglomerate. Hard line nationalist Russians blamed the Jewish/Israeli influence which had bought the company for about $300 million. It was worth about $40 billion. Bolshvouy considered this looting the entire Russian economy. A course of action was set by the military to regain the oilfields surrounding the Caspian Sea. In addition, a decapitation move toward Israel was decided upon. The battles from Serbia to Iraq became essentially the same war. The control of Central Asian oil by the U.S. oil companies and Israeli citizens, bypassing the Russians, necessitated a military response as a last resort. Initial plans were developed in 2005 after the Baku-Tbilisi-Ceyhan pipeline opened up to pump high quality Caspian crude from Russia under American control. It became a war of Russia's survival over trillions of dollars in oil and gas wealth.

In order to deceive U.S. Air Force satellites, massive tank movements were made in the fall of 2017 by covered barge down the Pechora River toward the central point of Volgograd, on the Volga River. President Gog loved this plan because he traced some of his roots (some real as well as some imagined roots) to the Cossack warriors that lived along the river. The communists, particularly under Stalin, had recruited soldiers heavily from these villages to turn back the Nazis in World War II. The President's name was found in the middle of the word Volgograd, and Volgograd was centrally located at the right position in the north for his planned invasion of the land bridge of Israel to control the Middle Eastern oil fields and their access.

From Volgograd, units would be sent amphibiously down the Volga, hidden in Astrakhan, and funneled into the Caspian Sea. They would then land in Azerbaijan and be sent over land just inside the Iranian side of the Iran-Turkey border. Iranians would assist and join, being told that the Jihad would end with the liberation of Jerusalem.

Troop transport world skirt Turkish airspace and airlift up to 50,000 airborne paratroops to airfields in Aleppo and Damascus in Syria. The Syrian government was still seething from the implications of the Bush Administration. Secretary of State Colin Powell had discovered the way that weapons of mass destruction were funneled out of Iraq into Syria and he caught them red-handed. The entire international community had ostracized President Assad's country. He began making secret arrangements to allow Russian troops to use Syria shortly thereafter.

Additional amphibious units would be assembled on the beach in Syria north of Tripoli and sent for a massive invasion of the Israeli port cities of Tel Aviv and Haifa. Haifa in particular seemed made for amphibious landing craft.

Russian aircraft carriers slipped through the Aegean Sea down south of Cyprus to support the amphibious landing. They launched

Mig 30s off their decks. The Mig 30s pounded Israeli defense installations into surprise submission. The invasion of Israel was underway.

Kings of the East

With a fierce and loyal army, Genghis Khan mapped out stunning new fighting strategies. For instance, he directed one flank to engage an enemy head-on while another flank secretly made its way around the skirmish. Then, to the enemy's surprise, his soldiers would appear suddenly hundreds of miles behind enemy lines, where least expected. But of course this was many years ago.

Aging General Ding Henggad had taken Chairman Mao and Deng Xiou Peng's visions and carried them out. Now was the time, before his death, to mark his place in history as the greatest Chinese man who had ever lived. Even though Kim Jong I1 of North Korea thought himself smarter, as early as 2004 Ding knew he could use Kim's arrogance to further the cause of the Peoples Liberation Army. There had been secret meetings about facing the common enemy of the United States. The ideas that were presented at the meetings had a clear purpose of winning control of all the major oil fields of the Middle East. In order to achieve this, however, they planned to mask their ultimate objective. They were going to stage many chaotic events designed to divert the attention and strengths of the U.S. political and military leaders while at the same time sparking hysteria in the media to create fear and confusion throughout all of the free world.

Ding played on Kim's arrogance perfectly, suggesting that North Korea take the "lead role" in operation "Red Glorification." Ding convinced Kim that in doing so North Korea would be rewarded with the lion's share of the oil won in the war which would be transported from the oil fields of the Middle East to Asia. North Korea would take care of both South Korea and Japan within its sphere of influence, drawing the United States into the hemisphere. With the over-commitment of troops to all areas of the globe already, the U.S. would then be spread so thin by deploying troops to the Korean theater that it would be at the point of breaking. And break it would. As soon as the decision was made, the Chinese general assured Kim of the success of the Peoples Liberation Army of China through Afghanistan, choking off the Strait of Hormuz, and controlling the Persian Gulf and the rich oil fields of the Middle East.

Ding's strategy worked perfectly on Kim, the dictator of North Korea, who is has egomaniacal stature of evil rivaling Hitler and Stalin combined. Kim's father and predecessor hated God because, in his opinion, the hundreds of millions of Christians in both North and South Korea caused the Korean War, the division of the country, and his lack of total control of a unified Korea. He had passed this hatred on to his son, who persecuted millions of Christians in Nazi-style internment camps until they died of disease or starvation or were killed. Like most notorious mass murderers, Kim was paranoid to the point of obsession. The object of this was, of course, the United States; However, Kim Jong Il was so afraid of the U.S. that he went and hid in a bunker during the entire Iraq War. He also fortified the defense of his death camps from outside invasion just in case U.S. paratroopers might drop in to free his enslaved citizens.

Ding convinced Kim that the U.S. was going to attack North Korea and that would set off a chain reaction which would be similar to the events in Iraq, with the impoverished citizens of his brutal regime actually assisting American forces in his overthrow, capture, or assassination. His only option to prevent this from occurring was a decisive, swift, and total victory through a pre-emptive and overwhelming surprise "blitzkrieg" attack. His deranged mind had considered this strategy previously. The possibility of loss and capture which befell Saddam prevented it from being anything other than war room plans. Now, however, with the full backing of China behind him, thoughts of dominating all of Southeast Asia became a workable plan in his sick, twisted mind.

In fact, Ding's persuasive strategies worked so well that Kim started calling him with wild ideas of massive troop movements and commitments by North Korean forces. Every day this little man with elevator shoes and Elvis hair got up to watch CNN and get hammered on Cognac. He wanted to watch CNN where he was the star! But not in defeats like Saddam! In his drunken stupor, he imagined the horror displayed on TV as it showed Tokyo vaporized by a Dong Fong nuclear missile. Next he fast-forwarded in his mind to a retaliatory strike by the U.S., which failed because of all the years of preparedness which he had put into building deep, hardened bunkers and a fiber-optic military communications network. Next, he imagined his surface-to-ship missiles destroying all the carrier groups from the U.S. Pacific Fleet. Then he saw Seoul's total capitulation within a day. Lastly, he saw himself walking onto the CNN set and shooting the anchorman right between the eyes with the cameras still rolling before an American audience that was collectively shitting its pants. With these thoughts, the demented demon drifted off to sleep.

Early the next morning, on the infamous day of January 18, 2018, as Kim Jong Il was awakening from his drunken Cognac stupor, an American RC-132S spy plane took off from Okinawa heading towards North Korea. Their mission was to chart the suspected launch of a North Korean version of the Chinese Dong Feng 31, a nuclear missile with a range of 8,000 km. It seemed like the routine missions that these air force pilots had seen many times before. The suspected launch was an elaborate, chest pounding of North Korean bellicosity designed to scare the pants off the peoples of South Korea and Japan. Perhaps because the American crew had done this so many times before, it had become somewhat boring as they got close to 200 km outside North Korean airspace, to see a pair of the newest Chinese fighter jets, XXJ-J12s approach them. The next part of the game was to turn around and have the potential enemy's planes chase them back over the Sea of Japan. But unbeknownst to them, this time was for real. The last thoughts they had as they saw two heat seeking missiles approaching them was, "Oh my God!" Their plane disintegrated in a gigantic fireball.

North Korea's offensive war plan was now in effect. Its goal was the destruction of the United States. As soon as the American spy plane was shot down, Kim Jong Il was filled with an adrenaline rush. He was almost gleeful as he gave the next set of orders. These orders were to launch Dong Feng nuclear-bomb-warhead missiles from their silos towards San Francisco. People in the city would be vaporized within minutes! Kim Jong was so excited that he pissed his pants.

Next came his full scale assault of South Korea. The most heavy artillery guns in the world, the 170 mm Goksan guns, came out of rails in caves of the north and began raining shells down on the U.S. bases at Yijong-BU, Paju, Yon-Chun, Munsan, Ding-Gu-Chun and Pochun at a rate of one million shells per hour. The bases were completely obliterated in 2 hours.

Next began the blitzkrieg that made the TET offensive of the Vietnam War look like an entire slow motion replay of "The Battle of the Bulge." Twenty mechanized brigades of Chun-ma-ho tanks crossed over the 155-mile stretch of the demilitarized zone. Each brigade had 31 tanks, 46 armored cars and 4 infantry battalions. These tanks had the ability to cross rivers under water 20 ft deep, had 155 mg guns, and could travel faster than 60 mph. They received little opposition from South Korean forces and made their way all the way to the outskirts of the capital, Seoul, which they completely surrounded. Then infantry units were sent in to occupy the city. Kim was in control.

The Third Red Revelation

General Ding of China had initially viewed Kim Jong Il's plan to engage the U.S. in war as crazy. But by the year 2010 he realized that his country had to import 100 million tons oil. By 2018 China could not supply itself with enough oil, water, or raw materials. This made it necessary to make a concerted effort to take the rich oil fields of Iran and Iraq.

The first order of business was to create diversions. Ding had his talons into enough places to be able to create widespread confusion and diversions to troop strengths and ultimate objectives. Part of the diversions would be to expand the effects of 9/11 to major financial centers where the Federal Reserve Banks are located. This would create total financial collapse of the stock, bond, and monetary systems of the United States so that even the political and military elite would be worrying about their own finances instead of the military end-game. Also, the sensational blasts would create frenzy and hysteria in the media which would break the will of the American people since almost no family would escape having a member killed.

Ding knew that Korean special force units were just crazy enough to carry it out. With the integration of Koreans into high levels of American society, no one could really tell good guys from the bad buys. Koreans are smart, driven, efficient, and hard workers. At his urging, North Korean special forces agents integrated into the south with new identities and secured jobs in the financial and hi-tech sectors. Then they immigrated to the United States where they were allowed to marry after finding a woman of U.S. citizenship and high social standing. Within a few years, they obtained citizenship themselves and basically escaped any suspicions by the INS or homeland security. However, they maintained their contacts in North Korea. They also had access to weapons of mass destruction, which other special forces smuggled over the Mexican and Canadian borders in the wide-open spaces.

The North Korean operatives had placed themselves well in Seattle, San Francisco, Los Angeles, Denver, Kansas City, Chicago, Dallas, Houston, Atlanta, Miami, Richmond, Washington, New York City and Boston. Their mission in each city was to find the tallest financial center building in the city and take it down in a 9/11 type of collapse using the Oklahoma City-type tactics of car bombs.

The high explosive C-4 that the North Korean operatives had available to them were much more devastating than the primitive fertilizer bombs previously used. Each of the Federal Reserve Banks would be blown up at the same time, creating a chaotic monetary system in which no one would be able to access cash or their accounts, even using ATM's. One Chinese military assessment of 9/11 failures cited the ability of the stock and bond markets to quickly re-open. This was the underpinning of American strength, the engine that drove the train. Coupled with the simultaneous attacks on the Fed Banks, an operative was to be inside both the Chicago Board of Trade and the New York Stock Exchange to blow them up at the same time. The president and the congress would be so tied up in the economic crisis that they would be unable to quickly approve any American military counter attack or even a defense of the United States.

The Red Sky

Major General Yang Huan, Chinese Deputy Commander of the Second Artillery of the Strategic Rocket Forces of the Peoples Liberation Army, wrote a paper for the National Defense Review in 1989. In it, he outlined the extent of Chinese nuclear missile capabilities at that time. However, in the 21st century the deployment of a missile shield by the United States eliminated any strength of a deterrent by Chinese missiles.

Therefore, the Chinese began work on developing an anti-satellite weapon that was designed to attach magnetically to U.S. satellites and then jam the signals, rendering the satellite useless. The U.S. military commanders were overly reliant on space-based information for mapping, geo-positioning, pinpointing, and destroying enemy targets in execution of war plans. That American weakness made the Chinese plan a brilliant strategy. The Chinese objective was to completely paralyze U.S. space-based fighting systems by attacking the vital vulnerable points in the information and weapons guidance systems. The Red Sky I Satellites program was developed and became successful in jamming signals from any U.S. satellite, whether it were a signal for communications, early warning, navigation, reconnaissance, or radar electronics jamming. The Chinese anti-satellite weapon was the size of a CD player and only cost about the price of a typical laptop computer. Multiple deployments of these weapons into space were easily achieved by rockets. These micro-satellites were packed into a large solid propellant Chinese version of the Soviet SS-25 rockets. After launch of these rockets, the warhead payload was blasted off its predictable trajectory through space and the atmosphere.

General Ding Hengaggao became the most successful military Chinese man since Chairman Mao Tse Tung. Mao had written in his little red book, "The capitalists will provide us the means to their own destruction." Ding took that as his mission as he successfully penetrated the Department of Commerce in the Clinton Administration, which allowed Loral to sell state-of-the-art guidance systems to deploy these micro-satellites. Also, Hughes was penetrated and Ding was able to secure whole satellites, which provide the Chinese Army with secure communications. These satellites provide cable TV to most of Asia for a fee and thus actually made a profit.

General Ding was the chairman of CONSTIND (Commission on science, technology, and national defense industry) The Vice Minister of CONSTIND, General Shen, met with Loral and Hughes. He managed to get his son Shen Jun a job at Hughes as the chief software engineer for Chinese satellites. There, his son was able to get access to satellite source codes.

General Ding's wife, Madam Nie Li, formed a company called Galaxy New Technology, which was allowed by the Clinton Administration to purchase secure fiber optic communications systems. These systems are able to withstand nuclear war and became the backbone of communications for the Chinese Army. Motorola was also compromised for satellite deployments. Their technology was used to double the number of nuclear warheads on the long-range Chinese nuclear missiles. These missiles were now also able to evade missile defense systems.

Johnny Huang had obtained much information regarding satellite positioning during the Clinton scandals. This information had reached the top generals within the PLAF (The Peoples Liberation Air Forces). The security of American defense satellites had been greatly compromised by this information leak. Security was also compromised by the PLAF's ability to launch and position nanosatelites in close proximity to American satellites. The Kahn-zing satellite weighs approximately 200 lbs and was launched from Jiuquan missile range. By and large the most important of our satellites is the Eagle Eye, which is positioned at 60 longitude, 30 latitude and stays in orbit above the Persian Gulf. Chinese launches had positioned a string of Kahn-zing in exactly the same orbit, circling the Earth and waiting for the opportunity to strike. Their purpose was clear: to deploy near the satellite, detonate and disable the Eagle Eye, and therefore to "blind" the ability of U.S. Air Force to anticipate troop movements of enemy forces based pictures taken from space.

And the Dragon Knocked the Stars from the Sky

The Chinese "Base 20" space launch facility is located in Jiuquan near the edge of the Gobi Desert in Kansu Province. From there, the Chinese coordinated their role in the attack that fateful morning in January 2018. The satellite launch center had put CZ-2F rockets into orbit and had masked the movement of the newest killer satellite by rail to hardened underground bunkers within yards of the launch pad. The CZ-2F was developed as a multi-pronged killer satellite with the mission of disabling all of the 600 defense satellites of the United States. These "eyes in the skies" had been the chief reason for the U.S. Army's victories in the Gulf War, Bosnia, Afghanistan and Iraq. Without them, in the view of Chinese military commanders, the U.S. Army would be reduced to age-old rules of combat and succumb to the laws of large numbers. This meant that eventually the U.S. would be encircled and defeated.

To the casual observer, it appeared that the Chinese were just launching the FY-IC weather satellite, but in reality, they were deploying the killer satellite. Once in orbit, multiple prongs would extend out. At the ends of these prongs were miniature CD–player-sized jamming devices with super epoxy pores to attach to U.S. defense satellites. They had small retro rockets on the ends which could fire and move them to exact positions around the target for attachment without detection. Some of them also had C-4 inside them so they were able to be detonated remotely.

However, the U.S. Space Force was acutely aware of this Chinese effort and had engaged in counter-deception of its own. Due to David Lion's development of the peace-ball killer satellites with larger sweeper capability, all 600 American satellites were protected. By the year 2010, each satellite was surrounded with a ring of four peace-balls. These peace-balls had magnetic siding and circled in outer orbits of 1 mile and inner orbits of ½ mile. Not only did they manage to sweep up 90% of the mini Chinese killer satellites but also they had managed to cloak their activity so that the Chinese mission commanders were fooled into thinking that attachments to the targets had been completed. (This would allow for later jamming and detonation). USAF commanders wanted to have each peace-ball be "full" before they used small retro-rockets to propel the peace-ball out from its orbit around the defense satellite. Once the peace-ball was a safe distance away in the outer exosphere, it would be detonated. Then sweeper battlefield vacuum satellites would spin and vacuum up the debris.

It was as if something genetically engineered within the military commanders of China awoke at the time of the great earthquake in Iraq and the evaporation of the Euphrates River. These natural disasters seemed to trigger a timetable for China's well-rehearsed invasion of the Middle Eastern oil fields to capture them for China's economic survival. Chinese military doctrine had evolved over the previous century but still rested on the basic premise that "wars are won on land by superior numbers." All other efforts – for example, air, satellite, amphibious, sea, artillery, and armor – were to support large divisions of infantry soldiers in wave technique. Specifically, Chinese military planners had numerically pegged a number of .61 as the margin of victory on any maneuver. This means that the winning force invariably has a ratio of 3 to 2 in order to achieve that victory.

After the economic attack by North Korea, the Americans would be tied up enough with actions on the Korean Peninsula and homeland security. American would not have sufficient forces to stop a Chinese advance through Afghanistan and Iraq. The number of Americans active in military service had dwindled over the previous decade because the U.S. economic deficit could not support the greater percentage of older people drawing social security and foreign troop deployment at the same time.

Early in the morning on the infamous day of January 18, 2018, at the same time as the North Korean attack on South Korea, Kang-Zing (satellite killers) were launched from the Jiuquan space facility. Over 600 of them were launched and were set on course for each one of the U.S. defense satellites. The express purpose of the satellite killers was to shut down American satellites by detonating so close to them as to damage communications abilities. This had been planned for over ten years. The Chinese were intent on destroying American satellites because the only strategic advantage the Americans had was in terms of the high ground of space and precision-guided bombs. The increasing dependence of the U.S. military on satellite topography, telemetry and final target guidance left this as the battle ground where the war would be won.

Success would mean that Chinese fighter jets could secure airspace over Afghanistan and Iran, leading the way for massive troop movements.

The Red Light of Europe

On July 16, 2001, as David Lion was having the beginning of the George Washington Vision, the presidents of Russia and China were meeting in Moscow and signing a treaty for good neighborliness, friendship and cooperation. Because of 9/11, most Americans overlooked the significance of this event, but it was the first treaty between the two countries since Mao Tse Tung met with Joseph Stalin right before the Korean War in 1950. The reason for the treaty was simple: to form an alliance against the United States and help each other through arm sales and technology transfers. The state-run newspapers in both countries called for an end to U.S. hegemonism and the establishment of a new international order.

Very shortly after the signing of the treaty, Russia's and China's armed forces began working together. The Russian Pacific Fleet missile cruisers and destroyers worked in tandem with the Chinese Eastern Fleet, as well as with the nuclear-capable Russian TU-22 Bombers. The whole objective was to complete the spread of weapons of mass destruction so that the U.S. military was spread so thin that it would be unable to respond to many different crises in different parts of the world simultaneously. The grand plan was the destruction of the United States.

From the beginning it was agreed that Russian military commanders would cross over Turkey in massive armor waves. Their goal was to secure the land bridge of Israel in order to secure that side of the Middle East. China would advance through Afghanistan and roll through collecting a temporary agreement with Iran. China's goal was to secure the majority of the Persian Gulf all the way to the Euphrates River in Iraq. They did not expect to meet stiff U.S. resistance until they reached Iraq.

In retrospect it appeared brilliant that President George W. Bush had insisted on the Iraq War in order to secure Iraq as a major staging base for the U.S Army and Marines. Bush was well informed on the George Washington Vision and Biblical prophecies and thus had considered his policy on Iraq in keeping with Washington's pact with God to position American troops in order to win the Battle of Armageddon.

In Biblical times, Armageddon was an enormous field outside Jerusalem named Megiddo. Both Napoleon and General George Patton are purported to have noticed that this field is so large that all the armies of the world could be assembled there for battle. In practical planning, the U.S. Army in Iraq would be trapped with the Chinese Army to the East and the Russian Army would be to the West. Since there would be many U.S troops committed to the Korean theater, there would be no troops left to break the circle in Armageddon and save the United States. With attacks on the continental United States broadcast on the U.S. news media, the will of the terrified U.S. population would be crushed and lead to capitulation. After that, both the Chinese and Russians would sweep into that vacuum of power to steal the oil resources of the Middle East, The oil they would control would greatly benefit their trade and commerce.

Red Sun Rising

"Now the number of the army of the horsemen was two hundred
million: I heard the number of them. And thus I saw the horses
in the vision; those who sat on them had breastplates of fiery red,
hyacinth blue, and sulfur yellow; and the heads of the horses were
like the heads of lions; and out of their mouths came fire, smoke
and brimstone. By these three plagues a third of mankind was
killed by the fire and the smoke and the brimstone, which came out
of their mouths." (The Book of Revelation)

General Ding and his top generals were ready on that fateful
January day in 2018. They gave the orders to activate all of the MAO
I parasite satellites which were attached to U.S. defense satellites.
Almost half of them were designed to detonate, while the others
were to jam the signals being provided to U.S. Forces on the ground,
in the sea, and in the lower stratosphere. This phase was completed
quickly as the units reported back with a near one hundred percent
success rate. It was unbelievable that things would be going so well.
Ding then emailed Kim Jong Il in Korea that the dirty deeds had
been done and it was zero hour to begin his havoc in South Korea.

Next, squadrons of XXJ-12 twin-engine fighter jets were
scrambled from southern airbases along the China border and broke
into airspace over Afghanistan. These are large twin-engine multi-
role fighters with stealth characteristics and which are powered by
two thrust vectoring engines for increased maneuverability. With a
tri-plane configuration, the mission of these planes was to clear out

Afghani airspace for what was yet to come. They expected little opposition form American F-22 warplanes because they thought that all of the satellites had been knocked out and the entire command and control structure would be wiped out by this time.

Next would come waves of SU-30MKK fighter-bombers, which can carry a wide range of precision-guided air-to-surface missiles, the KH-29T and KM-59MK. They would soften up any U.S. Forces on the ground in Afghanistan. Then, hundreds of type 90 II (similar to T-72s) tanks would roll across the sand accompanied by Z-8 (SA-321JA) Super Frelon and Z-9 (AS-365N) Dauphin helicopters loaded with infantry units. Finally, massive waves of infantry units would follow, fulfilling the ancient Chinese military doctrine that war is won on land with overwhelming numbers. This was to be the largest troop movement in world history with 200 million men.

The advance met little opposition, and within a week the People's Liberation Army of China was at the banks of the Euphrates River, providing half of the surrounding trap of the US Army in Iraq, while Russian forces were landing to provide the other half of the trap on the land bridge of Israel.

Top Secret Bombs

"And this shall be the plague with which the Lord will strike
all the people who fought against Jerusalem: Their flesh shall
dissolve while they stand on their feet, their eyes shall dissolve
in their sockets, and their tongues shall dissolve in their mouths."
(Zechariah 14:12)

When Zechariah wrote his prophecy, it must have been almost impossible to imagine human flesh dissolving instantly. However, in the 20th century, the human race developed the technology to accomplish this – the neutron bomb.

The neutron bomb has the same core as a fusion bomb, but the heavy U238 isotopes have been removed, so only the energy from the fusion core explodes. The power of the explosion is yielded from the massive flux of neutrons. Humans flesh is instantly vaporized. It only kills living things; no structures are damaged. There is no residual radiation, so it is safe to walk in the area within minutes after a neutron bomb blast.

Neutron bombs were developed in the late 1970's and early 1980's by the U.S. to be a counter-threat to the Soviet Union's large number of tanks and armored vehicles amassed in Eastern Europe. Neutron bombs could be deployed in the field in packages small enough to be put into artillery shells. All the occupants would be killed and the vehicles would be stopped in their tracks.

President George H. W. Bush publicly signed an authorization to eliminate the neutron bomb from U.S. arsenals. However, in top secret the U.S. military continued to work on the neutron bomb project in conjunction with their new electromagnetic bombs.

The electromagnetic bomb produces a very powerful burst of energy through an electromagnetic field which inflicts damage similar to a lightening strike. It uses explosively pumped flux compression generators like the virtual cathode oscillator. In effect, it uses a fast explosive to rapidly compress a magnetic field and then transfers that energy to enlarge the magnetic field. The effect is similar to the electromagnetic pulse produced following the detonation of nuclear weapons. In this way, an electromagnetic bomb renders all batteries and electronic equipment inoperable. EMP (electromagnetic pulse) weapons were developed by the U.S. military in order to incapacitate the enemy's computers, communication, and electronic equipment without using nuclear weapons.

American weapons researchers discovered that the acceleration of a high-current electron beam against a mesh anode produced a very powerful burst of radiation and high electromagnetic fields. Further research proved that the larger the bomb mass, the greater the area of the lethality. In early 2005, the U.S. Air Force began the production in of a 25,000-pound EMP bomb which could be dropped from B2 bombers. The code name for this bomb was "Big Daddy." These bombs were designed with precision guidance geo-position systems. The goal of the Big Daddy was to incapacitate the enemy's electronic systems at the start of any war (in effect to "fry" them) so that these systems were inoperable. The result would be a communications break down with chaos and capitalization ensuing.

Another kind of bomb developed by American weapons researchers was called the "Bronx bomb." It was developed in response to the bombing of the World Trade Center. The extreme foresight of the secretary of defense led the United States to begin this top-secret project. Its name is an ironic twist on the bombing of the World Trade Center, calling the project simply "The Bronx."

Both neutron bomb and EMP projects indicated the possibility that electrons could be split. In theory, the possibility of splitting electrons combined with the research in the neutron and the electromagnetic pulse bombs, led scientists to believe that charged electrons could produce enough energy and light to blind and scorch entire enemy armies and their electronic equipment. When electrons are split, a large amount of energy is emitted, creating the electron or "Bronx Bomb." If it were possible to split an electron and produce energy, it would prove that matter is indeed light. Electrons are the atomic particle with the most energy, and therefore they should yield the most light.

Underneath the city of Los Alamos, New Mexico, the Bronx Bomb was perfected in secret. The facility where it was built went down into the earth forty-two levels. There were tunnels linking it to nearby installations. Down under the electromagnetic research facility, scientists were beaming electromagnetic radiation at atoms. It was here that a new theory was discovered which states, "When an electron splits into a chargeon and a fluxon, a large binding energy is released." Scientists also smashed gamma photons into electrons, forming a particle with a spin frequency exactly equal to that of the photon from which it was formed. This proved that light and energy are the same. Using these theories, the United States of America was able to recreate sun scorch on earth in the form of the electron bomb. This was the ultimate weapon to be used against enemy soldiers.

An electron bomb releases blinding light upon detonation. The electromagnetic pulse fields then move in powerful waves away from the center of the blast for miles. The intense heat is similar to a lightening strike, but for a person near the blast, it more closely resembles being thrown into the sun. All flesh and blood within a hundred miles of the blast zone is vaporized. Vehicles and metal are completely melted into the ground and the ground melts and becomes molten lava. In the first tests at Los Alamos, New Mexico, observation towers were 50 miles away from the blast site. Several scientists were vaporized and their observation towers were melted because they had under-calculated the effects of their new Bronx bomb.

General Mark West

Major General Mark West had always been an all-American boy. He had short cropped red hair, had done MVP quarterbacking, had graduated from West Point, and had risen through armor ranks as a top Stryker Force Commander. So it was no surprise that he was named Centcom Commander in 2017. The Stryker was the successor to the M1 Abrams Tank. It was faster and more agile and therefore more able to repel and defeat Soviet, Chinese, and North Korean tactical use of hardware.

Major General West was a student of military history. He had studied both Lee's and Grant's troop movements in the Civil War and the tank movements of General George S. Patton and Field Marshall von Rommel in World War II. If World War III was going to happen on his watch, he was going to win it decisively.

Major General West went to the Cadet Chapel on January 1, 2018, to pray. As he knelt upon the kneeler, he saw a piece of paper on the floor. It was the program from the Christmas Eve service last month and had the words to the song "Silent Night, Holy Night" on it. He noticed the last verse:

> "Silent Night! Holy Night!
> Wondrous star, lend your light.
> With the angels let us sing
> Alleluia to our King;
> Christ the Savior is born,
> Christ the Savior is born."

Next he noticed the handwritten words, "The George Washington Vision." "Hmm," he thought as he began to pray. Since he had been promoted to Centcom Commander, he would soon be leaving his wife, Molly, and their kids at West Point and traveling to the Middle East. As always, he began his prayers with the "Our Father." As a converted Catholic, his faith was much fresher and more alive than most. As he was concentrating hard on his prayers, a vision came to him of a red background. Out of this came dust. Through the dust he saw advancing columns of armored vehicles and tanks. Then he saw a blinding light and all had vanished.

He quickly finished his prayers and exited the chapel. "Woo, I should give up drinking that Blanton's whiskey after dinner," thought the top tank commander in the United States Army. The next day he was on a plane to Tel Aviv.

Centcom Headquarters

After the end of the Iraqi War, the U.S. military decided to move Centcom (Central Communications) of the desert operations out of Qatar to deep below Tel Aviv in a top-secret underground facility which resembled a miniature Pentagon. The U.S. Army Corps of Engineers along with consultants form Israel had designed it to withstand World War III. It was located over two miles underground and had access points through underground-to-sea tunnels which could support submarine launches and arrivals. The facility was constructed with its own water and air regeneration capabilities. Enough food and supplies were stocked within it to last a year.

Centcom had access to all information provided by satellites. It also got information through hardened-fiber optic cables which led into ground-protected computers. The beach and ports were invasion-ready for a couple carrier task forces and the largest amphibious landing in the history of the U.S. Marines if necessary. It was built on huge springs to withstand deep blasts or earthquakes. In addition, large armadas of ships carrying army armored divisions could land up on top of Centcom. Results from all U.S. Air and Space Forces were all broadcast onto giant jumbo-tron screens as big as the screens in the outfield of a major league baseball stadium within the command center. In Centcom, all of the services had finally come under joint coordination and command all in one place.

It had seemed like a routine transaction when the Israeli Ministry of Tourism purchased a large tract of land just outside of Tel Aviv. Not even local residents questioned it when the largest warehouse in the world was built on the site. Inside the warehouse, there was a flurry of activity as the U.S. Army Corps of Engineers and the Navy Seabees began digging a giant hole, excavating for the biggest project in their collective histories. The U.S. Government had built underground facilities in the United States in years since President Dwight Eisenhower established a fund in for them in 1957. However, no underground facility of this magnitude had been built in a foreign country.

(Officially, none of the underground sites in the United States exists. The sites below the Greenbrier and Mount Weather in West Virginia were designed for the protection of the president, top officials, and members of congress in holes in the ground. These holes are so far down that they can survive a nuclear blast and insure the continuity of the U.S. government).

The money for building Centcom was authorized by the appropriations committee which allocated it to the Army and the Chesapeake Division of the Navy engineers as a top-secret item. After that, the project was assigned to the 30th Naval Construction Regiment (NCR) Underwater Construction Team 2 (UCT2). They specialize in building underwater pipelines and tunnels. Also, they were prepared to use deep-sea divers and scuba-men for underwater tunneling. They needed the best men to apply the advances in underwater tunneling techniques developed since the Chesapeake Bay tunnel was built in 1965. While the Army engineers were working above ground, the Seabees were just offshore the Tel Aviv Marina sinking air tight sections which would be an underwater submarine entrance to Centcom Headquarters. They were in a race with the Army to meet each other at the half-way point.

Above ground, electrically charged fences with razor wire on the top surrounded the entire area. There were guard posts at the entrances. Signs in Hebrew and Arabic said, "No trespassing as forbidden by law. Violators are subject to prosecution." Inside the warehouse engineers drilled through the sand and pumped the water out until they struck rock. After they hit rock, they used a new device called the "subterranean blaster." It used nuclear reactor heat pipes to melt the rock. Tunnels were bored to a depth of ½ mile. They led to a vast subterranean bunker resembling an underground city about

250 acres in size. It could support 50,000 troops and administrative personnel. The newest shuttle technology was used, employing tubes to shoot personnel and supplies to the destination bunker using the vacuum method. Centcom was made secure with the latest satellite receptors. In summary, it was a miniature underground pentagon.

The army got to the planned depth first, and then the Seabees linked up the underwater entrance. There were six air lock chambers through which trident submarines could bring their crews for personnel change and re-supply. The docking stations had hook-up tubes for their missile launches so that they could launch missiles from underground. After launch, the missile would travel up the long underground tube, out a portal on the ground, and up through the atmosphere to its target.

The Eagle Soars

The Eagle's sense of timing was identical to his father's. Therefore he felt the winds of war blowing long before anyone else. His desire to win the downhill in the Olympics was based on his premonition that the United States and the world were on the verge of World War III. His ski racing was progressing with the better results with each successive race.

It was January 10, 2018. John "Eagle" Lion was outside of Innsbruck, Austria, awaiting his chance to ski on the famous course where Franz Klammer had won the downhill gold in the 1976 Olympics. It was snowing. The flakes were coming down so thick that a ski racer would have to concentrate in order to keep from becoming lost on the course and heading off into the woods, catapulting to injury or death. At eighty or ninety mile per hour, there is no margin for error. The course was covered with about six inches of powder.

Powder was the Eagle's specialty. He had begged his father, David Lion, to take him out through the trees at Sugarloaf Mountain at every new snow when he was a young buck at the SCVA Racing School. Little did he know that it would prepare him for the biggest race of his life, the last downhill before the 2018 Olympics at Lake Tahoe. He was in a ritual tie in total World Cup points with the top Austrian skier in the world, Hans Hellsrunner, who had earlier called Eagle a "nose-picker." This had added fuel to Eagle's goal of winning the overall World Cup title. (This title is more important to a ski racer than even an Olympic gold medal).

His father had taught him, "Only Joe Namath talked junk about the opponent and won," referring to the cocky statements the quarterback had made prior to beating the Baltimore Colts in Super Bowl III. This had instilled in Eagle a sense of respect for even the weakest-appearing opponent, while inciting an inward fire burning fury to make a disrespectful opponent "eat his words." It seemed like there was almost a physical release of a testosterone-like hormone in his brain when he heard such trash talk. The comments made by Hellsrunner played right into Eagle's hand.

Eagle heard the countdown. He broke through the start wand at the top of the course, and all that he could think of was rage. The top of the course required large perfect skates under normal conditions, but in the two inches of snow that had fallen in the last hour, he knew that gliding and floating a flat ski would provide him with the most speed. Soon he was low into his tuck position, like an egg, with his hands stretched out in front of the visor of his red, white and blue eagle-embossed helmet. As he reached the steep middle part of the course, he pre-jumped the headwall and rapidly descended the downhill slope of forty-five degrees! He was gaining tremendous speed and flew through the midcourse timer with the fastest time ever clocked – over 100 mph! In such snow conditions this speed was not only unheard of but totally on the edge of loss of control because the soft snow would not allow a hard ski edge to dig in the correct direction. Not since Bill Johnson's victory in Sarajevo had conditions been so perfect for a true powder speed skier. The Austrians, while good at skiing on ice, were totally outclassed in these conditions. Only once in a blue moon did this happen. Little did the world know that Eagle had awoken early in the morning, couldn't get back to sleep, and had performed the ancient Native American ritual snow dance!

As he rocketed over the final headwall, he was on the verge of control. It was an exact picture reproduction of Franz Klammer's one ski off the snow, one high up in the air searching for a landing that graced the cover of Sports Illustrated in 1976. He landed it! Amazing! He returned down into the tightest tuck possible, got both skis flat, and sped through the finish line. He instinctively knew that was the greatest performance of his life. As he came to a complete stop, he pumped his pole dangling fists upward towards the heavens. He glanced at the scoreboard. The day's top time! He was in the #1 position!

None of the other skiers beat his time and he won the race, putting him in first place in overall World Cup points. The TV cameras swung over towards Eagle and a gorgeous blonde woman interviewed him, holding his skis so the whole country could see the brand. "I'd like to thank my God, my family, and my country," said Eagle.

The interviewer asked him, "Are you ready for the Lake Tahoe Olympics?" Eagle responded with a wry smile, "Well you can imagine…"

Watching the coverage from her Lake Tahoe Ski condo was China Doll. The phone rang. She knew what the call would mean. Her handlers realized the secret of possessing the holy spear and of unlocking the Biblical code, so they had dispatched China Doll to try to get the lance and the code so that China might rule the world. Intelligence sources had found out that Senator David Lion had possession of the code. The only way to get to him was by kidnapping his famous ski-racing son. She was immediately dispatched on this mission.

China Doll

Liu Lin was beautiful. She had wanted to be an actress ever since she saw her first Hollywood film. She had been trained by the Chinese government's "Dragon Lady" to gather intelligence. The famous "Dragon Lady" had been a double agent, sleeping with FBI Agents in the 1990's, in order to compromise American intelligence concerning the Chinese military involvement in weapons dealing and also concerning far ranging matters of homeland security.

Liu's skin was pure and white, earning her the alias "China Doll." She was trained to ski very well. With that training she could attract a top ski racer, especially if he had a reputation as a ladies' man. Her arrival would be timed to cross paths with the Eagle at precisely the time of the Olympics in January 2018 at Lake Tahoe. Once there, her mission would be to seduce him. Then, under the auspices of pillow talk, she was to gain information about the lance and the code as well as about his brother Hawk and top secret U.S. space defense systems.

It was January 17, 2018 when China Doll arrived at Squaw Valley, USA. She wove her way thought the crowd of skiers to the chairlift line. Up ahead of her she saw the familiar speed suits of the U.S. Ski Team – light blue under a dark blue backdrop of stars with red spider webs. She had studied photos and she knew that her mark, Eagle. He wore a namesake helmet. On the front of his helmet were the white head and yellow eyes of a bald eagle and the gray wings of an eagle were painted on the rear sides. She saw him and slid into line beside him. She said "Single!" as she paired up with him to get on the chairlift. He barely noticed her.

She was determined to change that, however, as she bent over and kissed him, hard, thrusting her tongue into his mouth and twirling it around like a helicopter blade as the dragon lady had instructed her. Meanwhile, she rubbed her hand on his crotch so as to generate arousal.

After about a minute of this, Eagle gently pushed her off and said, "Nice introduction. So what's your name?"

She looked seductively through the amber lens of her goggles, batted long black eyelashes and said, "China Doll."

"Well, China Doll, how about having international relations," said the Eagle.

"When and where?" She asked.

"9 p.m., Caesar's, Nero's 2000 Dance Club. See you on the dance floor." With that, the chairlift reached top of the hill and Eagle did two giant skate-pushes with his skis and sped off down the hill.

China Doll knew it was impossible to keep up with him. Besides, her objective had been achieved. She skied down to the bottom, took off her skis, and made her way back to her condo at the base of the mountain. She took a nap in anticipation of an all-nighter with a wild ski racer.

An Angel Opens Her Eyes

Angel Lion was flying United Airlines Flight 1045 from Boston to San Francisco. As she looked out the window, she saw the gray rocky tops of the Sierra Nevada Mountain Range all but covered in a white blanket of snow. Down below was Lake Tahoe where her brother John was going to ski in the Olympics. She was so excited about being reunited again with her two baby brothers. It seemed like just yesterday that she had been flying down Sugarloaf Mountain with both of them, gleefully laughing in their youthful exuberance about life.

Angel was smart too. She had read over 100 books in the fifth grade, surprising her teachers. This yearning for learning had led her to the discovery of her father's humble achievements in trying to use the power of clairvoyance to try to prevent the September 11, 2001 attacks on America. Like her overachieving brothers, Angel had an impressive background of many diverse talents and successes.

Her plane touched down at the San Francisco Airport and she hustled out to catch a small plane to Tahoe. As the small plane descended, she couldn't believe her eyes – she spotted the bluest, largest lake in North America at an elevation of 6264 feet! Angel was excited about meeting up with her brothers and skiing together once again. She reminisced back to the days when they all were in ski programs at Sugarloaf Mountain, soaking up all the sunshine and cool crisp air as they flew down the mountain.

The wheels bumping on the runway jolted her back to reality. She got her baggage and boarded a bus to the resort at Squaw Creek.

As the bus wound up the mountain, she saw the trails of the ski slopes. Suddenly a tingle ran down her spine! Her kid brother was going to be running (skiing) in the downhill, super G, and giant slalom in the Olympics! A childhood dream was coming true.

When she arrived, she saw the mirror-glass reflection of the snow covered mountains, the trees, and the hotel. She walked into the hotel lobby. "Angel Lion," she said to the desk clerk. The clerk responded. "Oh my, you're staying in the Sierra Penthouse. You're going to love it."

"Great," replied Angel, but she barely heard what the clerk said as jet lag was starting to creep into her body from the full day of traveling.

Her room was on the eighth floor and had two story windows which provided a panoramic view of the mountain. She plopped herself backwards on the bed in sheer wonderment. Gazing up at the mountain she drifted off to sleep. When she awoke, she had no earthly idea what time it was. She looked over at the phone and saw two blinking message lights. Had she slept through the rings? She picked up the receiver and asked the front desk for a playback. The first one was from Eagle, clowning around as always, imitating some foreign guy's voice and telling her to meet him at Nero's Club in Caesar's at 8 pm. He left his number for follow up details.

The second call was a mysterious women's voice which simply said, "Beware of the China Doll!" and hung up. "That's weird," she thought. "Must have been a wrong number."

When Angel arrived at Nero's, it was packed. She began using her extra-sensory perception to find her brother. "Now where would I be if I were John?" she asked herself. Immediately, she spotted the handsome ski racer with broad shoulders, a smiling face with cool green eyes, and auburn hair. He was chatting in the corner with several very hot woman admirers.

She busted right through them, ran up to John, and gave him a big bear hug, dispersing the crowd of women. He scolded her for a second with, "Now see what you've done. You've scared all my girlfriends away!" They both started laughing hysterically. It was like the time when they were both toddlers and began an all-star wrestling match in the middle of the public library. Their father had been too embarrassed to even claim them as a crowd gathered around to see these two-pint sized, giggling combatants gleefully flipping each other end over end. "Seems like old times," said Eagle. "Good to see you, John!" replied Angel.

"Let's take that corner booth behind you," suggested John. They both slid around the circular table to sit in the middle together. They could barely hear each other over the noise of the band as the waitress came over to take their drink orders. "I'll have a Gatorade, on ice" said Eagle. Angel ordered a beer.

When the band took a break, they could hear each other talk without shouting. "I've got a hot date, so I need you to help me look out for her," said John sheepishly to his older sister. She rolled her big blue eyes at him and said, "Oh no! Not again!" as they both started laughing.

Then some seriousness of their mother, Naomi, crept over her face as she began asking him twenty questions about her like, "What does she do?" and "Where's she from?" He could provide definitive answers to none of the questions. "Oh, well, he's just like Dad, messing with my controlling mind and in effect telling me he doesn't want to tell me. He's just being difficult," she thought. She had just one more question through, "O.K. I'll help you look for her. What does she look like?"

"Well, she's beautiful, short – about 5'3", with the fairest complexion of them all, and you might say she looks like a China doll." With that statement and the strange phone message she had received about a China doll, Angel instantly felt all the blood run from her face. The waitress brought the drinks and Angel took a large sip out of her beer. John noticed the change in her demeanor, so he asked her what was wrong. It was really starting to get weird and she did not want to upset him so she made up a story that she had to go into the ladies' room and that she would look for "China Doll" there. Eagle thought that was a great idea.

An even greater surprise awaited her as she entered the ladies' room. She saw standing there, primping her hair in front of the mirror, the whitest, most beautiful looking Oriental woman she had ever seen. In order to keep her head from spinning, Angel slipped into one of the toilet stalls. She sat down like she was taking care of business as usual, but instead peered through the crack in the stall door to view China Doll. What Angel saw was pure narcissism, as her subject literally made sure every eyelash and hair on her head was in place. Then she cracked a big red lipstick smile at herself that was at the same time equally sensual and sinister. She then primped her perky well-rounded breasts up under the tight red pullover spandex top she wore.

"Oh my God, what a slut," was all that Angel could think as her subject turned and walked out of the ladies' room. Not wanting to be conspicuous, Angel waited a few minutes before leaving. She walked across the packed bar and headed toward her table in the corner. As her eyes found the table where she had left her brother all alone, Angel was shocked to see China Doll already there. She was sitting close enough to John to be his wife.

Angel had to think about this. Inside her being, the DNA of the officer who had fought with General George Washington sparked her suspicions of the foreign woman. She stepped back, unseen by her brother and his "date," and walked over to the bar to recollect her thoughts for a moment. To make matters worse, a drunken skier who had been drinking since the lifts closed came over and tried to hit on her. "Can I buy you a drink, llovley lllady?" he slurred.

Angel looked at him with blue eyes of steel and snapped, "Go home and dry out." The man slinked away. Now, alone with her thoughts, she asked herself how the China Doll could have found her brother so fast. Also, had she been in the women's room preparing to snare a prey? Was this all a plan? Did she have accomplices? Angel thought the whole series of events too coordinated to be coincidence, so she figured the answer to all the questions was "yes." She went into her "secret agent mode" and began training her eyes on the rest of the patrons at the bar in a way that would not alert them that she was scanning the crowd. Much to her surprise, when she looked at a heavy set Hawaiian looking guy, he was staring at her! She stared back until the man looking at her looked away, basically saying to him, "I know you're looking at me, so I'm going to get a good look at you!" When she finally looked away, Angel was confident that the Hawaiian man did not belong in the picture of the ski mountain scene, nor did the China Doll. Therefore they might be a pair of outcasts.

She knew exactly what to do. She made herself white as a sheet by causing the blood to run from her face. She walked up to the table where her brother was sitting and stood there, wavering. Eagle saw her, and asked, "What's the matter, Sis?"

"I don't feel well," she said as she slumped to the floor, apparently passing out.

"Jessums," Eagle said as he flew out from behind the table.

As he kneeled over her, he could see her eyes roll forward, and she said, "I'm sick, Brother. Take me back to my room!"

"O.K., Angel," he replied.

With that, he lifted her into his strong arms and stood her up. Turning to the beautiful China Doll, he said, "Sorry. Catch you on the re-bound" and then headed towards the door. They walked to a Porsche turbo coupe that said "Eagle" on the license plates and got in.

"Thanks, Bro," said Angel as she put her head back on the headrest. She didn't say another word, but drifted off to sleep as soon as Eagle started driving.

Along the highway up ahead he could see a black vehicle turned sideways, completely blocking the road, forcing him to a dead stop. Eagle saw a man dressed entirely in black get out of the car and begin walking towards their car. He knew he didn't like the karma of what was going on, so he pulled a u-turn, nearly running over the black figure in the process. The speed skier in the Eagle came out when he saw the headlights of the car that had the dark figures in it give chase. He raced back up the mountain road they had just come down. Eagle knew all the turns. Angel was stunned into alertness now and figured they must be in the middle of something big, real big, but she didn't want to disturb her brother's driving at this critical moment.

He gunned the engine around the curvy road, sliding the car sideways around a hairpin turn, inches away from the guardrail. The pursuers were not so lucky, however, as their car flipped, rolled, tore through the guard rail, bounced down the mountainside and exploded in a ball of flames. Ever the dry wit, John Lion looked at Angel Lion and said, "Welcome to the Squaw Valley torchlight parade!"

Angel was very concerned about their well being now. She said, "Let's just get back to Squaw Creek safely." When they arrived at her suite, it was so spacious that the Eagle had a separate room upstairs for himself. Before they went to sleep, Angel replayed the message from the message center on her phone for her brother.

Again joking and being stupid, John said, "What? Was she a spy working for the FBI?" Angel looked at him and said, "A spy with a China eye!" They got silly and began laughing like they were four and five years old again. Little did they know in their childish simplicity how close they were to the truth. However, just the fact that they were together gave them a strong sense of security. After they had parted to their separate bedrooms, both of them got on their knees and thanked God before crawling into bed and falling fast asleep.

The Eagle awoke for a second only to see a dark figure put a sweet smelling rag over his nose and mouth. Then all was darkness. Was this just a vivid dream? When he awoke for a second time, he realized, much to his chagrin, that there was an incredible pain coming from his wrists which were bound behind him. His first thought was, "Shit. How am I going to be on time for ski race training?" The biggest races of his life were literally days away. His next thought was that he could be killed. He tried to see through the dark hood that was placed over his head. He felt like he was lying on the back seat of a car. Then he passed out again.

Meanwhile, back at her room at the Squaw Creek Hotel, the phone rang, awakening Angel. A voice on the other end said, "Get out of town. The dirty deed has been done." Then the caller hung up. She called up to her brother's room, "John, John," but there was no answer. She ran upstairs to find an empty bed.

When Eagle awoke in the morning, he realized that he was tied up and covered with a hood so that he couldn't see. He was sitting upright on a jump seat. He thought he could hear the drone of turbine engines. That combined with the feeling of pressurization led him to the conclusion that he was being transported somewhere by airplane.

He knew that he must stay awake so that he could try to access the numbers of hours he was away from Lake Tahoe. Then he could use that as the epicenter of his location. Hopefully he could assess where he was if he were able to view the sun's or stars' positioning. That was going to be impossible, however unless he was able to see. He began trying to work the hood off his head by craning his neck and rubbing the base of the hood across the top of the back of the seat. Apparently someone was watching him as he struggled. A dark figure came over and thrust the hood down snuggly around his neck once again.

It was the fateful day of January 18, 2018.

The Unholy Spear

Allah would kill them by his hand and he would show them their
blood on his lance
(the lance of Jesus Christ).

David Lion had done much soul searching about the vision he
had a few months prior to the 9/11 attacks. He wondered especially
about the Roman soldier standing over him pulling a spear out of
his side, so he began researching the subject of crucifixion on the
Internet. What he found astonished him – the lance of Longinus,
the Roman Soldier who had stuck his lance in the side of Christ,
had been in the hands of many of the rulers and conquerors of the
world!

It was said that this lance been unearthed when Helena found
elements of the cross and nails from the crucifixion of Christ. Atilla
the Hun was purported to have had it. Later Charlemagne and
Frederick Barossa had it during military victories. Napoleon was
said to have pursued it after the Battle of Austerlitz, but it eluded
him. A legend had been passed down for generations that whoever
possessed the "Holy Lance" would be able to conquer the world.

The spear finally ended up in the possession of the House of
Hapsburgs and was at the Hofsburg Museum. It was there that
a young Adolph Hitler saw the lance and was thrown into a state
of trance in which he felt as though he had held it before in some
earlier century. After Hitler annexed Austria, he had the spear moved
to Nuremberg. On April 30, 1945, Lt. Walter William Horn of the

U.S. Army captured the spear. Later that day, Hitler and Eva Braun committed suicide in a bunker and Germany surrendered. This ended World War II. The spear fascinated General George S. Patton, and he had its history traced. Within the year he was dead.

The spear was kept in the Hofsburg Treasure House in Austria until David Lion's obsession with it led to the American government making a bargain with the Austrian government in which Austria allowed the spear to be displayed for a while at the Smithsonian Institution. While it was at the Smithsonian, it was taken from its case and replaced with a very convincing forgery. It was then placed in the bottom vault of the Greenbriar bunker. The reasoning was not so much the fact the United Sates needed the lance for protection but to keep it from the radical elements of evil sweeping Europe at this time. Hitler had deceived the world and conquered many countries while the lance had been in his possession, so David knew instinctively that if the Anti-Christ were to emerge and get the lance in his possession, the world was in for another bad spell.

Unbeknownst to Senator David Lion, men employed by Gustav Caesar arrived to steal the sacred spear just moments after it had been crated and loaded aboard an express airliner bound for the Smithsonian Institution. Thus, the satanic power of the weapon that had killed Christ was effectively removed from the hands of this upcoming world leader. Once again the United States was responsible for keeping the world from evil. This is the lance that David Lion saw in his dream or premonition of the 9/11 attacks. David – and the United States – was in possession of the lance now.

Shattered Dream

The Eagle felt the plane land and then heard footsteps coming towards him. Perhaps he was breathing his last breath. Suddenly the hood was removed.

"Dad?" How could you do this to me? My race is in three days! A lifetime of training and races has gone into this race!," blurted out the Eagle.

"Son, something bigger that that is about to happen," replied Senator Lion.

"What? Like the end of the world?"

"Maybe," said the Senator.

"Get out!" groaned the Eagle.

"We've been watching Red Chinese Army sleeper cell units in the U.S. and all of them have been simultaneously activated. Something big is about to happen."

"Why did you kidnap me?" asked the Eagle.

"Actually, it was your sister's idea."

"Angel knew about it?"

"She organized it!"

"Why?" asked the Eagle in almost a whine.

"Well, you know that China Doll girlfriend of yours?"

"Cute, huh?"

"She's a special operative who was trying to get to you in order to gain intel on Hawk. She was either going to poison or kidnap you last night!" said the Senator.

"So what's next, California falling off into the ocean?" asked John.

"No, but you're close. We have reason to believe that there's going to be an attack!"

"But I was all the way up in the mountains. How would they have gotten me up there?" asked Eagle.

"Nuclear missiles," replied the Senator.

"Jessums....What about the final arms reduction talks?" asked Eagle.

"The president knows all about it."

"What about Hawk?" Concern for his brother was beginning override Eagle's distress over his skiing race.

"He's on high alert and ready for blast off!" said his dad.

"What about Angel?" Now he was concerned about his sister too.

"She's on her way back here now."

"Where's here?" asked the Eagle.

"We are underneath the Greenbriar Resort in the mountains of Virginia!"

Senator David Lion and his son Eagle were now safely under the mountains of Virginia at the Greenbriar Resort. David had stored the sacred spear in a safe place there. He knew capture of the lance would mean the loss of power just as Hitler had lost power within hours of the spear's capture by U.S. forces during Word War II.

Broken China Doll

On the fateful morning of January 18, 2018 at Lake Tahoe, China Doll was in a fix. It didn't take her more than a few hours to learn that she'd been outsmarted by U.S. Intelligence. How could this happen on a top secret mission? She was furious. She knew she was probably going to face dire consequences when she returned home. Her superiors were unforgiving, and this would mean the end of her career.

She contacted her computer reservations plant person who quickly found out where Angel Lion was staying. China Doll went to housekeeping at the Sierra Hotel. She found a poor housekeeper standing in the hall and forced her at knifepoint to open a room. Once inside the room, she made the housekeeper strip and took her hotel uniform. She told the poor woman to stand in the shower. Then China Doll came in behind her and with one quick motion ruthlessly slit her throat. She put on the housekeeper's uniform and pushed the cleaning cart to the Sierra Penthouse where she knocked on Angel's door. This was going to be easy, like killing a dove.

Little did she know the devil in Angel as her brothers did. Angel was all packed up and ready to go, so the knock at the door came as no surprise. Neither did the voice of the maid. Angel recognized the voice immediately from the night before as the same voice that was talking to Eagle as he was standing over her body while she was faking the act of fainting. Yes, she had been observing every sound that was going on around her.

"Oh, good. Come right in," Angel said to the maid, never taking her eyes off of China Doll. Once in the room, China Doll wheeled around brandishing her knife. Much to her surprise, however, Angel was ready and thinking. "Come to Mommy, you freakin' commie," Angel said as she swung her black athletic sport clothes bag at her attacker's head.

China Doll ducked and spun, wielding the knife towards Angel's ribcage. Angel blocked the killer blow just as Master Kim had taught her in Tae Kwon Do. She then grabbed China Doll's wrist, spun her around and forced the enemy's own blade into China Doll's chest. "Clean up this mess," Angel said to her as she departed. She ran down the stairway to call her dad.

"Dad?" Angel asked as the phone was answered.

"Yup, I thought It'd be you!" said the Senator.

"What?" asked Angel.

"I hired Russ months ago to be your guardian, Angel."

"Dad, so why didn't he protect me from China Doll?"

"What do you mean? He just called and said he was at the hotel picking you up."

"She beat him to me, and we fought," said Angel.

"Honey, are you O.K.? asked her concerned father.

"Yup, but China Doll is broken!" replied Angel.

"Good. Get the hell out of there because she might have back up."

"Where's Russ waiting for me?" asked Angel.

"Out front, and quite frankly, he's scared of you," replied the Senator.

"What???" asked Angel in amazement.

"You and your brother almost ran over him last night!"

"That was him?"

"Yup, and that car you blew up was his men's!"

"That's your son's fault, not mine," said Angel.

"Just like kids, always blaming the other," joked her father. "Anyway, just listen; he's outside the front lobby. Just get down there and get the hell out of Dodge."

"O.K. See you at home," said Angel.

"No, you're being flown to the 'Briar. Now go!" ordered her father.

Angel made her way down the stairwell, out the door and looked this way and that in a paranoid video scan of the area for bad guys. The only person she saw out front was a retired secret service agent with short-cropped hair leaning against his car with his arms crossed.

"Rusty!" she shouted to the man who had been a family friend for as long as she could remember.

"Get anybody killed today, sweetheart?" asked Russ.

"Well as a matter of fact..." began Angel.

"Hey, that was me you almost ran over last night," Russ said as he opened the car door for her.

"I know, I know. Dad already yelled at me for that," she said, sounding like a spoiled little rich child who had been out to late. "Besides my brother was the one who was driving, so you'll have to take it up with him!"

Russ Redson drove her to the Tahoe Airport where a small jet was waiting for them. They boarded it together, bound for the safety of the Greenbriar Mountain retreat dug deep below the resort in the mountains of Virginia. Their destination was in the same county where the Lions' ancestor Colonel Daniel Lion I had enlisted in the Virginia militia.

The Revelation

"And you will hear of wars and rumors of wars. See that you are not troubled; for all these things must come to pass, but the end is not yet." (Matthew 24:6)

On the fateful morning of January 18, 2018, President Glendon Rush was flying in Air Force One. He looked out over the wing of the plane at the snow covered Sierra Nevada Mountain Range. He was worried about the events about to unfold. Air Force One was almost to Lake Tahoe, California, the site of not only the upcoming winter Olympics but also where the Final Arms Reduction Talks were about to begin. He was to meet with delegations from Russia and China. His peace plan centered on demonstrations of his trump card, the laser-based weapon shield carried in supersonic space fighter planes. How futuristic it had seemed when President Reagan had first proposed the system back in the 1980's. It was a good thing that the Defense Department had secretly funneled the money to U.S. Space Command through different accounts so that not even the General Accounting Office was able to pick it up on the reports to Congress. It really was top secret, even within the government. It was especially good that nobody knew about the weapon shield because of the Chinese influence on the Clinton Administration. This influence set the Chinese missile program twenty years ahead of the American program, enabling China to reach the west coast of the United States with nuclear missiles.

President Rush was hoping he would not have to use his trump card. However, he did want to end the threat of nuclear war that had been hanging over the world for the greater part of a century. In fact, he remembered the last time he had been to Holy Confession. It was during the Cuban missile crisis when he was just a boy. His entire family thought, as did most of the world, that they might die in a nuclear holocaust on that day. Had things changed that much? The only big difference was that the U.S. had won the space race. Americans were in control of the higher ground. "We have satellites watching them all," thought Rush. "Heck, we can even read people's newspapers for them from space with that new TRW satellite if they're sitting on a park bench in Central Park."

Rush looked back to the table. It was laid out with fine linen decorated with embroidered stitching of the presidential seal – the eagle. Just then Chief of Staff Art Fleshman handed him a brown government envelope. It was so fitting that the envelope was stamped with bold red letters and eagle's talons. This sent a shiver up the president's spine. This document, when sent in motion, could save mankind. It was the George Washington Vision.

Rush went into the president's office in the Boeing 747-200B and locked the door. Not another person was in the room, not even a Secret Service agent. The red "war phone" rang. The president picked it up. It was the situation room at the White House calling.

The president held the phone to his ear. The voice on the other end was clear with military precision, "Sir, we've got to turn your plane around and head back to Washington. We've got a major situation. The Chinese have invaded Afghanistan and the North Koreans have launched a Dong Fong II missile over the Pacific Ocean heading for the coast of California toward the exact location of the missile summit." Four or five seconds went by, and then the president replied, "I have no choice but to put the final war plans into the computer. Advise all personnel up and down the chain of command."

"Yes, Sir," came the reply.

He felt a pain in his chest, and he wasn't sure if it were coming from the area of his heart or not. He hung up the phone and slumped to his knees, with his heart beating dysfunctionally. The president of the United States began praying right then, in the middle of the flight on Air Force One over the Sierra Nevada Mountain Range en route to Dulles Airport outside Washington, D.C. The missile summit was off, and the world was in danger. As he prayed, his heart resumed a normal beat. It was amazing for the most powerful man on the planet to be humbling himself to an unseen deity, imploring Him for assistance. He prayed "Our Fathers" so fast and hard that his head started reeling and he fell to the floor.

Next, in the previously empty and locked chamber, he heard a voice speaking to him what sounded like scripture. At that moment, he heard the voice saying, "Now the destiny of the United States is upon you, Mr. President." He thought he might be hallucinating, so he opened his eyes. Before him was a spiritual form. He cleared his eyes and focused. It was the voice and presence of General George Washington! The apparition said, "Quickly, unlock the code!"

The president opened up the brown top secret envelope. Within it was a computer CD disk with some writing on it. It looked like Greek writing, a code of some sort. This was the code that Isaac Newton had worked on and passed to America through the Lion family. It was magnetic and made to be scanned into the Department of Defense master computer.

The president did not really care about the disc. His trust was in God alone.

General Washington continued, "The United States is now under attack! However, because you have kept the sacred pact with the Almighty, he has allowed me to return to you to help guide the believers through the tribulation that is upon you now. Quickly, now, insert the George Washington Vision magnetic code into the Department of Defense computer!" President Rush immediately did as he was instructed. Across the land, Americans were mobilizing. "Let every child of the republic learn to live for his God, his land and union" (The George Washington Vision)

Once the president inserted the code into the Department of Defense computer, it began an irreversible sequence of events that had been prepared for the protection of the United States from the final peril. George Washington had witnessed this final peril in his vision. The disc activated the United States Strategic Command

266

computers. (USSTRATCOM is headquartered at Offutt Air Force Base, Nebraska). These computers went into the plans that were in the Biblical matrix to carry out the precise instructions for defense from the attack that had been foretold in the Bible.

USSTRATCOM is the command and control center for the U.S. Strategic Forces and controls military space operations, computer networks, and global strategy. The USSTRATCOM Command Center is housed in a specially designed, two-level, 14,000-square-foot reinforced concrete and steel structure. It contains the critical information management and communication systems to provide the USSTRATCOM commander an assured capability to manage forces worldwide. In time of war, the underground entrance is sealed off. An underground emergency power supply, a well supplying an emergency water source, and stockpiled rations allow continuous operations without outside support for an extended period of time. Electromagnetic pulse protection is provided for critical command, control, and communications equipment as well as supporting utilities. This allows the USSTRATCOM commander to continuously exercise command over American forces, even in the disturbed electromagnetic environment which would follow a high altitude nuclear burst.

The Command Center's group display and briefing support system provides the capability to display full motion videos and still frame imagery on eight large wall screens and individual video monitors. It also allows video communications between the Command Center and the weather and force status readiness centers. This system also has the capability to convert hard copy, 35 mm slides, or overhead transparencies into video. The Command Center also has rapid access to worldwide maps. Within seconds, vital operational data can be displayed on the large wall display screens or individual computer monitors. The primary system for storing and supplying this data is the USSTRATCOM Automated Command Control System. Information about weather, force movements, aircraft, and missiles is stored in computers, ready for immediate access. Field units continually update the data.

Using dedicated telephone circuits, the primary alerting system enables USSTRATCOM controllers to speak directly to approximately 200 operating locations throughout the world, including missile launch control centers. Through this "red phone" system, each unit receives coded messages giving notice of an actual or practice alert. The senior controller also has a direct line to the National Military Command Center in Washington, DC, and to the other major command headquarters. This system, called Joint Chiefs of Staff Alerting Network, allows the USSTRATCOM commander prompt contact with the president, the secretary of defense, the chairman of the Joint Chiefs of Staff, and other unified commanders.

Information shown on these screens instantly alerts the senior controller of an ICBM or SLBM attack against the North American continent or our allies. These systems, along with summary information and attack assessment from other military command, permit the USSTRATCOM commander to protect his force pending a presidential decision. Although the USSTRATCOM commander can launch aircraft for survival, only the president can order nuclear strikes.

Ride 'em, Cowgirl

The infamous day of January 18, 2018 was a big day in the remote parts of Nevada as well as for the president. Databyte Cowgirl was more than ready when she got the call that morning from a mysterious Air Force officer asking her to meet him at the local Jack-in-the-Box.

"I'll have the tacos," she said to the boy behind the counter. As she sat down to eat, she spied a very handsome man in his middle 40's wearing a leather bomber jacket and jeans. He came over and quickly slid into the seat across the table from her. He had what looked like a napkin with some writing on it. She stuffed the napkin in her pocket. The man smiled at her as he got up as quickly as he had come. "Wipe your mouth," he said as he left, just like her father would have chided her.

Upon hearing this, she choked on her food between bites of her taco. She had just been given the code to launch a malevolent computer virus against the Kujinator in order to protect all the American missile defense systems' computer codes! If she was successful, she could prevent the end of the world as we know it! She could not contemplate failure. Picking up her tray, she dumped the trash, sauntered out the door, and then walked at a brisk pace to catch up with the U.S. Air Force officer. They traveled to the Vandenberg Air Base, entering the underground hardened bunker.

Once safely behind locked doors, in a room which housed a myriad of computer servers, Cowgirl opened up the napkin. It said, "Kurtail Kuji." She began furiously pulling up and activating her stored files of algorithms into the Department of Defense computer. Each algorithm she entered was intended to stop a specific Kujinator virus destined for U.S. missile command systems computers.

An Airborne Hawk

While at Schriever Air Force Base, James "Hawk" Lion had become the top pilot in the 50th Space Wing, and he had taken the vision to heart. That vision was to enhance the capability of America and our allies to deter, and if required, to win future wars by the exploitation of space. Readiness and the vigilance of U.S. military forces were key. "We bring space to the fight," was their motto.

At the Joint National Integration Center, all services were brought together in the integration and deployment of missile defense systems. The space missile tracking system, known as "brilliant eyes," is made up of low level orbiting satellites which provide information on ballistic missile launches. When Hawk got intelligence from these guys, he knew it was real.

In the wee hours of the fateful morning of January 18, 2018 , "Code Red Dawn" awoke Captain Hawk Lion from his sleep. He felt a rush of adrenaline shoot through his body. This was what he had trained all his life for. He remembered back to age five, lying in his bunk bed as he was drifting off to sleep and listening to his father, David Lion, read to him from a book called *Stealth Space Fighter Jets*. It was about supersonic invisible space planes which defended the country. Young Hawk had been fearful and asked, "But what if there are aliens up there?" Without hesitation his father replied, "Then you shoot them down!" The boy had known the answer for a long time and it had become instinctive as an adult. He was being scrambled to the top secret launch facility at Vandenberg Air Force Base in California that day.

Hawk quickly made his way to the base, which had a vertical launch pad that was designed to launch an entire squadron of X44 Space fighter jets one after another. The atmosphere was tense in the briefing room. The Chinese had just launched killer satellites at our defense satellites! His job was to make sure his squadron supported the deployed peace-ball defense killer satellites. If they failed, it was Hawk's job to knock out the penetrating enemy with laser canons from his fighter jet. He and his fellow space fighters would launch immediately. Their flight would follow the 120-degree longitude over the North Pole. Then they would split up and follow all of the longitude lines of satellite positioning. "Gentlemen, it's show time! Mount your birds!" came the orders from the general.

Hawk was first on the launch pad, and he went through an abbreviated flight checklist. As he was doing that, his thoughts drifted for a second to his brother who was in northern California getting ready for the Olympic downhill ski race. He hadn't even had time to pop off a call to John. Perhaps Hawk had not even had enough time to read the paper, for he did not know that he president of the United States was en route to California for missile talks with delegations from China and Russia. (Both of those countries' delegates conveniently failed to make their flights).

It was before dawn on January 18, 2018, a day that the world will never forget. Hawk sat in the cockpit of his X44 space fighter plane. This plane represented the pinnacle of the world's highest technology from its best minds. Attached to his plane was a solid booster rocket. The whole combination was atop a launch platform which had been rolled out of the vehicle assembly building to the launch tower. (This was similar to the procedure used in the old space shuttle launches). Like all of the training missions, the launch was at night under the cover of darkness at Vandenberg Air Force Base in California. This was perfect for the launch path for a polar insertion southwest.

The spotlights shone on the launch tower and Hawk was strapped in tight. Through his retina-sensitive space helmet he ran through the pre-flight checklist with mission control in his earphones. As his eye spotted each gauge, panel, or switch, an automatic image was sent back to the flight computer. This accelerated the process.

Final countdown began. T minus 10, 9, 8, 7, 6, 5, 4, 3, 2, 1 – Blast off! As the G forces ripped his face back inside his helmet, he felt the tremendous acceleration of his craft and his body rapidly hurling down range past the gravitational pull and out of the earth's atmosphere.

Blast-off was achieved and he made his orbit window. Suddenly Mission Control called him to tell him that a North Korean Dong Fong missile had been launched from a base in North Korea outside Wonsan and was heading past Hawaii for California. Holy shit! One hell of a morning! Hawk made the split decision to handle it himself and told Mission Control, "No problem, I'll switch to the 180 degree longitude at the pole and detonate it just over the Tropic of Cancer in the North Pacific before we have to see if they are planning on hitting Honolulu or not. Get me a lock on exact intercept." Then Hawk added this afterthought to his message, "Control, leave original mission of Chinese space mines to Captain Elwell." Elwell had been a classmate of Hawk's at the U.S. Space Force Academy and his hit ratio was just shy of Hawk's, but Hawk trusted him and knew he could get the job done.

Hawk had flown this top secret mission before, a couple of laps around the world to check on all the defense satellites, peace-balls and Aries satellites that protected the United States from missile attack. This detour was no big deal. Within minutes Hawk arrived at his destination and had a lock on the Korean missile. He thought, "Fire!" as one X-43A supersonic missile headed towards the Korean missile to destroy it. "Locked on target......... locked on.......... locked on...."

BAM! A gigantic blinding light scorched through the darkness of space. Hawk braced himself for the pulsating waves indicating a nuclear detonation. Nothing came.

He heard the crackle of the radio in his ear, "Captain Lion, premature detonation of the hyper X missile on apparent enemy space mine. Enemy missile still on course. Fifteen seconds till downward descent arch pattern. You must intercept within that time frame or we lose the city of San Francisco!" A quick vision of the devastation of Hiroshima came to mind, with the Golden Gate Bridge gone and a twisted, mangled, black, and smoking series of threads in its place.

Hawk envisioned the scene further east in the mountains, with his brother's flesh burning off his body in a nuclear fallout windstorm. That was enough for him to summon courage for an immediate gut-check.

Hawk pulled his craft upward, helios-planing on the upper atmosphere, with the seconds ticking off. Ten seconds left, "Our Father, who art in heaven…Fire!" screamed Hawk into his headgear as another Hyper-X missile left its tube and headed towards the North Korean nuclear missile. Five, four, three, two, one…no time was left! Just then a supernova lit up the entire upper atmosphere of the parallel. Hawk peeled up so the radioactivity shield coating on the underbelly skimmed off the first wave of radioactivity and sped away at Mach 10.

People looking up at the sky from the Hawaiian Islands saw what looked like the sun exploding in the middle of the night. The entire Pacific Ocean reflected it as waves of radioactivity pulsed out from the epicenter of the blast. A young boy asked his mother, "Is that Jesus in the sky coming back?" His frightened mother responded, "I don't know. Now run and hide inside!" The radioactivity fell into the ocean., killing all sea life within a ten mile radius soon thereafter.

"Termination of enemy missile successful, Caption Lion," came the advice over the radio. Hawk thanked God. He was hoping there were no more missiles. As if his thoughts were magically connected to Mission Control, the answer came simultaneously, "No more enemy missiles on the radar screen."

Hawk had just saved millions of lives – the state of California, the president of the United States and the Olympic village where the Eagle was staying. As a true hero, however, he didn't let the magnitude of his achievement puff up his ego for even a nanosecond. He just responded, "Roger that!"

Bathe Seoul with Fire

Unbeknownst to the North Koreans, there was a massive series of tunnels that had been constructed by the U.S. Army Corps of Engineers all the way under South Korea to the coast. That day, the 17,000 soldiers of the 2nd Infantry Division were moving rapidly through the two-lane automobile and truck-capable passageways of the tunnels, making an exit at a town in the south. From there, they set up a southern defensive point from which they could defend the Sea of Japan and await orders.

Top military planners in the U.S. Armed Forces had secretly carried out the plans for neutron bombs which would just kill humans but leave the buildings intact, although President Bush Sr. was said to have ordered the destruction of such weapons. North Korean soldiers flooded into Seoul in an apparent victory. But what they found was a virtual ghost town. US military planners had evacuated all civilians to the coast along with American troops.

When the president of the United States had inserted the Code into the Department of Defense computer, it had set forth a set of preplanned events that were virtually unstoppable, and as the computer continued to update, the president approved each recommendation. The next request was to deploy neutron bombs on the occupying North Korean Army in Seoul. The invaders did not even hear the B1 Bombers high overhead Korean airspaces as they dropped their payloads of neutron bombs. The entire North Korean Army was vaporized in this way.

In his bunker in the north, Kim Jong Il shot himself in the head.

Centcom Rules

At Centcom headquarters, Major General Mark West was now calling the shots. Clearly, the red forces had bonded together to attack America as George Washington had predicted. The North Koreans had shot down our planes and launched a ballistic nuclear missile at California, and the Russians had started a major tank pincher movement on Israel. However, the foresight of U.S. military planners had put Major General West right in the "stopper" position. Now it was "do or die."

West decided to handle the major thrust of Russian armor around the Caspian Sea with his personal command. He moved the 101st Air Assault Division rapidly from Mosul, Iraq up to southern Turkey outside the town of Sanliurfa. Along with them went the 502nd Infantry Regiment and the 1st Battalion of the 320th Field Artillery Regiment.

From there, they made a short hop and surrounded the Syrian Town of Aleppo, which had become a staging base of Russian paratroop operations. The attack was staged at night, giving the 101st Division a distinct advantage with their night vision capability. Major elements of Russian forces were trapped and holed up in the Citadel atop the city. (The Citadel is an ancient sandstone fort with tops that looked like a medieval castle). Resistance was fierce, but at least they were pinned down. Aleppo was key because it is situated in the plain that stretches from the Orontes to the Euphrates. This location was strategically important to the tank movements to come. Ironically, it is the second oldest inhabited city in the world. The oldest city is the Damascus, Syria. Both ancient cities became the lynchpin for World War III!

The Russians had quietly slipped into the Tekkie Mosque complex in Damascus and turned its military museum into a command post. What they didn't understand was that the Americans had formed an alliance with Arab fighters who were the sons of those killed in Chechnya. Arab Muslim fighters, fueled by hatred of the Russians in sympathy with their Chechen brothers, armed themselves from secret catacomb caches of weapons hidden within the inner sanctuary of this holy place. Fierce gun battles took place behind the enemy lines within the complex. Russian forces were forced to evacuate or be killed, so they ran outside waving white flags of surrender to the American forces that had completely surrounded the outer perimeter of the complex. Their rationale was that they would rather surrender to the Americans than face brutality or beheading.

This was victory for Major General West.

The Koptenators

The idea for the koptenators was originally presented to Department of Defense officials by David Lion in 2004. He was sick and tired of seeing U.S. foot soldiers being killed in warfare and the resultant pain wrought on the surviving families. He proposed that the United States Department of Defense rely on robotic vehicles and super soldiers in place of humans. Here is David's fax:

2-12-2004
Lincoln's Birthday

Dear Mr. Rumsfeld:

As you may or may not know, per Isaac Newton's calculations on the Book of Daniel, the Chinese advance to the Euphrates River is slated on a timetable for the year 2018. It would be most advantageous for the U.S. military to hardwire those Jet Propulsion Lab Projects like the Mars rover to think like Norman Schwarzkopf. Then use them in place of soldiers and tanks in the battlefield of the future. Heavy armament robots would move like tank divisions, while lighter ones would be infantry or airborne soldiers, ready to deploy rapidly via parachute. Test them in California, then plan for permanent deployment along the Euphrates River in Iraq.

Son of the American Revolution,

David Lion

Top secret competitions were held between contractors who wanted to build this project. The winning entry was the koptenator. In the desert of California, giant robotic battles to the death were held. Playoffs and a championship decided the winner. Then U.S. Army personnel took over and armed the koptenator with renewable energy sources, stealth technology, tactical lasers, and electromagnetic bomb and pulse technology. In the core of each koptenator was a Bronx bomb.

The koptenator combined the success of the Mars rover, which could be operated on a virtual desert from millions of miles away, with the brains of the tank commanders that defeated the Saddam Hussein's' tanks in Operation Desert Storm. Hardwired into computers, these robotic tanks could out-think, out-maneuver, and defeat any opponent. With every major land battle in history pre-programmed into their memory banks, practice land battles became like a 3-D chess game in which teams of koptenators never lost to conventional forces in mock battles. Additionally, koptenators could be dropped behind enemy lines. This would allow them to kill many enemy combatants. If overwhelmed, koptenators were able to self-destruct with an even greater toll, with no human cost to the United States at all. These robotic tanks and soldiers did not rely on traditional armaments like M2 machine guns that would need to be re-supplied, but rather used electromagnetic pulse generators and laser cannons, which are self-generated. They had numerous computer chips, which allowed communication with command in addition to chromatic panels which made them appear invisible to enemy soldiers behind the lines they had penetrated.

When they arrived at the Euphrates River, the People's Liberation Army of China was quite perplexed to encounter no resistance from living, breathing U.S. Army personnel. Once the river dried up, there seemed to be no impediment stopping them. Much to their surprise however, koptenators were waiting for them in buildings, warehouses, bunkers and foxholes.

As the Chinese People's Liberation Army was advancing into and through Iran, American B1 Stealth Bombers airdropped thousands of koptenators behind enemy lines using parachutes to coordinate battle group movements and follow the Chinese Army until the enemy had reached the Euphrates River. In the large war picture, the PLA would be trapped in front and in the rear. In addition, the marines had modified their version of the devices called the pyle and arranged for amphibious landing on the ports in Iraq and Iran. They were transported by U.S. Naval ships that had traveled through the straight of Hormuz to the Persian Gulf. Additional units were deployed at the top of the Suez Canal to split the Islamic revolutions which were occurring in Egypt and Saudi Arabia. Order and control was established by the governments of both those countries.

Amphibious pyles were put in place on the beaches of Israel of Gaza, Haifa and Tel Aviv by landing crafts deployed from the Mediterranean Sea. The pyles were positioned in the rear of the Russian units that had landed on those beaches in the previous days.

The USS Mount Whitney was the command ship for the amphibious operation. The amphibious transport docks Green Bay and New York, both cast from the steel of the World Trade Center remains, provided the basing for the deployment of the pyles. These amphibious transports provided the ride to just off the shores of Israel, while the USS New Orleans and Mesa Verde were in the Persian Gulf. From the helicopter decks, CH-53E Sea Stallions and CH-46E Sea Knights provided the air drops of the pyles to the beaches. From there, the pyles set up their operations among themselves and began working their way across land.

In addition, the largest of all amphibious warfare ships (It is so large that it resembles a small aircraft carrier) the Tarawa Class USS Makin Island sailed into the Persian Gulf stocked with hundreds of pyles. She was known as the "pyle-driver." She and her crew dispatched her entire load up the Euphrates River bed with in 72 hours.

More landings of pyles were originated from four dock landing ships: the USS Harper's Ferry, USS Carter Hall, USS Oak Hill, and the USS Pearl Harbor. From each of these transport ships, four air-cushioned landing crafts were loaded with six fully armed pyles apiece and sent at high speeds to landing areas on the beaches.

All of these landings were done at night, with crew members using the top night vision technology goggles. Fire support and security for the landings was provided by AH-1W Super Cobra Helicopters.

The U.S. Air Force was not to be outdone by the Navy and Marine deployment of the new robotic super soldier koptenator units. B-2 Spirit Stealth Bombers were used to fly low (under enemy radar) through Turkish air space over Aleppo, Syria and the Caspian Sea. As their bomb bay doors opened, parachute-equipped koptenator units were dropped over target areas. Command and control units were dropped first, then the rest of the groups. Once all were on the ground, central command computers took over all movements. It looked like a large scale Mars landing on earth, complete with lethality.

Chinese military doctrine was based on the assumption that American military planners had used the threat of nuclear weapons as a paper tiger and they would not use it because of the premium placed on human life. This was a miscalculation of enormous proportions. To some extent, in the nuclear age this was true, but the reasons for not using nuclear weapon were more about retaliatory strikes against Americans and the damage that might be done by the lingering effect of the radioactivity on the world. The top-secret development of the electron bomb solved the problem of lingering radioactivity. With electron bombs, human armies could be in essence be "micro-waved" with no lingering effect to the environment. In fact, a study was done on how to roto-till the remains into the soil to produce a potent fertilizer where they lay, providing valuable nutrients for the soil to become fertile crop land in the post-hostile world to follow.

The koptenators annihilated the Chinese PLA at the Euphrates River. When this occurred, it brought about internal collapse of the entire Chinese chain of command. Every general placed the blame on another general. Some committed suicide, some shot each other, and some were killed by the people. The only ones who survived were the smart ones who converted to peaceful roles in society.

The Lake of Fire

I then saw an angel standing on the sun, and he shouted to all
the birds flying in the sky, "Come and join in God's great feast!
You can eat the flesh of kings, rulers, leaders, horses, riders, free
people, slaves, important people, and everyone else." I also saw
the beast and all kings of the earth come together. They fought
against the rider on the white horse and against his army.
But the beast was captured and so was the false prophet. This is
the same prophet who had worked miracles for the beast, so that he
could fool everyone who had the mark of the beast and worshiped
the idol. The beast and the false prophet were thrown alive into a
lake of burning sulfur. (Revelation 19:11-20)

General West called in Major General Davis, USMC, the
Joint Chiefs of Staff's top Marine. The Marines' defense of the
beaches of Israel was to begin. Marine pyles were loaded into jet
propelled armored amphibious vehicles. These vehicles would be
shot up through Centcom portals and would blast through the dirt
above Centcom Headquarters. After their launch from underground,
the vehicles became hover crafts and would begin high speed
land maneuvers. These units came up on the beaches of Haifa and
Tel Aviv, completely surprising the Russian units attacking the
beaches. American units surrounded the Soviets in Tripoli to the
North, springing out of the sand like unannounced dust devils.
Casualties were almost nonexistent, as the surprise was complete.

The enemy totally capitulated, deciding to surrender rather than to be annihilated.

The European Union army of Gustav Caesar was defending Nazareth and Jerusalem from the Soviet Army's thrust to Jerusalem. Within hours, Caesar flew into the area and declared himself the "Ruler of Jerusalem." General West sent envoys to talk with him, but the Americans were shot. Therefore West engaged the European Union tank division commanded by von Rommel and drew them to them open field of Megiddo using five divisions of koptenators. The European leader took the bait and somehow was convinced that the Americans could not handle the Russians, Chinese, and North Koreans simultaneously. He envisioned an overwhelming victory and a triumphant march into Jerusalem. Then he would fill the vacuum of power vacated by the United States, and his nation would become the world's only superpower. As his units arrived at Megiddo, USSTRATCOM computers released the Bronx bombs from the underground vertical tubes at Centcom headquarters.

There was an eerie silence in the field of Megiddo. It was the calm before the storm, just before Caesar and his men and equipment were completely scorched into the desert. Then the Bronx bombs hit. No living forms remained, and the sand was super-heated to form lava. It burned like a lake of fire for weeks, and when it cooled, all was encased in a hardened rock similar to cooled lava.

Major General West had suckered the enemies of the United States into the field of Megiddo and then dropped the Bronx bombs on them, vaporizing their entire armies.

Christ Appears in China

Liu Qinglin II was the son of a Chinese Christian evangelist-preacher. His father had healing powers and had been sent to a prison camp where he died in the 1990's.

When Liu was thirty-three years of age he unexpectedly received the gift of the Holy Spirit. He was reading about the George Washington Vision and how a spirit of the Lord had appeared to an American citizen to warn leaders of the upcoming war wrought by the hands of a few fanatical Muslims. He was alone in his room as he read about the spear piercing the side of the main character. (This was an analogy to Christ). This made Liu realized that visions could be divinely inspired.

Just as that thought occurred to him, a blinding light came into the room. It was so intense that he could not look directly at its source. He was overcome by a feeling of warmth, love and salvation. The spirit immediately infused into his brain a sort of code – some mathematical Biblical matrix code. He saw all of China's history flash before him in a nano-second, leading to the future in which he saw himself standing with Jesus Christ in front of a crowd of millions of people. Many of the people were pressing towards them in an orderly fashion in order to experience the "laying of hands" in which by his mere touch people could be healed of their afflictions. The joy that he felt at his ability to do this was other-worldly, unmatched by even his most pleasurable experience in life. In fact, he felt a mystical aura around himself, like the halos in the paintings of the biblical scenes during the Reformation. This dreamlike state continued until dawn, at which time Liu fell asleep.

When he awoke, he could not tell if it had been real or a dream, but it made such an impression on him that it seemed life threatening. It's a good thing he did not see an American psychiatrist, or he would have been diagnosed as bipolar! He got up and got ready for his day without any doubt in his mind that he could heal people. He went down to the main hospital in Moguqi and entered the cancer ward. He found a man with a tumor the size of a grapefruit protruding from his stomach. He touched it with both hands and gently squeezed the man's side as he recited the Lord's Prayer, feeling a magnetic energy pulsing through his hands onto the tumor. He could feel something happening, like the tumor was shrinking.

At that moment, he was interrupted by a hospital orderly who was a member of the communist party. Liu just turned and walked out of the room and into the next, in which he found a woman with a similar condition. He repeated the same procedure. The same orderly followed him and grabbed his arm. Liu broke free, ran down the hall, ran out the front doors of the hospital and onto the busy Main Street of Moguqi, and eventually ducking into an alleyway.

As he looked back up the street to see if he had been followed, his heart was racing so hard that he could feel its rapid pounding on the outside of his chest. He waited there a full twenty minutes to make sure no one had followed him. His pulse finally calmed down and he walked home. The next week he spent fearing that he was losing his mind and questioning what he had done. Would there be a knock at his door in the middle of the night? Would he be taken away to a death camp never to be seen again?

At the end of seven days, however, the Holy Spirit moved him to return to the hospital. He went first to the man's room, but he was gone. Then he went to the woman's room, but she was not there either. As he turned to go, unbelievably, the same orderly from the communist party who had tried to grab him during his first visit appeared behind him. He said, "We've been waiting for you!"

Liu was curious and asked, "What happened to the man and the woman who were patients in these rooms?" The orderly surprised him with the reply, "They both got up three days after you were here and walked away. They were completely healed – their tumors were gone!" With that, the orderly took Liu's hand, placed it on his own head, knelt down, and said, "Master, heal my iniquities!" Liu obliged, and in an instant felt some evil rush from the man's body, through his arm and out of his body. The orderly was overwhelmed with radiance and peacefulness as he smiled and told Liu, "Thank you." Then he turned and slipped away.

News of Liu's amazing powers spread throughout China's provinces, and people began flocking from all over to witness his curative powers being exercised on those who came to be healed mentally or physically. The government in Beijing became increasingly concerned because he was baptizing people by the thousands and converting many to belief in Christ. The government's chief worry was that this might spark a revolution against communist rule. They sent spies from the communist party to infiltrate the church groups and obtain information about how these supposed miracles were happening, but in every instance the spies were converted to become followers. The government's suppression techniques had the opposite effect of convincing more and more people to join Christian house churches.

Next, the government sent in troops from the People's Liberation Army to try to stop Liu's revival. The soldiers became converted also. This had a most negative effect on PLA war-planning efforts in the Middle East. Even some senior members of the PLA became closet Christians.

God appeared to be with this small group of messianic Chinese people, just as he had appeared to be with the Americans and George Washington during the American Revolution. However, America was doing its best to break its pact with God by questioning "under God" in the Pledge of Allegiance and arguing about whether the Ten Commandments had a place in an Alabama courthouse. God looked with extreme disfavor upon such actions and would have punished the United States with fire and holocaust where it not for a few devoted Americans still praying around the clock. America's false pretense of religion was causing it to teeter on the brink of destruction.

In contrast, the faith of the Chinese Christians was so complete and without question! That was the basis for the miracles which were occurring in China. The spirit was so clean and pure within the hearts of the new Chinese Christians and they had such simple unadulterated faith in God that the Holy Spirit poured itself fourth and great miracles were happening within China. These new Christians were kindred to the settlers in the early days of the formation of the United States of America when they were in a time of need and desperation. Prayers were answered and God seemed to be guiding China towards a new age of global awareness. The change did not come without persecution, however. People from the Chinese house churches were hunted down and arrested.

One night on a Chinese national holiday, hundreds of believers were being baptized in a river. This river was in a deep ravine in a mountain pass. The army was prepared for an arrest en-masse, and they had surrounded the group on all sides. Suddenly, in the darkness, the PLA saw an army of giant white spirits who appeared and waved long swords at the army. All the PLA soldiers were so spooked that they ran, leaving their guns and equipment behind.

The next morning when the newly baptized Christians walked out of the ravine, they saw guns and military gear strewn all about through the trails in the woods. The spirits who vanquished the PLA soldiers were the spirits George Washington had witnessed in his vision.

An emergency envoy had been sent to Beijing on a mission of trying to secure a peace. The diplomats were met with indifference at first, but they persisted. At the eleventh hour, as things seemed to be hopeless, and agreement was made to secure enough oil for China's growth from the Iraqi oil fields. A peace agreement was drafted and signed by the representatives of both countries.

Soon there were reports that people throughout China were having visions of a fatherly figure that people thought to be God. Upon reflection, these people were asked to draw what they had seen. The results were startling in their similarity. They appeared to be visions of General George Washington praying at Valley Forge! The Chinese military could not accept this, so they began persecuting and arresting any and all that laid claim to having this vision. However, after the great destruction of the Chinese Army at the Euphrates River, these people were freed and news of their visions spread throughout the land. These people were considered to be divinely inspired leaders and were given high positions in the new government.

The changes brought about by the revival and visions were not without struggle however. A factional outbreak similar of the conflicts of Thomas Jefferson and Alexander Hamilton occurred. There were divisions of opinion about the direction that China should take, with the main conflict being between agrarian farming or banking and commerce. With American assistance, these divisions never came to bloodshed as both philosophies slid together seamlessly and worked together.

The conversion of China was part of the third and final section of the George Washington Vision being fulfilled as the spirits joined together to assist with the destiny of the United States.

The Chinese military had tried to use the powerful large market of China to control prices of commodities and U.S .Treasury bonds. After revival came to China, the new Christianity that spread rapidly through the country spilled over into business, bringing new ethics with it. These new ethics turned the country once again into an honest trading partner. No boundaries existed as the free flow of goods and capital between the United States and China brought a rapidly increased standard of living to millions of Chinese peasants.

When those in the Muslim world heard of the miracles within China, they remembered and believed teachings regarding the Mahdi, especially where the Mahdi says that when he reappears, the earth will be engulfed with the divine light.

"Thereafter imam continued as such: he is the one whose reappearance shall coincide with the call of the caller from the sky such that all the inhabitants of the land shall hear this cry: 'Know that the Hujjat (proof) of Allah has appeared near the house of Allah. So follow him since the truth is in him and with him. The word of Allah too refers to the same.'"

With such wonders as those in China happening, many Muslims converted to Christianity.

Lion's Den

Across the world, many people saw the events that had transpired so rapidly as a sign of the apocalypse, and they began flooding the churches throughout all the continents. As people knelt in fear of God and his mighty retribution on mankind's iniquities, perhaps this giant outpouring of the Holy Spirit was heard in some way by God. If it hadn't happened this way to show God our sincerity no one would have been saved.

Senator David Lion took great interest in the revitalization of Christianity in China and had in previous years sent envoys over to help support the growth of churches. His plan was so simple as to be miraculous: In order to have peace on earth, convert the most largely populated country to Christianity. He felt as though this was his divine purpose in life, much as President Ronald Reagan felt compelled to defeat the evils of communism. In a sense both were disciples of Christ in their world view. Part of each man's philosophy was to convert as many people as possible.

Senator Lion walked to his personal safe by his bunk in the Greenbriar. Within the leather case was the object that quite possibly had controlled the outcome of military power in the world since the time of Jesus Christ. He locked the Holy Spear in the safe. He knew the U.S. had won World War III because the lance had been in its possession. This war had been destiny, pre-planned by God. It was at its core a fight over the scarce resource that everyone was pursuing – oil, the ooze which is the breakdown of all living matter which God made. David's experiences also had taught him that a similar truth exists in the spiritual realm. It had something to do with the dissemination or the splitting of the individual's own atomic energy upon death. This leads to a collection of souls upon death into a cosmic force which keeps the balance of power between good and evil so that evil cannot overtake good on this earth.

David had gradually accepted, as his forefathers had, the task of carrying on the George Washington Vision. He knew that if the members of his family kept themselves as true as they could to the commandments of God and applied them in everyday life to lead their families and their country in thoughts, word and deed, the Lions would be able to achieve a spiritual victory as well as a decisive military victory for the United States over the forces of the ungodly in this world.

Was this victory preparing mankind for eventual rule of this earthly world by the true ruler of the world, Jesus Christ or His Father? Was it preparing men to be wise spiritual governors? David knew that only God knew the answers to these questions. If the Second Coming did not happen during his or his children's lifetime, they would all leave the world a better place through freedom of religion and other American ideals. "Could it be true?" the eldest Lion asked himself. "Is the destiny of the United States to protect freedom on the globe until Jesus Christ's return to earth?" That would make the world a better place, even if Christ's return never happened.

David Lion emerged from the bunker with Eagle and Angel. They had prayed nightly for the cessation of hostilities and apparently their prayers were answered. The United States armed forces had fought the armies of the communist forces that had attacked her and had won. Thank God and the spirit of the George Washington Vision. But what would lie ahead for this great nation? What evils must she be prepared to meet?

Across the continent, at Vandenberg Air Force Base, Hawk finally landed his space fighter plane to end the last of his many missions around the earth. He joined the love of his life, Databyte Cowgirl. Perhaps hope for the future lay within the newly conceived form inside the womb of Databyte Cowgirl. Could it be the next generation of Lions who would fend off a greater evil yet to come to the world?

AFTERWORD

This is a true writing up to the present time, with only the names changed to protect the innocent and guilty parties. If you don't believe that this book is based on fact, look up the Kujinator , X44, the U.S. Space Force, the Spear of Longinus, the Greenbriar bunker, or Databyte Cowgirl on the Internet. David Lion exists in the true sense, and so does Father Mathias. So do the descendents of the American Revolution who hold George Washington's vision to heart and thank all the men and women of the United States Armed Forces who protect our freedom daily. These are the people who preserve our future. Whether or not this can be achieved depends on the ability of the country to rise above the flesh and to maintain a spiritual plane in which they will be able to identify evil in all forms and be vigilant enough to combat it in even its smallest forms. To do so will mean a spiritual re-evaluation; this will be the next stage of man's evolution: Moral, intuitive, evolutionary – that is man. That is also the next paper David Lion wrote. Who knows what is in the Biblical Code for the future? Only God the Father.

APPENDIX A
The START Treaty

Intermediate-Range Nuclear Forces Treaty
Message From the President of the United States

The Treaty between the United States of America and the Union of Soviet Socialist Republics on the Elimination of their Intermediate-Range and Shorter-Range Missiles, Together with the Memorandum of Understanding and Two Protocols, Signed at Washington on December 8, 1987.

Letter of Transmittal

The White House,
January 25, 1988
To the Senate of the United States:

I am transmitting herewith, for the advice and consent of the Senate to ratification, the Treaty between the United States of America and the Union of Soviet Socialist Republics on the Elimination of Their Intermediate-Range and Shorter-Range Missiles (the Treaty). The Treaty includes the following documents, which are integral parts thereof: the Memorandum of Understanding (the MOU) regarding the establishment of a data base, the Protocol on Elimination governing the elimination of missile systems, and the Protocol on Inspection regarding the conduct of inspections, with an Annex to that Protocol on the privileges and immunities to be accorded inspectors and aircrew members. The Treaty, together with the MOU and the two Protocols, was signed at Washington on December 8, 1987. The Report of the Department of State on the Treaty is provided for the information of the Senate.

In addition, I am transmitting herewith, for the information of the Senate, the Agreement Among the United States of America and the Kingdom of Belgium, the Federal Republic of Germany, the Republic of Italy, the Kingdom of the Netherlands, and the United Kingdom of Great Britain and Northern Ireland Regarding Inspections Relating to the Treaty Between the United States of America and the Union of Soviet Socialist Republics on the Elimination of Their Intermediate-Range and Shorter-Range Missiles (the Basing Country Agreement), which was signed at Brussels on December 11, 1987.

The Basing Country Agreement confirms that the inspections called for in the Treaty will be permitted by the five Allied Basing Countries. The Report of the Department of State discusses in detail the terms of the Basing Country Agreement. Also attached for the information of the Senate are the notes exchanged between both the German Democratic Republic and Czechoslovakia and the United States. The notes acknowledge that these countries agree to the United State's conducting inspections, under the Treaty, on their territory. Identical notes are also being exchanged between the Soviet Union and the five Allied Basing Countries.

The Treaty is an unprecedented arms control agreement in several respects. It marks the first time that the United States and the Soviet Union have agreed to eliminate, throughout the world, an entire class of their missile systems. Significantly, the elimination will be achieved from markedly asymmetrical starting points that favored the Soviet Union. The Treaty includes provisions for comprehensive on-site inspections, including continuous monitoring.

APPENDIX B
David Lion's Letters to National Leaders

This is the actual unedited text of letters which David Lion sent to the national leaders. Some of them were written before 9/11 on August 11, 2001. David called this day "the day before Pearl Harbor."

To: Secretary of Defense, Donald Rumsfeld, Pentagon
From: David Lion
Date: August 11, 2001

Dear Sir,

I've been thinking about some of the greatest problems facing the satellite defense program. I've enclosed some sketches of them. Conceptually, maybe some of these ideas will help. Thank you for being a great American. Make sure you get your sleep, because this is going to be a marathon.

Sincerely,

David Lion

To: President George W. Bush
From: David Lion
Date: August 11, 2001
Re: Satellite Defense Initiative

Mr. President,

Enclosed please find my paper from 1981. Much of its predictions have been fulfilled. As Ike said, "Only an alert and knowledgeable citizenry can compel the proper meshing of the huge industrial and military of defense with our peaceful methods and goals, so that security and liberty may prosper together."

That concerns my last recommendation made in 1981, but it is reiterated at the bottom of the page in today's context. I don't know why it has come out now, but my fear of our enemies using nuclear extortion, or even a missile attack is imminent. Please get the satellite missile defense system to a flawless state and demonstrate it before our enemies launch a missile.

Sincerely,

David Lion

To: Donald Rumsfeld, Secretary of Defense
From: David Lion

Dear Sir,

I believe missile usage to explode things is wholly useless when trying to prevent either enemy missiles with nuclear or biological agents from dispersing their poisons or in the case of domestic hijacking. Smart, super-fast missiles could be outfitted to capture enemy missiles or hijacked planes. Missiles could be equipped with retractable, expand-o-bands which could be used similar to an oil filter changing wrench after "lasso-ing" the target to clam onto and tighten. After that, Mission Control can redirect the flight to a water landing, rafts deploy and a carrier pickup. The band would be inter-woven like a "Chinese finger trap" for non-slippage, perhaps in a wrap around the wings harness fashion. The problem is to have something hold during the re-direct firing. Maybe using multi stages on X43 would help with redirect. Scenario #2: Domestic type hijacking.

To: Greg Smith, Curator of the Smithsonian Institution, MRC 311
From: David Lion
Date: August 11, 2001
Re: "A house of cold warriors civil war...Start Treaty...Star Wars Defense...Peaceful Demonstrations"

Dear Sir,

Many of the things you have in your Air and Space Museum my father, Col. (Ret.) David Lion, U.S. Army helped design. The landing gear on the lunar module. The map duct-taped by U.S. astronauts over the lunar rover. Since he was the Corps of Engineers man from MIT, he had even picked astronauts to be in the Space program.

My father was my idol as a little boy, and I think all American boys should have such a leader to follow. He bought me the Doubleday Science Service books on rockets (please see enclosed). I have used this book to teach my own sons. Taped in the front of this book is a picture of what my children call "Granddad's rocket". It is the Pershing II. It was my father's final assignment to make this the "smartest rocket in the world" and he did, and he went to NATO and showed them. I believed that this rocket's deployment could end mankind. I was determined to have my voice heard, but my father said, "The world doesn't care what David Lion, Jr. is thinking about nuclear war." I thought differently and entered the *Bulletin of the Atomic Scientists* Editor's Essay contest on eliminating the threat of nuclear war in Europe. Regarding your exhibit on the START Treaty: The paper contains an outline of the Treaty written many years before the treaty.

My paper did not win the contest, but in a recent move, I found the original written in 1981 and to my surprise it contains on pages 3, 4, and 5, the foundations of the Start I treaty in which the Pershing II is mentioned as being the land-based missile to be removed. This was many years before the treaty. To my further surprise, on the essay, page 5, I outline what is now known as "Reagan's Star Wars Defense Initiative" many years before his speech. Its purpose was the pursuit of peace.

My point is that together, at our dinner table, we debated many things, and provided some of the framework for world peace. Sons, listen to your fathers. Daughters, listen to your mothers. And parents, listen back.

The cause of peace meant so much to me that I used my excellence in the sport of skiing to train for the Winter Olympics in Sarajevo in 1984. I was known as the "speed demon of Purgatory." I wore the enclosed "Wildcat jacket" as my identifying uniform and I skied on the VR 17's (Jean Claude Kily's) which bear the American flag, known as the American Flyers. Any and all who ski with me experience "flight training" for a few brief seconds until I, as a rocket man, am gone from sight. As a purist athlete, I chose Jim Thorpe as my model, and would accept no money. No money, injuries, and the birth of my first daughter wore me down. I quit, but this paper lives on.

Like nuclear war threatened to end the whole world 20 years ago, the biggest threat to the United States of America right now is the disintegration of the world into rogue states that are planning to launch nuclear weapons.

The reason that this paper was rediscovered was for its final recommendation: Develop the satellite missile defense system to a flawless state and then demonstrate it to the world, so that any nation preparing to launch missile aggression against the U.S., in any form, will fall short.

Sincerely,

David Lion, Jr.

Note: Later in that week in August, 2001, Mr. Smith called David and told him that his paper was "prophetic" and that it would be included in the papers of the Smithsonian Institution.

To: President Bush
From: David Lion
Date: West Point Graduation May 2002
A West Point Speech Draft: An inspiration for a nation

West Pointers Determine the Boundaries
of Peace Through Victory in War

George Washington awoke from a terrifying dream. He stood, ashen faced in front of his secretary and recanted it. "Our country was enveloped in this volume of cloud, and I saw these vast armies devastate the whole country and burn the villages, towns and cities that I beheld springing up." (George Washington's prophecy) This was so terrible that he wanted to find some meaning to it.

George Washington found West Point to be the bastion of freedom, and the key to the Revolutionary war. He waited there until the British had withdrawn from New York City, to assure the war was over. His lieutenants proposed that he become king, but he would have none of it. His was a pact with the Almighty. He had not taken Communion during the war because it conflicted with "Thou shalt not kill'". Upon the death of officers, he took out of his pocket a little prayer book which he had personally written prayers which we would read. One prayer which he had written, during the war, asked the Lord to forgive him for the vileness of his own requests. He was indeed blessed, ending up being grazed by bullets several times, but never seriously wounded.

After the War, in order to preserve peace and Freedom, in the 1790's, Washington was convinced of the need to build an Academy at West Point. Congress would not appropriate the money. If pro is the opposite of con, progress is the opposite of Congress. It was finally appropriated and signed under Thomas Jefferson.

At his funeral, Harry "Lighthouse" Lee, his number one cavalry officer would proclaim, "George Washington was First in War, First in Peace, and First in the Hearts of his countrymen". His son, Robert E. Lee, would be so inspired by a visit to his house in Virginia by the Marquis de Lafayette that he would decide to attend the U.S. Military Academy. Ulysses Grant would set the record of horse jumping on a wild horse no other cadet would ride. As a true gentleman, Grant would not accept Lee's sword at the surrender at Appomattox Courthouse. The Cause of Freedom was involved and West Pointers had determined it.

Let us not be arrogant as George Custer was and underestimate the strength, numbers, destructive capability and will of our foes. For many lives are at stake by your decisions. One has only to go to the hilltop at Little Big Horn to see the markers of where all his officers fell to see the cost of his miscalculations.

General Pershing's Crusaders led us into WWI, and again the U.S. Army helped secure world peace. On the European continent overshadowed by the evil of Adolph Hitler, SS troops and Nazi Fascism, the birth of American Freedom had three deliverers standing in the mud of France: Patton, Bradley, and Eisenhower. The Manhattan Project was directed by Gen. Leslie Groves, class of 1918. On the battleship Missouri, General Douglas MacArthur accepted the unconditional surrender of the Japanese. "Pax-Americana" had been established for the world by West Pointers. They had made a world Super Power.

General MacArthur's fear of meeting the Chinese at the battle of Armageddon led us to stop them at the 38th parallel, establishing the best ally in Southeast Asia in South Korea. Imagine if the entire country was Communist North Korea. A vision by a West Pointer has given us the most powerful friend in the region.

Also, we must strive to know our foes, and establish friendly relations and trade with them as soon as we can. If we had just known that the Vietnamese were really farmers that thought the original helicopters which came to assault them were tractors, we could have been their best helpers by dropping American-made tractors on giant parachutes.

War could have given way to trade. As it is, millions of Vietnamese have immigrated to the U.S. because they know freedom is here, not in a communist country.

Ed White, an Apollo astronaut on the first American space walk, did not want to come back in the spacecraft and end his work, paid the ultimate price for the program when his rocket burnt on the pad. This led to deep questioning of the program, but we persevered.

The lunar model, the eagle, was referred to as "Mule on the Moon" in a thesis at the U.S. Army war College by David Lion as Buzz Aldrin USMA popped out and secured the highest ground for the United States. Michael Collins, another graduate flew around the moon in the command module and picked Neil Armstrong and Buzz up.

In the Super Bowl, we award the Vince Lombardi Trophy. It is a testimony to a man of excellence who received his early and formative training under the great Army coach Red Blaik at West Point. It is now the most watched Event in the world.

When Freedom was threatened in the Gulf War, a West Pointer named Norman Schwarzkopf delivered a stunning left hook to the overwhelming numbers of Saddam Hussein's forces, and it was the biggest rout in the history of warfare.

On a hot May afternoon in 1991, President George Bush, with Barbara by his side, spoke at the graduation and was supposed to hand out just the first hundred or so diplomas. In gratitude, he rolled up his sleeves and delivered every last one of them. His was a gratitude to each and every soldier for their sacrifice to their country. If you are sent into battle, I promise you our victory will be overwhelming.

What we realize is that you are the best of the best, the products of American freedom and equality, of teamwork, ingenuity. But you have chosen to possibly sacrifice all ultimately for the United States. We are at war. The enemy missed its mark, delivering a superficial blow just under the ribcage in an evil act of insane cowardice. For just up the River Hudson lies the Heart of the Heart of America. You.

The Corps of Cadets at the United States of Military Academy at West Point. Your hearts beat red, white, and blue. True. You have inherited your commands directly from the vision of George Washington. There are those among you today who will determine the peace and the freedom of the entire world. You will be the leaders that shape the boundaries of freedom. You will be challenged to your limits but as those graduates who have gone before you, you will persevere, and triumph on the battlefield against all those foes of Freedom. Your country, your leaders will stand behind you. All of our allies, impressed with the leadership will stand behind you, and united we are more powerful than all of those who would wreak ruin on us in a jealous rage. The enemies are insane murderers, their leader no different than Hitler.

We will never let George Washington's nightmare of the Union being destroyed come to pass. War is the American opportunity for a better world once peace is achieved. God bless America. You are the ones who will stand beside her and I will help you guide her through the night with the light form above. War will give way to peace and trade in the greatest American Century yet to come. Godspeed.

To: President Bush
From: David Lion
Date: May 29, 2002

Mr. President,

In an effort to complete the Strategic Defense Initiative,
or SDI, donations could be obtained from billionaires like
Ted Turner and Warren Buffet.

Sincerely,

David Lion

Date: 10/20/02
To: Secretary of State Colin Powell
From: David Lion
RE: Constitutional Warfare....of Iraq...of Palestine

1. Arabic translators to "rewrite" the constitution in personal terms and make it look like it were written by Iraqi hands. Hussein=George III. Rewrites also of the Declaration and Articles of Confederation.
2. Staple a tea bag to each copy (optional)
3. Airdrop millions over the country.
4. Apply personalized copies over other bad situations, over Yasser Arafat's controlled people. These are the seeds of self-determination.

David Lion

November 26, 2002

3 Situations: 1) Recession2) Stock Market   3) Social
Security

Dear President Bush:

The Stock markets have either put in the right shoulder
on a massive head and shoulders formation of all time, or a
double bottom of near time, with a cup and handle formation
to rocket off of 200 day moving averages. You can assure
the end of recession, stock doldrums and fix social security
by year's end.

Federal Employees Retirement System (FERS) already
has a track record on the C fund which you can show on TV
with a laptop. The fund can be expanded to include social
security options of all those so electing. The C fund will
become one of the larger mutual funds, leading the market
in a powerful advance. Confidence in the market by the
president will spill over to the average investor, as they
move back to stocks. You should do this before January,
which has always the biggest run-up. #41 lost the election in
'92 at the debate in Richmond, when a lady asked him about
the recession and he looked like he was from outer space.
Godspeed. Please have Andrew send a card to my mom:
Mrs. Alice Lion, VA.

David Lion

11/26/02

Situation: Paying for the cost of war.

Dear President Bush:

My father helped your father end the Cold War. Now they have sold little pieces of the Berlin Wall, at a big profit.

The U.S. mint should sledgehammer the pieces of the World Trade Center into stones, put them in little leather pouches and sell them with the inscription, "Lest we forget who threw the first stone."

All profits would go the U.S. Treasury. If we could do it in time for Christmas, it would be best for sales.

Sincerely,

David Lion

February 2003
To: Donald Rumsfeld
From David Lion

Approach - Constitutional warfare/Iraq

Millions of leaflets must be dropped to the population of Iraq showing Saddam gassing his own people. The U.N. Delegation should show ghastly reminders of this inhumanity. The USA must be seen as liberators of a people to self-determination from the evils of this dictator. He wants to be seen as a Martyr for Islam, (Do not let him. But he is purveyor of a perverse hoax in the oppression of his people. Need to have "Truth Flyers"

1. Exhibit A
2. Saddam drinking wine.

Inscription: "He says he's true to Islam" But he is not.

3. Saddam swimming in a palace swimming pool side by side another picture showing an Iraqi Civilian lying in a pool of blood.

> Inscription: "Saddam uses the blood of his people so he can swim."
>
> It would be best if we had some wise sayings directly from the Koran.

2/6/03

To: Mr. Colin Powell
Re: Nobel Peace Prize

Excellent! Excellent! Excellent job!

One last chance for peace may exist. In sales, you have to answer the client's, "What's in it for me?" question. Saddam has no out. His back hurts so much he can hardly walk or sit without pain. An American neurosurgeon can fix him at a neutral location, like Turkey. He could bring his own guards and recovery time would be only 2 weeks, under his people's supervision. He would then be able to return to Iraq to be leader only if he comes clean on all WMD, and stops all torture and had Democratic Elections for a parliament, not him. In return, he will be guaranteed an oil deal with exclusive rights at $25.00 bbl (lifetime). But it could start at $20.00. Vice President Cheney should know the price. It should be secret so OPEC doesn't flip. U.N. could supervise humanitarian $ usage in Iraq. U.S. economy would boom by the 4th quarter 03. You and Cheney can broker this deal. Tell Jane sorry I was gruff with her that day. Again, unbelievable job.

Godspeed,

David Lion

February 11, 2003

To: President Bush, General Colin Powell, and Hon. Donald Rumsfeld
From: David Lion
RE: Nobel Peace Prize

Imagine 40 years ago if the U.S. Army had airdropped a million John Deere tractors over North Vietnam but gave all the keys to the U.S. infantry? Trading partners instead of impoverished peasants of a totalitarian regime would now live there.

Now imagine the future oil company, IRAQO, owned by the people of Iraq. We need to make up stock certificates in Arabic for 100 shares each and drop them in the millions over Iraq. On each would be the phrase, "given only to those who helped themselves." Also attached would be a resolution that the president of the new company would be the Iraqi who brings in Saddam, dead or alive.

Board members would consist of those who assist (50% Iraqi's who helped bring in) 50% to NATO countries who assist. Eventually, many years buyout to Iraqi control. Preferred oil contracts would be given to NATO members, say, $15 per barrel, then U.N. Members. American people mandated it when they voted in oilmen to solve this problem in advance. Amazing Grace.

3/4/2003

Dear Mr. Rumsfeld:

Shares of Iraqco could have cusip #s on them that could be read by electronic scanners. Every military unit dropping or distributing shares would have a pre-coded agent #, so that they would receive a commission or incentive based on the # of shares redeemed. This would be bonus pay. Heavily fortified redemption centers would have scanners. If an Iraqi brought information on WMD or even small arms cache, they would be rewarded, if true and successful interdiction, with more shares.

Good Luck,

David Lion

Colin Powell's Birthday in Baghdad Airdrop
CC: Mr. Bush, Mr. Rumsfeld, and General Myers

March 4, 2003

My pen cost 7 cents but it can beat Saddam's words. That's because it was made in the U.S. of A. It can make the hearts and minds of the people give up Saddam's body.

Let it snow in Baghdad with leaflets with quotes from the Koran relating to his evil. Hadiths can be quoted. We can help them. Five prayers/day can be dropped to them.

In summary, daily we can drop a passage from the Koran to produce a tartil which will add up to a month long (or whatever) chain of consciousness that will conclude that Saddam is evil, anti Muslim, and anti God.

In Chapter 100:

The clatter! What is the clatter and what shall teach thee what is the clatter?

The day that men shall be like scattered moths, and the mountains shall be like plucked wool-tufts, then he whose deeds weigh heavy in the balance shall inherit a pleasing life, but he whose deeds weigh light in the balance. Shall plunge in the womb of the pit. And what shall teach tee what is the pit?

A blazing fire! - Goes Saddam!

April 2003 (Before the run to Baghdad)
To: Donald Rumsfeld
Pre-Baghdad airdrops please have translated.

The American Objective

Our founding fathers, realizing that democracy was the closest man-made from of government, whereby the collection of wills would form the consensus which is God's will, gave us freedom.

On 9-1-2001 American freedom was violated in 3 important ways:

1. The freedom to fly
2. The freedom to invest in stocks and bonds.
3. The freedom to defend our country.

That assault was wrought from jealous freedom haters.

We, the people have seen our form of government topple torturous tyrants like Hitler before. Our self-depreciating Freedom Fighters under arms and uniforms are in Iraq to give their lives, possibly, so that Iraq may have a constitutional convention which will give every Iraqi the right to attend based on the will of the people. Towns and villages will elect local leaders whom will be sent to the Baghdad Congress in order to form a more perfect government for the people of Iraq. These leaders will write the Iraqi constitution providing Iraqi Freedoms, which, will never be violated by a Hitler man again.

This is a gift from the American people to compensate for our great sadness and loss of our own people's lives and freedoms. Glorious ceremonies will be held for those Iraqi and Americans/Coalition forces, which died during that struggle to free the country from Hitler Hussein.

Lay down your arms, people of Iraq, and we will not hurt you. Give up the evil one Hitler Hussein, who had blasphemed in the name of Islam with the blood of his people. Bring us his body so that we may complete a gift of freedom to you. Do not die for the evil one in an everlasting fire. Lay down all your chemical weapons so you will not die but rather choose life and freedom.

Date: April 10, 2003

To: Mr. Rumsfeld:

Re: Allah will condemn suicide bombers

Separate Killers from the Population

In Islam, committing suicide is a grave sin, turning one's back on Islam altogether. It is an affront to Allah, the giver of life. A person who commits suicide actually puts himself on the same level of Allah, saying to him, in effect: "You have given me life and I take it away."

This is totally unacceptable. In a Qudsi Hadith, Allah is quoted by his messenger as saying: "My servant has affronted me with regard to his life and I, therefore, forbid him entry into heaven."

The women:

Except those who join in a group between whom and you there is a treaty (of peace), or those who approach you with hearts restraining them from fighting you as well as fighting their own people. If Allah had pleased, he could have given them power over you, and they would have fought you. Therefore if they withdraw from you but fight you not, and (instead) send you (guarantees of) peace, then Allah hath opened no way for you (to war against them).

David Lion

In the summer of 2003, David Lion could see that poverty was breeding despair in Palestine and faxed the following letter to Secretary of State Powell.

June 19, 2003

To: General (Ret) Colin Powell
From: David Lion

As a struggling entrepreneur, I scrimped and saved every penny as my grand-mommy had taught me she had done to survive the depression. The difference was that I invested those pennies into business.

Current problems in Iraq and Palestine could be worked out by Muhammad Yunus' econometric model.

Yunus, with the help of his graduate students, dug further and found 41 other people in the village suffering a similar fate. With a total of just $27, their lives could be changed, he calculated.

Please find him and get him to start this type of banking in Baghdad and Palestine.

As you and I understand, poverty brings despair. Deep despair brings violence. Thus the root of all wars is economics. Peace can be achieved on a grass roots banking level.

Sincerely,

David Lion

Date: August 8, 2003

To: Donald Rumsfeld
Re: Iraq

Dear Mr. Rumsfeld:

1. Attacks on U.S. Troops might be eliminated entirely if we offer $500.00 for each RPG Launcher turned in.
2. The Humvee has a bad casualty rate. Eliminate them from the field. Maybe "Conan" will buy them all for California (Arnold)
3. Tap the oil surplus fund to provide greater benefits to families of those killed in Iraq. Like Sgt. Pokorney's wife and little girl.
4. Increase the army to 10 divisions. We will need them.
5. Promote within the ranks, using meritocracy. If in doubt, ask one's self, "What would George Washington do?"

Sincerely,

David Lion

Date: December 5, 2003
To: General (Ret.) Colin Powell
From: David Lion
RE: Troop Morale

As my ancestor was shackled aboard a British prison ship, as the irons bit close to the bone what vision would sustain him?

I suggest to you, Sir, none other the promise of freedom given to him by General George Washington himself!

Now our troops need your vision.

Great P.R. would be for leaders to go to Iraq for Christmas and read these letters on national TV. Look what spending Christmas with troops did for General Washington. Also, give the Iraqi's some money for Christmas, but be wary of attacks!

Godspeed

David

April 2004
To: Mr. Donald Rumsfeld
Dear Sir:

I have read the Iraqi constitution and I believe the founding fathers would be most proud of what we've done.

Radical Islamic clerics feel a sense of non-inclusion in this process. It is at a critical point, whereby if they surrender now and only now, they will be given some hope of inclusion. This can be watered down with time. But we need all their RPG's now, piled up and arranged neatly for us to crush. Similarly, all their AK 47s, in neat piles. Only after that, they will be allowed inclusion (promises, promises.) All hostages must be freed. If they do not surrender, Allah will incinerate them in a fiery furnace.

Reward moderates with money and jobs. Start giving them the Halliburton jobs. Iraqi's will not kill or kidnap Iraqi's as much over time.

For what it is worth,

David Lion

August 11, 2003
To: Hon. Donald Rumsfeld, Secretary of Defense
From: David Lion, Son of Son of Soldiers
In Unrestricted Warfare, by Chinese Cols. Qiao Liang and Wang Xiangsui

1. Correctly predicted 9/11
2. Outlined Chinese Military Strategy
3. Along multi-channels

My wife handed me a little refrigerator magnet of New York, with the twin towers and an American flag on it. I flipped it over and saw "Made in China" on it. My shoes were made there, as well as my calculator. I am against trade protectionism, but at what level are they trying to exert financial warfare? Currency rates? Treasury Bonds?

Given the success of General Ding in obtaining missile technology, we should not underestimate their ability to deploy hacker detachments and bury computer viruses like the Kujinator and the North Korean. It is disturbing that they can come and go on L-1 visas! Stop 'em

Take care,

David Lion

Then Jesus came to them and said, "All authority in heaven and on earth has been given to me. Therefore go and make disciples of all nations, baptizing them in the name of the Father and of the Son and of the Holy Spirit, and teaching them to obey everything I have commanded you. And surely I am with you always, to the very end of the age." (Matthew 28)

When the whole country mourned the loss of President Ronald Reagan, David Lion felt a sense of loss that was hard to describe the former president who had used his ideas in the "Star Wars" speech. He felt a seed of peace that he might plant with Secretary of State Powell and help ease the pain that the elder statesman must have been feeling at the loss of such a great leader, so he faxed the following letter:

6/9/04
To: General (Ret.) Colin Powell
From: David Lion
Re: Dutch

Please do not be sad for Mr. Reagan, because he is in heaven, with the Father. He would want me to tell you, "Things happen for a reason that is determined by God and as individuals we have a divine purpose."

In his memory, I think we should convert China's leadership to acceptance of Christian Churches. My inside sources tell me that persecution is prevalent, as they view it as a precursor to revolution. It is important because of the size/weight of the China market.

Malevolent forces (see *Unrestricted Warfare*) of the Chinese military could be used to crash our markets (See charts: cotton, copper, soybeans). The support of churches in China would encourage ethics in trading. Mr. Reagan's divine mission was to convert communism to Christianity. He did the Soviet Union. Now you must free China. Then free North Korea also, with China's assistance. (Reverse Domino Effect)

David Lion

Other information:

"World Powers Weighing Weapons Safeguards"
Nation's Newspaper, May 28, 2002

"MOSCOW - The apocalyptic prospect of international terrorists obtaining nuclear, chemical and biological weapons caused U.S. and Russian officials and analysts to meet Monday to help draft possible new safeguards. Former Sen. Sam Nunn and Sen. Richard Lugar of Indiana, who together drafted the decade-old U.S. effort to help contain the threat of weapons of mass destruction in the former Soviet Union - described the threat of "catastrophic terrorism" as possibly the gravest challenge to global security.

'We are in a new arms race,' Nunn said at a conference organized by the Nuclear Threat Initiative, a foundation he is co-chairman of along with CNN founder Ted Turner. 'Terrorists and certain states are racing to acquire weapons of mass destruction, and we ought to be racing together to stop them.'

The Nunn-Lugar program has assisted the former Soviet republics of Ukraine, Kazahkstan and Belarus eradicate nuclear weapons and aided Russia in expensive efforts to dismantle nuclear weapons, secure nuclear and chemical stockpiles and find civilian jobs for weapons scientists.

Despite the programs' success, Lugar said it might not pass further funding in Congress because of Russia's failure to provide full information about activities in the chemical and biological weapons area.

Nunn said the threat of weapons of mass destruction falling into the wrong hands 'extends well beyond Russia and the former Soviet Union,' noting that some 20 tons of highly enriched uranium remain piled up at 345 civilian research facilities in 58 countries."

David's thoughts on President Dwight Eisenhower:

President Dwight Eisenhower set a goal to keep the peace and worked determinedly to achieve it. Coming into office in 1953, Eisenhower knew the last thing America needed, on the heels of World War II, was an arms race with the Soviets. With Eisenhower's help, the U.S. had emerged from the war as military superpower and started the research on tactical nuclear weapons as a deterrent. As president, Eisenhower was determined to be a peacemaker and strengthen America's role as the world's only commercial superpower.

APPENDIX C
David Lion's Drawings of His Defense Ideas
Such as the Peace-Ball

"Each wheel was exactly the same and had a second wheel that cut through the middle of it, so that they could move in any direction without turning. The rims of the wheels were large and had eyes all the way around them. The creatures controlled when and where the wheels moved – the wheels went wherever the four creatures went and stopped whenever they stopped. Even when the creatures flew in the air, the wheels were beside them. Above the living creatures, I saw something that was sparkling like ice, and it reminded me of a dome." (Ezek. 1)

PERHAPS EZEKIEL SAW THIS SATELITE DEFENSE SYSTEM!

Permanent Space Development Of Satellite Defense

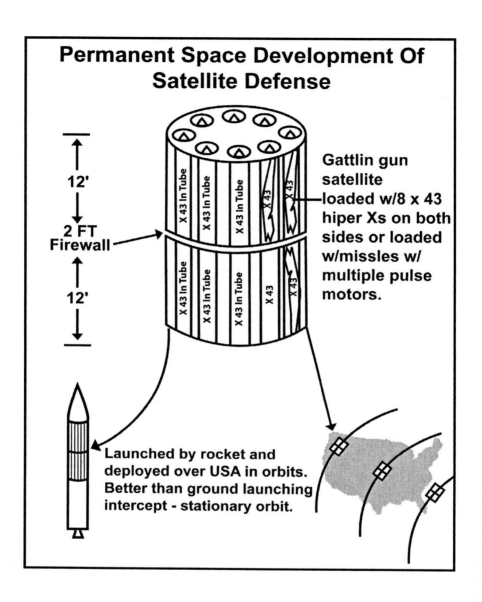

12'

2 FT Firewall

12'

X 43 In Tube
X 43 In Tube
X 43 In Tube
X 43

X 43 In Tube
X 43 In Tube
X 43 In Tube
X 43
X 43

Gattlin gun satellite loaded w/8 x 43 hiper Xs on both sides or loaded w/missles w/ multiple pulse motors.

Launched by rocket and deployed over USA in orbits. Better than ground launching intercept - stationary orbit.

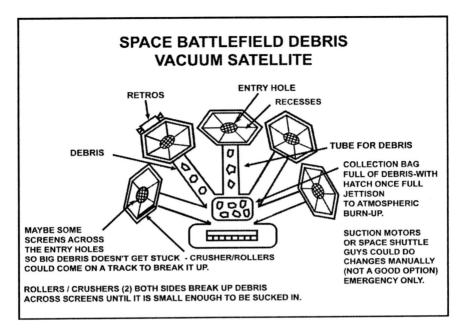

SPACE BATTLEFIELD DEBRIS VACUUM SATELLITE

RETROS

ENTRY HOLE

RECESSES

DEBRIS

TUBE FOR DEBRIS

COLLECTION BAG
FULL OF DEBRIS-WITH
HATCH ONCE FULL
JETTISON
TO ATMOSPHERIC
BURN-UP.

MAYBE SOME
SCREENS ACROSS
THE ENTRY HOLES
SO BIG DEBRIS DOESN'T GET STUCK - CRUSHER/ROLLERS
COULD COME ON A TRACK TO BREAK IT UP.

SUCTION MOTORS
OR SPACE SHUTTLE
GUYS COULD DO
CHANGES MANUALLY
(NOT A GOOD OPTION)
EMERGENCY ONLY.

ROLLERS / CRUSHERS (2) BOTH SIDES BREAK UP DEBRIS
ACROSS SCREENS UNTIL IT IS SMALL ENOUGH TO BE SUCKED IN.

Immediate deployment in satellite battlefield where debris is floating around. They spin and "vacuum" the area. Hexagonal collection areas sloping inward to a hole, opening to the powerful suction vacuum tube which brings the debris to the center collection bay.

1) If you have no money, and want to keep the satellite, eject the collection bag when full to be burnt on re-entry.

2) If you have a lot of money, send the whole unit down when full. Probably will take a lot less development of sensors to know when full, to eject bag, to re-inflate a new one, etc.

Phase 1 - Production - Cheap, available for mass production quickly. 2400 are needed.

2) Cost = Cheap.

Phase 2 - Deployment - 1st ones manually from space shuttle bay. 4 per shuttle.

2 ARE HOMING IN ON ERRANT PLANES

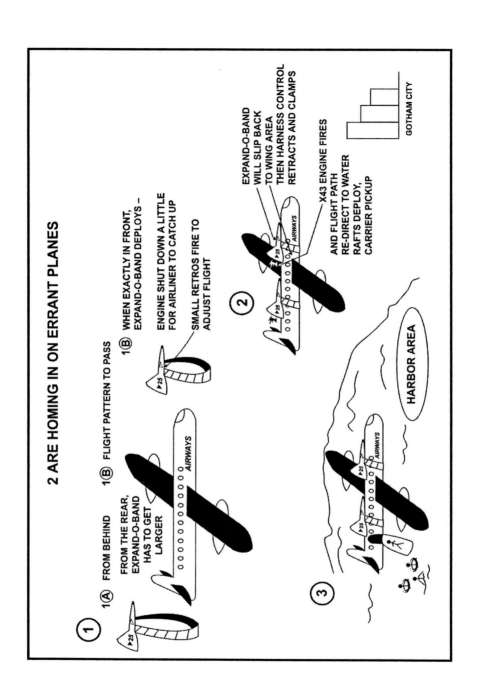

1 FROM BEHIND

1Ⓐ FROM THE REAR, EXPAND-O-BAND HAS TO GET LARGER

AIRWAYS

1Ⓑ FLIGHT PATTERN TO PASS

1Ⓑ WHEN EXACTLY IN FRONT, EXPAND-O-BAND DEPLOYS –

ENGINE SHUT DOWN A LITTLE FOR AIRLINER TO CATCH UP

SMALL RETROS FIRE TO ADJUST FLIGHT

2 EXPAND-O-BAND WILL SLIP BACK TO WING AREA

THEN HARNESS CONTROL RETRACTS AND CLAMPS

AIRWAYS

X43 ENGINE FIRES

AND FLIGHT PATH RE-DIRECT TO WATER

RAFTS DEPLOY, CARRIER PICKUP

3 *AIRWAYS*

HARBOR AREA

GOTHAM CITY

326

PEACEBALL (KILLER SATELLITE)

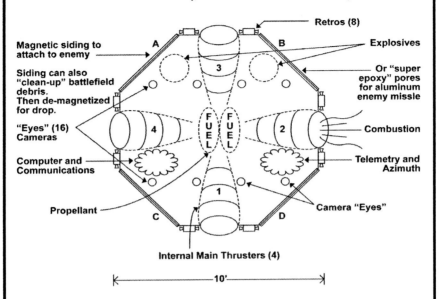

Retros (8)

Magnetic siding to attach to enemy

Siding can also "clean-up" battlefield debris. Then de-magnetized for drop.

"Eyes" (16) Cameras

Computer and Communications

Propellant

Explosives

Or "super epoxy" pores for aluminum enemy missle

Combustion

Telemetry and Azimuth

Camera "Eyes"

Internal Main Thrusters (4)

|← —————— 10' —————— →|

ADVANTAGES: WORKS IN GROUPS OF 4.

1) SPHERICAL SHAPE ALLOWS IT TO STAY IN PERMANENT ORBIT AROUND SATELLITE, EMULATING OUR MOON, SATELLITE.
ALSO, EXIT FROM ORBIT EASIER TO ACHIEVE TO ATTACK ENEMY SATELLITES.

2) SLIGHTLY FLATTENED (SUPER EPOXY POROUS) MAGNET SIDES TO AFFIX TO ENEMY ICBMS OR SATELLITES (A-D) THRUSTERS/RETROS DIRECT COURSE.

3) ONCE ATTACHED, THRUSTERS DRIVE IT INTO SPACE FOR DETONATION.

327

ABOUT THE AUTHOR

Daniel Lion's books have won world wide acclaim from readers. His advice has reached the top leaders of the world as he hopes to have an impact that will help stop the world hurtling towards chaos and disaster. As the true descendent of a man who fought under General George Washington, he is bringing forward the hope that this nation can overcome any adversity as it was founded, under God.

Printed in the United States
38294LVS00004B/145-147

9 781420 810790